THE ADVENTURES OF NATHAN T. RIGGINS

THE ADVENTURES OF

Nathan T. Riggins

BOOKS FOUR, FIVE, AND SIX

The Last Stubborn Buffalo in Nevada

Never Dance with a Bobcat

Hawks Don't Say Good-bye

STEPHEN BLY

CROSSWAY BOOKS

A DIVISION OF
GOOD NEWS PUBLISHERS
WHEATON, ILLINOIS

The Adventures of Nathan T. Riggins: Volume 2

Copyright © 2001 by Stephen Bly

Published by Crossway Books
        a division of Good News Publishers
        1300 Crescent Street
        Wheaton, Illinois 60187

Cover design: Cindy Kiple

Cover illustration: David Yorke

First printing 2001

Printed in the United States of America

ISBN 1-58134-234-9

Library of Congress Cataloging-in-Publication Data
Bly, Stephen A., 1944 -
    The adventures of Nathan T. Riggins / Stephen Bly.
      p.   cm.
    ISBN 1-58134-235-7 (v. 1 : trade pbk.) — ISBN 1-58134-234-9
(v. 2 : trade pbk.)
    1. Children's stories, American. [1. Frontier and pioneer life—Nevada—
Fiction. 2. Nevada—Fiction. 3. West (U.S.)—Fiction. 4. Christian
life—Fiction.] I. Title.
PZ7.B6274 Ad   2001
[Fic]—dc21
                                  00-011985

VP		13	12	11	10	09	08	07	06	05	04	03
15	14	13	12	11	10	9	8	7	6	5	4	3	2

For
Miranda Alicen Bly

BOOK FOUR

The Last Stubborn
Buffalo in Nevada

ONE

Nathan T. Riggins felt foolish dressed in his Sunday clothes on a Friday afternoon.

"Hey, Nathan! What are you doing?"

"I'm waiting for a stage. What does it look like?"

Colin Maddison, Jr., (with two *d*'s) carried his canvas coat in his hand as he sat down on the rough wooden bench in front of the Nevada Central Stage Line office.

"Where're you going? Where are your parents? They're not letting you go off on the stage by yourself, are they?" he quizzed.

"I'm not going anywhere," Nathan mumbled.

"You're waiting for someone, right? Is it your mom? Your grandparents? Listen, if someone famous is coming in on the stage, I ought to know about it," Colin insisted. "I mean . . . my dad's the president of the bank, and surely he—"

"I don't want to talk about it." Nathan sulked, rubbing his fingers through his light brown hair and replacing his hat on his head.

"You're waiting for someone you don't want to wait for?" Colin pressed. "Did your mother make you come wait for some old aunt or second cousin? That's okay. I'll wait with you."

"You don't have to stay. And I'm not waiting for a relative. And, no, my mother didn't make me do anything."

"Well . . . if your mother didn't make you, why are you here?"

"I was wondering the same thing." Nathan sighed. He stared north down Main Street and glanced at the green mountains in the distance.

"Hey, you want to go hunt some rabbits?" Colin asked. "Maybe you'd let me ride Onepenny."

"I can't go hunting, Colin. I promised Leah I'd wait at the stage."

"Leah! Leah made you do this? Come on, Riggins. You aren't going to let some girl with freckles run your life, are you?"

Nathan tugged at his collar trying to release his tie. Then he sprang up, ambled across the wooden plank sidewalk, and gazed at a mule-pulled freight wagon creaking towards the Galena Mercantile.

"I'm not letting Leah run my life. I just made her a promise, that's all. And I've got to keep my word."

"So Leah's expecting company, and you're the one to meet the stage?"

"Yep."

"Well, who is it?"

"Who is what?"

"Who is the person you're waiting for?" Colin shouted waving his hands in the air.

"Some friend of Leah's."

"Ah hah!" Colin jabbered. "Now I get it. Some cute girlfriend of Leah's is coming to town, and you slicked up to make a good impression."

"Hardly."

"What's she look like? Is she our age? Did you get to see a picture of her?"

"He. It's a he."

"You're waiting for a boy?" Colin gasped.

"Yeah, and it's about the dumbest thing I ever did." He jammed his hands into his pockets.

"Why did you agree to it?"

"'Cause Leah was crying, that's why," Nathan reported.

"Well, anyway . . ." Colin banged his boot heels as he sauntered closer to Nathan. "What's this guy's name?"

"Kylie Collins," Nathan mumbled.

"What! Here in Galena? The infamous Kylie Collins?"

"Yeah, the guy Leah 'ain't ever goin' to marry nobody else but.' Mr. Kylie Collins himself."

"Why in the world isn't Leah here?" Colin asked.

"It 'ain't proper to look over-anxious,'" Nathan quoted.

"Leah said that?"

"Yep."

"This is stupid," Colin chided.

"I already said that," Nathan reminded him. "How about you going for a walk or something? Don't make a big deal out of it."

"You've got to be kidding! I wouldn't miss this for anything on earth. I can see the story in *Frank Leslie's Illustrated Weekly* already. 'Fight to the finish in the streets of Galena, Nevada, as two lads battle to the death for the hand of the lovely Miss Leah Walker!'" Colin giggled.

Nathan scowled. "I think your mother is calling you for supper." He motioned toward the bank.

"Forget it, Riggins. I'm staying right here. You can't sucker me."

"Well then, there's no use telling you about the factory-made creme fills shipped all the way from St. Louis that just came into the Mercantile," Nathan added.

"Creme fills?"

"Mine were raspberry . . . but they have lemon, orange, strawberry, and cherry."

"Riggins, if you're lying . . ."

Nathan turned back to the bench and sat down. "Do I ever lie?"

"Dark chocolate or milk chocolate?"

"Both."

"How much do they cost?"

"Two for a nickel."

Colin stared down Main Street toward the north. "I don't see the stage."

"Me either."

"I think maybe I should go check out those creme fills." Colin grabbed his coat and hurried down the sidewalk.

Nathan leaned back on the bench, jerked his tie loose, and unbuttoned the top button on his white shirt. He crammed the black silk tie into his shirt pocket and then walked into the stage office.

"Mr. Olivera, how late is the stage now?"

The short man in the green trousers and tall boots pulled out his pocket watch.

"It's a good hour late, Nathan. Must have got stuck crossing the river again. It's been a bad week for that. All this spring runoff slows the route down."

"Stuck? How long will it take to get it unstuck?"

"Tuesday last they didn't roll into town until 5:25."

"5:25! I can't wait that long. Maybe I'll ride out to the river and see if I can lend a hand."

"I wouldn't go in those clothes," Mr. Olivera cautioned. "There's lots of mud at the river."

Within fifteen minutes Nathan had run home, changed clothes, left a note for his mom, and saddled Onepenny. He had just led his spotted horse out of the Lander County Livery and parked him next to the corrals when a scream caused him to spin back toward town.

"Nathan T. Riggins, you promised me that you'd wait for the stage!" Leah cried. She held up her long dress and ran down the dusty street.

"I did wait!" he hollered.

"But you ain't waitin' now! And where's them nice clothes you promised?"

"Leah, you saw me! I waited right there for over an hour. The stage is late. Mr. Olivera said it might be stuck in the river again, so I'm ridin' out to see if I can help them get it going again."

"Why ain't you wearin' your good clothes? You don't want Kylie to see you lookin' like that, do ya?"

"I don't care if Kylie ever sees me at all." Nathan mounted Onepenny and turned him north. "It's you he's coming to visit, isn't it?"

"It certainly is . . . and I'm going with you."

"You are not."

"Am too!" she insisted.

"You can't go . . . it isn't proper for a girl to look too anxious."

"Who said that?"

"You did."

"Well . . . I lied. Come on, Nathan, please? You know I been waitin' a year for Kylie to come visit . . . please, let me ride with you!"

"Leah, you are the most aggravating girl I've ever met!" Nathan reached down, grabbed Leah's arm, and pulled her up behind him on the horse. She fussed at keeping her dress pulled down while sitting side-saddle behind the cantle.

"Well, that's jist because you ain't met many girls!" she finally replied.

About a half-mile out of town, Nathan's gray and white dog, Tona, trotted out of the sagebrush and took up the lead, just a few steps ahead of Onepenny.

Leah laced the loose leather strings behind the cantle of Nathan's saddle around her wrists and shook her hair loose as she bounced along in the mild spring breeze that blew from the northwest.

"Nathan, ain't them hills pretty?"

"Yep."

"You are really going to like Kylie—honest," she insisted.

"That's what you keep saying."

"Now you ain't jealous, are you? I mean, I always told you that I ain't never going to marry nobody but Kylie Collins."

"I'm not jealous, Leah. I know you're in love with this Kylie boy."

"I didn't say I loved him," she corrected.

"But you're going to marry him someday!" Nathan pointed out.

"Yeah, but I never did say that I loved him, so don't you go puttin' no words in my mouth!"

"But how could you—"

"The trouble with you, Nathan T. Riggins, is that you jist don't understand women."

Lord, I don't know about women . . . but I know I don't understand this girl!

The snows of winter and the heavy rain in early April had decorated the mountains north of Galena with dark green grass. It was bunched here and there between the sage, but from a distance the landscape all looked solid green to Nathan. It was his first spring in Nevada, and he marveled that the barren hills could look so lush. Even the tailing piles scattered by the diggings of frustrated miners sprouted grass among the rusts and yellows of discarded gravel.

"You know, Leah, when all the mines are played out, this sure would make good country for a cattle ranch."

"Are you going to be a rancher when you grow up . . . or a lawman like your daddy? I sure hope you won't be a lawman."

"Why?"

"'Cause you'd bring your wife nothin' but aggravation and worry—always wondering if you would get shot or somethin'. Jist like when your Daddy got shot last winter."

"He's all right now," Nathan reminded her.

"Sure, but it was mighty close."

"Well, I'll probably be a rancher . . . or maybe governor," he teased.

"Governor? Boy, that'll be the day. Governor Nathan T. Riggins." Leah paused for a moment and then said softly, "I'd vote for ya."

"Women can't vote."

"Well . . . it won't make no difference. You wouldn't win. My daddy says all them politicians is crooked, and you don't ever cheat, lie, or nothin' like that."

For about an hour they bounced along with only brief conversations. Finally, Leah waved her hand at a dark ribbon of foliage stretching out ahead of them.

"Look!" She pointed at the trees. "There's the crossing!"

Two rapping sounds caused Nathan to pull Onepenny up.

"Someone's shooting!" he cautioned.

"It's a holdup! They're shootin' at the robbers. We better hurry and help them."

"I don't think it's a holdup," Nathan commented. "Look, they're pulling the wagon out of the mud . . . and over there those men are target-practicing or something."

"Maybe Kylie's shootin'. Did I ever tell you what a good shot he is?"

"No, but I did figure out he is perfect in every way," Nathan mumbled.

"Are you sure you ain't jist a little bit jealous?" Leah asked.

Nathan didn't bother answering. He rode straight toward the stagecoach.

"Hi, Mr. Davis . . . did the stage get stuck again?"

"Nate . . . you ride out from town? Miss Walker . . . are you two out for a little picnic?" He raised his eyebrows.

"We ain't on no picnic," Leah replied.

"We were worried about you being so late," Nathan informed him.

"Well, I sure appreciate the concern. I just pulled her out. Now as soon as I scrape the mud off and get the passengers reloaded, we'll be back on the road."

"Is that the passengers up on the knoll?"

"Yep, three fellas. Two are headed to Austin, and the other's gettin' off in Galena."

"It must be Kylie!" Leah exclaimed.

"I don't reckon I heard a name," Mr. Davis reported. "Say, will you two ride up there and tell them to come on back now. They ain't going to bring down that old boy at that distance with handguns anyway."

"What are they shooting at?"

"Oh, that bull buffalo that's been wandering around out here all winter."

"Buffalo! Thunder? They can't do that!" Nathan hollered. "That buffalo belongs to the Rocky Mountain Exposition Company!"

"Well, it's been a nuisance all winter. It rammed this stage last week! It's crazy!"

"I got to stop them!" Nathan spurred Onepenny, and the spotted horse burst into a gallop with Nathan's dog, Tona, barking ahead of them. Nathan took a hard left turn when he hit the mud at the edge of the river. He heard a scream and felt Leah losing her grip around his waist. She tumbled off the back of the horse, but Nathan didn't look back.

Lord, don't let them shoot Thunder! It wasn't his idea to get stranded out here!

Nathan could see two men and a boy standing on a hill with smoking revolvers in their hands.

"Hey! Stop! You can't do that! Don't shoot him!" he screamed. Tona sprinted at the men barking incessantly.

The three looked surprised as they turned to stare at Nathan galloping up the hill. Nathan figured the boy in the middle to be a couple of years older than himself.

That's Kylie Collins? He's not much bigger than me . . . and he's not all that strong.

"I say," one of the men called to Nathan, "what's all the screaming about? You startled that bison. How will we shoot it now?"

Nathan stood in his stirrups and looked out across the prairie at Thunder, who stood about a hundred yards away, facing them, but no longer retreating.

"You can't shoot that buffalo . . . it belongs to the Rocky Mountain Exposition Company of North Platte, Nebraska."

"You're lyin'," the blond-haired boy answered. "You can't own a buffalo!"

One of the men raised his pistol to fire another shot.

"No . . . wait!" Nathan insisted. "I'm telling the truth. You see, Dakota Williams and his Rocky Mountain Show were on the train going to San Francisco last fall, and Thunder —that's the buffalo's name—busted out of the cattle car and ran off. They couldn't catch him, so they had to go on. But last winter I found him, and I've been bringing him a little feed now and then. I wrote to Mr. Williams, and he said that they would pick up Thunder on their way back to North Platte in the spring."

"That's absurd," the man said and again lifted his gun.

Nathan spurred Onepenny in front of the man blocking his view.

"I say . . . move that horse!" the man commanded.

"Look," Nathan reasoned, "Mr. Davis said it's time to load the stage."

"Not without downing that bison," the man insisted.

"You can't kill it with a handgun from here. You'll just wound it and make it mad. Then it will charge you, and someone will get hurt."

"Well, that would be one way to get it close enough to shoot," the boy chimed in.

"Nobody's going to shoot that buffalo!"

The boy took two steps to the left of Onepenny and raised his gun. Nathan dove out of the saddle and knocked the boy to the ground. The revolver tumbled into the sage. Tona pounced into the fight barking and biting at the other boy's heels.

Both boys struggled to their feet. Nathan ducked, but the fist still caught him in the side of his neck just below his left ear. The blow made him stagger back.

Oh, man . . . he's bigger than me!

Diving below the next wild swing, Nathan tackled the

boy to the ground and threw a punch to the midsection. He felt his knuckles sink into the soft flesh below the rib cage. Suddenly, a knee slammed into Nathan's stomach, and he rolled over trying to catch his breath.

The other boy was on his feet, and Nathan recovered in time to grab a shoe as the boy kicked at his side. He twisted the foot sharply to the right, and the boy let out a piercing scream just about the time Nathan heard two guns fire.

"You busted my ankle!" the boy cried. "You broke it!"

The boy stumbled back and fell to the ground clutching his ankle.

"My word!" one of the men shouted. "That beast is actually going to charge us!"

Tona was still barking as Nathan looked up to see Thunder begin his charge from across the prairie. The two men ran for the river.

"Wait! Uncle Jed! Help me!" the boy yelled as the buffalo pounded toward them.

Nathan leaped into the saddle and stationed Onepenny between the buffalo and the boy on the ground. The spotted horse spun his hindquarters toward the charging animal.

"Stay, Onepenny . . . stay!"

Tona barked.

Onepenny nervously pranced.

Thunder shook the prairie.

The boy on the ground cried.

Nathan prayed.

The buffalo ran straight at Nathan and then, only twenty yards in front of them, suddenly swerved off to the left and pursued the men running toward the river. He didn't slow until both men dove headfirst into the swollen stream.

Then Thunder pulled up, peered at the men, turned, and

slowly walked back out into the prairie, never glancing back at the confusion behind him.

Nathan jumped down and patted his horse's neck. "That-a-boy, Onepenny . . . good horse! You stayed with me again, didn't you."

Tona slinked off into the sage eyeing the buffalo.

"I can't believe it!" the boy on the ground marveled. "You and that horse blocked off that stampeding buffalo!"

"Onepenny's a good horse. We've had run-ins with that old boy before."

"Look," said the boy wiping the tears from his cheeks, "I'm sorry about the fight. I was . . . you know . . . mad."

"Well, just don't go shootin' animals for the fun of it. He really does belong to Dakota Williams."

"Can you help me back to the stage? My ankle is busted."

Nathan slipped the reins over the saddle horn, and Onepenny trailed along behind them. Nathan let the boy hold on to his shoulder as he limped back to the stage.

It wasn't until they got to the stage that he remembered Leah. She was hunkered down on a log trying to wipe the mud off her face.

"You ruined my good dress, Nathan T. Riggins!" she cried. "Look at this! Look at this! How could you do this to me?"

"Leah, I'm sorry . . . it's just that they were shooting at . . . Thunder." He noticed that the boy was staring at Leah.

"Oh, yeah . . . listen. Eh . . . this really is Leah Walker, and her dress was very pretty, and before I dumped her into the mud, she looked great!" Nathan stammered. "'Course there's no need for me to introduce you two. I'm really sorry, Leah. I know this isn't the way you wanted it to go."

"What are you talking about?" She sniffled.

"I know you wanted to look pretty for Kylie and—"

"That ain't Kylie!" she whispered

"It isn't?" Then he turned to the boy. "Who are you?"

"Eh . . . Mason DeLaney. Who's she?"

"Leah Walker, a friend . . . a good friend of mine."

"Well, I ain't your friend no more! You treat me bad, Nathan T. Riggins. You really treat me bad!"

Mr. Davis finally got his passengers loaded up. Leah, partially clean, rode behind Nathan as they began to trot back to town.

"Say, you two!" Davis shouted. "I jist 'membered. I got a letter for each of you in the dispatch."

"A letter?" Leah smiled.

"Yep. Here they are." He swung down off the stage and handed them up to Nathan. "Ain't no reason for you to wait until I get to town."

T W O

Onepenny trotted beside a wagon rut toward Galena as Nathan and Leah bounced and ripped their letters open.

"He ain't comin'!" she moaned. "They're goin' straight to Silver City from Fort Hall, and they ain't comin' down here!"

"I don't believe it!" Nathan shouted.

"You'd better believe it. It says so right here."

"Man, this must be my lucky day! It's an answer to prayer!" Nathan laughed.

Leah reached up and wiped a tear from her cheek. "Nathan, you ain't got no right to be funnin' me about this!"

"Wait until I tell everybody in town!" Nathan shouted waving his letter back at Leah.

Suddenly, Leah wound up and slugged Nathan in the right arm, causing him to clutch the saddle horn to keep from sliding off the horse.

"What did you do that for?" he hollered, rubbing the ripe bruise.

"'Cause you're making sport of me and . . ." Now the tears were streaming down her face. "And cause I'm all covered with mud, and Kylie ain't comin', and cause I cain't learn my lines to the play, and—"

"Kylie's not coming to see you?" Nathan asked.

"Of course he ain't! I read you the letter."

"Oh, yeah . . . your letter. Who was it from?"

Leah brushed her long brown hair back from her eyes. "I told you it was from Kylie! Weren't you listenin'?"

"I, eh . . . I guess I got sidetracked with my letter," he admitted.

"Who is your letter from?" Leah spoke softly now.

"It's from Dakota Williams," Nathan reported.

"Honest?"

"Yep. So what happened to Kylie Collins?" Nathan stood in the stirrups and stretched his legs.

"You really weren't makin' fun of me, were you? Nathan, I'm sorry I hit you." Leah reach up and rubbed Nathan's arm where she had clobbered him.

Nathan pulled up Onepenny and stopped. Then he turned and glanced at the tear-streaked freckles across the bridge of her nose. "Have you been crying?"

"Yeah."

"I'm real sorry, Leah. Honest, I am." Nathan tried to comfort her.

"Listen, all I said was that Kylie and his parents are goin' on to the Idaho mines, and they ain't comin' down."

"I know how much you were looking forward to this. Maybe he can come down in the summer."

"Yeah . . . maybe," she murmured.

Nathan spurred Onepenny, and they trotted toward town. Both were quiet for a minute.

"She'll be really mad at me," Leah finally said.

"Who?"

"My stepmother. She told me to save this dress for church. I snuck it out and wore it anyway. She can get mule-cross when she's mad."

"Why don't you stop at my house and let my mother wash it out for you? She's good at getting mud out of my clothes."

"Nathan?"

"Yeah?"

"If you weren't funnin' me, then what were you hollering about?"

"Oh! It's my letter. Listen to this!

Dear Master Nathan T. Riggins,

I received your note concerning my buffalo, Thunder, on April 4. I appreciate your seeing that he had plenty to eat this winter. Unfortunately, the Rocky Mountain Exposition Show was rained out for twenty-one straight days, and I had to disband the company.

Not all is lost. I've been elected Mayor of Stockton and plan to settle here for a while. All of this is to say that I will not be coming back through Nevada to pick up Thunder. So here is my offer. I will sell Thunder to you for the price of $1.00. Just sign both copies of the bill of sale, and mail one copy to me with a dollar, and the buffalo is yours.

If you learn how to keep him in a pen, you're a better man than I am.

Yours truly,
Dakota Williams

"Can you believe it? I'm going to own a buffalo!"

"Why?"

"Why, what?"

Leah grabbed Nathan's waist as Onepenny picked up the pace. "Why do you want to own a buffalo? You goin' to butcher it?"

"Butcher it? Are you crazy?" Nathan moaned. "Haven't you been reading the newspapers? They're shooting all the buffalo on the eastern slope and plains. Daddy says some-day buffalo will be as rare as a cool day in July. And I'll own one. Me, Nathan T. Riggins, buffalo rancher."

"One buffalo don't make a ranch," she protested.

"Leah, you just don't have any vision. Can't you see? I'll be the only kid in Nevada who owns a buffalo."

"You're the only kid in Nevada that wants one."

"Look, you don't understand, do you? I own a buffalo! Not even old Kylie Collins can say that!"

Leah was quiet for a few minutes.

"Nathan?"

"Yeah."

"You was just a little jealous of Kylie, weren't ya?"

Nathan was silent.

"Yeah," he finally admitted. "I was a little jealous."

"Thanks, Nathan," she whispered.

"For what?"

"For sayin' you was jealous. It makes me feel good."

"I wasn't lying."

"I know—you don't ever lie."

Nathan thought for a moment he could feel Leah hold-ing tighter to his waist. Then she turned loose and grabbed the saddle strings.

"Were you serious about your mama washing my dress?" she finally asked.

"Sure. She's good at that kind of thing."

"What do you think she'll say?"

"About the dress?"

"No, about the buffalo," Leah said impatiently. "What will your parents say when you tell them you own a buf-falo?"

"Oh, I'm sure they'll be impressed by my ingenuity."

"You did what?" Nathan's mother roared as she scrubbed Leah's dress across the washboard.

"I bought Thunder, the buffalo, for only a dollar. I already mailed Mr. Williams the money, and I've got the bill of sale—see. It's all legal and—"

"What in the world are you going to do with a buffalo?" she grilled.

"Why does everyone keep asking me that?" Nathan complained. "Nobody ever asks, 'What are you going to do with a dog?' or 'What are you going to do with a horse?'"

"Dogs don't require a corral and four tons of hay! And you can't ride a buffalo! If he stampedes again and runs over a wagon or something, you will now be responsible," his father lectured.

"That's just the point. I'll keep him safe in a corral, and he won't bother anyone, and no one will bother him."

"What corral?"

"Shipley's. The bank owns the place now that the Shipleys moved to Arizona Territory, and Mr. Maddison said I could use the corral until the place is sold."

"That corral won't hold a newborn calf, let alone a 2,500-pound buffalo," Mr. Riggins insisted.

"But me and Colin and Leah can patch it up. Don't you see, Dad? Galena will be the only town in Nevada with its very own buffalo."

"And I'm the marshal in Galena. If that animal causes trouble, I'll shoot it. Have you got that clear?"

"Yes, sir! Does this mean I get to keep him?"

"Until we get hungry enough to butcher it. But I'm not going to help you bring it in. If you can sweet-talk it into

Shipley's corral, then you can keep it. I'm not paying for hay, and I'm not haulin' manure. Do you understand?"

"Yes, sir. As soon as summer vacation starts, I can double my hours at the Mercantile. I'll buy plenty of hay this summer."

"You've got to get him rounded up first," his father reminded him.

"David," Mrs. Riggins asked her husband, "do you think Nathan can bring that buffalo in by himself? I mean, would it be safe?"

"I think," Marshal Riggins said as he pulled on his hat, "that if he can't get it to town, it doesn't belong to him." Then right before he left the house, he turned back. "And whatever you do, don't try to rope it."

"Yes, sir . . . I'll remember," Nathan blurted out.

By 8:00 A.M. Saturday, Nathan had his crew rounded up. Leah, wearing an old dark dress and a hat pulled down on her head, rode a roan mare. Colin, sporting his woolly chaps and spurs on his boots, rode his father's buckskin gelding.

Nathan tied Onepenny to the Shipley corral gate. Tona had already sniffed the corrals and was turning circles in preparation for a nap in the shade.

"We got to build fence first," Nathan reminded them.

"It looks all right to me," Colin offered.

"It wouldn't curb a calf," Nathan responded. "Your dad said we could use those rails in the barn." Nathan waved his hand at a stack of long boards.

"He did?"

"Yep. Come on. You guys hold a rail up, and I'll nail it tight."

While Leah held one end of the board, Colin hoisted the other. With both hands clutching the hammer handle, Nathan pounded twenty-penny common nails to attach the rail to the posts.

"There are forty-one loose boards in this corral and eleven that are missing completely. Did you know that you'll have to drive in seventy-three nails? If each one takes about ten blows, Nathan . . . you'll have to pound nails 730 times to finish the job," Colin called out.

"Yeah . . . thanks, Colin," Nathan moaned. "That should keep me busy for a while."

"How does he figure all of that out?" Leah asked.

"Why does he figure all of that out?" Nathan countered.

"Hey," Colin yelled, "it's boring holding boards. When are we going to go cowboying?"

"When we have a buffalo-tight fence," Nathan called back.

"You think this will hold him?" Leah asked.

"A five-rail fence of rough-cut two-by-eights nailed onto railroad ties sunk four feet into the ground—yeah, it will hold him. Thunder's kind of peaceful as long as you don't get him riled."

"Colin's right. It is boring just standing here."

"You want to drive the nails?" Nathan rubbed his hands. They were already turning red and sore.

"Nah . . . hey!" Leah looked up with a wide grin. "Let's practice our lines for the play."

"Now?"

"Yeah. 'My maidens and I will fast too, and then I will' . . . 'I will' . . . Don't tell me. I'll get it. 'I will' . . . Aghhh! I never remember that line. I told Miss D'Imperio that I shouldn't have this part. Why did she make me Queen Esther? She knows I don't speak good."

"I don't like my part either," Colin yelled from the other end of a board. "Haman's not all that bad. I don't think it's fair that he gets hung!"

"Nathan, what comes after 'I will'?"

"'I will go to the king, which is—'"

"'Which is not permitted by the law,'" she squealed. "'And if . . . I perish, . . . I perish!'" She bowed low as she completed the line, which caused the weight of the board to shift to Colin, who promptly dropped it on his toe.

"Oh, man! Quit fooling around down there," he cried out. "I nearly broke my foot!"

"'The enemy is this wicked Haman!'" Leah grinned.

"It's not funny!" Colin called.

"Colin's right."

"I'm sorry, Colin," Leah apologized.

"Come on. Let's get this done and go buffalo hunting," Nathan encouraged them.

As it turned out, they ate the noon meal at Nathan's house. Then they mounted up for the ride out to the river with a flour sack stuffed with hay tied on the back of Onepenny. Tona trotted ahead of them.

When they arrived at the stage crossing, they searched the hillsides and cottonwoods but saw nothing.

"Maybe someone captured him," Leah suggested.

"Maybe the Indians shot him for food," Colin added.

"Yeah, and maybe he wandered off to find people who treat him nicer," Nathan replied. "Leah, you ride up on that bluff and see what you can see. Colin, you ride downstream. And I'll look upstream."

Within minutes, Colin screamed. Leah and Nathan raced to where Colin sat on his horse.

"There he is!" he shouted. "He's getting a drink!"

"What do we do now, Nathan?" Leah asked.

"Eh . . . you and Colin go way over by that tallest cottonwood. When he comes out of the river, don't let him head that direction. Me and Onepenny will cut him off from this direction. Then he'll have to start moving toward town. I figure once we get him moving, we'll just hang way back and graze him toward town."

"So we just ride over there and wait for him to come back out of the river?" Leah asked.

"Yep. He surely can't stay in that one position very long," Nathan predicted.

Actually, according to Colin's pocket watch, Thunder stayed in the mud along the river for one hour and eleven minutes more. Nathan, Colin, and Leah were all under the same cottonwood tree, sprawled on a fallen log and studying every movement of the animal.

"I don't think he's leaving the mud," Colin said.

"Maybe we should throw something at him," Leah suggested.

Nathan paced in front of the other two. "No, that would aggravate him, and he'd charge right at us."

"Then see if you can get him to come out and eat some hay. Isn't that why you brought it?" she urged.

"I was saving it for an emergency," Nathan protested.

"Riggins, this is an emergency!" Colin hollered. "If we don't get him out of the river, we'll waste the whole afternoon."

"Okay. Take positions on both sides. Me and Onepenny

will ride straight up to the bank of mud and scatter some hay."

When the other two were in position, Nathan rode toward the buffalo. Thunder stood at a forty-five-degree angle to the river. He could turn toward the water or glance back at the intruders. Most of the time he stared at Tona, who was content to bark at a considerable distance from everyone.

"Thunder! Look . . . it's your dinner! Come on, boy . . . come on! It's mighty good hay! Come on!" Nathan called.

The big bison glanced up at Nathan, still thirty feet away, and then stared at the hay on the river bank. Finally, he started to yank his right front foot out of the mud, but nothing happened. Over and over, the buffalo struggled to move one of his feet, but he remained rooted to that one position.

"He's stuck!" Leah called to Nathan.

"Man, we would have been waiting forever!" Colin griped. "Did you guys bring anything to eat? I'm hungry."

"Look, we are going to have to get him out."

"How?" Leah asked.

"Well . . . I'll . . . eh, I'll toss a loop over him and drag him out. I've seen them do that with cows."

"Didn't your daddy say not to rope him?" she protested.

"That's only when he's out running around. After we pull him out of the mud, he won't feel like running anywhere."

"Is your rope long enough to reach?" Colin asked.

"It is if I wade in there a little."

"Don't get Onepenny stuck," Leah warned.

Nathan pulled his rawhide *riata* off his saddle and made a big loop. He rotated the rope three times above his head and sailed the loop toward the buffalo's head.

The rope slapped up against the buffalo's nose, and the animal flipped it down in the mud.

"Almost, Nathan! Just a little further," Leah encouraged.

On the fourth attempt, the loop circled the buffalo's huge head, and Nathan pulled his end tight. The powerful animal jerked his neck back and almost yanked Nathan out of the saddle. Quickly he tied off the other end of the rope to his saddle horn.

"I'll just see if Onepenny can back him out of there. I'll keep at the end of the rope. When Thunder gets to the river bank where the hay is, he'll stop and eat. Then I'll see if I can flip the rope off."

Following Nathan's command, Onepenny began to back up the river bank until the rope stretched, strained, and groaned. But the buffalo didn't budge. Trying to avoid getting pinched between the tight rope and the saddle, Nathan spurred Onepenny up the river bank.

Just about the time he expected the rope to break, Leah let out a yell, "Keep going, Nathan! He's got a back leg loose!"

Then a front.

Then the other back.

Then a front.

And then the back ones were stuck again.

One step . . . tight rope . . . straining horse . . . slurping mud sounds . . . then another foot . . . then stuck again.

Very slowly, Thunder made his way to dry ground.

"You did it!" Leah shouted. "Nathan did it, Colin!"

Nathan, still almost thirty feet from the buffalo, struggled to untie the rope from his saddle horn. The buffalo in the meantime shook himself off like a dog after a bath, took one bite of the hay, and then, as if it were a sudden decision, bolted at full speed past a startled Nathan and Onepenny.

Frantically, Nathan still tried to untie the rope.

"Stay, Onepenny! Shut him down! You can hold him!"

The spotted horse dug his back feet into the soft ground and shifted his weight back. When the buffalo hit the end of the rope, he had picked up full speed.

In an instant the cinch on Nathan's saddle snapped in two, and the whole saddle, with a panicked Nathan clutching the saddle horn, went flying into the air.

As he fell to the ground, he could hear Leah scream, "Turn loose! Nathan, turn loose!"

The warning wasn't needed. When he slammed into the ground, he lost his grip and rolled into the sagebrush. Staggering to his hands and knees, he watched as buffalo, rope, and saddle disappeared into the northern Nevada horizon.

THREE

Nathan!" Leah called as she rode toward him. "Nathan, are you hurt?"

With effort, he stood to his feet. His face felt fiery pain. There was a dull throb in his right leg, and a sharp pain shot through his arm. "I think I hit my elbow on a rock or something—that and scraping my face in the dirt . . . I'll be okay. Can you believe that he broke the cinch?"

"What do we do now?" Colin asked as he joined them.

"Go get my saddle back." Nathan dusted himself off and looked for his hat. "Where's Tona?"

"He was last seen chasing your saddle through the brush."

Nathan grabbed the reins on a waiting Onepenny. He spread out the maroon-and-black-striped Navajo saddle blanket, then grabbed a handful of the spotted horse's scraggly mane, and quickly pulled himself up on the horse.

"You goin' to ride bareback?" Colin asked.

"Until I find my saddle." He nodded.

"Where you learn to do that?" Leah asked.

"What?"

"Pull yourself up without a stirrup."

"A girl showed me."

"That Tashawna? Miss Show-off?"

"Nah, it was a Nez Percé girl named Eetalah. Why did you mention Tashawna . . . you aren't a little jealous, are you?"

"I ain't got one bit of jealous in me, and you know it, Nathan T. Riggins!"

Nathan kicked Onepenny, and they trotted off into the sage. A saddle dragged through the desert leaves a distinct trail, and they had no trouble finding the barking Tona and the buffalo. The shaggy-haired, short-horned, huge-headed, brown-eyed bison stood in a small meadow grazing on bunch grass and keeping one eye on Tona who still barked at the saddle.

"I'll try to get that rope untied," Nathan explained. "You two ride over by those rocks. That will give the buffalo something else to think about besides me."

Tona ran to his side when he climbed off Onepenny. Nathan could feel his boot heels sinking into the sandy prairie soil. Working quickly, with Thunder always in view, Nathan untied the rope and pulled back his gear.

The hay in the flour sack had scattered along the way, leaving a civilized trail in a primitive land. Nathan tied his saddle on the back of Leah's horse and remounted Onepenny.

"Now, let's move him toward town. He won't trot along like a cow, but we can graze him in that direction. Colin, you ride on the north side, and, Leah, you take the south. Give him about fifty feet and try not to make him angry."

"Where will you be?" Colin quizzed.

"Tona, Onepenny, and me will sweep along at the back. We'll be the ones to make him move. You two just keep him from drifting south or north."

"What about your rope?" Leah asked.

"I'll have to leave it until later."

With Leah and Colin in place, he rode Onepenny right at the buffalo. When they got within twenty feet, Thunder turned and stared at them. Nathan felt his stomach churn.

He's going to charge!

Then the buffalo looked back to the west and began to trot along through the sage.

"All right! That-a-boy, Onepenny. We bluffed him!" Nathan called.

Soon a pattern developed. The buffalo would wander about fifty steps in the general direction of town and then stop to eat grass and stare at his pursuers. Then Nathan would ride at him, which caused him to scoot on through the sage to another grassy morsel where he'd stop and repeat the process.

"This is getting really boring!" Colin hollered.

"Yeah, but it's working," Nathan called back.

"At this rate we won't get there until tomorrow."

"What's the rush? We've got all afternoon."

Leah held her hand up to shade her eyes. "Nathan, can I say my part in the play again?"

"Yeah . . . go ahead."

"Give me my cue."

Nathan held Onepenny back and let the buffalo eat. "Da te da te da . . . 'and who knows whether you have come to the kingdom for such a time as this?'"

Leah rolled her eyes toward the sky and spoke the words in a monotone, "'Go, gather together all the Jews in Shushan, and fast for me, and neither eat nor drink three days, night or day—'"

Then there was a long pause.

"Don't tell me!"

Nathan began to move the buffalo again.

"Oh, yeah! 'My maidens and I will fast too, and then I will go to the king . . . go to the king . . . to the king . . . the king.'"

"'WHICH IS NOT,'" Colin shouted. "For heaven's sake, Leah, we all know that line!"

"'Which is not permitted by the law; and if I perish, I perish!'" she stammered.

"Well, I'm going to perish at this speed," Colin complained. "I'll get him moving!" He turned his horse toward the buffalo and trotted right at him.

"Wait! Colin, no!" Nathan shouted waving his arms.

With sudden movement from the right, the buffalo stampeded to the left—right at Leah who was bowing in the saddle at the imaginary applause from her theater audience.

Her roan mare bolted at first sight of the charging buffalo. Leah tumbled off the back of the horse and bounced across the prairie.

Without hesitating, Nathan charged the buffalo. The animal veered to the west of Leah just enough to miss running right over the top of her.

"Colin, you idiot! Follow that buffalo!" Nathan shouted as he jumped down to the girl lying motionless next to the sage.

"Leah? Leah!" He knelt and tried to lift up her head. "Leah . . . are you all right? Leah? Say something!" Nathan pleaded. He gently brushed back her long brown hair.

One eye blinked opened and stared at Nathan. He saw her lips move, but he couldn't hear any words.

"What?" He leaned his ear close to her trembling lips.

Suddenly, she hollered, "I said, if I'm going to perish, I ain't going to perish fallin' off another horse!"

Nathan jumped back at her shout and dropped her head into the dirt.

"I'm sorry," he apologized.

Leah sat up and brushed off her dress. She sucked air and tried to talk. "Nathan T. Riggins, I'm going home. Every time I ride out with you, I get dumped. It's hard to be ladylike when I keep falling off a horse."

"Yeah . . . maybe we've done enough for one day."

"Done enough? We've only moved him two miles closer to town."

"At this rate we'll get him there in just five more days," Nathan calculated.

"I ain't got that many arms and legs to break, and you ain't got that many saddles."

"I'm not giving up. I just got to figure a different tactic."

"Yeah, and next time it won't involve me!" she insisted.

Nathan led Onepenny and walked Leah across the prairie to where her horse was standing. She stooped over with her hands on her hips, still trying to regain her pattern of breathing. He left her standing and crawled up on Onepenny.

"Wait here and rest. I'll go get Colin. Then we'll go back to town."

Nathan rode through the sage following the hoof prints of Colin's horse. The hot spring sun glared off the hillside in the breezeless afternoon. He was surprised at how far the buffalo had run. He grabbed tight to Onepenny's mane as they worked their way down a steep *barranca* and along an almost dry streambed. Then the track crossed the little creek and climbed a sheer bank on the far side. Nathan had to pull back on the reins to keep Onepenny from running up the incline. Even before Nathan made it to the top, he could hear Tona's barking.

Cresting the ridge, Nathan was surprised to see a small one-room cabin that was leaning so much it looked as if it would collapse at any moment.

Colin was on his horse facing the building about fifty feet away. Tona was close to the open door barking with unceasing fury.

"Where's Thunder?" Nathan yelled.

"In the cabin," Colin replied.

"Inside? You're kidding me!"

"Look. See your rope coming out the doorway? I saw him run right into that cabin."

"What's he doing in there?"

"How should I know? Maybe he's cooking supper. I'm sure not going in to find out! How's Leah?"

"She's all right . . . eh . . . we're going back to town."

"Giving up on the buffalo? Now that's the smartest thing you've decided in—"

"I'm not giving up! I just want to figure a better method."

"Yeah . . . whatever. Just make sure the next plans don't involve me," Colin replied.

Nathan slid down off Onepenny. "I'm going up to take a look at what he's doing."

"On foot?"

"Yeah. Is that all right with you?"

"Sure, I'll just scrape up what's left of you and carry it back to your mother in a bucket."

Nathan ignored the comment and slowly approached the cabin. He noticed that the door was off the hinges and lying across the front porch, which consisted mainly of broken boards.

The rear end of the buffalo was in full sight, but Nathan couldn't see the head of the animal. As he approached Tona, the dog quit barking and waited by his side. Taking one step at a time, Nathan watched for any sign of movement and tried to keep his spurs from jingling.

If he turns for that doorway, I'm running! Lord, keep me from doing something really, really dumb.

Nathan walked all the way to the porch before he could see the whole animal. For several minutes he just stared.

"What's he doing?" Colin yelled from his position of safety.

"He's just licking the dirt."

"What?"

"He's just licking the dirt. You know, the cabin has a dirt floor, and he's in there licking it."

"Buffaloes don't eat dirt!"

"No, not eating . . . licking. You know, like a salt block? That's it! I'll bet that's a salt lick! You know, where the mineral content's real high! I read about those one time."

"He's really just licking the dirt?"

"Yep." Then Nathan turned to go back to Onepenny. As he did, he slapped his leg and called, "Okay, Tona!" Suddenly, the dog flew into an outrage of barking and dove through the open doorway after the buffalo.

"Tona! No!" Nathan screamed. "I didn't mean attack! I meant come on, let's go home! Tona!"

There was a rumble, a snort, and an explosive crashing of timber as the buffalo butted his way right through the end of the building. Boards and splinters flew everywhere, and Tona was at the big animal's heels.

Nathan jumped back. With a loud crash the entire cabin collapsed into a rubble of broken boards and fractured shingles.

Colin rode up leading Onepenny.

"Did you see that?" Nathan shouted. "Did you see that? He brought the whole building down!"

"We better go catch Tona before he chases that buffalo all the way back to—"

"Hey," Nathan interrupted, "that's the direction of town, isn't it? Let's go get Leah, and then we'll see how far they run."

Nathan and Colin rode back across the prairie, down across the creekbed, to the place they had left Leah.

"Where is she? Did she go home already?" Colin asked.

"Leah? Hey . . . where are you?"

A panicked feeling hit Nathan as he looked down at the tracks in the dirt.

"She probably went—," Colin began.

"Look! Look at those tracks! Someone rode by here . . . no, there were two of them . . . then three. They took Leah with them! They're headed east. Galena is west."

"Maybe they were friends of hers," Colin offered.

"We're friends of hers. She wouldn't desert us. I can't believe I left her out here."

Dropping the reins, Nathan stood straight up on the saddle blanket.

"Can you see her?" Colin pressed.

"I think there's some movement over across the prairie, but it might just be a dust devil. Colin, you ride back to Galena and tell my dad what happened. I'm going to follow this trail."

"What about Tona?"

"He'll take care of himself."

"What about the buffalo?"

"Forget the buffalo. We have to find Leah!"

Nathan clutched Onepenny's mane and kicked the pony's sides as they loped down the trail of the three horses.

Lord, I don't understand. I mean, she was winded, so I just left her there for a minute to go get Colin . . . how could she? . . . Lord, I keep getting Leah into tough situations. It's not fair. She shouldn't even be out here! She's just got to be all right! Please, Lord.

The tracks made a sharp left turn and headed straight

toward the mountains. He wiped the sweat from his forehead and replaced his hat.

I've got to find her before we reach the mountains. I can't go in there alone.

Nathan kicked Onepenny into a gallop. It was all he could do to hold on and not get bounced off. The horse slammed into his backside like a paddle during a spanking. Then he saw a grove of cottonwoods tucked up against the hills—and a stout set of corrals with fifteen to twenty horses milling in various pens. He was surprised no one was with the horses.

Horse thieves? Maybe they stole Leah's horse. Maybe they shot her and left her back there on the prairie!

A well-worn trail stretched away from the corrals back up into a canyon. The entry was narrow, and Nathan felt as if he were entering a trap. He slowly rode Onepenny deeper into the shadows. A cool, comfortable breeze drifted out of the canyon, and Nathan could smell sweet grass somewhere up ahead. Finally, the trail broke into an open meadow covered with green grass and purple wildflowers.

He stopped the horse the minute he spotted the small log cabin at the back of the meadow. It stood against a massive sandstone cliff, and a thin trail of smoke feathered skyward from the chimney. Nathan thought he could see three horses tied in front. One was Leah's roan mare. He left Onepenny grazing back in the shadows and crept through the tall grass on his hands and knees.

My saddle is still on Leah's horse . . . if I can sneak up close and pull my rifle . . . maybe . . . Lord, please don't let anything happen to Leah.

A natural spring seeped into the middle of the meadow, and Nathan soon was dragging himself through mud.

I've got to get there quickly . . . really quick!

Once he reached the yard, Nathan crouched behind a stubby tree and looked for movement in the cabin. Then he crept over to Leah's horse. Carefully standing up so the horse would block the view of anyone in the cabin, Nathan quietly unsnapped his rifle from the scabbard. Creeping up to the front porch, he crawled under the unshuttered window. Nathan held his rifle toward the door as he strained to hear what was going on inside. He could hear muffled voices and whispers, but they seemed to be coming from a back room.

Lord, I'm just a kid. What if I run in there, and they just shoot me down? Then I haven't helped Leah at all. And what if I don't? What if she needs me right now?

Suddenly, the front door opened. Nathan threw the gun to his shoulder, but he had no idea what he would do next. No one appeared at the door, but a brown ball of fur tumbled out onto the porch, and the door was once again slammed shut. The little fur ball jumped to its feet, yipped once at Nathan, and then trotted over to him.

A puppy? These horse thieves keep a puppy in there?

The pup excitedly sniffed Nathan's boots.

Tona! He smells Tona!

Nathan reached down and scratched the little dog's head. The big-footed, flop-eared pup rolled over on its back.

"You want your stomach scratched, huh, boy?" Nathan whispered. "I wish you could tell me what's going on in there."

The pup crawled up on Nathan's lap and settled down, closing his eyes in the warm afternoon sun. Nathan petted the dog a few more times and then set the sleeping puppy on the front porch. Slowly, Nathan pulled himself up to the window, hoping to get a quick peek inside.

Just as he got his left eye even with the glass window, he spotted a kid with his face to the window looking out at him. In panic, Nathan fell to the porch and scurried around to the side of the building.

He saw me for sure! They've got some other kid in there and . . .

Then he had a sinking feeling—the kind he always got in class when he went to the chalkboard to do a problem and everyone in class could see him do it wrong.

It was me! Riggins, you idiot, that was your reflection in the glass! Oh, man, I hope nobody ever finds out about this.

The puppy had trailed him around to the side and stayed underfoot as he made his way back to the front porch. He had just about gotten up enough nerve to peek through the window again when an agonizing scream echoed out of the back room.

Nathan jumped to his feet, cocked his rifle, and kicked open the front door. He burst through the dimly lit, unoccupied front room and barged into the back room waving his rifle and shouting, "Leah! Leah!"

He stopped immediately in his tracks when he saw what was happening in the room.

"Leah? Dr. Stanton? Oh no . . . that lady in bed . . . she's having a . . . a . . ."

"Nathan T. Riggins, you get out of here right now," Leah scolded. "Cain't you see she's having a baby! Go on! Go on!"

"Horse thieves . . . where's the horse . . . it's a real baby!"

The voices sounded distant to Nathan, and all in the room looked as if they were standing far away at the end of a tunnel. Above a dull hum, Nathan heard Leah yell, "Don't you go fainting on us, Nathan Riggins. Doc Stanton and me is busy enough with tending to a . . ."

Then everything went black.

FOUR

The voices were familiar. A man . . . a woman . . . another man . . . a girl. The girl was talking to him. But it was dark. And she spoke softly. Persistently.

Nathan knew he should be saying something.

But he couldn't remember where he was.

Leah!

He sat straight up opening both eyes wide.

"Leah?"

"Well, if it ain't the world's bravest boy! It's a good thing Doc Stanton didn't need you to help out. When it comes to deliverin' babies, you're 'bout as valuable as a sack of taters!"

"Baby? That lady was having a baby!" Nathan looked around and realized he was now in the front room of the cabin.

"That lady is Mrs. Dodge, and you sure didn't help none runnin' in there waving a gun and shoutin'! What was you yelling about?"

"Horse thieves . . . I mean . . . I thought you'd been kidnapped or something."

"And you was comin' to rescue me?" Leah asked.

"Eh . . . well . . . yeah, I guess that was it."

"Well, I was waiting out there for you and Colin, and all of a sudden Doc Stanton and Mr. Dodge come galloping along. Doc shouts to follow him cause he's going to need my help."

"You?"

"I helped him deliver Mrs. McNeil's baby last December, or don't you remember?"

"Eh . . . I guess I forgot."

"Well, Mrs. Dodge was havin' a real tough time with a breech birth, and so Mr. Dodge rode for the Doc, and I came to help."

"But you're just a girl—a kid . . . you don't . . ."

"I know a whole lot more things than you think I know, Mr. Nathan T. Riggins!"

"How about the baby? Is he . . . eh, she . . . is it all right?"

"*He* is doing very well, thank you. Christopher Carson Dodge. But Mrs. Dodge is pretty much worn out. Doc Stanton has to get on out to the Konesky's, so they asked if I would spend the night here. Just in case I could be some help."

"Really? They want you?"

Leah tilted her head and let slip a half-grin, half-frown. There was something about the expression that startled Nathan.

It's like Leah . . . but it's not Leah. It's . . . it's like an older Leah. It's like she isn't a kid anymore.

"Nathan?"

"Uh . . . yeah?"

"You was starin' at me."

"Oh . . . maybe . . . you know, I'm still a little fuzzy from fainting."

"Well, I need you to tell my daddy that I'll probably be here until after dinner tomorrow. Then I'll ride back."

"By yourself?"

"You could come out and ride back with me if you want, but I ain't afraid to ride by myself, mind ya."

"Yeah . . . after church I'll come out." Nathan stood to his feet and picked up his rifle and his hat.

Doctor Stanton came out of the room with Mr. Dodge and left some final instructions for Leah.

"Well, son," he said resting his hand on Nathan's shoulder, "I think we can leave now."

"Yes, sir, I'm sorry for barging in there like that, Mr. Dodge. I was looking for Leah."

"No problem, son. I'd have acted the same way if I thought my Sarah was in danger. You got a mighty fine girlfriend here. She's a stander. If I was you, I'd keep the other boys away from her, if you catch my drift." Mr. Dodge grinned.

"Well, he ain't my—," Leah began.

"Yes, sir, I think I will," Nathan interrupted.

He borrowed a cinch from Mr. Dodge, and Leah walked with him across the meadow to where Onepenny stood munching on the grass. As he repaired his saddle, Leah asked, "Did you really break in there thinking you'd have to shoot your way out to rescue me?"

"Yeah."

"Thanks. You're a good friend. I ain't never had many friends that good. I mean, I ain't never had *any* friend that good."

"Well, a person's got to stick by his friends—right?"

"Yeah." Leah watched Nathan mount up and stand in the stirrups to get the saddle well set. "Nathan, you know, if you wanted to . . . I mean, if you ever needed to say to someone that you was my boyfriend, I promise I won't get mad at you."

Nathan smiled. "Okay, but I better not tell old Kylie Collins that."

"Now jist 'cause I said you can call me your girlfriend don't mean I'm goin' to marry you!"

"Here comes Doc. I'll see you tomorrow." He turned toward the oncoming horse and spurred Onepenny. Just when he reached the rocky, narrow exit of the canyon, he turned and waved to Leah, who still stood shading her eyes by the cottonwood.

She waved back.

When they reached the horse corrals, Doc Stanton stopped and let his horse drink from the springs.

"Well, Nathan, you head on back to town. I've got one more stop to make."

"Doc, what's with this pen of wild horses?"

"Well, Mr. Dodge breaks horses for the army up at Fort Hall. And he says there isn't enough water for them all up in the canyon, so he leaves them down here unless he expects some trouble. You'll talk to Mr. Walker for me, won't you? I don't want him worrying about Leah."

"I'll go tell him."

"Well, I'll see you back in town."

"Yes, sir."

After watching Doctor Stanton ride out of sight, Nathan returned to the prairie and took the stage road back to Galena. It was a good half-hour before he remembered Colin. *Oh no! I told Colin to send my dad out with some men to rescue Leah! He'll be riding out here for nothing.*

Nathan spurred Onepenny to a fast trot and pulled his stampede string tight against his chin. Expecting to spot his dad at every rise and turn, he was surprised when he caught sight of Galena in the distance.

"Maybe I missed him," he moaned to his spotted horse.

He was planning on riding straight to his father's

office, but a noise off in the sage to the left caught his attention.

"Tona? Hey, Tona!"

Nathan jumped down to grab his gray and white dog.

"You just came on home? That's a good boy! What are you barking at? My rope! All right! You drug my rope all the way home?"

Nathan grabbed the end of the rope and began to coil it neatly.

"We'll go back out tomorrow afternoon and get that old boy. I think he'll move for us if we catch him in a good mood. Hey, you must have caught this on a . . . sage . . . oh, no!"

Nathan had rounded the tall sagebrush, and suddenly he was not more that ten feet away from 2,500 pounds of very tired buffalo. Thunder, still wearing Nathan's rope like a necktie, lay in the dirt, lathered up and panting.

"Eh, excuse me . . . I think I'll just . . . walk on back out of here," Nathan stammered.

At a safe distance Nathan remounted Onepenny and circled the beast.

"Tona, did you run him all the way to town? I don't believe it! Did Colin help you? He probably kept you going toward town, didn't he? Where is Colin? I bet he rode on in to get Dad. I told him to forget about the buffalo. Anyway, come on Tona; we can let that old boy rest awhile."

Nathan rode straight to his dad's office and explained the situation with Leah. He was surprised to find out that Colin hadn't come by yet.

"He was awful hungry," Nathan added as he left the marshal's office. "Maybe he went over to the Mercantile to buy some of those creme fills."

Nathan stopped by Mr. Walker's barber shop and told

Leah's father where she was. Then he swung by the Mercantile, but no one had seen Colin.

Did he go home for supper without even sending any-one out to help me and Leah? What if there really had been trouble? What if we had been kidnapped by horse thieves? What if we were shot and bleeding in some lonely cabin? What if the Indians carried us off to make us slaves in their secret camp? What if . . . Lord, I've got to stop reading all those stories in Frank Leslie's Illustrated.

Nathan picked up a fresh sack of hay at the Lander County Livery and rode by the Shipley place.

"Well, Tona, our corral sure looks stout enough. I guess we'll know soon enough."

Nathan took about six trips to the Shipley well with an iron-handled wooden bucket and filled a small water trough in the corral. Then he opened the gate wide and propped it that way with a rock. He crawled back up on Onepenny.

"Now if Mr. Thunder will just march into that pen, I'll have me my buffalo."

And if he doesn't, he'll probably stampede through town terrorizing every man, woman, and child. . . . I ought to go find Colin and make him help me finish this job. But if I can do it myself, I bet no one else in this whole town ever penned a buffalo single-handed.

As he rode back out of town, he noticed a wagon stopped out in the sagebrush near where he had left the buffalo. When he came closer, he could read the faded sign on the side—Hawthorne H. Miller, Photographer, Author, Lecturer. He was startled to see the wagon parked not more than twenty-five feet from the buffalo. Thunder gawked warily at a man in dirty gray frock coat moving quickly to set up his equipment. He hummed and sang as he worked.

"'Tenting tonight, tenting tonight, tenting on the old camp ground . . .'"

"Excuse me, Mister."

"Oh . . . my word, you startled me, son. I'm terribly busy at the moment. Just wait 'til I'm through. Say, maybe you'd like to help me. Could you hand me that black box, the little one there."

Still mounted on Onepenny, Nathan lifted the box out of the wagon and handed it to the man.

"Mister, you better be careful. That—"

"Son, I know exactly what I'm doing. You are speaking to none other than Hawthorne H. Miller! I'm sure you've read my books and seen some of my photographic exhibits."

"I've never heard of you."

"Oh . . . well, I suppose things are primitive out here. Ah, so much the better. More people will be delighted to purchase such historic photographs."

"Mr. Miller, I'm not joshing you. If that buffalo decides to run, he'll bust your camera, your wagon, and your body like it was a matchstick."

"Well, he looks rather docile. Besides, I tied the end of that rope to the wagon wheel. Just how far can he get?"

"A wagon wheel? He'll rip that off and drag it all the way to Utah."

"I hardly think so." Miller pushed his rounded crown hat back and glanced up at Nathan sitting in the saddle. "What makes you an expert on buffalo?"

"I'm not an expert. But Thunder there is my buffalo."

"What do you mean, your buffalo? People don't own buffaloes."

"I do. That's my rope on him, and I've got a bill of sale

right here in my pocket. I bought Thunder from Dakota Williams."

"Dakota Williams!" Miller roared. "Thunder? This is the famous buffalo, Thunder? My word, I saw him at the Rocky Mountain Exposition in North Platte last fall!"

"Well, he belongs to me now, and I can't let you take a picture of him."

"Hmphh. I suppose you want a sitting fee. It's an outrage, but I'll . . . I'll give you fifty cents for permission to photograph the buffalo."

"Nope, I don't want—"

"Oh, my word, is there no respect for art? Money-hungry children just don't . . . oh, all right. One dollar, but not a copper more. Do you understand?"

"Mr. Miller, you can't photograph him right now for all the money in the Comstock. I've got to get him into a corral in town first. Then you can photograph him for free. If you flash that pan, he'll run off, and I'll have to start all over."

"Obviously, you know very little about this buffalo. Thunder was raised as an infant by Dakota Williams and used to eat scraps at the family table. I read it in the broadside advertisement for the Exposition. Look at him! You could probably get him to roll over and let you scratch his stomach. Say? I wonder if you'd like to be in the picture? You could—"

"I'm not getting close to him, Mr. Miller. I don't care what you read in some flyer—he's about as wild and stubborn as they come. He's charged me on more than one occasion, and I just saw him level a cabin about five miles down the road. Like I said, as soon as I get him penned, I'll let you photograph him through the gate or something."

"Corral? Penned? Anyone can photograph a buffalo in

captivity, but out here in the wild—what a shot! 'The Last Buffalo in Nevada!' Tremendous! Splendid!"

Miller returned to setting up his equipment.

"Mr. Miller, you can't do it. I won't let you do it. He's my buffalo, and you can't go scaring him off!"

"Son, you annoy me. If you persist in being distractive, you leave me no choice but to report you to the local constable."

"You mean the marshal in Galena?"

"Is that the name of this town?"

"Yes, sir."

"Well, then, I will surely report you to the marshal of Galena!"

Nathan reached over and pulled his rifle out of the scabbard.

"I s-say," Miller stammered, "no young ruffian will threaten me!"

"How about going to get the marshal? Tell him his son, Nathan, won't let you scare off his buffalo."

"Your father is the marshal? My word, what kind of town is this?"

"Look, Mr. Miller, I really don't want you to scare the buffalo. So just pack up your gear and slip out of here before he makes kindling out of you and your wagon."

The man stared at Nathan for a long moment. Then he shrugged. "Well, if that's your decision . . . of course it will take me a few moments to break it all back down."

"I'm sorry, but it's just got to be that way."

Miller fumbled with some of the gear and then put the little black box back into the wagon.

"'Tenting tonight, tenting tonight, tenting on the old camp ground,'" he sang.

Nathan watched the buffalo intently. He thought

Thunder was about to make a move. When the massive bison lifted his head, Nathan called out, "Watch out, Mr. Miller. He's getting up!"

"Splendid!" Miller called and ducked under the black canvas at the rear of the camera.

Nathan glanced at the standing buffalo and backed Onepenny away from the wagon.

"Mr. Miller, get out of there!" he hollered.

Then it dawned on him what Miller was doing.

"No!" Nathan yelled.

Black powder flashed.

Nathan held his breath.

Thunder charged.

Hawthorne H. Miller, with terror in his eyes, dove back under his wagon. The two mules hitched to the wagon panicked and attempted to pull away Miller's hiding place. Thunder clipped the side of the camera, jumped over Miller, and headed for the open prairie.

At least the rope will break!

It didn't.

Instead, the spokes of the wagon wheel snapped like dry twigs, and the huge metal rim bounced like an anchor following the buffalo. The photographer's wagon overturned, and the mules halted. To Nathan's surprise, Thunder ran about a hundred steps out on the prairie and then stopped.

"Mr. Miller, are you all right? Are you hurt?" Nathan slid off Onepenny and ran to the man still crouching in the dirt.

"My word, the animal's a killer! My plates! Did he break the plates?" He rushed to the toppled camera. "They're still intact! I must hurry. I must hurry. Charging buffalo! Oh, splendid. Yes . . . yes. Hurry, son, help me set up my dark tent. I'll need to develop this and . . . well, don't just stand there! Get me my large valise!"

"Mr. Miller, I'm going to try to get my buffalo into a pen. You can do anything you want."

Miller seemed to ignore both Nathan and the recent near disaster. "'Tenting tonight, tenting tonight, tenting on the old campground,'" he sang as he packed his camera over to the tipped wagon.

Nathan mounted his horse and trotted out to Thunder. The animal took several steps away from him, but the weight of the wagon wheel caused him to stop again.

"Tona, I don't think he can go too fast dragging that wheel. Let's keep him moving toward town."

With Tona barking, Onepenny and Nathan put continual pressure on the buffalo. The huge beast reluctantly retreated closer and closer to the Shipley corral and the open gate.

By taking it slow and allowing the animal plenty of rest stops, Nathan maneuvered the buffalo right next to the corral gate. But try as he might, Nathan couldn't get the buffalo to walk in. Every time he put on a little pressure, Nathan could see the animal searching for a direction to run back to the prairie.

"Tona, if we push him, he'll run away. Maybe I'll leave you and Onepenny here and go scatter some hay in the corral. Perhaps he'll go for the hay."

Nathan debated in his mind the wisdom of crawling off his horse this close to the buffalo. As he was still thinking about it, Tona ducked under the bottom rail of the corral and put his front paws on the water trough. Still keeping an eye on the buffalo, the dog began to lap water.

Hearing the noise of the dog drinking, the big buffalo

spun toward the gate opening and trotted right into the corral and over to the water.

"Tona! You did it!" Nathan jumped off Onepenny and quickly closed the gate and slid a four-by-four board into the locked position.

The dog hustled out of the corral. Nathan untied the wagon wheel, which still lay outside the gate. He lifted it up and rolled it over to the fence, leaning it against a rail.

"I don't know how I'm going to get that rope off," he mumbled to Tona.

He gazed through the rails at the enormous animal as it slurped the water. Then he grabbed the sack of hay and dumped it over the fence into the corral. When the buffalo had his fill, he backed away from the trough, shook his head violently back and forth, flipping the rope to the ground. Then he began to chomp on the hay.

Nathan retrieved his rope by pulling it under the rail of the corral and was tying it back to his saddle horn when Mr. Maddison walked up to him.

"Well, I see you boys herded up that buffalo after all!"

"Yes, sir." Nathan beamed.

"Well, he's a majestic animal. Did you name him?"

"Dakota Williams called him Thunder, so I'm just going to keep that name."

"Sounds good to me. He's the only buffalo in Nevada Where did Colin go? I told his mother I'd send him on home, and I can't seem to locate him."

"Well, he came on in before me. We sort of . . . well, it's a long story. Anyway, he was supposed to go see my dad, but he didn't. So he's either at home or down at the Mercantile sampling those creme fills."

"I just left the Mercantile and the house. He's not at

either place. And his horse isn't back at the livery. I thought for sure he was with you."

"You mean, Colin hasn't it made it back to town yet?" Nathan glanced back out at the prairie. "I really thought he could find his way back."

F I V E

As he and Mr. Maddison scurried through Galena looking for Colin, Nathan related the whole story of the buffalo roundup, Leah's disappearance, and Colin's return for help. But although they looked everywhere, they found no trace of Colin.

"Mr. Maddison, I don't kn-know what to say," Nathan stammered. "We were just across the creek from the Galena road. I know Colin couldn't have missed it. Besides, he's a good rider. I came up that road myself, and I didn't see him."

"You're right." Mr. Maddison took a deep breath and sighed. "He's quite capable of getting himself home from there. That's the problem. Who else did you see on the road?"

"Well . . . there were a couple freight wagons . . . and a photographer—Mr. Hawthorne Miller. That was his rig out by the Shipley place."

"I'll get my horse and check with Miller. Nathan, I'll need you to ride out with me and show me where you saw Colin last. It could be he's just lost."

"Yes, sir. I'm going to tell Dad. Maybe he can come with us."

"Yes, please do that!"

Mr. Maddison scrambled toward the livery as Nathan dashed for his father's office. In a matter of minutes, Marshal Riggins, Mr. Maddison, and Nathan were riding out of Galena.

"David, I really appreciate your coming out with me."
Mr. Maddison nodded. "It could be just a dawdling youth."

"Nothing would make me happier," Mr. Riggins
replied. "It seems strange he would lose his way so close to
town."

It was thirty minutes later when Marshal Riggins
stopped the other two.

"You see that trail? A wagon rolled across here this
afternoon heading north, and it had a horse tied to the rear.
See that extra set of prints?"

"Could that be Colin's horse?" Nathan asked.

"No tellin'. This main road has had too many wagons
and horses today to be able to distinguish any one track. If we
don't find anything better, then we'll come back and take a
look at this."

When they finally reached the river crossing, the marshal made a troubling discovery.

"Indians. Maybe a dozen . . . one lodge . . . see where the
travois poles drug in the dirt?"

"Indians?" Mr. Maddison choked. "We don't have any
Indians around here . . . do we?"

"Not normally. They usually keep themselves up at Ft.
McDermitt or at Duck Valley, but they were obviously here."

"I met some Shoshone Indians out here somewhere last
year," Nathan recalled. "I think the chief's name was Pie-a-
ra-poo'-na. He had a young Nez Percé girl with him named
Eetahla."

"You saw Indians out here today?" Mr. Maddison
asked.

"No, that was last year. I didn't see any Indians today."

Marshal Riggins turned his horse up the trail to follow
the Indian sign.

"I say, David, is it advisable to follow the Shoshone?" Mr. Maddison questioned.

"If it were my boy, I'd follow them even if they were the James gang!"

"Yes . . . yes, you're quite right." Mr. Maddison pulled a snub-nosed Colt out of his coat and spun the chambers.

"Now we aren't lookin' for trouble. Colin might not be with them at all," the marshal cautioned.

"I can't see any trail of a shoed horse," Nathan complained to his father.

"Nope. I don't see one either. But I do see that the travois is rigged in such a way as to brush out tracks. So we'll follow this trail for a while anyway."

Marshal Riggins led the way, leaning over in the saddle to study the signs in the dirt. Mr. Maddison rode next, keeping his eyes on the horizon looking for riders . . . or one particular rider. Nathan rode last. When his father wasn't watching, he slipped his rifle out of the scabbard and laid it across his lap.

The air was perfectly still—the sky clear. Nathan could hear nothing except the soft plodding hoofs on the Nevada dirt and the occasional squeak of saddle leather or the tinkle of a jingle-bob on his spur.

They had just reached the top of the first hill when they saw a teepee rigged up next to a tiny creek. Several people were around a fire that burned in front of the lodge. A dozen horses milled nearby.

"Do you see Colin?" Mr. Maddison asked nervously.

"Nope. But they see us. Three of them are standing on this side of the fire toting guns. We might as well ride in."

"Will there be shooting?" Mr. Maddison asked.

"I would certainly hope not," the marshal replied.

Three Indian men, packing rifles, met them at the edge of camp.

"We are looking for a lost boy," Marshal Riggins called out. "Have you seen him out here anywhere?"

The Indian with the barrel chest answered, "A white boy?"

"Yes."

"How big?"

"Just about this boy's size." He pointed to Nathan.

"I will ask."

He turned to speak to the others and then walked back into the teepee.

Suddenly a young girl darted out of the lodge and ran their way.

"Nathan!"

"Eetahla! Father, this is the girl I was telling you about."

"You found your mother and father?" she asked him.

"Yes . . . eh, you didn't get to go back to your people?" Nathan quizzed.

"No, but I am happy. Did you come to carry me off?" she teased.

"No," Nathan joked, "I'm not rich enough yet."

"But you have a beautiful pony. He is one of ours—a Nez Percé horse."

"Yes, I know, and his name is Onepenny."

"Did you know that I have a new name?" She beamed.

"What's wrong with Eetahla? It's a very pretty name."

"Yes, but I was given another name when I was baptized."

"Baptized?" Nathan questioned.

"Yes, yes, it was very exciting. We wintered near Ft. Hall, and a Bibleman and his family were also wintering there. He came to our lodge often and told us about God and Jesus and the Holy Ghost."

"And you were baptized?"

"Yes, many of this band were baptized. He gave me my very own Bible, and as soon as I learn to read, I am going to study it."

About this time the young man emerged from the teepee and returned to Marshal Riggins.

"None of us saw a boy. However, there were two men in a wagon trying to sell us very poor goods. Perhaps they saw the boy."

"What men?"

"White men with little round hats and soft hands. They had broken muzzle-loading guns, worn-out blankets, and whiskey. We would not trade with them for those things. They were very angry and threatened to shoot us with their revolvers."

"What did you do?" Mr. Maddison asked.

"We took away their bullets." The Indian smiled showing a tooth missing. "We gave them an old buffalo robe for all their bullets. It was a very good trade."

"Where did you last see them?"

"Near the buffalo cabin."

"Buffalo cabin?" Marshal Riggins asked.

"I know where it is!" Nathan shouted. "That's where Thunder found a salt lick and tore down a whole cabin!"

"Well, lead us there."

Then the marshal turned to the Indians.

"Listen," he said to the spokesman, "it was reported that a herd of pronghorn antelope are just north of here near Three Bear Mountain."

The Indian quickly translated the words to the others.

"That is very good news!" He nodded. "If we see the boy you are looking for, we will make him go home."

"I'd appreciate it," Mr. Maddison responded as he turned his horse to leave.

Eetahla stood next to Nathan's horse. "If we find the boy, I will make sure he is safe."

"Thanks." Nathan smiled. "I'm glad you were baptized."

"Yes, and next time you must let me ride Onepenny!" she shouted as he turned and waved good-bye.

When they were out of sight of the Indians, Colin's father asked, "Do you believe them?"

"The Indians?"

"Yes."

"Yep. There was no reason for them to lie."

"What about those traders?"

"Obviously some riffraff that just got off the train from the East. It wouldn't hurt to check them out—providing we can find them."

Nathan led them to the now-destroyed cabin on the salt lick, and they rode ever-widening concentric circles around the cabin until they found wagon tracks.

"That's what I thought. These are the same tracks that crossed the Galena road."

"Where are the horse tracks?" Nathan asked. "You said there was a horse tied to the back of the wagon."

"You're right, Nate. There's no horse tied to it here. Let's follow these wagon tracks!" Marshal Riggins spurred his horse, and the other two followed down the dusty trail through the sage.

The shadows from the horses stretched long to the east, and Nathan figured they had no more than an hour of daylight left when they plodded up a mountainous draw leading to a clump of piñon pine trees. They would have to turn around very soon to make it back to the Galena road before dark.

Within a couple hundred yards of the trees, the marshal stopped. "Nathan, if we are following someone who doesn't want to be followed, then that grove of trees is where they will make a stand. You stay here. If you hear shooting, I want you and Onepenny to race to Galena. Get Deputy Hailey to round up a half-dozen good men and then come back out here—even if it's dark. Have you got that?"

"Yes, sir. I'll stay right here unless I hear shooting or you signal me up."

Nathan slipped down off Onepenny and readjusted his saddle. Then he walked the horse out away from the sage so that he could see his father and Mr. Maddison from where he stood on the trail. He glanced at them, then at the small grove of trees up the draw, and then at the surrounding countryside. What he saw was mile after mile of sagebrush, treeless, high-desert basin, rolling hills, and a few jagged mountains.

It all looks the same . . . Austin . . . Eureka . . . Galena . . . Elko . . . Wells Station . . . White Pine . . . it's just Nevada—that's all.

Lord, I'm really worried about Colin. I shouldn't have let him . . . but I really thought . . . Lord, don't let anything happen to Colin, please!

As Nathan saw the men approach the grove of trees, he remounted Onepenny.

"We'd better be ready to ride, boy." He patted the spotted horse's neck, which felt warm and moist.

Suddenly, he heard a voice–shrill, distant, and obviously anxious. It sent a chill right down Nathan's back.

"Nathan!" He heard it a second time.

He spun in the saddle and pulled his rifle from the scabbard.

"Nathan! Over here!"

His gaze searched the horizon, bouncing off green hills and gray sage, but he couldn't locate the voice. "Colin?"

"The rock! Behind the two rocks!"

About a hundred yards away, Nathan noticed a granite outcropping of rocks almost concealed by tall sagebrush. He spun Onepenny in that direction and trotted toward the voice. As he approached the rocks, Colin's hatless head popped up from behind the rocks. "Don't come any closer!" he shouted.

Nathan reined up. "Colin, are you all right?" he called.

"Yeah . . . not really . . . well, sort of!"

"What?" Nathan began to ride around the rock.

"Stay there!" Colin shouted.

"Why? What's going on?" Nathan could only see Colin's head appearing above the rocks.

"Well, I had a little trouble on my way back to Galena. You see, I met these two traders—at least they claimed to be traders—in a wagon. They said they had some goods I might be interested in."

"But it was a bunch of junk, right?"

"Yeah. Did you see them too?" Colin questioned.

"Nope, but the Indians mentioned them."

"Indians? You mean there're Indians out here?"

"Colin, go on; what happened?" Nathan prodded.

"Well, naturally, I wasn't about to trade for inferior merchandise, and I told them so."

"That didn't make them real happy, did it?"

"No. They were quite indignant. One of them insisted on having my woolly chaps. When I refused and began to ride off, they grabbed my horse and forced me to come with them."

"Where did they take you?"

"Up to that grove of cottonwoods."

"Then what happened?"

"Then," Colin fumed, "they stole my horse, my saddle, my chaps, my boots . . . and my other personal items. They rode off laughing, leaving me in the trees."

"Other personal items?" Nathan questioned. "You mean, like your shirt, suspenders, and britches?"

"I mean you had better toss me that blanket rolled up on your cantle."

Nathan untied the blanket behind his saddle. He threw it over the rocks, and soon the blanket-wrapped figure emerged.

"Did they beat you up or hurt you?" Nathan asked.

"No, but they should be hanged anyway."

"That was your father and mine riding up there," Nathan announced. "I should signal them."

"Couldn't we just ride back to town? I mean, the fewer the people who know, the better."

Nathan scowled, lifted his rifle into the air, and fired off two rapid shots. In a matter of moments he saw the dust of two riders coming toward them out of the cottonwood grove.

"I'm glad you're safe, Colin. I was really worried about you being hurt or something. The Lord really answered my prayers."

"Well, next time pray that I'll still have my clothes on!"

"Next time? Do you plan on making a habit of this? What were you doing down here anyway, instead of staying up in the trees?"

"I was hoping to sneak along the sage toward town and then to go home after dark."

"Why didn't you signal me sooner?"

"I was back over against those hills, and I couldn't tell who was with you. From that distance, I could spot Onepenny, so I knew it was you. But I wasn't sure of the other two. I had to come closer and make sure Leah wasn't with you."

"Leah? Yeah, that could have been real interesting!" Nathan laughed.

"Riggins, if you ever, ever tell anyone in Galena about this, you will suffer a slow and tortuous death, I promise you!"

Colin was mounted on Onepenny behind Nathan when they met their fathers on the trail. After a few minutes of explanation, they turned their horses back toward Galena.

"Marshal, you have to catch them and see that they are hung," Colin insisted.

"Well, son, the punishment I'll have to leave to a judge and jury, but I will try to trace them down. I'm not about to ride up in those mountains after dark, but I'll get a couple of men together in the morning, and we'll pick up the trail. I'll wire up north too. They sound like the type bound to show up at a saloon sooner or later."

No one talked much on the return trip. It was after sundown when they rode down the rutted, dusty Main Street. The ever-pounding presence of the Shiloh stamp mills echoed in the distance. There were no shouts from the saloons, no shots in the street, no freight wagons creaking—not even a barking dog.

It was exceedingly calm.

But no one seemed to notice.

Nathan rode Onepenny out to Shipley's to check on Thunder. Tona crouched at the buffalo's gate as if it were his assignment in life to watch the beast.

"Well, Tona, he looks fed, settled, and asleep on the hoof. You really don't have to sit here all night."

Tona tilted his head and whacked his tail in the dirt. But he didn't budge, even when Nathan rode back to town. Nathan put Onepenny away for the night in the corral next to the livery and walked toward home.

Lights flickered out of the shops and houses.

Nathan heard the sound of his boot heels slapping the wooden sidewalk.

Then the sound of a shot came from across town.

He heard a man's shout.

A woman's high-pitched laughter.

And a curse.

A crowd flooded into the street, then ebbed back into the Cimarron Club.

Just a typical Galena Saturday night!

S I X

On every Saturday at 5:01 P.M., 284 mostly single male employees of the Shiloh mine got paid, as did those who worked for the Ratchet, the Elmira, and the Double Donkey. By 5:30 p.m. cowboys from the 707, the McGuire, the Pronghorn, the Running R, and the Circle XL ranches would hit town with a galloping thunder. And by 6:00 P.M. citizens could count on the first report of fights.

Despite all this confusion, Sunday mornings were usually calm at the Riggins home. Nathan's mom busied herself in the kitchen with the last details of Sunday dinner. His dad spent Saturday nights sleeping at his office or patrolling the streets.

On this particular Sunday morning, if town was quiet enough, Marshal Riggins and two deputies would ride out to try to locate the traders who had stripped Colin. Church would not start until 10:00 A.M.

Nathan always brought in extra firewood on Saturday nights and was allowed to sleep late on Sunday mornings—not that he was always sleepy. With a cotton flannel sheet pulled up to his neck and only one quilt on his bed, he opened his eyes and stared at the ceiling.

Maybe I could charge a nickel each for any who wanted to come see Thunder. If I got, say, twenty customers per day, that would be a dollar a day! A few handbills around town, maybe a big sign over by the stage stop—Nathan T. Riggins Presents Thunder—Nevada's Last Buffalo.

"Thunder!" Nathan groaned as he sat straight up in bed. "I've got a buffalo to feed!"

"Nathan," a voice shouted, "haul out here as quick as you can!"

"Dad?" Nathan hopped across the floor pulling on his britches. "Dad? I thought you went out looking for—"

"A busy night. But I'll be riding out soon. You get dressed and go get that buffalo of yours."

"Thunder?"

"Yeah, he just ate the mayor's entire garden and has chased about every horse on Main Street."

"How'd he get loose? What's he doing out? Where is he?" Nathan pulled on his boots.

"I don't know how he got loose, but he's only a few minutes away from being Sunday dinner," his father reported. "I'm leaving to track down Colin's abductors, so you'll have to round him up by yourself."

"Nathan," his mother called, "don't be late for church!"

Running out into the street, Nathan heard dogs barking furiously over on the west side of town. He sprinted most of the way and found Tona and a small pack of dogs penning Thunder against a remnant of a wooden fence behind Mrs. Gregory's house.

"Tona, what happened? How did Thunder get here?"

The dog didn't answer.

Nathan's sudden presence gave the dogs added confidence. They stalked toward the buffalo, who spun around and ran right through the fence, scattering boards everywhere. Then he cut down an alley and routed out two cowboys sleeping on the bench in front of Big Leonard's. He trotted past the row of privies toward the hills behind town. Nathan turned and ran straight for the livery.

Tossing his saddle on Onepenny, he quickly climbed aboard and raced after the buffalo. Tona met them by the back of the burn pile.

Nathan had only come within a hundred feet or so when the buffalo ran straight at him. Nathan cut Onepenny to the right and avoided the charge. But Thunder turned and rushed them again.

"Man, no matter where we turn, he's coming right at us! Hey, that's it! He can just chase us back to the corral."

Nathan zigzagged Onepenny right and left all the way back to the edge of town and Shipley's corral. Thunder ran after them—sometimes charging, sometimes trotting, sometimes walking. When they reached the corral, Nathan saw that the gate stood open.

"Somebody let him out! Someone had to open that gate, Onepenny!"

To Nathan's great surprise Thunder trotted right into the corral and over to the water trough, which was almost dry. Nathan slid down off Onepenny and quickly closed the gate.

On the way back to the house, he spotted Mr. Mercee loading something out of his blacksmith shop. Within a few minutes, Nathan had a piece of chain dragging in the dirt behind him. He swung into his yard, dropped the chain, and raced into the house. He emerged a few minutes later with a key lock in one hand and a piece of toast in the other. He crammed the toast into his mouth as he raced back to Shipley's corral dragging the chain. With the corral gate secured and locked, he stowed the key in his pocket and rode Onepenny home.

Nathan scrubbed his face and neck, changed his clothes, cleaned his fingernails, and was ready to walk to church when his mother emerged from the bedroom.

"I trust you took care of that buffalo business?"

"Yes, ma'am. He's in the corral, and the gate is chain-locked. He won't be eating up anyone else's garden."

Nathan was surprised to see Leah sitting with her stepmother in church. Sliding in next to her, he whispered, "What are you doing home already?"

"Doc Stanton was out all night and rode back by this morning, so I just rode in with him."

"Are Mrs. Dodge and the baby . . . you know, okay?"

"Yep. She was up cookin' breakfast," Leah murmured as the worship service began.

After church Nathan told Leah about the morning's dash to recover Thunder.

"He's rather a bother, ain't he?" she commented.

"Actually, if folks would just leave him alone, he'd not—"

"But that's the bother in it. Folks ain't goin' to leave him alone. They ain't never had a buffalo in Nevada before."

"I don't expect any more trouble," Nathan mumbled. "Did you hear what happened to Colin?"

"I saw he wasn't in church."

"Some outlaws stole his horse and saddle and stuff, but he wasn't hurt."

"When?" she gasped.

"Yesterday . . . on the way home. While I was out there at the Dodge place looking for you."

"Stuff? What do you mean they stole his stuff?" she asked.

Nathan shrugged. "You know . . . his woolly chaps and—"

"They stole those? What on earth for?" She smiled.

"Beats me, but outlaws aren't always known for being smart," Nathan replied.

"What else did they steal?"

Nathan started to walk on toward home. "What do you mean, what else?"

"You know. Did they take his boots?"

"Yep."

"His . . . eh, shirt?"

"Yep."

"His—"

Nathan interrupted, "Look, if you want to know what they stole, you just march up there to his big house on the hill and ask him yourself!"

"Well, you don't have to get uppity!"

"The important thing is that Colin's not hurt, and he's back home," Nathan explained.

"Did your daddy go riding after those men?"

"Yeah, but he can't chase them any further than the county line."

"Nathan, after dinner could you and me practice sayin' our lines? Miss D'Imperio wants me to have them all memorized by this Wednesday, and I need some help."

"Yeah. I'll meet you over at Shipley's," he suggested.

"Why Shipley's?"

"'Cause there's nobody there but Tona and a buffalo," he answered.

"Thanks, Nathan. And remember," she giggled, "if I perish, I perish!"

When Nathan finished eating a dinner of fried chicken, boiled rice, canned stewed tomatoes, baked acorn squash, and warm bread pudding with raisins and brown sugar, he asked to be excused. Miss D'Imperio, who rotated her meals among the parents of Galena, had eaten with them. She and Nathan's mother were discussing quilt patterns when he cleared his dishes off the table, left the house, and walked toward Shipley's.

Leah joined him in front of the Mercantile.

"I saw Colin's mother, and she said his feet were so sore he couldn't put on his boots. That's why he didn't come to church," Leah reported. "I used to walk barefoot all the time. It ain't so bad."

"Well, Colin probably isn't used to it."

"Did you tell Miss D'Imperio what we were doing?" she asked.

"Yep."

"What did she say?"

"She said she had found the perfect material for your costume and was going to work on it tomorrow night."

"Really? She said that?" Leah beamed.

Nathan turned quickly to stare Leah in the eyes, and then suddenly he blurted out, "'Don't think that you can escape in the king's house, any more than all the other Jews. For if you don't speak out, then someone else will deliver the Jews, but you and your family will be destroyed. Who knows, but perhaps you have come to the kingdom for such a time as this?'"

Leah's smile faded, and she replied with arms waving, "'Go, gather together all the Jews in Shushan, and fast for me, and neither eat nor drink three days, night or day. My maidens and I will fast too, and then I will go to the king . . . to the king . . . the king, WHICH is not permitted by the law; and if I perish, I perish!'"

Suddenly she hugged Nathan and danced around in a

circle shouting, "I did it, Nathan. I did it and you didn't have to help me at all!"

Realizing what she was doing, Leah pulled her hands away from Nathan and blushed. They continued walking, neither speaking for a moment.

"Nathan? Did you ever wish you had a brother or sister?"

"Yeah, sometimes."

"You and me—we're kind of like a brother and sister . . . ain't we?"

"I suppose so."

"Ya know, we ain't knowed each other for a year, but it seems like it's been a long, long time, don't it?" Leah nodded.

"Yep."

"Nathan, I got a question for you. Now I know that Queen Esther needed to break one of the laws of Shushan to try to save her people, but didn't she know that the Lord would save her? I mean, if she really trusted the Almighty, she wouldn't have to worry about perishing, right?"

"I don't know, but it seems to me," Nathan shrugged, "that people ought to do what God wants them to do—no matter what. I don't think He always guarantees we'll have a happy ending."

"You mean, she could have obeyed God and got killed anyway?"

"I think maybe that's a question for Reverend Clarenton."

"Yeah . . . but . . . you mean she was really afraid? I thought maybe those lines was just melodramatic. You think she really was scared of dying?"

"Why not?"

"It makes my lines kind of scary, don't it?" she said, eyes wide.

Suddenly, Nathan began to run. "What's that? What's happening at Shipley's?"

Wagons, horses, and people crowded around the corral. Nathan raced toward the barn with Leah a few steps behind. Tona ran out to greet him. As he approached, he noticed the repaired wagon of Hawthorne H. Miller. The photographer had set up his camera and was taking pictures of people posed in front of the corral by the captured buffalo.

"What's going on here?" Nathan shouted.

From under the black canvas at the back of the camera Miller shouted, "Get out of the picture, son. You'll have to wait your turn!"

Nathan jumped back, and the powder flashed as a picture was taken. Thunder paced back and forth, irritated by the confusion outside the corral.

"Now, son, if you'll just—"

"Mr. Miller, what are you doing with my buffalo, and how did that top rail come off the corral?"

"The Riggins lad. My word, of course I'll take your picture. After all, he is your buffalo! Just wait in line behind these other fine people." Then he turned to the crowd gathered there. "That's right, folks, you can have a photograph of your whole family with the legendary buffalo, Thunder. Why, you can send this to the relatives back East. What sport it will be! Yes, just line up behind the little blonde girl here and have your cash dollar ready!"

"Mr. Miller," Nathan insisted, "you can't pester my buffalo like this! If he gets mad, he could sail right over the top of this short rail!"

"Nonsense. You have him chained in there quite nicely, may I add. And you did give me exclusive rights to photograph him in the corral, didn't you? You are a lad of your word, I presume?"

"I said you could take a picture, but not set up a circus!"

"Son, you're slowing things down. You run along. I do have a present for you."

Miller reached into the back of his wagon and removed a photograph and handed it to Nathan. "Came out rather well, wouldn't you say? That's your copy."

Nathan stared at the large picture of Thunder charging Miller's camera.

"Let me see, Nathan!" Leah tugged at the photograph.

He handed it to her. "That is a really great picture, Mr. Miller."

"Fine. Now you two run along. I promise I'll replace the rail as soon I accommodate these outstanding citizens. And if anything's open in town, go buy you and your very attractive girlfriend a sweet!" He handed Nathan a quarter.

"Actually, she's not my—"

Suddenly, Leah grabbed him by the arm and kicked him hard in the shin.

"What did you do that for?"

"You were about to say something stupid." She wrinkled her nose and the freckles danced. "I saw Mr. Welenky open his store for the foreman of the Circle XL. Maybe we can catch him and buy a licorice."

"Mr. Miller," Nathan called, "this is the last day for taking pictures."

"Thank you, son. I will see that you get the rest of your royalties."

"Royalties?"

"Yes, Hawthorne H. Miller is a professional. I don't expect to make money off your animal without you getting a profit. Say about five cents for every photograph sold?"

"Five cents?" Nathan coughed.

"He wouldn't consider it for less than a dime!" Leah put in with a fake scowl.

"Actually, I didn't think—"

"Now, Nathan, don't be greedy," Leah interrupted. "Ten cents will be just fine."

"My word," Miller fumed, "I should say so. Yes, yes, a dime it will be. Now go on . . . go on."

Leah pulled Nathan back away from the crowd and toward town.

"You ain't no good at all at bargainin'," she teased.

"A dime for doing nothing? That doesn't seem fair."

"Well, I sure do hope you marry a money-smart girl 'cause you're going to need help, Nathan Riggins!"

Sunday evening seemed too quiet to Nathan. His mother was reading *Moby Dick*, trying to find the symbolism that Miss D'Imperio had suggested it contained. His father was still out on the trail. The streets were hushed because the miners and cowboys were either broke or sleeping it off— or both.

He had no school assignments left, no book he wanted to read, no game to play, no chores to do. He took a piece of leftover chicken from the hamper and ate it standing in the open front door watching the evening sunset. The sky was blue as a robin's egg, but the blue was fading, and the breeze felt cool, as if you were fanning yourself with a wet rag.

The skin of the chicken was especially crisp and the meat juicy. "Mother, you know . . . sometimes Galena can really be boring!" Nathan returned to the kitchen and wiped his hands on a flowered towel.

"What, dear?"

"I said, there's nothing to do!"

"Yes, that's why I like Sundays so much. Don't you think it's nice to have one day when we aren't so busy?"

"Oh, I guess. Say, can I walk over to Colin's? I want to see how he's doing."

"Yes. Take that basket on the table back to Mrs. Maddison, would you?"

"Yes, ma'am."

Nathan cut across the street, up the alley, and down Main Street where he picked up Tona. After several raps on the door, Colin appeared, peeking out a crack in the curtains. He flung open the door.

"Nathan," Colin groaned, "what do you want?"

"Hi, Colin. Hey, this is for your mother. And I was just wondering how you were doing. I mean, I haven't seen you all day."

"Well, I've spent the day demanding that we move to another state."

"What?"

"At a minimum I'm dropping out of school."

"You're what?" Nathan gasped.

"Don't you see? I can't walk through town ever again. Everybody knows. Everyone will laugh!"

Nathan relaxed and shifted his weight from one foot to the other. "You didn't have any choice about giving your stuff to those outlaws. It could have happened to anyone."

"But it didn't happen to anyone. It happened to me!"

"Colin, no one in town knows but your dad, my dad, and me."

"You told Leah, didn't you?" Colin accused.

"I told her about you losing your horse and stuff, but I sure didn't mention you needing my blanket."

"You really didn't tell Leah everything?"

"Nope."

"Honest?"

"I don't lie, Colin."

"You promise that you will never ever tell another living soul in this town—cross your heart and hope to die?"

"I promise."

"Well," Colin said sighing, "I guess I could try one more day of school just to see how it goes."

"Great! We couldn't get along without you. You make a great Haman!"

"Oh . . . the play! If I'm going back to school, I've got to learn my lines! Bye, Nathan!"

Suddenly, the door slammed with Nathan still staring at the curtained glass. He turned slowly. As he walked across the street, he saw Mr. Mercee, the blacksmith.

"Nathan, did that piece of chain work for the buffalo?"

"Yes, sir. Thank you. Say, Mr. Mercee, I was wondering. How would a person build a corral guaranteed to be buffalo-stout? I mean, I know Thunder can bust out of a railroad car, and he ran right through an old cabin."

"I saw a corral built using railroad rails for posts and one-inch-thick flat-iron bolted on for cross pieces," Mr. Mercee reported. "I don't think a train could have steamed out of that pen."

"Wouldn't that cost a lot of money?" Nathan asked.

"It sure would if you used new material. But a place like the Shiloh or one of the other mines has lots of scrap iron around. Maybe a fellow could make a deal with them. You fixin' on upgrading the corral?"

"I don't know," Nathan responded. "It's just that Thunder attracts so many people. I'd feel safer if he were more secure."

"Well, son . . . if you ever need my help with such a project, let me know. I think having a resident buffalo might be good for Galena."

"Yes, sir."

"Anyway, Nate, don't worry. I saw the corral this afternoon. It looks plenty stout to me."

Nathan had just left Mr. Mercee when a cowboy ran up the ally and pulled a Henry repeating rifle out of the scabbard on a blood-bay horse standing at the rail.

"What's going on?" Nathan shouted.

"There's a buffalo going wild out behind the Cimarron Club. He just leveled the outhouse, and he headed for the water tank!"

"What are you going to do with that Henry?" Nathan hollered.

"Shoot him, of course," the man yelled as he ran back up the alley.

SEVEN

Nathan sprinted past the cowboy with the rifle and reached the back of the Cimarron Club. He couldn't believe his eyes. Before a gleeful watching crowd, Hawthorne H. Miller was trying to subdue Thunder with a cane in one hand and an open umbrella in the other.

Seeing Mr. Norco, owner of the Cimarron, Nathan shouted, "Don't let them shoot my buffalo!"

Ned Norco, who could lift two men off the ground at a time, grabbed the pursuing cowboy by the neck and relieved him of his rifle.

"Don't mind Rawley. He's just sore 'cause he was in the outhouse at the time!" the big man shouted.

Seeing Nathan, Miller stopped chasing the buffalo to catch his breath.

"Riggins! Thank heavens, you're here. My word, get that brute back in the corral, would you? At least back into what's left of the corral."

"What's left of it? What happened?"

Leah ran up to Nathan.

"Well, this . . . this monster, this buffalo of yours tried to jump right over the corral!" Miller huffed.

"Leah," Nathan ordered, "go saddle Onepenny and bring him here! I'm afraid one of these men will shoot Thunder if I leave." Then turning back to Miller, he probed, "So Thunder jumped out? I told you it was dangerous to take down that top—"

"No, he didn't jump out!" Miller interrupted. "I said he tried to jump out. Actually, he hit the rails and sort of . . . you know . . . busted his way through."

"Through the two-by-eights?"

"Like they were matchsticks."

Nathan was relieved to see his father ride up and send the crowd back into the Cimarron Club. Then the marshal came over to Nathan and Miller. The buffalo stood silently staring at them from fifty feet away.

"You spent all day, and you haven't got him penned yet?" the marshal asked.

"I corralled him this morning, but he busted out again this evening," Nathan explained.

"Marshal, it's my fault actually. I'm afraid I underestimated the animal's ferocity."

"And who are you?"

"Hawthorne H. Miller, photographer, lecturer, and author. No doubt you've read about me."

"I've never heard of you." The marshal shrugged. "But if you're responsible for that buffalo escaping, then you're responsible for rebuilding the Cimarron Club outhouse. Is that clear?"

"Yes, sir." Miller nodded. "Say, it would be a splendid photograph to have father and son posed next to the Galena mascot. I could run get my wagon and—"

The glare from Marshal Riggins's eyes silenced Miller.

Nathan's father reached into his black leather vest and pulled out his pocket watch. "Nathan, I've got to send a couple wires out. Get this animal back into the corral, and do it immediately."

"Yes, sir." Nathan glanced at his father sitting, as always, straight up in the saddle. "Ah . . . did you find those men who stole Colin's belongings?"

"Nope. We tracked them to the county line, but I don't have any jurisdiction further than that. That's why I need to wire up to Elko County. Chances are, they will be trying to peddle things there tonight."

The marshal rode back toward the center of town, tipping his hat to Leah as she rode up on Onepenny. Hawthorne Miller retreated to the Cimarron Club, leaving Nathan, Leah, Onepenny, Tona, and several other barking dogs to confront the buffalo. Nathan climbed up into the saddle, and Leah slipped on behind him.

"What do we do now?" she asked.

"Well . . . I think this will work!" He spurred Onepenny toward the buffalo and then veered him off at the last minute. Once again Thunder started chasing after them. Within a few minutes he had led the buffalo back to the Shipley place. With Leah still mounted, Nathan dropped down and unlocked the gate.

"He'll just come through those busted boards again," she warned.

"Not until he's through eating," Nathan replied. He grabbed a couple arm loads of hay from the barn and scattered them on the side of the corral furthest from the broken rails.

He had just exited and remounted Onepenny when the buffalo trotted back into the pen. Again Nathan jumped down and locked the gate.

"Leah, I need to talk to Mr. Mercee. I think maybe he can put an iron rail or two over here and keep Thunder penned. But I need you to sit on Onepenny right in front of this break until I come back. I don't think he'll try anything with you two blocking the path."

"What if he tries to escape?"

"Then get out of his way because you couldn't stop him if you wanted to."

It was almost dark when Mr. Mercee finished bolting two flat-iron top rails to the Shipley corral.

"There you go, son. They'll hold him for a while. Once he really tries though, he'll snap those posts off at the dirt line."

"Thanks, Mr. Mercee! I'll try to figure a better setup."

He rode back to the livery and left Onepenny and then walked Leah to her house. When he reached his own house, his mother and father were sitting at the kitchen table. From the serious expression on their faces, he knew they'd been talking about him.

It was his father who spoke. "Nate . . . this buffalo thing. It's just not working."

"Dad, this is just the first day. I'm sure—"

"Nathan," his mother broke in, "we just don't have a secure enough place. Wouldn't it be better for him to run out on the prairie?"

"Mother, he'd be shot in a week."

"Son, animals don't live forever. Besides he lasted all winter."

"But he didn't choose to be out here! It's not fair. There must be a way to keep him safe!" Nathan insisted.

"Well," his mother added, "if we had a zoo or something, then everyone could enjoy watching him."

"A zoo! Yeah, Galena could build a zoo and—"

"Nathan, Galena isn't large enough for a zoo. Maybe Virginia City or Sacramento."

"No, not California. He's the only buffalo in Nevada.

How about Carson City? Don't you think the state capital should have a buffalo?" Nathan suggested.

"Well, that does make a lot more sense than keeping him here in Galena," his father agreed.

"You could write to the governor and tell him you'd like to donate a buffalo for the cultural heritage of the people of Nevada," his mother suggested.

"Wh-what?" Nathan stammered.

Mrs. Riggins laughed. "I'll help you write the letter."

Actually, it turned out to be Miss D'Imperio and his friends who wrote most of it. When Nathan told her about it the next day at school, she decided it would be a good lesson in grammar and government for the older students. They spent three days working on the text and form. By the end of class Wednesday, a carefully printed letter was inserted into an envelope addressed to "The Honorable John H. Kinkead, Governor of the State of Nevada, State Capital, Carson City, Nevada."

Nathan walked home from school, which met in the back room of the Welsh Miners' Hall, with Leah and Colin.

"You going to take that letter to the post office?" Leah asked.

"Nope. They don't send the mail out until the morning stage. I'm going down to the Overland office and see that this gets on the evening stage to Battle Mountain Station. They'll put it on the train there, and it could be in Carson City by tomorrow."

"Well, I'm going to the post office," Leah announced, "because I just might be gettin' some mail!"

"You really didn't tell her, did you?" Colin whispered as Leah crossed the street.

"Nope."

"Well, I think maybe we won't be leaving Galena after all."

"Great! This calls for a celebration. I'll race you to the Mercantile. Loser buys the factory creme fills!"

"Riggins, you cheat. You can't start running! You didn't say one, two, three, go! Riggins!"

The voice was fading behind Nathan as he crashed through the Mercantile door. It was always the same. He always won. Colin always cried foul. And Nathan always bought his own candy.

Both boys were sprawled on the bench in front of the Mercantile debating the merits of dark chocolate lemon creme fills versus light chocolate ones when Leah ran up with a letter in her hand.

"I knew it! I knew it! Look here! I got another letter from Kylie!"

"Kylie who?" Colin asked with a wink at Nathan.

Leah stuck out her tongue. "He says he'll be comin' to visit after all. His daddy can't come down, but he'll be on the stage from Silver City and should get here Wednesday next."

"When did he write the letter?" Colin asked.

"Eh . . . Saturday. Why?"

"Then that means he's coming in today," Colin informed her.

"Today! No, not today! I'm not ready. I'm not . . . today? Are you sure?"

"Today is Wednesday." Nathan nodded. "Doesn't this Kylie have to go to school?"

"He's smart enough without school," Leah bragged. "Nathan, you've got to go to the stage office and wait for him!"

"Oh, no, I already spent one afternoon looking like a fool," he protested.

"Please, Nathan, please? I have to go put on my new brown dress, comb my hair, wash my face, and . . . Please, Nathan, just wait until I get there. I promise I'll hurry! Didn't you say you wanted to get that letter on the stage? Well, just keep an eye out for Kylie, that's all. Please, please, Nathan?"

Nathan sighed and shook his head. "Okay, but this is the last time I do this. Understand?"

"Thanks, Nathan!" Leah hugged him around the neck and then took off running toward home.

"Nathan," Colin began, "do you understand girls?"

"Nope."

"Good."

"Why?"

"'Cause neither do I, and I was afraid maybe I was all alone. Are you going over to the stage now?"

"What time is it?"

Colin pulled out a pocket watch. "Almost 3:30."

"Well, the stage doesn't come in for forty-five minutes. I think I'll check on Onepenny and Thunder first."

"And I'm going to check out mother's pantry," Colin added. "I'll see you at the stage!"

Nathan perched in front of the stage office, letter in hand, at 4:00 P.M. Neither Leah nor Colin had arrived. A well-dressed man with shining black boots and a straight-handled cane sat down next to him.

"You waiting to ride the stage, son?"

"No, sir, I've just got an important letter to send out."

The man turned and smiled. "You writing to some cute little girl?"

"No, sir, I'm writing to the governor . . . see?" He held up the envelope. "It was kind of a class project."

"Yes, well that's very good of you. I'm sure John will be pleased to hear from you."

"John? Do you know Governor Kinkead?"

"Yes, indeed. We have dinner together about every Monday evening."

"Are you somebody important—like a judge or something?" Nathan asked.

The man laughed. "Oh, no, I'm not very important at all. My name's Pennington. I happen to own a railroad."

"You own the railroad?" Nathan gasped.

"I'm afraid so, but it's not that important a position. Especially when times are tough. Say, I will be seeing the governor this Saturday. Would you like me to hand-deliver it?"

"Yes, sir! Thank you!" Nathan handed the man the letter. "Say, I was wondering . . . how much would it cost to ship a big animal from Battle Mountain Station to Carson City?"

"How big an animal?"

"Say, a buffalo."

"A buffalo? A buffalo! You have a buffalo?"

"Yes, sir, I bought it from Dakota Williams."

"That buffalo? You have Thunder?"

"Yes, sir." Nathan smiled.

"Son, I wouldn't let that animal within two miles of my rail car! Do you have any idea of the damage he did to our train?"

"He busted out of a freight car."

"He ripped up two freight cars and then charged the engine. He broke so many steam pipes and fittings that the engine was inoperable. No, no, I'm afraid railroad rules state that absolutely no buffaloes can be shipped alive."

"Maybe there can be exceptions to the rule?" Nathan asked hopefully.

"Not hardly. I made the rules!" the man insisted. "Listen, son, why on earth do you want to ship a live buffalo anyway?"

"It's in the letter. Since Thunder is the only buffalo in Nevada, I thought he ought to be in a zoo or something in Carson City."

Mr. Pennington sat up straight on the edge of the bench and leaned both glove-covered hands on the cane.

"Son, that's an excellent idea! Why, if the governor doesn't want him, I'll build a pen at the railroad office . . . yes, yes, something for the easterners. My, won't that be something! Indeed, it's a splendid idea, simply splendid!"

"Then you'll ship him on the railroad after all?" Nathan pushed.

"Oh my heavens, no! You'll have to deliver him of course."

"Deliver him?"

"Yes, yes, you know, like driving cattle or something."

"Mister, if he was calm enough to drive like a cow, he wouldn't have jumped through your freight car."

"I suppose you're right. But still it is a good idea. Perhaps a freight wagon? A stout one of course. Look, here comes the stage!"

"You'll take the letter to the governor?"

"Yes, indeed, and I'm serious about wanting that buffalo in Carson City."

Several people climbed off the stage and unloaded their luggage.

"Now remember," Mr. Pennington continued, "you be

figuring out how to get him to Ormsby County, and I'll take care of the rest."

"Yes, sir. Thank you, sir."

Nathan stood watching the stage, now teamed with six fresh horses, roll out of town. Two men, a woman, and a boy were carrying baggage down the wooden sidewalk when he remembered. *Kylie! I forgot to look for Kylie Collins! Leah will kill me!*

He raced after the departing stage passengers. "Kylie! Kylie!" he screamed.

Suddenly, a tall, broad-shouldered man with shaggy blond hair spun on his spur-jingling boot heels and drew his revolver, pointing it right at Nathan! Nathan's hands shot straight up. "Don't shoot, Mister. I'm not packing a gun!"

The man looked up and down the sidewalk. "Who shouted at me?"

"You're Kylie?" Nathan gasped. The man looked about six feet tall and about twenty-five to thirty years old.

"You yelled at me?" The man's grim expression relaxed, and he reset the hammer of his revolver and jammed it back into his holster.

"Eh . . . yes, sir, I was sent here to meet you."

"Who knew that I was coming?"

"Leah."

"Who?"

"Leah Walker. You wrote her a letter, and she's been expecting you."

"I don't think I know any Leah Walker. What's she look like?"

"You know . . . kind of long brown hair and some freckles . . . and about as tall as me . . . a real pretty smile and—"

"How old is this Leah?"

"Twelve. But almost thirteen."

"What? Son, you've got the wrong Kylie."

"You're not Kylie Collins?"

"Nah, I'm Kylie Rowtane. Most call me Kid Rowtane."

"Kid Rowtane? Like in the Gold Hill shootout?"

"That's me."

"Kid Rowtane pulled a gun on me—and I lived?" Nathan stammered.

"It's your lucky day. Next time be more careful who you run up to from behind."

"Yes, sir. I will," Nathan stammered. "Ah . . . Mr. Rowtane, was there a Kylie Collins on the stage?"

"Nope."

Rowtane turned and walked on down to the hotel.

"Who was that?"

Nathan whipped around to see Leah in her brown Sunday dress standing behind him.

"Eh . . . that was Kid Rowtane."

"The gunfighter? You know him?"

"Yep."

"What was you talking to him about?"

"Kylie."

"Kylie wasn't on the stage, was he?"

"Nope. But Kid Rowtane was, so I, eh, asked him if he had seen a Kylie."

"And what did he say?"

"Nope."

"I knew it. Wednesday next is next Wednesday. Not today. You'll just have to wait for him next week!"

"Oh, no, not me," Nathan groaned. "But, listen, I did meet Mr. Pennington—you know, the one who owns the railroad? He said he would make sure they'd have a place for Thunder in Carson City if . . ." Nathan's voice trailed off.

"If what?"

"If I'll deliver him to Ormsby County."

"Deliver him? You mean like ship him on a train?"

"I mean, like pack him across the state. The train won't ship buffaloes—especially Thunder."

"Pack him?"

"Yeah, in a wagon."

"You can't keep him in a stout pen. How are you going to haul him in a wagon?"

Nathan walked along the sidewalk and waited for several rigs to pass before he crossed the street. "Mr. Mercee said he could build a buffalo-stout corral if he had the material. Maybe he could build a buffalo-stout wagon."

"Well, I'm going to go change my dress," Leah informed him.

"Why? It looks very nice."

"Of course it looks nice. That's why I'm saving it for Kylie!" she huffed.

As Nathan explained the situation, Mr. Mercee's eyes gleamed with the challenge. Soon he was sketching out a design on the back of a used piece of brown paper.

"It will work!" he exclaimed. "It will work! Of course you'll need iron wheels, lots of axle grease, and maybe four mules to pull it, but it will work, Nathan. Providing it doesn't rain and you don't hit sand."

"Yeah, but what will a wagon like that cost?" Nathan asked.

"Well . . . let's see. For such a patriotic cause I'll donate my labor; and for supplies, if we buy some of the things used, why, it can be built for two hundred dollars."

"Two hundred dollars? Two hundred dollars!" Nathan moaned. "Where in the world will I come up with two hundred dollars?"

"Well, if you do, I'd be honored to build such a wagon. 'Mercee's Buffalo-Tight' we'll call it. I might get orders for others. Of course they'd cost more," he mumbled, "much more."

Nathan walked toward his house without glancing at anyone around him.

Lord, I should have never brought him in. I should have let Thunder wander out there on the plains until he ended up as a robe around some Indian lady or supper for some cowboys. Two hundred dollars! Lord, it would take me five summers to earn that much.

He didn't notice the men in a heated discussion in front of the Cimarron Club until one of them grabbed his shoulder. Nathan glanced up to see Hawthorne H. Miller.

"Riggins, my boy—just the lad I need to talk to. The boys and I have been talking, and I've got a splendid idea. How would you and your buffalo like to make two, three, maybe even five hundred dollars?"

E I G H T

"Five hundred dollars!" Nathan choked. "You've got a way I can legally make five hundred dollars?"

"Well, at least two hundred, but perhaps more," Miller blustered, throwing his arm around Nathan's shoulder.

"Now here's the situation." Nathan squirmed out from under the man's arm. "Perhaps we should find a private place to talk," Miller suggested.

"How about my dad's office?"

"The marshal? Ah, yes . . . of course."

They crossed the street and walked to the jail. Deputy Hailey sat behind the desk.

"Nathan, your dad headed home after sending those wires. Who's this guy?"

"I am Hawthorne H. Miller—respected writer, photographer, and—"

"Well, I ain't never heard of you."

"Mr. Hailey, this man has a deal for me. How about you listening to it?" Nathan requested.

Nathan and Miller sat down in chairs across from the deputy.

"Now here's the arrangement," Miller explained. "The boys from Rocking R just drove up 2,000 head of cattle from Mexico for the army to feed the Indians at Fort McDermitt. But while they were in Mexico, several got in a high-stakes poker game. Well, they ended up winning a prize fighting bull."

"You mean the type that's trained for the bullfights?" the deputy asked.

"Exactly. And they drove it up here with the rest of the animals."

"What are they going to do with it? Bullfights are illegal in the states," Nathan questioned.

"Now just wait, I'll get to it. Anyway, the boys say this is the meanest bull they ever been around. He'll charge every one and everything in the corral. He's hooked half the boys at the Running R. They've been trying to figure what to do with him, and we came to a solution. Here's the deal. We build a big corral, set up some bleachers, and then sell tickets."

"Tickets to what?"

"To the bull versus the buffalo."

"What?"

"The two animals will be put into the arena to fight it out. Winner takes all—so to speak."

"That's crazy!" Nathan exclaimed.

"It would draw a crowd," Deputy Hailey conceded.

"That it will. And we can make handbills and distribute them all over the county. We'll charge one dollar. It will be a real money-maker. And your part will be guaranteed. No matter how well your buffalo does or doesn't do, you get the same amount. I'll put it all together. All you have to do is show up and supply the buffalo. What do you say, son?"

"I say it sounds crazy!"

"Are you turning me down?"

"Not necessarily. I just said it sounds crazy. I don't want to hurt the buffalo."

"Well, what's it going to be? I need to know."

"I'll have to think on it awhile, Mr. Miller."

"You what?"

"Miller," Deputy Hailey interjected, "he said he'll think about it. I'll walk you to your hotel room. Need to make my rounds anyway. You go on home, Nate. Talk it over with your folks."

"Splendid!" Miller mused. "We'll stop by the Cimarron for a nightcap. I'm buying."

"You are going to your room," Hailey stated bluntly.

Hawthorne H. Miller was still mumbling protests when Nathan hurried up the now-darkening street toward his house. He spent almost two hours talking about the offer to his mom and dad, and as he crawled into bed, he still hadn't decided what to do.

"Nate?"

"Yeah, Dad."

"Your mother and I will support your decision. But he's your buffalo. It's your call."

"Yes, sir. I know."

"Maybe you better spend some time talking to the Lord about it."

"Yes, sir."

His dad blew out the lantern, and Nathan stared at the darkness.

Lord . . . it's me. This whole thing is crazy. I mean, I want to do what's best for Thunder. Now I think he would live longer and be more protected if he was in Carson City, but I can't get him there without this money from facing a bull. If I don't do something pretty soon, Dad is right. He'll break out of Shipley's and someone will shoot him.

And if he gets hurt or killed by that bull, it will be all wasted effort. Lord, I wish I knew who would win the fight. Then I'd know what to do.

Nathan's mind drifted to the buffalo . . . to Onepenny . . . then to Leah. Suddenly his lines in the play came to mind, and he instinctively mumbled, "'And who knows whether you have come to the kingdom for such a time as this?'"

Suddenly he sat straight up in bed.

"Lord, if I'm going to make a mistake, I'm going to make it trying to do what I think is right—not by doing nothing at all!"

Hawthorne H. Miller holed up in his hotel room all the next day. Nathan was anxious to talk to him, but he was not taking any visitors. It was after school about 4:30 P.M. when a telegram was brought to Nathan's front door.

"Is it for me? Is it from the governor?"

"No." His mother frowned at him. "It's for your father —from the sheriff up in Elko County. Dad must be around town somewhere. Please, go find him. It might be important."

Nathan found his dad helping the Jorgensens reset the wheel on their wagon.

"Dad, you got a wire from Elko County. Maybe it's about Colin's horse!"

"My hands are greasy. Read it to me."

Marshal Riggins, Galena

 Two men answering your descriptions were incarcerated here on Sunday night for drunk and disorderly conduct. They were released Monday morning and told to promptly exit the city, which they did. They go by the names Hollis Gray and Lorenzo Mourning. Gray is sporting a pair of woolly chaps.

Sheriff Dan Peters,
Elko County.

"Drifters . . . probably won't see them in this area again," his dad commented. "How about you taking that wire to Mr. Maddison?"

On Thursday Nathan reported to Miss D'Imperio and the class about talking to Mr. Pennington and about the bull/buffalo fight suggested by Mr. Miller. On Friday the whole class discussed a plan, and by the time Nathan, Leah, and Colin met with Mr. Miller, Nathan was ready.

"Well, son," Hawthorne Miller questioned, "what are these other youngsters doing here? Isn't Thunder your buffalo?"

"Yes, sir, but we decided to make a class project out of this."

"Class project? What do you mean?"

"Well, it's sort of a class project to get the buffalo to Carson City, and we see this as a school fund-raiser."

"Yes, yes, of course . . . that will look good on the handbill! Then you have agreed to stage the contest?"

"Not until our terms are met."

"Your terms?"

"Yes," Leah answered. "We have a list of requirements."

"A list?" Miller gulped.

Nathan nodded and informed him, "Yes, I will agree if:

1. *The school will be given a minimum guarantee of two hundred dollars.*
2. *The exact purse will be split with 40 percent going to the Rocking R, 40 percent to the class project, and 20 percent to Mr. Hawthorne H. Miller.*"

"A mere 20 percent?" he huffed.

Nathan hardly looked up. "I'm not through.

3. *Mr. Miller will pay for all publicity and printing costs for promoting the event.*
4. *Mr. Miller is the exclusive photographer of the event and will be allowed to sell his services during the show.*
5. *The bull/buffalo match will be preceded by a trick riding act, by two songs from the school Glee Club, and a performance of the play,* The Queen Makes a Stand."

Miller ran his fingers nervously through his graying hair and nodded. "A multi-act show . . . yes, yes, that's good, but—"

"There's more," Nathan continued.

"6. *The contest will be held in the stockyard next to the Lander County Livery, which Mr. Petterson will donate for that purpose in exchange for the exclusive right to board the horses of all folks who ride in for the event.*
7. *The bleachers will be built by the Galena Mercantile and the lumber will belong to them after the event. This they will do for free in exchange for being given the exclusive right to sell refreshments to those watching the performance.*
8. *At any point in the match should the hands for the Running R or Mr. Nathan T. Riggins signal to quit, the animals will be separated, and the other side declared the winner.*"

"Well," Mr. Miller puffed, "I can see you have given this quite some consideration. And to tell you the truth, several of your ideas are splendid, simply splendid. However, others are quite impossible. To begin with, the distribution of ticket money I cannot accept—"

"Mr. Miller," Colin announced in a tone born into

bankers, "the points of this agreement are not open to negotiation. You can accept them or reject them. We will give you until 5:00 P.M. to answer."

With that, Nathan, Colin, and Leah marched out of the room. They giggled all the way down the sidewalk.

"You did real good, Colin." Leah smiled. "You've done your daddy proud!"

"Time for a creme fill!" Nathan shouted and dashed for the Mercantile.

"Nathan!" Colin called, "Hey, wait up! I'm not buying! Did you hear me?"

At 5:01 P.M. Hawthorne H. Miller signed his yet-to-be-famous signature on an agreement right next to Nathan's and Miss D'Imperio's. After Miller left, she turned to Nathan.

"Congratulations, young man. You did a good job."

"Now all I have to do is keep Thunder penned for two weeks!"

"And practice your lines for the play," she reminded him.

"And practice my trick riding," he added.

On the following Tuesday, Nathan received a letter from the governor accepting Thunder for the state of Nevada and inviting Nathan, Miss D'Imperio, and other representatives of the school to come to Carson City and meet with him when they brought the buffalo.

On Wednesday Galena, Battle Mountain Station, Austin, and most of Lander County were plastered with handbills trumpeting the great bull/buffalo fight and talent show. That day Nathan T. Riggins also waited again at the stage office to welcome the mysterious Kylie Collins.

Collins did not arrive.

On Thursday the Galena Mercantile began to build bleachers that would seat one thousand people next to the stockyards.

On Friday Colin broke out with a rash over most of his body. That same day, convinced by mounting enthusiasm for the great event, Mr. Abel Mercee began to build "Mercee's Buffalo-Tight #1" in front of his blacksmith shop.

The following Monday, a meeting of parents and community leaders decided that, pending a positive outcome from the great event, Miss D'Imperio, Nathan, Colin, and Leah would travel to Carson City with the buffalo and meet the governor personally. Mr. Mercee was the unanimous choice to drive the wagon west, since he was the only man alive who would know how to repair the wagon if necessary. His acceptance speech in front of the Cimarron Club lasted almost thirty minutes and effectively cleared the street.

The Shiloh mine and the other smaller ones all declared the coming event a holiday and planned to shut down so miners could attend. Word spread that mines in other towns had also decided to halt operations for the one day.

The cowhands at the Rocking R soon spread the news to outfits from as far away as Idaho and Wyoming. Marshal Riggins enlisted twelve men to act as special deputies for the coming weekend. And most of the saloons in town ordered extra supplies.

Hawthorne H. Miller, anxious to attract a larger crowd, added several more events to the program—Mexican music, Basque folk dances, an Oregon man and his trained dogs, a

Hangtown man doing trick shooting, and a wild horse-break-
ing contest.

On the Tuesday before the great event, the stage lines
announced they would run four extra coaches on Friday and
Saturday to bring folks down from the Battle Mountain
Station train depot.

As the excitement grew, Colin, Leah, and Nathan grew
nervous. On the Wednesday afternoon before the performance, the three sat in the empty bleachers overlooking the
freshly whitewashed stockyards.

"Nathan, I couldn't sleep last night. Every time I'd close
my eyes I was in front of a thousand people, and I couldn't
remember my lines."

"Yeah, it's been worrying me too, Leah. Even if we
remember our lines, who could hear us in this big crowd
anyway?"

"Maybe we'll be lucky and nobody will show up,"
Colin suggested as he scratched his rash.

"They have to show up! That's how we'll raise the
money for the trip!" Leah huffed. "I ain't never been to
Carson City before."

"I almost met the governor once," Colin boasted.

"I don't know why we had to have the play out in the
arena. It was supposed to be just for parents and such," she
complained.

"Miss D'Imperio said it's a great opportunity to teach
a Bible lesson to all the miners and cowboys," Nathan
reminded her.

"What lesson?" Colin asked.

"You know—that there are some times a person just has
to stand up and do what is right regardless of the conse-
quences," Nathan responded.

"Yeah," Leah blurted, "and that we've all been put on

earth for a purpose, and we better stand up when it's our appointed time!"

"Do you really think anyone will hear that message?" Colin replied sarcastically.

"If I don't forget my lines!" Leah replied.

"And if they can hear us," Nathan added. "Come on, let's try it again."

"Oh, boy, we've gone over this two dozen times," Colin groaned. "We all know our lines."

"Come on, Colin." Leah grabbed both boys' arms and led them down the steps.

On Friday night Nathan didn't even bother closing his eyes. He stared at the dark ceiling and thought about wild horses, school plays, buffaloes, bulls, Onepenny, iron wagons, Carson City, and a girl with freckles.

Lord, this is real important to all of us, but especially to Leah. Could you help her tomorrow? She doesn't think she can do anything very well . . . and she really wants to impress her father and stepmother. Please, Lord, help Leah and all of us not to mess up.

Saturday morning was a blur. People had begun streaming into Galena Friday night, filling up hotels and setting up tents on the west side of town. By the next morning the streets of Galena were clogged with wagons, horses, stages, and pedestrians.

There were rumors of reporters from as far away as San Francisco and St. Joseph. General Miles sent his last minute regrets for canceling his plans to attend. Trouble with the Sioux kept him in the Dakota Territory. And the famous actress and singer, Lynida Tuloski, was rumored to be in town to watch the performance.

Nathan got up before daylight. He and his dad moved Thunder to a pen next to the stockyard. True to form, the buffalo chased Onepenny right into the new corral. Fresh hay and a half-bucket of sweet oats kept him quiet for most of the morning.

The cowboys from the Rocking R ranch herded the bull, which they nicknamed Lightning, into town. The big, sharp-horned brindle bull trailed fine and only turned unruly when anyone or anything entered his corral. During his fourteen hours in Galena the bull had gored two horses, killed one dog outright, and lamed another when it flung the mutt twenty feet into the air.

Mr. Hawthorne H. Miller scurried through the crowds like an overwrought mother. He split his time running from the ticket booths to the barn that served as a backstage room for all the acts. With a large megaphone that he had gotten from some actors down in Austin, he directed the crowd and the cast.

At 10:00 A.M. the stands were empty.

By 11:00 they were half-full.

And by noon there was not a seat left for the 2:00 P.M. performance.

Nathan, Leah, Colin, and all the others gathered in the barn by 12:30, with Miss D'Imperio giving last-minute coaching and finishing touches to the costumes.

Leah whispered, "Are you ready?"

"I think so. Are you?"

"Yeah . . . I guess. Nathan, would you pray for me?"

"Sure. I'm going to pray for all of us."

"No, I mean, would you pray just for me . . . right now?"

"Here?"

"Yeah?"

"Out loud?"

"Please!" Leah pleaded.

He cleared his throat and then began, "Ah . . . Lord, it's me, Nathan. We're all nervous here . . . and Leah, well she's really nervous. But we think we're doing the right thing—the right thing for Thunder, for the school, and for ourselves. But help us not to do anything that will make us ashamed. And 'specially help Leah remember her lines. Amen."

"Amen." She smiled, leaned over, and kissed Nathan on the cheek.

"What'd you do that for?" he demanded.

"It don't mean nothin'!" she insisted. "Thanks for praying."

Tension continued to build and reached its climax when Hawthorne H. Miller rushed into the barn at 1:53 P.M. shouting, "Line up, everyone! There's 1,212 paid customers waiting for a show!"

At exactly 2:00 P.M. the Galena Miners' Band began to play patriotic numbers. They ended with the "Star Spangled Banner" and Rena McGuire riding her palomino around the stockyard carrying the American flag. Just as the number concluded, her horse swung close to the pen where the bull, Lightning, was kept. He charged at the fence that separated them, making a terrible banging noise. Rena's startled horse reared up on his back legs, but she stood in the stirrups and waved the flag anyway—all of which brought thunderous applause from the audience.

Next came the wild horse riding. Six teams of three

men each, including one team from the Running R, entered the arena on foot. They had to rope and saddle one of the six wild horses turned loose at the other end and ride one complete circle around the arena. The action was fast, turbulent, comical, scary, and skillful. The crowd loved it.

After that, Nathan, wearing a new bright blue shirt his mother had made for the occasion, raced out of the barn into the arena aboard Onepenny. He stood up on the saddle and trotted the spotted horse around the arena waving at the crowd. Then he sat down and worked the horse backwards, sideways, and through a number of spins. Finally, he raced Onepenny to the far end and brought him to a sliding stop. Then he called Leah out of the barn.

She walked out toward the middle of the arena just as they had practiced. Several men set out two barrels and placed a wooden plank across them. Right on cue, Leah's hat slipped off her head, but she continued to walk to the barrels. Nathan galloped across the dirt, leaned over, and scooped up her hat without even slowing down. The crowd roared its approval.

Then Leah climbed up on the plank and lay down, propping her head up on her elbow and smiling at the vast audience. Nathan swung Onepenny around one end of the arena and spurred him to a gallop, running straight at the reclining Leah. A gasp went up from the crowd as they sensed what was about to happen. Leah pinched her eyes shut. Nathan stood in the stirrups and leaned forward, and Onepenny leaped over the barrels, the plank, and Leah with plenty of room to spare.

At this, the crowd jumped to their feet and roared and applauded for several minutes, giving Nathan, Leah, and Onepenny time to bow three times. Finally the three exited into the barn.

It took Hawthorne H. Miller screaming through his megaphone to get everyone's attention again for the dog act, the school Glee Club's medley of songs about mothers, and the Basque folk dancing. Then the trick-shot artist amazed them with his skills. His assistant tossed five glass balls into the air, and the man, riding horseback, blasted each one out of the sky before any hit the dirt.

When it was finally time for the play, Miss D'Imperio introduced the story of Esther, and the drama began. Everyone shouted out the lines on cue, and while Colin said all of his in a stilted monotone, no one missed a beat.

Not even when Leah caught her heel in her long dress and almost fell to the dirt.

Not even when Colin stopped in the middle of his lines and scratched his rash.

Not even when Nathan's costume tore as he bent low before the queen.

The day had been so hectic he hadn't even tried to remember his lines. They just seemed to roll out of his mouth. Before he knew it, he was calling out, "'And who knows whether you have come to the kingdom for such a time as this?'"

Leah, with hands folded over her heart, cried out, "'Go, gather together all the Jews in Shushan and fast for me, and neither eat nor drink for three days, night or day; my maidens and I will fast too, and then I will go to the king . . .'"

Nathan held his breath.

"'. . . which is not permitted by the law; and if I perish . . . I perish!'"

Applause and whistles rang through the bleachers, and Nathan winked at Leah. He had never seen her look so happy.

Thanks, Lord. Thanks a lot.

The play rolled to its conclusion with the hanging of the wicked Haman and the triumph of Mordecai, Queen Esther, and the Jews. In a burst of hometown pride, the people of Galena led the rest of the audience to stand to their feet and clap.

Back in the barn, Nathan pulled on his old clothes and brought Onepenny near the door. He could hear Hawthorne Miller on the megaphone building up the featured event.

"You riding back out?" Leah called up to him.

"Not unless Thunder needs help," he replied. "You did superior, Leah. Really grand!"

"Yeah. You did pretty good yourself."

"Well . . . this is it. We'll see what Thunder can do."

"What do you think will happen?"

"I have no idea, Leah—no idea at all."

According to a prearranged plan, Nathan's dad opened the gate and let the buffalo into the arena first. He started to trot across the huge corral, but suddenly he glanced up at the cheering crowd. He sat down on his haunches. His rear end was on the dirt, but his front feet held his massive head high.

Then the cowboys from the Running R let the fighting bull run into the arena. Instantly sensing the buffalo's presence, the bull pawed, snorted, and circled the arena once on a trot. The second time around he looked at Thunder eye to eye and suddenly spun and dashed full steam right at the buffalo.

"Get up, Thunder!" Nathan screamed from the barn door where he and Leah were watching. "Stand up! Don't let him hit you sitting down!"

The collision of the two skulls sounded like a rifle shot. The bull bounced back about six feet, and Thunder remained passive on his rear. The entire audience of 1,212 rose to their feet, screaming at the top of their lungs.

Reeling back to the rail, the bull circled the buffalo once more. This time he trotted several laps around the rim of the arena before turning and making a ferocious dash toward the buffalo.

Thunder stood to his feet and lowered his head. The audience gritted their teeth in anticipation of the horrible crunch. Once again it sounded more like an explosion than a collision.

The bull bounced back fifteen feet, staggered to keep its balance, and retreated to the rail. Thunder, now up on all fours, stood immobile in the middle of the arena. With the crowd's roar at a near-deafening level, the bull circled the arena several more times. He stopped to glance at Thunder several times and then continued his circling.

For a while Nathan thought maybe the contest was over. He kept looking at the Running R cowboys, but they were busy yelling insults at their bull.

Finally, coming around to the buffalo's back side, the bull pawed the dirt, snorted, and once again charged. This time Thunder spun on his hoofs and ran headlong into the charging bull.

The shattering crash silenced the crowd completely. The bull, thrown some twenty feet away, pitched and wobbled, fell to its knees, struggled back to his feet, and then staggered toward the fence. Again the animal circled the arena, not looking at the buffalo, but only at the fence.

"What's he doing?" Leah called.

"Looking for a gate to get out." Nathan smiled.

Finally, the bull cut across the arena on a dead run away from the stands full of people, leaped the back fence, taking the top rail with him, and headed out into the sage-covered prairie east of Galena.

Thunder stood still as the crowd tossed their hats, fired guns into the air, and shouted. Nathan noticed the buffalo's left eye blink twice and then stay shut.

"What's Thunder doing?" Leah shouted.

"I think he's taking a nap!" Nathan laughed. "We're going to Carson City! We're really going!"

He grabbed Leah by the waist, and they danced around the barn.

NINE

On May 4 at 9:00 A.M., "Mercee's Buffalo-Tight #1" rolled out of Galena, Nevada. In the four-wheeled iron pen was a 2,500-pound buffalo. Leah Walker and Miss D'Imperio rode next to Mr. Mercee, and Nathan Riggins and Colin Maddison, Jr., (with two d's) rode their horses alongside the wagon.

Tona was locked in the woodshed behind the Riggins house, scheduled to be released the next day. The plan was to take six days to travel to Carson City. Then there would be a ceremony with the governor and a guided tour of the capital. Miss D'Imperio, the children, and the two horses would return on the train (a trip donated by Mr. Pennington) to Battle Mountain Station. Mr. Mercee would either sell the wagon in Carson City or drive it back to Galena.

The first evening they camped in Star City, where they were welcomed at the school like conquering heroes. In Lovelock the next night, they formed a parade down Main Street, with the iron wagon and buffalo winding up at the county courthouse. The third night out, they slept on the ground south of the train tracks at Hobner's Well—the last drinking water before crossing the eastern part of the Carson Sink on the way to Ragtown. They laughed, giggled, and talked into the night until Miss D'Imperio finally announced it was time for bed.

They fastened the horses and mules to a picket line, and Thunder sprawled on the straw with his legs tucked under him in the iron wagon. Miss D'Imperio and Leah used a small tent. Nathan, Colin, and Abel Mercee slept next to the wagon. Originally they considered sleeping under the wagon, but neither boy liked the idea of a 2,500 pound buffalo perched above them.

It was well after dark when a stiff breeze from the west began to blow. The temperature began to drop, and Nathan could see clouds rolling across the star-covered sky. Mr. Mercee stood barefoot on his bedroll studying the clouds.

Nathan crawled out and pulled on his boots.

"Is that a storm rolling in?"

"Yep."

"Will it rain?"

"Could be. We can't take a chance. We better move out."

"In the dark?"

"It's better than sitting here. Wake Colin. I'll signal the women."

With the whole crew dressed and partly awake, Mr. Mercee addressed them. "If it rains, this sink will fill up, and we'll find ourselves in a lake instead of a dry lake bed. If the ground between here and Ragtown gets wet at all, this wagon will bog past its axles, and I doubt if anything short of a locomotive could pull it out."

"What are you suggesting?" Miss D'Imperio asked.

"We need to make a run for Ragtown tonight. The closer we get, the closer we'll be to someone who can help us if we do get stuck. So load up all the drinking water you can. I'll hitch the team."

"How can we see where to go?" Leah asked.

"Nathan and that spotted horse can lead the way. I'll need Mr. Maddison, Jr., here to ride the lead mule and call back Nathan's directions."

With a cooling wind and a sense of urgency, they packed up quickly and began the trek across the lake bed. Nathan had brought only a light ducking jacket, and he now had it buttoned at the neck and the collar turned up. His hat was screwed down and held in place by a horsehair stampede string. He leaned over Onepenny's neck and kept peering into the blackness of the night, searching for any faint sign of previous wagon tracks.

He shouted directions, which were echoed in the wind by Colin and repeated with a shout by Abel Mercee. Leah and Miss D'Imperio huddled under a blanket and tried to doze off amid the shouts. Only Thunder relaxed. He slept peacefully as long as the wagon rolled.

Sometime in the middle of the night—somewhere in the middle of the Carson Sink—it began to rain. It was just a few drops . . . just a sprinkle . . . then a little more . . . then a little more.

"Head us toward any high ground you can find!" Mercee shouted.

"Head toward high ground!" Colin repeated.

"Toward high ground!" Nathan answered.

The wagon began to sink a bit into the mud, and the mules struggled to pull it. In the brief seconds when lightning lit the sky, Nathan thought he spied some low-lying hills to the south. He signaled the wagon toward them. He wasn't at all sure how far away they might be.

The rain slapped his face now, and the mules were taking one labored step at a time. The wagon wheels left foot-deep slimy ruts. Nathan suddenly felt an incline under Onepenny's feet. He climbed up what turned out to be no more than a mound. But it was a mound big enough for a wagon and several horses.

Now soaked to the bone, he rode back and grabbed the lead mule's halter, helping to pull its head up the hill.

When the wagon crested, he stopped the team and rode back to Mr. Mercee.

Shouting through the rain, he explained the situation. "If this lake bed gets some water in it, we're better off up here!"

"You're right," Mercee shouted. "We'll stop here! Set up the women's tent. I'll tend to the mules."

"Tent?"

"At least it will get the wind off them!"

"Yes, sir!"

Sloshing in the mud, Nathan put up the little tent, and the drenched women stumbled inside. Both of them had dry clothes in a valise they had brought, but they huddled close, trying to overcome the cold.

Mercee, Riggins, and Maddison threw a tarp down in the mud and crawled under the right side of the wagon. None of them mentioned the buffalo above them.

"I don't see why we can't all get into that tent!" Colin whimpered.

"It ain't proper!" Mercee bellowed. "I've got firewood slung under here, but it wouldn't burn in a downpour like this! We'll have to wait it out."

All three pulled wet blankets around their soaked shoulders and tried to think of dryer days.

A good hour before the sun came up, the rain stopped, and a warm southern breeze began to blow. Immediately, Abel Mercee pulled out the wood and built a fire. Within minutes around the blaze, Nathan felt warmness return to his fingers and face. The women stayed inside the tent while the men changed into their driest clothing. Then everyone gathered around the fire to dry out their wet things.

"What are we going to find at daylight?" Nathan asked Mr. Mercee.

"Well, we'll either be on an island in a lake, or the lake bed will soak all the water in, and there'll be powder on top."

"Powder?" Colin asked.

"Alkali! It leeches right up out of the ground and dries the moisture. But it can be tricky—dusty on top and sticky gumbo one inch below."

"How close are we to Ragtown?" Miss D'Imperio asked.

"I'm not sure. Maybe morning will tell."

It didn't.

The sun came up. The warm southern wind continued to blow, but they could see only alkali in every direction.

No trees.

No sage.

No grass.

No roads.

No houses.

No chocolate creme fills.

Nothing.

After a big breakfast of boiled eggs, sausage, and beans, they all stood by the fire and stared south.

"It's crusted up, Nathan," Mr. Mercee noted. "I believe a horse might walk out there."

"You want me to try it?"

"Yeah, ride south to those next hills, climb them, and take a look. Come back and tell me what you see."

Dry powder covered the barren, white ground that a few hours earlier had been slick with a slimy mud. The crust held under Onepenny's hoofs. Wind blew the white dirt all around, and soon Nathan's lips were chapped and his eyes burned.

He reached the hills in less than an hour and from the top could only see more alkali . . . and on the distant horizon what looked like trees.

"If there are trees, there has to be water! Good water!" he shouted at his spotted horse. Staring back the way he had come, he could barely make out the wagon. He tried to determine a straight line between the trees to the south and the wagon to the north. Then he piled dry alkali chucks on top of each other for a marker.

Turning to ride back, he thought he saw a dust devil blowing near the wagon. Then he realized that it was riders coming up from the south.

"They can help us pull that iron wagon over to the trees! But where in the world did they come from?"

He wanted to gallop up and join in the greetings, but he knew that the crust would only hold Onepenny at a fast walk. Coming within sight, he noticed two new horses tied behind the iron wagon and a stranger working with the harness of the lead mule. No one else was in sight. The man tipped his hat as Nathan rode up.

"Howdy!"

"Where is everyone?" Nathan demanded.

"Now which everyone did you mean?" The man grinned.

"Mr. Mercee, Leah, Colin, Miss D'Imperio!" he called, slowly reaching over to unbutton his rifle scabbard.

"Leave it, boy!" a voice shouted from behind the wagon. Suddenly, a man wearing woolly chaps stepped out holding a short shotgun on Leah and Miss D'Imperio.

"Climb off that spotted horse!" he demanded.

"Mourning and Early?" Nathan mumbled.

"Well, isn't that nice. The boy knows our names."

"Leah, Miss D., are you all right?"

"Be careful, Nathan. These men are dangerous," Miss D'Imperio warned.

"Oowhee, listen to the schoolteacher. We are armed and dangerous, boy."

Nathan climbed off Onepenny and stepped toward Leah.

"Where's Mr. Mercee and Colin?" he asked.

"The blacksmith bumped his head on the end of my shotgun, so he's napping it out under the wagon," one of the men said.

"And Mr. Pink Cheeks is up there with the buffalo!"

"Pink Cheeks?"

"They put Colin in with Thunder," Leah explained.

Nathan stared into the cage and saw a tied, gagged, and frightened Colin standing next to a hay-chewing buffalo.

"Colin identified them as soon as they rode up, and there was a scuffle. Mr. Mercee took several blows to the head," Miss D'Imperio informed him.

"Now there is no need to worry, boy. We'll leave you and your friend up there with the buffalo. We'll just take the horses, mules, belongings, water, and womenfolk. You can have all the rest." They laughed.

"The women?" Nathan shouted.

"Why, we want to make sure they're good and safe — right, Early?"

"That's right. I sure do like that horse, boy. I think I'll have him for my own."

"You can't—," Nathan started to yell and then found himself looking down the barrel of a drawn and cocked .45. He stood in place while the gunman mounted Onepenny.

"Stay, Onepenny, stay!" Nathan yelled.

The man kicked his spurs into the spotted horse's flanks, but Onepenny didn't move.

"Nathan, I don't know what to do!" Miss D'Imperio moaned with a high, tight voice.

"Stay, Onepenny!"

The outlaw kicked the horse again, and this time the horse began to buck.

"Nathan," Leah yelled, "'who knows whether you have come to the kingdom for such a time as this?'"

She's right, Lord! I couldn't live with myself if I didn't try something!

He finished, "'And if I perish . . . I perish.'"

On the third buck the outlaw flew off Onepenny's back. Before he could get to his feet, Nathan jumped into the saddle and spurred Onepenny out into the alkali flats. To Nathan's surprise the ground held up fine.

"I'll shoot him!" one of the outlaws shouted.

"Don't hit that horse! I still want that horse!" the other demanded.

One of the men ran to the back of the wagon and began to mount his horse to pursue. Nathan plowed toward the other outlaw. By dropping to the right side of the horse, Indian-style, Nathan made it impossible for the man to shoot him. In the confusion both women broke free and began to run out into the Sink.

Gaining on the confused gunman, Nathan leaned way forward in the stirrups and gave Onepenny the command to jump.

He's never jumped over a man before. I don't think he can do it. I hope he can't do it!

Onepenny's flying legs caught the man in the chest, knocking him violently to the ground. The man didn't move.

Nathan spun toward the other man, who fired a wild shot and climbed onto his horse. Pulling his rifle out of the scabbard, Nathan raced after him. But the man's horse hit a bog only a few feet from the wagon.

The horse came to a complete stop.

The outlaw didn't.

He flew headlong into the alkali dust.

Nathan sprang down off Onepenny and jammed the barrel of the rifle against the back of the man's head.

"This thing is cocked, Mister, and I'm mighty nervous. If you so much as wiggle, the hair trigger is going to go off, and I won't be able to stop it! Leah!" he shouted. "Bring me a rope."

Within minutes Nathan had both men tied, hands and feet. Miss D'Imperio helped Mr. Mercee sit up next to the wagon. He had several red welts on his face and head. As Nathan walked over to them, Leah ran up and hugged Onepenny. "Old Onepenny really came through, didn't he?" She smiled.

"Onepenny? How about me?"

Speaking under her breath, Leah replied, "I can't hug you in front of Miss D'Imperio. It wouldn't be proper!"

Nathan nodded and went over to the others. Miss D'Imperio jumped up and gave Nathan a big hug. He winked at Leah when he caught her eye.

"Nathan," Miss D'Imperio said, "it might seem foolish later on—whenever I think about it—but that was about the bravest thing I've ever seen. I've never needed to be rescued before, and I hope I never will again, but I thank the Lord that you and your spotted horse were with us!"

"I just had to try something. Those lines me and Leah said . . . well, we weren't play-acting today."

Then a frantic protest came from the iron cage. Nathan

crawled up and pulled Colin out. Finally, untied and ungagged, Colin shouted, "Kill them! They deserve to be shot and left out in this barren land!"

"Don't mind him." Nathan grinned. "It's Colin's reaction to every personal injustice."

It was noon before Mr. Mercee pronounced the dirt dry enough to hold the weight of the wagon. When they pulled out this time, all took their original places, except that Thunder now had two passengers in the cage with him and two horses trailed behind the wagon.

After refilling with fresh water and washing their faces at the spring near the clump of trees Nathan had spotted early that morning, they continued south. About sunset a group of concerned citizens from Ragtown rode out and found them. A big party was planned for that night, and the hosts had been worried about the travelers.

With Mourning and Early in the Churchill County Jail, and after a bath and a change of clothes, they all went to the party.

Miss D'Imperio visited with a long line of young men.
Mr. Mercee talked wagons with several local merchants.
Leah wouldn't let go of Nathan's arm.
And Colin hovered over plates full of cookies.

T E N

The state of Nevada, searching for an excuse to celebrate, found it in the "Last Buffalo Capital Expedition," as it was now being called in the newspapers. The capture of Early and Mourning—two otherwise petty thieving misfits from upstate New York—was described as a heroic battle for Nevada's cultural heritage.

When "Mercee's Buffalo-Tight #1" swayed out of Ragtown, they had twenty-six well-armed outriders as escort. By the time they reached Gold Hill, the party had swelled to over a hundred. After a parade through every dusty street of Gold Hill, the mayor of Virginia City insisted that they come on up the mountain to the "Queen City of the Comstock."

A series of hurried telegraphs to Governor Kinkead postponed the Carson City festivities one day and allowed them a trip to Virginia City. By the time they creaked their way into the famous mining town, Fourth of July bunting draped the buildings. Miners, gamblers, shop clerks, and families crammed the wooden sidewalks.

Nathan waited aboard Onepenny for the Virginia City Marching Band to line up and lead the procession. He rode up to the wagon and looked at Leah and Miss D'Imperio.

"I don't get it. This is really not such a big deal, is it, Miss D'Imperio? I mean, a buffalo is a buffalo."

Miss D'Imperio opened her salmon-colored parasol to shade her eyes. "Nathan, Nevada's a tough state—hardworking men and women. Everyone's trying to make some money, and most plan to leave as soon as they make their fortune. Not much future for a state like that."

She pulled off her white gloves and held them in her lap. "But you and Leah and Colin—you represent the future of Nevada. You might be the first children to do something, anything for the betterment this state. Your determination to get the buffalo to Carson City is telling folks, 'Hey, this is our state too!' I think it's made people believe Nevada is more than just a mining camp. You've inspired some folks to think beyond the daily grind. You gave them a breath of fresh air, and in a mining state there isn't much fresh air."

That evening at a picnic, the Galena group sat at honored places. Miss D'Imperio presented a short talk on how the whole school had worked on the project. And Mr. Mercee was allowed to make a pitch for his buffalo-tight wagons.

Right after a big breakfast the next morning, they started out toward Carson City. Most estimates placed the number of people traveling with them in excess of five hundred.

Under Mr. Pennington's planning and leadership, Carson City was ready for the Last Buffalo Capital Expedition. A stout iron corral had been constructed a block south of the capital building. A large, freshly painted sign marked the location. It gave special thanks to the "Galena School, Lander County, and their teacher Miss Angelica D'Imperio."

When Leah read the sign, she turned to Nathan and whispered, "I didn't know her name was Angelica! Did you?"

"Nope," Nathan replied. "But it fits, doesn't it?"

They unloaded Thunder, and he trotted around the entire corral, occasionally testing the strength of the iron posts with a head butt.

The parade in Carson City was the largest and most

orderly of the trip. Mr. Pennington decided to spread out the Galena group in order to lengthen the procession.

First came Nathan on Onepenny, then Colin, now sporting his famous woolly chaps. Then, in a special coach donated for the occasion by the Sierra Vista Carriage Works, Leah Walker would roll along wearing a bright yellow dress given to her by Marquette Millinery. Following Leah, in an open coach that had been used at the governor's inauguration, came Miss D'Imperio, wearing another Marquette creation of off-white and lavender.

Finally, with an escort of fifty musket-carrying men dressed in buckskins from the Ormsby County Mountain Men Association, would come Mr. Abel Mercee, his all-iron wagon, and Thunder—"the last buffalo in Nevada."

At the final minute Nathan was handed an American flag to carry. He decided to stand in the saddle as he rode down the street waving the flag. But then he had second thoughts.

Lord, this is all . . . you know, kind of out of hand, isn't it? Help me to enjoy the fun of it all, but not take it too serious. It's sort of a good day to be me . . . and Leah and Colin and Miss D'Imperio and Mr. Mercee . . . and even Thunder. Thanks, Lord, from all of us.

The parade was late in starting. Something created a disturbance in the rear. Nathan rode back to Colin.

"What's happening back there?"

Colin shrugged, "I don't know . . . maybe Mr. Mercee's having trouble with the wagon. Say, Nathan, do you really think I should wear the woollies? I mean, it's a might warm on a day like this. Yet they are rather glorious-looking, don't you think?"

"Eh . . . sure. Definitely wear them. I'm going to check this out."

"But you'll need to hold your place," Colin insisted.

"You hold it for me," Nathan called. He trotted up the parade route. "Leah, you look . . ." His voice faded.

"I look what?" She squinted her eyes and wrinkled her nose.

"You look about sixteen years old and extremely pretty," he blurted out and hurried past her. Miss D'Imperio was visiting with a tall, strong-looking man on a beautiful black horse, so Nathan just tipped his hat and rode on.

Once he made it past the Mountain Man club, he found Mr. Mercee and several men on horseback trying to get Thunder out of his corral and into the wagon.

"Nathan!" Mercee shouted. "We can't get him to move. Perhaps you could help!"

"I can't blame him. Six days in that jail cell, and he has no intention of returning. Maybe we should just leave him corralled."

"My heavens, no!" exclaimed Mr. Pennington. "The whole town is waiting to see Thunder roll down Carson Street."

Nathan handed the American flag over to Mr. Mercee and rode Onepenny into the iron corral. Thunder, who had absolutely refused to budge for all the others, glanced up at the spotted pony. Nathan ran Onepenny right at the big buffalo and then, as usual, veered off to the right. True to form, Thunder waved his head at the horse and began to trot after him.

Nathan circled the corral twice with the buffalo trailing behind. Several days cooped up in the wagon had stiffened the old buffalo, and Nathan could see him slowing down, yet trying to chase the spotted horse. As he rounded the open gate, Nathan grabbed the American flag and shouted at Mr. Pennington, "Get the parade started! Thunder isn't going back into that wagon!"

Parade participants parted as Onepenny with a flag-waving Nathan proceeded up Carson Street, Thunder trotting behind. While the rest of the parade struggled to catch up, the crowds lining the streets cheered in wild enthusiasm.

Thunder, bewildered by all the confusion, followed the only familiar sight—the spotted horse—straight up Carson Street, around the corner on East William, and back down Stewart to the corral.

He and Nathan finished the parade route well ahead of the others, but no one seemed to mind. With Thunder happy to be back with his hay and a bucket of sweet oats, Nathan led Onepenny out of the corral and then closed and locked the big iron gate.

Everyone was either still in the parade or watching it, so Nathan slid down off his horse, loosed his cinch, and led the spotted horse to the water trough.

"Well, Onepenny, we did it, didn't we? I think I'm going to miss that buffalo. He looks sort of lonesome. You're about the only friend he has!"

"Hey, cowboy, do you always talk to your horse?"

Pushing his hat back, he looked up to see a girl riding a tall black horse.

"Tashawna?"

"Hi, Nathan."

"What are you doing h-here?" he stammered.

"I live here, remember?"

"Oh, yeah, I guess I forgot."

"Out of sight, out of mind." She smiled.

"What?"

"Oh . . . nothing. Listen, this was a great parade. I

couldn't believe it was really you when I read it in the paper. You're a hero!"

"Yeah. It's all kind of silly, isn't it?" he admitted.

"Enjoy it, I say. There'll be enough bad days that will come along. That's what my daddy always says."

"Your dad! The black horse! Your father's in Carson City now?"

"Yeah. He came here about two weeks after me and Mom. Of course he doesn't live with us."

"He doesn't? Where does he live?"

"Down there in that granite building."

"The Nevada State Prison?"

"Yeah . . . but only until next December."

"So he turned himself in for that stage robbery?"

"Yep. He said it was the proper thing to do."

"Well . . . how . . . how are you and your mom getting along?"

"Mama's working for a doctor, and I'm taking care of some horses for Mr. and Mrs. Pennington. We'll get by."

"That's great, Tashawna!"

She climbed down off her horse and tied him to a rail. Then she and Nathan walked over to the corral and peered through at Thunder.

"You know what I kept thinking about when I saw all of you riding in the parade?" she asked.

"What?"

"Well, if we'd have listened to your advice and stayed in Galena, maybe I'd be right out there with you."

"Yeah." Nathan nodded. "I'm sure you would have. You could even have done some trick riding or something!"

"Hey, I'm taking some singing lessons. Isn't that something?"

"You told me you'd be singing at the opera house some day."

"Yep. Miss Tashawna Cholach—on stage!" She giggled.

"You've got to save me some tickets, remember?"

"I promise."

Nathan noticed that others from the parade were starting to pull up to the iron corral behind them.

"You know, Nathan, someday . . . someday I'm going to be in a grand parade too. I won't be just a country girl from some remote ranch. I won't be some stage robber's daughter. I'll be famous!"

"Tashawna, I sure hope your dreams all come true . . . and they don't disappoint you when they do. Listen, when you ride in that parade, be sure and look in the crowd 'cause I'll be there cheering you on."

"Who knows? Maybe Nathan T. Riggins of Lander County will be riding with me. Maybe he'll be governor by then."

"I doubt that," Nathan mumbled.

"Nathan, can I ride Onepenny—just for old time's sake?"

He took off his hat and swept it low in front of Tashawna. "Miss, I'd be delighted to have you ride my talented pony!"

"Uhhum!"

Nathan turned around to see Leah, carrying a yellow parasol, standing behind them.

"Oh! Hi!," he called. "Wasn't the parade spectacular?"

"Up to this point," Leah huffed, tugging to make her dress feel more comfortable.

"Oh . . ." He turned to Tashawna. "You remember—"

"Your dear little friend from Galena!" Tashawna smirked.

"This is," Nathan's voice sounded deep and deliberate, "my girlfriend Leah."

A burst of joy swept across Leah's face, lighting her eyes and lifting her smile. She stepped up to Nathan and slipped her arm in his.

"Nathan, darlin', the governor is expecting us for a cookout at his house. Perhaps your friend, Miss Curlylocks, wouldn't mind putting Onepenny in the stable when she's through with her ride."

She tugged Nathan over toward the smiling governor, Mr. Pennington, and the others.

Leah glanced back at Tashawna.

Nathan didn't.

If he had, he would have seen both girls sticking their tongues out.

BOOK FIVE

Never Dance with a Bobcat

ONE

Look at that one, Nathan. Don't it look like a lady in a fancy dress dancin'?" Leah pointed.

"It looks like a big scoop of mashed potatoes!" Colin intruded. "All it needs is some gravy poured over the top."

"Colin, all you ever think about is food!" she scolded.

Nathan T. Riggins tugged on a stalk of wild oats growing in the little meadow above Galena, Nevada, and began to chew. The base of the stem was still moist, and it tasted sweet as he ground it between his teeth.

"I think Colin's right. I'm hungry . . . reckon I'll go check on dinner."

"You boys is always hungry! Why, I'll bet it ain't 10:30 yet," Leah chided them as she wove a purple wildflower into her long brown hair.

Looking at his pocket watch, Colin countered, "It happens to be 10:48! Besides, growing boys need plenty to eat."

"Well, jist 'cause you two grew a few inches taller than me, it don't mean nothin'. Kylie Collins is taller than both of ya!"

Nathan continued watching the clouds. *Oh, yeah . . . good old Kylie, the Perfect.*

He glanced over at the other two. "Summer's kind of boring, isn't it? You know . . . in a nice sort of way? Do you think Miss D'Imperio will be back next September to teach?"

"She promised," Leah replied. "I just know she'll be back."

"Are we going to go eat, or what?" Colin pressured as

he began to roll up the cuffs on his long-sleeve white cotton shirt.

"Yeah. Let's see if we can find something in the pantry." Nathan stood to his feet, brushed off his gray britches, and led the others back toward town. His dog, Tona, scurried along in the sagebrush ahead of them.

"Well, I'm going to the San Francisco Millinery. Mrs. Sewell said she might have some work for me this week," Leah announced.

"You know, I need a better job," Nathan commented. "A couple hours a day at the Mercantile doesn't keep me very busy, except when a new load of freight comes in."

"Well," Colin huffed, "I just work one hour a day cleaning the bank, and I can tell you right now, that's plenty for me!"

Tona let out with a warning bark. It was one of those yelps that seemed to start in his tail and build until it exploded out his mouth. Suddenly Nathan realized that there was some commotion in town.

"What's going on?" Colin stretched his neck to try to see around the buildings into Main Street.

"It ain't payday at the mines, and it ain't Saturday night," Leah added as the three broke into a trot.

Tona sprinted ahead of them and disappeared among the buildings. Nathan led the trio past the Oriental Supreme Chinese Laundry, in between Wainwright's Variety and David Isaiah's Tailor Shop, and up onto the wooden sidewalk in front of Angus McGregor's law office.

Ahead he could see a crowd gathering around a tandem freight wagon rig stretched diagonally across the street blocking traffic in both directions. The freighter, with hands in the air, sat on one of his stout wheeling horses, with five teams of mules stretched out ahead of him. He was shouting at a man on the ground who waved an old Henry repeating rifle.

Nathan pushed his way through the crowd and came to a stop between a man who smelled like a saloon and a woman who smelled like spring flowers. The jerk-line still lay across the freighter's lap, but he didn't lower his hands toward the revolver in his belt. The sweat and dust of a week on the road blotched his clothing.

The man on the ground wore a dark blue shirt caked with dirt. His left boot was worn through and wrapped with a broken latigo. His hat was ripped to the crown. His red, tired eyes searched the crowd as he talked.

"Push-Bill, you ain't leaving that rig alive until I get my goods!" he shouted.

"You cain't have nothin' till them wares is paid fer, and ya know it!"

"My name is on the bill of ladin'; they belong to me!"

"It says cash on delivery! You can read, cain't ya?"

The man with the gun screamed, "But I'm good for it!"

"From what I hear, you couldn't buy a thirsty man a cup of water!"

"When I get my goods, I'll be able to cash more ore than anyone in the state of Nevada."

Suddenly, the man next to Nathan shouted, "Wobley, your diggin's pinched out and you know it! Give it up."

Spinning toward the detractor, the man called Wobley fired his gun into the air above Nathan's head.

Women screamed.

The crowd scattered.

Colin froze.

Nathan pulled Leah between the freight wagons.

And Push-Bill reached down for his revolver.

Someone's going to get shot! Lord, help us!

Nathan shoved his floppy brown felt hat in front of Leah's eyes.

"What ya do that for?" she protested.

"Someone's going to get shot!" he whispered.

She shoved the hat aside and peered around the wagon. "Here comes your daddy!"

Marshal Riggins, standing taller than Nathan had ever seen him, marched in between the two gun-waving men.

"Wobley, give me that rifle!" he commanded, as he stretched out his left hand, his right hand remaining on the polished oak grip of his still holstered revolver.

"Marshal, this man won't give me my goods! So don't press me. I swear I'll shoot you and him both!"

"You're not shooting anybody today!" Marshal Riggins replied.

"Your daddy is wearin' them shootin' eyes!" Leah whispered.

"What?" Nathan murmured.

"Miss Patsy told me you can tell if a man is goin' to shoot by lookin' at his eyes. Your daddy's sportin' shootin' eyes, and them fellas know it."

Without taking his focus off Wobley, the marshal called out, "Push-Bill, you holster that gun, slide down off that wheel horse, and go inside the Mercantile. Do you hear me?"

Lifting himself off the horse, the freighter groused, "He don't get them goods, do you hear, Marshal? He don't get them until—"

"Push-Bill, get inside!" the marshal thundered.

"Yes, sir . . . I'm goin' . . . don't let that weasel shoot me in the back, Marshal."

Ignoring the freighter, the marshal looked straight at Wobley. "Give me the Henry."

"Nope, I won't. I got to have them supplies. Don't ya

see? If I don't get 'em, I'm busted. I'll shoot ya, I swear, Marshal. That diggin' is all I got in this world; I ain't goin' to lose it now."

"Wobley, give me the rifle!" Marshal Riggins repeated.

Nathan strained to see his father's eyes.

Leah's right. Daddy won't back down now! Lord, help him! There's nothing in those wagons worth anyone getting shot over . . . especially Daddy.

"Marshal . . . you don't understand!" the man pleaded.

"Wobley, look around you. There isn't a man on this street that hasn't gone belly-up in the mines once or twice. I lost every penny I had to my name at Willow Creek. Pull yourself up and go on."

"Yeah, that's easy for a man with a job, a fine wife, and a family to say. I ain't got nothin' . . . nothin'! Do ya hear me?"

"Wobley, I'll tell you what you have. You have two choices. Either you're going to die right here on this dirty street in a dusty, little, no-account Nevada town . . . or you can hand me that rifle. Now if you give me that gun, I'll see that you get a bath, a shave, and a hot dinner at the New Orleans Hotel. Then you can leave town and find yourself something better. It's your turn. Choose."

"It ain't fair!" Wobley hollered. "If I'd a had them supplies six months ago, I'd be the one living up on the hill in that big house!"

"Wobley, give me the gun, or I'm going to shoot you. But I'm not planning on missing dinner 'cause of you."

"Do I get my gun back when I leave town?"

"Yep."

"You goin' to throw me in the hoosegow?"

"Nope."

Wobley took a big deep breath and sighed.

"There ain't goin' to be no shootin'," Leah whispered, putting one hand on Nathan's shoulder and pointing with the other. "Look at your daddy now."

Nathan could see the tense lines relax. He had seen it before hundreds of times.

Leah's got it straight! It's all over.

"Marshal, kin I order one of them black Louisiana steaks?"

Nathan's dad cracked a generous smile. "Wobley, you can order a double helping of okra if you want. Now hand me that gun."

"You can have the gun," Wobley said with a nod, "but I ain't eatin' no slimy okra. I'd just as soon take lead!"

The marshal seized the man's gun, and people streamed out from hiding places and milled in the streets. The hushed conversations soon burst into a roar.

"You goin' to lock him up, Marshal?" someone shouted.

"Nope. He's got a good-bye meal coming. But he doesn't get it 'til he takes a bath. Now you folks go on and do something constructive instead of standing and staring. Nate! Come over here."

"Yes, sir," Nathan replied.

"You go into the Mercantile and tell Push-Bill to get out here and park these wagons someplace else. Then head on home and tell your mother I'll be taking dinner at the New Orleans Hotel."

"Yes, sir. I will." Nathan sensed someone was standing behind him.

"Miss Leah," the marshal said, nodding at her, "you're looking mighty fine today. Those flowers look right handsome in your hair."

"Thank ya, Marshal. It's a pity your son didn't inherit

your keen eyesight." She wrinkled her nose at Nathan and then continued, "That sure was a brave thing you did—backing down Mr. Wobley like that."

"He's not bad. It just hits a man hard when he's worked so strenuous and lost everything."

Nathan banged his boots into the worn wooden sidewalk as he scurried into the Mercantile shouting, "Push-Bill, it's all over! Daddy says to move that team out of the road!"

"Thanks, son. Your daddy's a good man." Push-Bill rubbed his chin and peeked out the front door. Finally, the freighter ventured out onto the sidewalk.

"Say, son . . . you want to make a few dollars this afternoon?"

"Yes, sir!" Nathan shouted.

"Well, after dinner come on around to the back of the Mercantile. I'll hire ya to help unload these wagons."

"I'll be there!"

Nathan scrambled over to Leah waiting outside and escorted her toward her house. She grabbed Nathan's arm and skipped across the dusty street.

"I betcha when you get older, you'll be brave like your daddy," she declared.

"I hope so, but I'm not too sure," Nathan admitted.

"How come you didn't want me to watch?" she asked.

"'Cause there are some things a woman shouldn't have to see."

"You sayin' I'm a woman?" she teased.

Nathan caught himself looking carefully at Leah. "You know what I meant." He blushed.

"Well, next time why don't you ask me before you go shovin' an old sweaty hat in my face?"

"I do have something to ask you." Nathan grinned.

"Oh yeah? What's that?"

"Well, you said a person could tell whether another was about to shoot by looking at his eyes."

"Yep. That's what Miss Patsy told me."

"Well," Nathan quizzed, "how did you get so chummy with Miss Patsy? My daddy says if he ever catches me over on Murphy Street, he'll tan me so hard I'll have to sleep standing up."

"Well, Miss Patsy don't spend all her time over on Murphy Street. I help with the fittin' on her dresses. She says when I get more . . . you know, more mature, she'll give me some of her old ones. So there!" She dropped Nathan's arm and ran up the stairs of the house without looking back.

Nathan spent little time scraping down a plate of hot beef stew, a fist-sized chunk of bread, and a very large helping of peach cobbler. He quickly carried his dishes to the kitchen counter, waved at his mother, and rushed out the door. Finding Push-Bill Horn rolling back the canvas tarps on his wagons, Nathan climbed up on the front one and began to help. Most of the products were in wooden crates, but Nathan enjoyed reading about the contents just the same.

The entire front wagon was full of mining gear. There were gauges, fittings, pulleys, reducing screens, bolts, and big odd-shaped boxes bearing the printed warning, "Do Not Open! For Shiloh Mining Company only!"

It took over an hour for the two of them to unload the wagon. Nathan's arms pained as they turned toward the second one. In it he found bolts of cloth for Mr. Isaiah, ready-mix paint for Central Nevada Sign Painting, a box of buckles for the livery, a crate of dishes packed in sawdust for the New Orleans Hotel, four one-hundred-pound sacks of sugar for the Deluxe Bakery, a rattling crate for the Modern Stationers . . . among other unidentified boxes.

When both wagons were empty, Nathan plopped down on the tailgate of the back wagon, panting.

"You a little tired, son?" Push-Bill asked.

"Yeah . . . I don't . . . you know . . . do that much lifting most the time."

"You still going to school, ain't ya?"

Nathan jumped down from the wagon and walked up to Push-Bill. "Yeah . . . I mean, no. I'm going to school, but we don't have class again until September."

"September, huh?" Push-Bill yanked himself back up on his wheeling horse. "Well, listen. I need a helper during the summer. I'm plannin' on haulin' freight all summer up to 10. I'll need a lad like yourself to grease axles and to wrangle the mules. It will be nine days out, then three days back here in town. After that we'll start all over again. You got a horse?"

"Yes, sir."

"Is he sound?"

"Yes, sir."

"Good. Well, if you supply a horse and bedroll, I furnish the grub and a fresh bed at 10. And I'll pay you $9 cash every trip."

"You will?" Nathan gulped.

"Yep."

"Push-Bill . . ." Nathan paused. "Eh . . . what's this 10? You said you're freighting to 10. Ten what?"

"10. That's the town. 10, Nevada. It's up there near the Owyhee. Ain't you heard about that strike?"

"The town's name is just 10?"

"Yep. I guess them old boys got tired of inventing

names, only to have the town go bust anyway. So this one they just call 10. Do you want the job?"

"When are you going to roll out?" Nathan asked.

"In three days."

"I'll have to ask my parents, but if they let me, I'd like the job."

Push-Bill picked up the jerk-line and slapped it against the teams. "Say, can you shoot a gun?" he called back.

"Yes, sir. I shoot a carbine pretty fair!" Nathan hollered. Then he thought to call out, "Why?"

The creak of the wagon wheels drowned out the teamster's reply.

Late that night, with Nathan tucked underneath a single flannel sheet, he heard his mother and father debating whether or not to allow him to accept the job. He could tell they disagreed. Most of the night, Nathan didn't agree with himself either.

Lord, I really, really want the job . . . but I'm scared. I mean, it's hard work . . . and kind of dangerous . . . I think. And I'd miss Mom and Dad and Colin and Tona . . . maybe I can take Tona with us . . . and I'd miss Leah. Leah!

Lord, it's kind of confusing.

By breakfast the next morning, four factors convinced Nathan to accept the summer job.

First, his father said it would be a good way for him to build up some strength and learn a little about freighting.

Then his mother said he could go, but he had to promise to read his Bible, keep his hands and face clean, and eat some fruit and vegetables every day.

And Push-Bill Horn, whom he saw at the corrals when he went to feed his horse, Onepenny, told him he could bring Tona as long as the dog didn't cause them any bother.

But the last and deciding factor tumbled into place when he ran into Leah at the post office.

"Nathan! Look here! Guess who I got a letter from?"

"Ulysses S. Grant?"

Leah stuck out her tongue and danced around on the wooden sidewalk. "No! It's from Kylie! Kylie Collins!"

"You mean the one who never shows up on the stage?" he teased.

"I mean the one I ain't never goin' to marry anyone else but him."

"Is he promising to come see you again?"

"He's coming," she announced, "sometime this summer!"

"Tell him hello. I'll be gone," Nathan informed her.

"You goin' away the whole summer?"

"Yep."

"You ain't either," Leah fumed. "You're jist jealous!"

After a heated seven-minute explanation, Leah was in tears. "Nathan, you cain't go now. Kylie is really coming to see me. You got to be here. It's very important!" she sobbed, brushing away tears with the back of her hand.

"Leah, if it's all that important, I'll . . . I'll make sure I visit with him when I'm back in town. It will only be nine days. I really don't understand the—"

"You don't understand nothin', Nathan T. Riggins!" She turned on her heels and stomped back toward her father's barbershop. While Nathan stared in puzzlement, Leah turned around and sneered. "And you can tell your mother I ain't comin' to no party neither!"

"What? Party? What party?" Nathan choked.

Instantly, Leah cried out, "Oh, no! I didn't say nothin'!" Then she hauled up her dress above her ankles and ran home.

"Nice work, Riggins. You certainly charmed her this morning!"

Nathan turned to see Colin walking up.

"Party?" Nathan mumbled.

"What did you say?" Colin asked.

"What's this about a party?"

"Hey, it wasn't my idea." Colin shrugged. "I told them there was no way of keeping it a secret. 'He'll find out, so why not just make it public?' Oh, no. No one would listen. It was your mother and Leah that dreamed it all up."

"Dreamed up what?" Nathan pressed.

"The surprise birthday party, of course . . . my word, wasn't that what we were talking about?" Colin gasped.

"Tomorrow's my birthday," Nathan mumbled.

"Everyone in town knows that," Colin assured him.

Nathan was silent for several moments.

"I didn't know," he confided.

"Well, there you go. Now you know. We don't have to go around whispering anymore."

"I think I might have hurt Leah's feelings," Nathan worried. "Maybe I'd better go talk to her."

"Why the big rush? You've got all summer," Colin insisted.

"That's the problem," Nathan sighed. "I've only got three days."

TWO

On Tuesday, June 22, 1878, Nathan T. Riggins had his almost-surprise thirteenth birthday party.

His father presented him a hand-tooled scabbard for his carbine and a box of scatter shells for "shooting snakes."

His mother handed him a copy of *The Adventures of Tom Sawyer* and four pairs of socks.

Colin gave him a full pound of St. Louis creme-filled chocolates and then proceeded to eat half of them himself.

Leah surprised him with a rich green shirt that she had made.

"I ain't too good at it yet, but I think that color will look awful princely on ya," she said blushing.

It seemed to Nathan that every kid in Galena was there at his party. They laughed, ate, ran, played, ate, sang, opened presents, and ate again.

The sun had just dropped behind the western hills when the party ended and Nathan walked Leah home. They sat down on a faded wooden bench in front of her father's barbershop.

"That was a good party, Nathan . . . even if I almost ruined it." Leah sighed.

"It sure was. I really like my new shirt. I'm impressed."

"You know, I'm making myself a dress out of that material. Maybe sometime we could wear them at the same time."

"Sure. How about when I come back home in nine days?"

"Kylie might be here," she reminded him.

"I know, that's why I want to wear it."

Leah wrinkled her nose and exclaimed, "You going to try to make him jealous?"

"Isn't that why you wanted me to be here when he arrived?"

She lowered her head. "Yeah . . . I guess."

"You know what, Leah . . . I think that party was kind of sad, too."

"Sad? Why you ain't that old, Nathan."

"You know how we ran around and played games and laughed at each other? Well, how many more birthdays do you think we'll act that way?"

"Everything's changin', ain't it?"

He glanced at her eyes and nodded. "Yeah, sort of like we're supposed to be grown up—"

"But we ain't yet!" she interrupted.

"I'm not sure I want to quit being a kid."

"You know, Nathan, before you moved to town last year, I hated being a kid."

"Really?"

"All I could think about was getting old enough to get married and move out on my own. But this last year . . . I especially liked this year. You made it fun 'cause you always treat me nice. I mean, most of the time you treat me nice. And you bought me them shoes, and you never teased me about the way I talk or that I don't read very good."

"Well, I'll have to admit, Leah, it's been about the best year of my life. I learned a whole lot about the West and about Indians and horses and gold mining and buffaloes and stuff. I learned to trust God more, and I sure learned that He gives me special friends like Leah Walker."

She reached over and put her hand on top of Nathan's

as it rested on the bench between them. He turned his hand over and gripped hers.

"Can I really wear that new shirt in front of Kylie?"

"Yep."

"What if he gets jealous?"

"He'd be the first boy who ever got jealous over me!" She feigned a pout.

"No, seriously . . . what if he's really jealous?"

"Then he'll beat you up." Leah shrugged.

"That's a fact I reckon I'll have to ponder."

Nathan stood and released her hand. "I guess I better get back home and pack a few things. We're leavin' at daybreak, you know."

"I see you in nine days then?"

"Yep."

"Good-bye, Nathan. Say a prayer when you think about me."

"Sure!" He walked about five steps and then turned. "Leah?"

"Yeah?"

"It felt good, didn't it?"

"What?"

He hesitated. "You know . . . holding hands."

"Yeah, it did." Then she straightened up and teased, "Now go on home . . . cowboy!"

He could see her watch him through the twilight shadows as he disappeared down the street. But he could almost hear her mumble in a monotone under her breath, "But I ain't never goin' to marry nobody but Kylie Collins."

And if he could have seen through the Nevada dusk, he might have spotted the tears that traced paths down her cheeks.

Promptly at 6:00 A.M. on Wednesday morning, two tandem wagons pulled by one team of stout wheel horses and five teams of mules rolled out of Galena headed for the upper reaches of the Independence Mountains and the mining town of 10, Nevada.

The spokes of the wheels were a faded red; the boxes were a dust-caked blue, with the name "J. Murphy" almost worn away. Only the bleached canvas tops looked new. A matched pair of white mules pulled in the lead, and the big horses were teamed next to the front wagon. Push-Bill Horn sat astride the left wheeler whom he called Rosie.

Tona alternated between leading the procession and following the spotted horse. Nathan rode Onepenny alongside Push-Bill. He waved good-bye to his dad and searched the street to see if Leah had come to see him off.

She hadn't.

It took Nathan only about thirty minutes to realize that freighting was a very slow business.

"What's the schedule, Push-Bill? How far do we travel today?"

"Today 17.5 miles, 15.2 tomorrow, 12.6 the next, 14.5 the following, and 5.4 tough miles up Wild Horse Canyon. That puts us into 10 by Saturday noon . . . providin' we don't have troubles with outlaws, Indians, flash floods, broken axles, snakes, or women folk," he roared.

By the time they reached camp that night, Nathan figured it had been the longest day in the history of the world. *Just one plodding step after another! One hour . . . then stop to let the animals relieve themselves. Two more hours . . . then a thirty-minute break to let them eat. Another two hours, and*

*it's dinner time. Unhitch the whole team and let them graze.
By 1:30 P.M. back on the trail until a half-hour break two
hours later . . . finally two more hours and then camp for
the night. Lord . . . I guess this is kind of how work is supposed to be.*

Nathan's job had been mostly greasing the hubs, scouting ahead for Push-Bill, and tending mules during the breaks.
He was amazed at how the freighter seemed to know exactly
the mood of each animal and how to coax the best out of it.

But it was around the fire as they ate their supper, after
tying the horses and mules to a picket line, that he learned
the most.

"Now, Nate, don't you ever picket Whitey and
Snowflake next to the other mules. They don't get along with
them. Seems they consider it below their dignity to associate
with an ordinary swing mule. That's why I always put Rosie
and Roanie in between them. Those two hosses seem to git
along with all their cousins.

"Ya see, being in the lead tends to spoil an animal quick.
They don't never want to go back to the line. Can't say that
I blame them though. Up there in the lead you get to gaze
across some mighty winsome country. But the rest that's stuck
in the pack . . . well, all they ever get to see is the rear end of
the animal ahead. And that ain't much of a view even for a
mule.

"You done a good job today, Nate. I appreciate the help.
It gets a might lonely out here hauling freight by yourself. In
the old days, a man wouldn't set out unless he had a dozen
teamsters pullin' with him. But things is changed. It's more
settled now, at least until we git to 10."

"Do we have a place like this to camp every night?"
Nathan asked.

"Nope. Tomorrow we'll make it to Bobcat Springs,

which is as purdy a place as you'll find in Nevada. Then we have a couple of meager nights in the mountains, especially Friday night in Wild Horse Canyon. But by Saturday night we'll be at the Colorado House, eatin' steaks and drinkin' . . . " Push-Bill looked over at Nathan. "Eh . . . drinkin' coffee, yes, sir."

Nathan stared across the campfire and up at the quickly darkening sky. He could already see the twinkle of several stars. "Push-Bill? Do we sleep under the wagons or by the mules?"

"Both. You take the wagon, and I'll guard the mules. But you sleep with that carbine handy."

"You think there will be trouble tonight?"

"Yep."

"What makes you say that?" Nathan asked.

"'Cause ever' time I decide that there ain't no trouble, it comes an' looks me up for sure. So I figure on trouble ever' night . . . and, by golly, it don't ever come."

"So what is the trouble we're planning for—that won't come? Indians?"

"Probably not. We jist got to watch out and try and keep the animals from gettin' spooked or scattered. I'll go settle them down. You can turn in if you want to."

"I promised my mom I'd do some readin'," Nathan informed him.

"Well, never disappoint your mama, son. Even old teamsters know that."

As Push-Bill Horn was walking toward the animals, Nathan called out, "What time are we getting up?"

"I'll roust you out. 'Course if we was camped by Echo Canyon, it would be different."

Nathan dug in his bedroll for his Bible.

"What's Echo Canyon?" he asked.

Push-Bill Horn sauntered back by the fire and squatted down. He picked up a small stick and began to scratch on the ground.

"Well, son . . . you've no doubt been next to a canyon wall a time or two where you had an echo. You shout 'hello there!' and pretty soon those words bounce right back at you."

"Sure," Nathan said with a nod, "like up on Lewis Mountain!"

"Yeah, that's the drift. But Echo Canyon is up on the Yellowstone. It's so deep and wide that the echoes are almost like magic. Why, one night me and Old Jim Bridger were up there—"

"You know Jim Bridger?" Nathan gasped.

"Bridger, Carson, Fremont—I know'd 'em all. But as I was sayin' . . . me and Old Jim was up on the Yellowstone, camped right on the rim of Echo Canyon. Now you ain't never seen a canyon like it, exceptin' you was in Arizona. And this one on the Yellowstone is an echo canyon too! So I was all tucked into my roll nice and smooth when Old Jim started hollerin' at the top of his voice down into the canyon."

"What did he yell?" Nathan asked.

"He screamed, 'Push-Bill, get out of bed, you lazy bum; it's morning!'"

Nathan pulled off his hat and ran his fingers through his hair. "I thought you said it was evening."

"It was. That's why it was so strange. Well, Old Jim comes shuffling back to the fire and crawls under his blankets without explaining nothin'. Naturally, I don't insult him by asking questions. Well, son, I was sound asleep dreaming of wild horses or something jist before daybreak, and all of a sudden this eerie voice comes rolling out of the canyon.

"What did it say?" Nathan pressed.

"'Push-Bill, get out of bed, you lazy bum; it's morning!' That's when I woke up, and, sure enough, Bridger was sittin' at the fire boilin' coffee. He said there's an eight-hour delay on that echo if you know'd how to do it."

Nathan stared up at Push-Bill who was sporting a five-day beard. Suddenly a smile broke across the freighter's face.

"Nate, don't you go believin' one word from a teamster's mouth when he's sittin' around the fire at night! We ain't got nothin' to do but pull a few stretchers."

After Push-Bill went to bed, Nathan read the first chapter of the book of Matthew, then put up his Bible, slipped off his boots, and climbed into the bedroll under the lead wagon. Tona slept only a few feet away.

He thought about cool breezes, bright stars, wagons that creaked slowly, and Leah Walker. He figured he was tired and would probably fall asleep quickly.

He was right.

Nathan didn't really feel wide awake until the first stop the next morning about two and a half miles from their evening camp. After that he was back in the grueling routine . . . riding . . . walking . . . greasing the hubs . . . tending mules . . . and plenty of sweat. The insides of his knees rubbed raw on the ducking britches, his right arm cramped, and his back ached whenever he slouched in the saddle. No wonder cowboys are always 'sittin' tall.'

By the time they rolled into Bobcat Springs, he knew it would be a long dusty summer, and he figured he would have honestly earned every penny he made. After supper Nathan lay on the ground with his bedroll as a pillow under the small part of his back. The smell of fried meat still lingered in the cooling night air. The conversation turned to bobcats.

"I been coming though this canyon for eighteen months," Push-Bill announced, "and I only seen one bobcat in here. 'Course that's 'bout what should be expected."

"How come?" Nathan had his pocket knife out and was trying to cut a matted fur ball off Tona's back side.

"Them bobs is mighty quick fellas. They're 'bout as sneaky as a Texas outlaw as far as keepin' out of sight. Then they don't run in packs neither. Always alone. Oh, a mama might have her cubs for a while, but when it's time to kick 'em out, they're all on their own.

"Now I want to tell ya, them is mean animals. Don't you ever dance with a bobcat. Do ya savvy? If they want to run, let 'em run, but don't pin 'em down. They'll jump ya. And they never lose a fight."

"Never?" Nathan pressed.

"Nope. They'll fight ya until they win or die . . . but they won't slink away a loser."

"How big are they, Push-Bill? They aren't as big as Tona, are they?"

"Nope. Now a cougar can grow that size, but a bobcat is about half the size of your dog."

Nathan pulled off his right boot and rubbed his toes. "What do they eat out here?"

"Rabbits, mainly, I suppose. Rodents, birds . . . maybe a baby deer or antelope. I ain't never seen it myself."

Sitting up, Nathan jammed his boot back on his foot. "When's the best time to spot one?"

"There ain't no good time," Push-Bill lectured. "But I suppose right before daylight if you scanned the water's edge, you just might catch sight of one coming in for a drink."

"Push-Bill, how do I know you're not just telling windies like you did last night?"

The teamster pushed back his dirty hat and grinned from ear to ear. "Ya don't, son . . . ya don't!"

It was still dark when Nathan felt a boot in the side, nudging him awake.

"Nate . . . if you want to have a chance at seeing a bobcat, you'd better slip on down to the water nice and quiet."

Nathan bolted straight up. "Did you see one?"

"I didn't look," Push-Bill replied, "but it will be your only chance this trip."

Nathan considered it fortunate that Tona had wandered off into the brush somewhere. He figured with his dog along, he would never get close enough to see a bobcat. At this time of the year the springs were no more than a small pond surrounded by grass, with a few bushes tucked on the south side. After sloshing through the mud, Nathan squatted in the brush and waited for more daylight.

He waited.

And waited.

And waited some more.

His legs began to cramp, and some kind of small, but fierce flying bug was feasting on the back of his neck.

What am I doing here? Is Push-Bill playing a trick on me? Maybe this is all a joke. He said that I shouldn't believe anything he said around the campfire at night. He played me for a sucker. It's like going on a snipe hunt! It's just a game for greenhorns!

Nathan had resigned himself to going back to camp to face Push-Bill Horn's laughter, when sudden movement along the water's edge caught his eye. His nerves jumped tight, then relaxed as the supposed bobcat turned out to be a rabbit eating the green grass on the water's edge.

I wonder what a bobcat looks like. . . . well, they have to have a bobbed-off tail . . . and, eh, look like a cat!

Suddenly a reddish-brown spotted blur flashed in front of his eyes, pounced on the rabbit, and, with a savage flip, broke its victim's neck. For a split second the animal hovered over the dead rabbit and glared at Nathan. A cold chill hit him as he glimpsed the animal's yellow-green eyes.

Bobcat!

Instantly, the animal and its breakfast disappeared into the brush.

Nathan gulped a big deep breath.

It was a bobcat!

"Push-Bill!" he shouted as he ran back for the wagons. "Push-Bill, I saw one! There was a bobcat down there. I really saw one! It wasn't a stretcher, was it?"

The freighter glanced up from his nearly boiling cup of coffee and grinned.

"'Course it ain't no stretcher. This is Bobcat Springs. What did he look like?"

"Well, he was about twice the size of a big house cat and reddish-brown, mostly brown, with a white-looking belly and dark brown streaks and spots, sort of like a leopard . . . and a short tail, maybe four to six inches, and a broad face . . . and strong—he looked like a regular cat with muscles!" Nathan paused long enough to catch his breath. "And he had yellow-green eyes!"

"You got that close, did ya?" Push-Bill asked.

"Yeah, I was in the bushes not more than twenty feet away."

"Don't ever plan on gettin' closer unless you have your

gun pointed and you consider yourself a good shot. Bobcats will fight anything, anytime. They don't get along with nothin' on this earth except themselves. Sort of like freighters I guess." He smiled.

Nathan bristled with excitement as he stirred up the fire and piled some beans on his tin plate. He could instantly taste the fire of Push-Bill's "Loredo Juice" seasoning.

"So now you've seen a bobcat," the old freighter mused, ignoring Nathan's gasping for cold air on his scorched tongue. "I'll tell ya somethin', and this ain't no stretcher neither. There ain't one man in a thousand who's ever seen one that close, no sir."

"It was kind of scary," Nathan admitted, grabbing for his canteen. "I mean, it's just a little animal, but his eyes looked . . . well, they sort of reminded me of my dad's eyes the other day when he thought he was going to have to shoot Wobley."

"How's that?"

"Determined to fight and win," Nathan replied. "That bobcat took one look at me and was determined to fight and win."

"Yep, I reckon he did."

Nathan's eyes watered as he finished his breakfast and rinsed off his plate with some boiling coffee. "Push-Bill, where are we headed today?"

"Well, we'll swing near the Rialto ranch and then start the climb up Wild Horse grade."

"The Rialto ranch?"

"Yep. Don't seem possible that anyone would try to make it up in this remote place, does it? Hope them girls is o.k."

"Girls?" Nathan quizzed.

"Yep . . . I hear the mama and daddy died a few years

back, and their seven girls is trying to keep the place going all by themselves."

"Seven girls? How old are they?" Nathan pressed.

"I ain't rightly sure, but it's a fact there'll be a passel about your size. But don't let your tongue loll out; we ain't goin' back in there."

"Why not?"

"'Cause the road's bad, and I hear they have a tendency to shoot at anyone who comes up the driveway. They is a cautious bunch any way you cut it, if you get the drift."

T H R E E

At the first stop out of Bobcat Springs to rest the animals, Nathan caught sight of what looked like trees at the base of a barren mountain range on the western horizon. Other than the blue sky, they offered the only color in the sand-brown landscape of the northern basin.

"What's over there?" He pointed.

"That's the Rialto ranch."

Nathan's eyes shot back and forth. "You mean all those girls you told me about?"

"Yep. Providin' they haven't starved, got carried off by Indians, or died of pneumonia."

"Maybe we ought to go check on them," Nathan suggested.

Push-Bill stared him right in the eyes and then snorted, "Wagh!"

"What I mean is," Nathan hurried to explain, "somebody ought to check on them." He looked away.

"I know exactly what you mean. I ain't that old!" Push-Bill roared. "One of these days . . . on the return trip maybe we'll mosey off that way. But the quicker I get these goods to 10, the more money I make. That boom will last till Christmas at best. After that, everyone will be broke or consolidated."

"Consolidated?"

"Right now there's a thousand little claims, none of them big enough to run a full-scale operation. So some San

Francisco company of bankers and lawyers will come in and buy them all out and put in one or two mines, open some company stores, and put us all out of business."

Nathan swung his left leg over the saddle horn and now sat sideways facing Push-Bill as the freighter remounted Rosie. "How big a place is 10?"

"Anywhere from 200 to 2,000." Push-Bill gazed at the horizon. "Look up there . . . here comes a pilgrim from that direction now."

Nathan eyed a man walking down the road. He carried a small pack on his back and a four-foot walking stick in his right hand. His felt hat had the entire top ripped off, and his jacket was patched, his boots worn clear through so that several toes showed. His scraggly beard showed flecks of gray.

"Ho! On the wagon! May I have a word with you before you roll on?"

"Pull out your carbine and watch the horizon, Nate," Push-Bill cautioned.

"He doesn't look dangerous."

"Nope, but he might be a setup for others. You keep a lookout, and I'll deal with this old boy."

Nathan laid his carbine across his lap and kept it pointed in the direction from which the man had appeared. The steel trigger guard felt hot to his touch.

"I say," the man shouted, "this is as fortunate for me as it is for you, my friends!"

"How's that?" Push-Bill growled.

"Well, excuse me, Colonel, but I have something I would like to show you. You are headed to 10, aren't you?"

"What if I am?"

"Now . . . we just might be able to help each other out.

You see, I've spent the past several weeks in the town and have purchased interest in several mining claims. But now—"

Push-Bill spat a wad of tobacco juice into the dirt between them and wiped his mouth on his sleeve. "And you want to sell them to me for some inflated price?"

"No, sir . . . I would never try to pull that on anyone, especially one as knowledgeable as yourself. I would like to sell them at an extremely modest price. You see, I lost my horse back up the road a spell and have need to reach Battle Mountain Station to talk to my bankers. But I will need a horse and supplies to reach the railroad."

He reached into his coat pocket and pulled out a wad of papers. "You see, I've got a few feet in the Lucky Seven Mine, some in the Alligator, the Pretty Nugget, the Root-Hog-Or-Die, the Pennsylvania Dutch, the Broken Nose, the Cedarwood, twenty-five feet in the All-Is-Lost (now that's a fine piece) and—"

"So you're going to make me a good deal by letting me buy the works for a surprising low amount."

"Yes, sir, I am. Just cause I'm in a bind, and I could let go a few of these admittedly small parcels, but I assure you they are rich ones. I'll sell, say, eight of them to you and your son for . . . $20 cash and a horse."

"Mister, I was in Californy in '49. After that there was Kern River, Fraser River up in the British possessions, then the Comstock. I've been from Florence to Prescott hauling goods. I've heard every spiel known to man and a few made up by the devil himself. I didn't buy claims then, and I'm not buying any now!" Push-Bill cracked the jerk-line and the wagons began to roll.

"Son . . . forget the cash." The man turned toward Nathan. "I'll just trade you straight across—these valuable claims I mentioned for that spotted pony of yours."

"Mister," Nathan replied, "I wouldn't trade this horse for every claim on Mt. Davidson." He spurred Onepenny ahead, then reined up, and spun him back to the man on foot.

"I'll give you a dozen strips of beef jerky for those claims," he called out.

"You drive a hard bargain, son . . . but it's a deal!"

Nathan reached into his saddlebag and pulled out the jerky, which was wrapped in a worn linen cloth. The bundle felt greasy in his hand, and he could smell the aroma of peppered meat. The man handed the tattered papers up to Nathan and reached out to shake his hand.

"What's your name, son?"

"Nathan T. Riggins."

"Well, Nathan T. Riggins, they call me Washoe Willy. Sure hope them claims bring you better luck than they brought me. Where's the next watering hole?"

"Two and a half miles straight ahead. It's called Bobcat Springs."

Nathan watched Washoe Willy trudge on down the road. Then he turned Onepenny toward the dust cloud of the wagons and galloped up to Push-Bill's side.

"Did you buy them claims?" Push-Bill asked.

"Yeah."

"What did you give him?"

"Twelve pieces of beef jerky."

"You got suckered, boy."

"They probably aren't real, are they?"

"Maybe. Maybe not. But even if they're real claims, they're claims to an empty hole."

Nathan looked through the papers. "This one—the twenty-five feet of the All-Is-Lost—is drawn up and signed by some California lawyer. It looks official."

"California lawyer? That's the most worthless of them all! Ain't good for nothin' but startin' a fire."

Nathan tucked the papers into his saddlebag. "Well, I'll just keep them anyway . . . sort of a souvenir."

"Well, I'm glad you got it out of your system. When we get to 10, there'll be a man on every street corner selling claims, and I don't want you to be an embarrassment."

"They have street corners in 10?" Nathan quizzed.

A loud roar boiled up from Push-Bill Horn. "Hah! Those streets, or what you might call streets, is so crooked there ain't a corner in the whole town! No sidewalks. No city parks. And no law. You'll see when we get there."

"When will that be?"

"Good Lord willin', it'll be noon Saturday."

It was closer to 3:00 P.M., Saturday, June 26, 1878, when Nathan first caught sight of 10, Nevada. All morning long lines of traffic going into town had increased. Horses, wagons, and stagecoaches rolled past them. And Push-Bill lived up to his name, shouting his team past several oxen-pulled freight wagons.

Nathan marveled at the height and steepness of the terrain they now climbed. Treeless, the naked peaks of the mountains huddled under a streaked powdering of leftover winter snow. Halfway up the side of the steepest one clung the town of 10, like a barnacle to a ship's hull.

Nathan stared in amazement. How could anyone build on something so steep? The back of every building perched on stilts, and many builders hadn't bothered to make them level. Nathan figured that over half the buildings were canvas-topped, and tents were scattered anywhere there was ten feet of flat space.

The crowd got thicker as they approached the city. By the time they reached the first building, what street there was left was so filled with people that Push-Bill had to pull to the side and stop.

"Nate!" he shouted. "You watch this rig. I'm going to see who's buyin'."

Nathan tied Onepenny to the wagon and climbed up on Rosie, taking the teamster's position. From that height he studied the people who crammed 10. The crowd was mostly male, mostly bearded, and mostly scroungy. Many looked like typical miners and prospectors—here to dig ore, hoping to strike color. The rest seemed intent on peddling something to the others—everything from mining gear to meals, from frying pans to gold pans, from baked goods to alcohol. Off to one side he saw several men waving slips of paper, haggling and shouting insults.

He face lit up when Push-Bill Horn wound his way back through the confusion. Soon they had plowed through town and parked the wagon next to a faded, unpainted building that sported a crudely painted sign—Jacob's Goods & Services. While Nathan turned the teams out into a nearby corral that sloped dangerously downhill, Push-Bill Horn supervised the unloading of the wagons. By the time Nathan returned, the freighter had emptied the wagons and stuffed his poke with gold.

"What are you going to do with that?" Nathan asked.

"Ship it off to Galena by Wells-Fargo. I don't carry no more than travelin' and repair money. We'll spend the night down at the Colorado House," he announced. "Got a good friend there who always saves me a clean bed."

From what Nathan could see of the crowd at 10, he

doubted that there could be anything clean in the whole town. After a brief stop at the freight office, they arrived in front of the Colorado House just as the sun dropped behind the towering mountain to the west. Nathan pushed through the throng and peeked into the window of the two-story, wood-framed building. The entire downstairs was a huge, bolted dining room with long rows of rough-cut tables set with tin plates, forks, and knives. Benches lined each side.

While Nathan was still staring at the place, Push-Bill fought his way back through the crowd on the raised wooden sidewalk and handed him something that looked like a poker chip.

"What's this?" Nathan shouted above the roar.

"It's your supper token," Push-Bill explained. "When you hear the bell ring, shove your way through this mob, hand that to the big man with the gray beard, and then dive for a spot at one of them tables. You start eatin' as fast as you can, and when you hear the bell ring, you got to quit. If you don't stop, you'll get throw'd out on your ear and never be allowed back inside."

"You're joking!" Nathan gasped.

"Are you hungry?"

"Yeah!"

"I'm not stretchin' ya, son. So don't come crying to me if you go hungry."

He had barely finished speaking when Nathan heard a faint bell ring and a roar from the crowd of men. It reminded him of his father's descriptions of charging into battle during the war. Now, armed with ravenous appetites, they stormed the tables of the Colorado House.

Nathan didn't bother keeping track of Push-Bill. He tossed his token to a huge, gray-bearded man and dashed to a table. He squeezed in front of an empty tin plate between two very large, dark-skinned men. They looked to Nathan like veterans of many supper battles as they shouted above the roar of the diners, "Waiter! Over here! Pork and beans! Coffee! Hot coffee! We got to have bread! Beefsteak! Eggs! More eggs! Potatoes! Where's the potatoes? Gravy!"

Nathan found himself shoving down food as fast as he could scrape it into his mouth. As the two big men kept the food rolling to their table, Nathan crammed down a plateful of cobbler, but in the mass confusion he couldn't tell if it was peach or apple.

As he furiously scraped the fork across his plate, he heard the bell again. Immediately the diners started to exit. Nathan had never viewed such a scene of destruction. Piles of empty dishes, upturned coffeepots, mounds of silverware, bread, meat, and bone fragments littered the tables.

The rough wood floor looked like a city garbage dump as smelly men picked their teeth and belched their way out the door. Though it was now dark and the streets more crowded than ever, Nathan was relieved that supper was over.

Push-Bill Horn grabbed Nathan by the shoulders and dragged him to the edge of the crowd.

"Is it always this way at the Colorado House?"

"Nah," Push-Bill laughed. "It's usually swarmed on a Saturday night. I guess business is trailing off."

"Trailing off?"

"Yep . . . I remember one run up here, I had to wait out in the street until midnight before I could get to the door."

"I don't understand," Nathan pressed. "Why did we have to hurry out?"

"'Cause they got to clean it up for the next shift, of course. They run six breakfasts, ten dinners, and eight suppers. The man with the gray beard—that's Henry McSwain, probably the richest man in 10."

"Where are we going now?" Nathan asked.

"Out to tend the stock—" Push-Bill suddenly pointed to the darkening mountain. "Did you see that?"

"What?"

"That lightning! It'll be here in no time."

"Rain in the middle of summer?"

"I mean a gully-washin', snake-drownin', cave-in-pro-ducin' downpour like these mountains are famous for."

Nathan studied the murky clouds. "When do you think it will hit?" The air felt heavy to him.

"In about an hour I suppose. Anyway, we'll be holed up in a nice room at the Colorado House by then. I told you McSwain was a friend of mine. We bushwhacked together from St. Louis to Denver. He took his funds and a one-third bonus for not returnin' and disappeared up in the San Juans. Next thing I knew he was a shopkeeper, then a hotel man."

After they cared for the animals, Push-Bill and Nathan tied the tarps down tight on the empty freight wagons. Nathan stored his saddle and personal items in one of the wagons, and Push-Bill tossed his gear in the other. Tona slept under the lead wagon and refused to venture any closer to town.

As they threaded their way back through the crowd, Nathan heard thunder rolls. A few faint drops sprinkled his face. He remembered his own grimy neck and wondered what his mother would think. Or Leah!

One of McSwain's exhausted workers led Push-Bill and Nathan up the outside stairway to the hotel above the restaurant. It opened to the street level above them. Nathan was shocked to step into one gigantic single room. Two hundred fifty wooden boards—two-by-six-foot, propped up like cots and laid out in rows—filled the entire room.

No sheets.

No mattress.

No pillow.

No privacy.

In fact, they couldn't find one empty place.

"We can't sleep here!" Nathan groaned. "There's no room!"

The worker shrugged. "Just wait a little while. Some of these men have slept all afternoon. As soon as they get up, you can have their beds."

"The lad's right," Push-Bill roared. "I'm a good friend of McSwain's, and he promised me a decent room!"

"Oh . . . well, why didn't you tell me that in the first place? You must be referring to the layout room."

"The what?" Nathan asked.

The worker led them back down the stairs and out to a small rectangular building next to the Colorado House. Two identical front doors framed a twelve-by-twenty-four-foot building which looked to Nathan like two separate hotel rooms.

The man pushed the door open, glanced into the shadows, and pulled it back closed. "That one's full." Then he walked over to the other door and looked inside.

"You're in luck, boys! There's plenty of room here. And only two dollars a night."

In the flickering light of a kerosene lantern that hung near the door Nathan saw a stark, bare, windowless room with absolutely no furnishings. Four men sprawled on bedrolls along the far wall.

"Where's the beds?" Nathan asked.

"It's a layout room, I said. You just take your own bedroll and lay it out on the floor anywhere you would like."

"What happened to the beds they used to have in these rooms?" Push-Bill bellowed.

"They got all busted up, so we pulled them out. You going to take it or not?"

"How many men do you cram into this?" Nathan questioned.

"Not more than twenty-five. No, sir, McSwain is real particular about that."

"Twenty-five?" Nathan gasped.

Push-Bill glanced at Nathan. "Well, let's you and me sleep in the wagons tonight."

Nathan felt like a man sentenced to hang who had just received a pardon. They raced back to the wagons. A driving rain blasted their faces, and mud clung to their boots. Nathan hunkered into his bedroll, listening to the downpour pound the taut canvas top. This time Tona climbed up into the wagon with him.

Nathan had pulled off his boots, but left the rest of his clothes on. His saddle made a stiff, cold pillow. Tona crawled onto the bedroll at his feet. Nathan was soon asleep.

It was a crazy dream—like the ones you have right before you wake up in the morning. Nothing made any sense. At first Nathan was riding Onepenny and chasing a bobcat about the size of a steer. When he lassoed the bobcat and pulled the rope to dally it on the saddle horn, the massive animal jumped right up at him knocking him off the saddle. He hit his head on something hard.

In the dream when he came to, he was in a small crowded cabin that belonged to the Rialto sisters. Each wore the same kind of blue calico dress, and each looked quite a bit like Leah.

He entered a small kitchen. There on a very large table

were piles and piles of meat, potatoes, carrots, and bread with so much gravy poured over the top of them that it ran off the side of the table and dripped onto the floor.

Suddenly, the Rialto sisters disappeared. Only Leah remained in the room. "Nathan T. Riggins!" she commanded. "I want you to eat every bite!"

Nathan groaned as he lifted his fork, but was pleasantly surprised to wake up in the wagon, daylight breaking across the top of the canvas.

The storm had ended.

It looked like a clear summer day.

Tona was out exploring.

Nathan's stomach ached from last evening's meal.

His neck felt stiff and smarted.

He yanked on his boots and peered around at the almost-deserted street on the back side of 10. As he climbed down off the wagon, he noticed that the mules and horses anxiously milled around the corral. They all moved toward him, as if expecting to be fed.

I didn't think I'd get up earlier than Push-Bill. Maybe he went down to the Colorado House for breakfast. Not me. I'd rather wait 'til dinner. I'll just eat some jerky . . . no! I traded that to Washoe Willy.

Nathan looked for tracks in the mud around Push-Bill's wagon to see what direction he had traveled. Finding none at all, he climbed up on the wagon and pulled back the canvas.

"Push-Bill!" he cried out. The freighter was tied with ropes and a bandanna gagged his mouth. Nathan pulled down the bandanna and began tugging at the knots in the ropes.

"It's about time you stirred around!" Push-Bill shouted. "I was beginning to think you'd leave me in here 'til noon! They's as good as dead . . . I hope they've said good-bye to their Marys because they are absolutely, thoroughly, completely, without hesitation, unequivocally, exceedingly, comprehensively dead!"

"Who?" Nathan implored.

"Those three blackguards who stole my poke, that's who! And I know who they are. Anyway I know one of 'em!" Push-Bill Horn dug through his supplies and grabbed a handful of shotgun shells. Pulling his short-barreled scattergun out from a box in the wagon, he turned to Nathan.

"Get that Winchester of yours, boy. It's time to do a man's work!"

FOUR

I'll kill 'em . . . I'll kill all three of 'em!" Push-Bill raged.

Nathan scurried through the thin crowd of early morning stragglers, chasing after the freighter. His boots felt stiff, and he stepped carefully, trying to avoid the larger mud puddles. He carried his Winchester in one hand and with the other caught hold of Push-Bill's sleeve.

"Push-Bill! Wait! Wait up! Couldn't we just tell the town marshal?"

"I don't need no lawman to settle my beefs. Besides, there ain't no lawmen up here!"

"None at all?"

"Nope."

"But how do you know who took your money?"

"'Cause he came askin' for a loan, but when I refused, he and those two others got the jump on me."

"Who did it?"

"Quickly."

"Quickly what?"

"The polecat's name is Quickly. But his name is going to be dead—real soon now."

"Is Quickly his first name or last?"

"He only has one name, and it's definitely going to be the last. We was partners up on the Boise."

"And now you're going to kill him?"

"No man steals from Push-Bill Horn . . . ever!"

"'Vengeance is mine, saith the Lord,'" Nathan quoted. "I read that in the Bible yesterday."

"Well, I figure sometimes the Lord is sort of busy over in other parts of the world and needs us to help level things out," Push-Bill tried to explain. "Anyway, don't you go quoting out of the Good Book at me. I didn't hire no preacher to ride the wagon."

"I'm not going to shoot anyone," Nathan protested.

"You won't need to. Just keep an eye on my back side and don't let anyone sneak up on me. I'll do all the rest."

"Where are we goin'?" Nathan asked.

"To the Bucket of Blood."

"The what?"

"The saloon. It's where Quickly always gambles. Right now he's undoubtedly losing my money! He's a lousy gambler."

"How can you kill a friend?"

"He ain't a friend no more. Besides, it's a matter of principle. If you let one man rob you blind, every fool in the district will try the same. In this country you can't let that happen."

Push-Bill shoved his way into the Bucket of Blood Saloon & Gambling Establishment. Nathan slipped inside the doorway and stood in the shadows against the wall. This Sunday morning the building was almost vacant. Chairs were stacked on the tables, the long wooden bar was empty, and the only light came from outside, beaming through the windows and doors. Dust hung in the air along with the smell of alcohol and stale smoke.

At the back of the room, five men sat around a card table. From their looks, Nathan guessed they'd been playing all night.

Lord, I don't know what I'm doing here. Don't let Push-

Bill shoot anyone . . . and don't let him get hurt . . . don't let anyone get hurt. That money isn't worth anyone's life!

Push-Bill, holding his shotgun straight in front of him, approached the table. One of the men spotted him. They all stood up, wide-eyed and reaching for their guns.

"Don't try it, boys! This scattergun will hit you all. I want to know where Quickly is, and I want to know right now!" Push-Bill shouted.

"Now, Push-Bill, don't get all riled. Quickly's gone south."

"Gone south! What about those two with him?"

"One tall and the other kind of dark?" the man asked.

"Them's the ones!" Push-Bill growled.

"They're a hard pair. Quickly paid 'em off, and they claimed they was driftin' up toward Montana."

Push-Bill eased off the scattergun. The men around the table began to relax.

"What do you mean, paid them off?" the freighter asked.

"Ol' Quickly got slicked out of $300 in a card game. They set him up, but we could never see how they done it. Anyway, they was a threatenin' to shoot him if he didn't raise the money. I guess he lifted yours."

"I'll kill him!" Push-Bill insisted.

"Yeah . . . he kind of figured that. That's why he lit shuck," one of the men at the table added.

Just then a man dressed in a black vest and narrow black tie came in from a back room.

"Push-Bill!" he called.

The freighter whirled around, threw the scattergun to his shoulder, and pointed it at the man.

"Whoa . . . not so fast," the man cautioned. "I've got

something for you. Quickly asked me to give this to ya." The man handed him a large certificate.

Push-Bill hesitated and then slowly lowered the gun. He cautiously reached for the large, stiff piece of paper.

"He said it was to pay you back for the loan," the man added.

"Loan? Loan! He lifted my poke!" Push-Bill looked the paper over. "One hundred feet in the All-Is-Lost!" he roared. "He lifted my poke, and he wants to give me this worthless mining stock? What did he do, find this in the trash?"

"Now . . . Push-Bill," one of the men soothed him. "That's a mighty rich prospect. Some boys think that'll be the biggest mine in the region if they can get it developed."

"I'll kill him!" Push-Bill snarled. "You tell him if he sticks his skinny head into the state of Nevada again, I'll ring his neck like a chicken's and stew him in boiling oil!"

"I'll tell him." The man in the vest nodded.

Push-Bill wadded up the mining claim and threw it across the room. As soon as he banged out of the door, Nathan ran to retrieve the claim. He tried to smooth it out and stuffed it into his pocket as he ran after the freighter.

"That's the last night we're sleepin' in 10," Push-Bill announced. "The town's so noisy you can't hear a bush-whacker sneak up on ya! No, sir, I ain't goin' through that again."

"What do we do now?" Nathan asked.

"We hitch up the wagons and hightail it back to Galena for another load."

"What about your money? How much did you lose?"

"$300. But I ain't lost it yet. I told ya, I'll kill Quickly next time I see him. Now let's get some breakfast at the Colorado House. I've still got a couple tokens."

"Is there anyplace else to eat?" Nathan squirmed.

"None that you wouldn't be embarrassed to meet your mama in."

After a battle for breakfast, Nathan and Push-Bill scooted toward the corrals. Nathan noticed a well-dressed woman holding up her ankle-length skirt to cross the muddy street. He stared a moment. In this town of males, she looked as out of place as a sheepherder at a cowboy convention.

She looks like she's going to . . .

"Sunday! This is Sunday, Push-Bill! I promised my mama that I'd go to church if we were in town on a Sunday."

"Well, there ain't no church in 10."

"Where's that lady going?"

"Oh, them Methodists meet out at a brush arbor for singin' and shoutin'."

"Can I go?" Nathan asked.

"Well, if you trade your rifle for a Bible, they might let you attend. I'll go get some supplies for the return trip."

"You're out of money," Nathan reminded him.

"But I ain't out of credit!" Push-Bill stormed down the street.

It was just past 1:00 P.M. when Push-Bill and Nathan finally left 10. With the mules rested, the wagons empty, and the trail stretching downhill before them, they moved along at a steady clip. At the first stop Nathan swung down from Onepenny and began to grease the axles. Push-Bill ambled over to him.

"How did you get along with them Methodists?"

Nathan glanced up. "Nice people. One man said we could stay in his cabin if we ever needed a place to sleep. They all said I should come back and bring you with me."

"Me?" Push-Bill bellowed. "I don't fit in with no singin' Methodists!"

"Yeah, that's what I told them," Nathan teased.

"You did? Now why'd ya tell them that?"

"Because," Nathan laughed, "I've heard you sing!"

The trip back to Galena was routine.

No Indians.

No bushwhackers.

No trouble with the mules.

No vagrants selling mining claims.

It was so boring that Nathan shouted with joy at the top of his voice when he caught the first glimpse of the town. After greasing the wheels one last time, he mounted Onepenny and raced to town with Tona leading the way.

His first thought was to race all the way home. However, as he approached town, he decided to take a tour first. Tona cut through an alley and headed to the Riggins house, but Nathan and Onepenny trotted down Main Street.

As he passed by the bank, the front door banged open. A shout blasted out into the street.

"Nathan! When did you get back? Man, you're dirty! Didn't you ever wash? What was 10 like? Did you see any gold? My father says there's lots of gold in that place! What are you doing, Riggins? Are you lost?"

"Colin!" Nathan waved. He rode Onepenny to the rail

by the bank and slid to the ground. "I just had to look around at Galena. It's kind of peaceful—did you know that?"

"Peaceful?"

"Compared to 10."

"What's 10 like?"

"It's like payday at the mines, the fourth of July, a riot, a circus, and the confusion we had when Thunder fought the bull—all rolled into one day, and then it repeats itself over and over."

"Did you find any gold?" Colin asked. "Was it lying in the streets and stuff?"

"If they had any streets." Nathan laughed. "The only thing lying in them are drunks and garbage." Nathan looked up and down the sidewalk as he talked.

"I say, Riggins, are you looking for someone?"

"Colin . . . have you seen Leah?"

"She's probably with good ol' Kylie."

"What? Kylie Collins is here? Actually in Galena?"

Colin threw his arm around Nathan's neck and tugged him toward an alley speaking in a low, hushed voice.

"As a matter of fact, he's been in Galena for a week. The two of them are always together. In the Mercantile, at the livery, in church, over at the bakery . . . say, did you know the Deluxe has a new baker from San Francisco? You should try the pineapple pastry!"

Nathan heard very little of the rest of what Colin said. It was as if someone had slammed a fist into his midsection.

He ached all over.

His stomach cramped.

He felt a little dizzy.

Remounting Onepenny, Nathan left Colin still rambling on about the new cook. He purposely didn't ride past Walker's Barbershop, but took the alley between Slausen's

Dry Goods and the faded red siding of the Oriental Cafe. His mother ran out to meet him as he tied Onepenny off in front of the house.

"Nathan! Where were you?" she called, throwing her arms around him. "Tona made it home several minutes ago!"

"Eh . . . mother . . . I'm kind of dirty. You might not want to—"

"Well, I certainly think your mama deserves a hug."

"Yes, ma'am . . . but couldn't we do that inside?"

"Oh, yes . . . you wouldn't want anyone to see . . ."

"Mother . . . it's not that," he began. Then his face lapsed into a smile. "Well, actually, it is that, isn't it?"

"Of course it is." She laughed. "Your father is at the office. Did you stop and see him?"

"Not yet."

"Did you eat well on the trip? Was there any trouble? Is it hard work? Or perhaps a little boring? Father said freighting is so slow it would bore him to tears. I hope you kept up your reading. Did you read, Nathan? I hear 10 is awfully wild. A man came through town just the other day with such horrid reports. But I suppose you didn't stay in town long enough to have trouble—just unload and leave. Anyway, you wash up, then come in and tell me everything that happened."

He did.

It took Nathan two hours to boil water and take a hot bath, put Onepenny up at the livery, bring in some wood for the stove, and tell his father about the trip.

"Well, I ran across Push-Bill down at the freight office," Marshal Riggins told him. "He said you were the best worker he's had on the trail in five years. I'm proud of you, son. Maybe this summer job will work out real nice."

"Did he mention the problem with Quickly?" Nathan asked.

"Yep. Push-Bill's a prideful man . . . figures it's up to him to settle the score."

Nathan crawled up on the top rail of the corral fence and looked his dad in the eyes. "What will happen next?"

"In time Push-Bill will cool off, but for now don't you go backing his play. Just tell him you got no stake in it and stick to your job. He'll understand. Push-Bill has a lot of sand, but he's not the type to go around shootin' people."

Nathan pushed back his hat. "Unless he gets desperate enough . . . like Mr. Wobley."

"Pride and desperation can be a tricky combination to handle," the marshal agreed. "Now," he asked grinning, "where are you headed all decked out like a cowboy on a Saturday night?"

"Oh . . . you mean, the shirt?" Nathan blushed.

His father poked him in the ribs. "I mean, the new green shirt, clean fingernails, hair slicked back."

Nathan jumped down off the rail and scratched the toe of his boot in the dirt. "Well, Leah made this shirt for my birthday, remember? And I was . . . you know . . . awful dirty. So I thought I'd just clean up and scout around town."

"Well, if I were you, I'd scout down near the stage office," the marshal suggested.

"Why?" Nathan asked.

"Because that's where I last saw Leah."

"Was she alone?" Nathan pressed.

"Nope."

Nathan wanted to ask more—*Was she with Kylie?*

What does he look like? How was she acting? Did she ask about me?

But he said nothing.

Leaving his father, Nathan walked back up to Main Street and turned east. He could see the afternoon stage pulling away in the direction of Battle Mountain Station. He thought he saw a green dress in the crowd.

As he got closer, he spied Leah, still a few blocks away, strolling his direction with her head down. Nathan ducked into the two-foot-wide alley between Cormack's Clock Repair Shoppe and the Eat Here and Die Saloon. After Leah walked by, Nathan crept up behind her.

"Excuse me for being so forward, miss, but that's a beautiful dress!"

Breaking out of deep thought, she spun around and stared wide-eyed.

"Nathan! You're home!"

"For three days." He smiled. "Where's Kylie?"

"He's gone. You just missed him! He was on the Battle Mountain stage."

"Sorry about that. I heard you two had a real good time."

"Where'd you hear that?" Leah demanded.

"Eh . . . you know . . . from Colin."

"Colin don't know nothin' about nothin'!"

Nathan tried to study Leah's eyes, but she kept glancing down. "You mean, you and Kylie didn't have a good time?"

"I didn't say that neither," she huffed.

"B-but I thought—," Nathan stammered.

"Nathan T. Riggins, how come you was gone when you should have been here, and you're here when you should be gone?"

"What?"

"You heard me," she fumed.

"You want me to go?" he asked.

When Leah looked up, tears streamed down her cheeks. "I want you to make up your mind!"

"Make up my mind? Make up my mind about what?" Nathan repeated. "Are you crying?"

By now the tears dripped from her cheeks and stained her new green dress.

"No, I ain't crying! And don't you ever go around sayin' I was!"

Suddenly, Leah hiked up her long skirt and ran down the sidewalk toward her father's barbershop. For several moments Nathan stood staring blankly down the wooden sidewalk filled with all sorts of people but not Leah Walker.

Nathan saw her only once more in the next three days. She seemed to be avoiding him.

Lord, I don't understand. Nowadays every time I talk to her, she runs away crying. We didn't used to have to have a reason to see each other. We just sort of talked and played and ran and laughed . . . but now it's different. It's like every conversation has to be important. I want to grow up, Lord, but I don't want to have to give up having fun.

"Let's roll 'em out!" Push-Bill shouted at 6:00 A.M.

Dust hung heavy in the air. Nathan couldn't see a cloud in the sky. What breeze there was already felt warm. As they wound their way past the last few buildings of the city, he smelled bacon blended with the aroma of the sagebrush. Tona trotted beside Onepenny. Both appeared happy to be once more making tracks.

On the first trip out it had all seemed like a great adventure.

Now it just felt like work.

And this time Nathan didn't look back as they left Galena behind.

FIVE

Nathan spent the first day out thinking mostly about Leah—about how they always argued and how he missed her in spite of it. He thought about how pretty her hair had looked all summer and how warm her hand felt when he held it.

He spent the second day thinking about dust, heat, thirst, bushwhackers, vengeance, justice, and gold.

They pulled into Bobcat Springs in the late afternoon and soon had the animals tended and camp organized. Right after licking up the remnants of Nathan's second plate of beans, Tona disappeared into the rocks west of the springs.

Push-Bill Horn sat back from the small fire and loaded his pipe. "Did I ever tell you about the time me and Jim Bridger went elk huntin' up on the Yellowstone?" he quizzed.

"I reckon you didn't," Nathan said with a wide grin.

"Well, son . . . it was in late October of the year, and we was looking forward to hanging some elk for the winter. So ol' Gabe and me followed sign up over a steep ridge that neither of us had ever crossed. Now we had just hiked out of the trees into a clearin' when we spotted him. Standing not more than a hundred feet away was the biggest bull elk I'd ever seen. I was already frettin' on how we would ever carry it back to camp.

"Well, ol' Jim, he wants to take it, so he throws his rifle to his shoulder and fires a round. Now Jim Bridger was a mighty fine shot, and I was shocked to see that he had completely missed the elk. Jim was furious, but startled, because that elk didn't even flinch. It didn't bolt, jump, or even look our way. About now I'm figurin' we ran across a deaf elk.

"So Jim, he loads her up and takes aim for another go. I watch in disbelief as he misses that elk again. I start to shoot the thing myself, but ol' Jim is so sure enough furious that he charges right at the elk, plannin' on hitting it over the head with the barrel of his rifle.

"Well, son . . . Jim hadn't run twenty feet until he runs face first into a solid glass mountain! It was just like that black obsidian, but this here was a rare, clear obsidian. No wonder he couldn't hit the thing! But not only that, the glass mountain acted as a magnifier. And instead of that elk bein' a hundred feet, we figure it was more like twenty miles away!

"If you ever get up into the Yellowstone, make sure you look up that glass mountain. . . . 'Course you can't see it, but you can run into it, that's certain sure!"

By the time Push-Bill finished his story, Nathan was doubling over with laughter. He was trying to grab enough air to talk when Tona's piercing cry sent shivers down his back.

"Tona's hurt!" Nathan yelled. He grabbed his carbine out of the scabbard and raced around the springs.

Lord! Not a snake bite again! Please, Lord, don't let him get bitten by a snake.

Nathan leaped over some boulders, his left foot coming down on loose gravel, and he tumbled into the rocks. The Winchester crashed into the granite, and he reached out to break the fall with his right hand.

Slamming into the rocks, he felt the skin rip away on the palm of his hand. He staggered to his feet and clutched his wound. It felt as if he had dragged it through a cactus patch. Brushing back tears and smearing blood on his face, he searched for his carbine and then raced toward Tona's shrieks.

Stumbling over the crest of the rocks, Nathan spotted Tona flung on his back down among the boulders. Standing over him was a bobcat. The animal had ripped Tona's thigh, a jagged ugly wound, and would have torn off the leg completely had it not been for Nathan's approach.

The animal's eyes blazed at Nathan. He slammed the carbine to his shoulder and grabbed the trigger guard lever to cock the gun. The fierce pain in his hand prevented him from setting the jammed lever.

It's stuck! It got jammed in the fall!

He charged the bobcat, hoping to clobber it with his carbine barrel, but the animal darted out of sight, leaving the wounded Tona behind.

"Tona!" Nathan sobbed. "Tona!" He bent down low to lift the animal out of the rocks, and the gray and white dog viciously snapped at him.

"Tona, it's me! Nathan! I'll help you, boy."

Laboring for breath, Tona growled at Nathan.

"It's all over for him. Let me put him down, son."

Push-Bill towered on the crest of the rocks, revolver in hand.

"No!" Nathan pleaded. "No! He'll pull through! I know he will!" The tears flowed so heavy now he couldn't see clearly.

"Son . . . you got to put him out of his pain . . . it ain't fair. You go on back and I'll . . . "

"No! You're not killing my dog!" Nathan shouted. "Come help me! We've got to get him back to camp! Help me, Push-Bill . . . please!"

Push-Bill Horn holstered his gun and, with a speed that amazed Nathan, grabbed Tona's nose and clamped the dog's jaws shut. Then with a gentleness that didn't seem to fit his big, calloused hands, he picked the bleeding dog up and began to carry him back to camp.

Scrambling to keep up, Nathan wrapped his bandanna around his own bleeding hand. Push-Bill laid the dog by the fire and gently folded the ripped hindquarters back to its original position.

"It's torn to the bone, son . . . I'm mighty sorry, but you've got to help him out. He's been too good a dog to let him go on and suffer."

Tona was silent, struggling for every short breath.

"No! I can't, Push-Bill, don't ya see? I just can't! Isn't there anything we could do?" Nathan pleaded.

"Well . . . a man could always pour whiskey in the wound and sew it up . . . but I ain't got a drink, and I don't have no needle and thread."

Nathan searched around wildly with his eyes. "How about in the wagon?"

"Son, them goods is buttoned down tight. I can't go spreading them across the desert lookin' for somethin' that might not even be there."

"We have to do something!" Nathan's hands and arms began to shake, and he couldn't make them stop. He felt like a person who was being held under water against his will.

Push-Bill grabbed him by the shoulders and shook him hard.

"Nate! You listen to me. Get hold of yourself! You got to let go! The good Lord don't let us keep them animals forever. It was bound to happen sometime. Let him go, son . . . let him go!"

"No!" Nathan sobbed. "I can't! I just . . . won't!"

Push-Bill threw his big arm around Nathan's shoulder and let out a deep sigh. "Son, we'll wrap them wounds up tight with some rags. Then you pour some water into his mouth every half-hour or so . . . if he's alive in the morning, we'll put him under the belly of that wagon with the firewood and take him with us."

By dark Tona was wrapped in a sack that read "Quaker Mills, Akron, Ohio." Nathan's hand displayed a clean bandanna, and Push-Bill had straightened the hammer on his Winchester carbine.

Nathan had a little cup of water by the sleeping dog, and every half-hour he forced Tona's mouth open and poured in a teaspoon or so.

Push-Bill broke a long silence.

"Son . . . you got to remember that Tona's just a dog. He got hurt doin' exactly what dogs are born to do—chasin' a cat."

"It isn't fair! I should have kept him at home!"

"In a pen? Now that wouldn't have been fair. Dogs is meant to roam and explore and get themselves into mischief."

"If I had it to do all over again, I'd still leave him at home."

"And if that dog had it to do all over again, he'd go right back after that bobcat. But life don't back up. It just rolls on."

Nathan tried to stay awake to keep Tona from dehydrating, but around midnight he slipped off to sleep. A couple of times during the night, he heard a noise and woke up enough to see Push-Bill giving Tona a drink.

Right before sunup, Nathan stole out of his bedroll, pulled on his boots, checked on Tona, grabbed his carbine, and slipped out into the rocks next to the springs.

Ninety minutes and two shots later, he shuffled back into camp. The sun blazed over the eastern mountains, and Push-Bill was beginning to hitch the team.

"Where's Tona?" Nathan shouted. "He didn't . . . You didn't . . ."

"He's barely alive, so I tucked him on top of the firewood."

"Will he make it to 10?"

"Only the Lord can give you that answer," Push-Bill declared. "I suppose you were bobcat huntin'?"

"Yep. I'm going to kill him!"

"You mean, you didn't have any luck jist now?"

"Nope. I never even saw him."

"Then why are you so dead set at killin' him?"

"It's a matter of principle. It's a matter of justice. An eye for an eye . . . and all that."

"Well, now . . . I believe the Good Book was written for people—not critters. Besides, that dog ain't dead yet."

"It doesn't matter," Nathan insisted. "I'm going to kill that bobcat anyway!"

"'Vengeance is mine, saith the Lord.' Seems like a lad told me that recently," Push-Bill reminded him.

Lord, just let me have one clean shot at that cat!

"This is different," Nathan insisted.

A few miles out of Bobcat Springs, Nathan spotted trees against the base of the distant mountains.

"Is that the Rialto ranch?" he asked.

"Yep."

"I'll bet they have needle and thread—maybe even some alcohol for the wound."

"I reckon they do, but we cain't pull over there now. I've got to keep these wagons rollin' to 10."

"Let me carry Tona over there on Onepenny."

"We got to move on up the trail!"

"I'll catch up. You just keep them rolling. Please."

"I don't know if I should turn you loose with that band of girls."

"I won't pester them, honest!" Nathan pleaded.

"It weren't them that I was worried about!" Push-Bill explained. "But if the wounds don't kill the mutt, the dust under that wagon will. I'll let you go, but you got to catch up by midafternoon . . . ya hear?"

"Yes, sir!" Nathan shouted, jumping off Onepenny to gently retrieve his dog.

Tona didn't protest. He didn't open his eyes. His tongue and his nose were both dry and caked with dust. Nathan poured a little water into the dog's mouth, and Tona tried to swallow, then gave up, coughed, and drooled most of the water out the side of his mouth.

The dog cradled in his lap, Nathan pulled off the trail and rode toward the distant trees. His mind drifted back to when Tona first followed him into Willow Creek. For a while he relived all the events of the preceding year. Abruptly, he came back to the present. What had looked like a flat valley all the way to the ranch now dropped down into a ravine.

Lord, you've just got to help Tona. I need him. Sometimes it seems like he's my best friend. We've been through everything together. Bears and snakes and outlaws and coyotes and bulls and blizzards and buffaloes . . . please, Lord!

Climbing out of the dry, ancient riverbed, Nathan studied the trees. They seemed even further away now than when he had begun.

One other thing, Lord. Help me kill that bobcat. I want to get even, Lord. Just give me a chance to get even!

Nathan calculated it took over an hour more to come close enough to see any buildings near the Rialto ranch. He was surprised to discover that the trees were not cottonwoods scattered along a creek or spring, but rather a row of scrub cedars. They'd been carefully planted beside a mile-long drive that led to a neatly maintained two-story house.

Tona hadn't opened his eyes for several miles. Nathan constantly searched the dog's neck for a heartbeat.

"Hang on, boy . . . you've got to hang on!"

He had ridden about halfway up the drive when a girl's voice from behind caused him to jump.

"What you want, boy?"

He spun around and glanced down the barrel of a shotgun perched on the shoulder of a brown-haired girl who looked about his age.

"Eh . . . is this . . . is this the Rialto ranch?"

"Maybe it is and maybe it isn't. What do you want?"

"Look, my dog got ripped up by a bobcat back at the springs. I need to get him fixed up and thought maybe you could help."

The girl, clothed in a faded dress with the sleeves pushed up to the elbows, stepped up to Nathan but didn't lower her gun. "What's that dog's name?"

"Tona."

"Tona? That's a dumb name," she announced. Then she lowered the gun a little and stepped up to look. "He's hurt bad, isn't he?"

"Yeah. Can I get some help?"

"Maybe . . . it's up to Sal. You walk that horse to the house and keep those hands in front of you. You try to pull a gun, and I'll blow you out of that saddle quicker than you can blink." Then she turned to the cedars and hollered, "Come on, girls, let's take him home!"

Three younger girls stepped out of the trees. The two oldest looking ones also carried guns. All three wore long, yellow calico dresses.

"What's his name, Nan?" the tallest of the three, with ink-black air, asked.

"Boy, what's your name?" the leader quizzed.

"Nathan. Nathan T. Riggins from Galena. Eh, what's your name?"

"We're Rialtos," she informed him.

"I'm Jerri," the black-haired one offered.

"And I'm Nina," the little blonde girl added.

The smallest took off running toward the house and shouted back, "I'm Babylon, but everyone calls me Babe!"

"Babylon?" Nathan mumbled.

"What of it?" Nan growled.

They traveled several more minutes without speaking. Nathan glanced occasionally at the girls who whispered and giggled as they skipped along beside him. Finally, black-haired Jerri tugged at his pant leg.

"Hey, boy . . . how old are you?"

"Thirteen."

"When's your birthday?"

"A couple weeks ago. Why?"

"He belongs to Cape!" Nina giggled.

"Cape?"

"She's our sister," Nina answered. "I told you he was too old for you, Jerri!"

"Well," Jerri huffed, "he's too young for Nan!"

"And he's too skinny," Nan added, never lowering her shotgun.

Nathan arrived in the well-kept yard of the Rialto ranch with Tona still in his lap. To the side were two large barns, corrals with several animals, a chicken coop, and a smokehouse. Out back he thought he saw a large garden and some fruit trees. Standing on the front porch was the little brown-haired girl called Babe and two other girls.

Glancing at the oldest of the girls, who looked to Nathan to be about sixteen, he said, "I've got a dog that's ripped up pretty bad, and I was wondering if anyone here could help get him stitched up?"

"He's yours, Cape," Nina shouted. "He's thirteen, and Jerri's too young."

A blonde-haired girl with blue-green eyes squinted into the morning sun and stared at him. She didn't say anything, but turned to the front door of the house.

"Go get Sal," the oldest called to her. Then she turned to the others. "Nina, you take Babe and fetch some water so this boy can wash up. Looks to me like his hand is bleeding. Jerri, go dig him out something to eat. Nan, you take his horse out to the barn. Boy—"

"My name's Nathan T. Riggins."

She walked over to him. "*Boy*," she emphasized, "give me that dog." Tenderly carrying Tona, she climbed up on the porch with Nathan following behind. As they reached the top step, the front door swung open, and a young woman who looked a lot like Miss D'Imperio, rushed out carrying several empty flour sacks.

"Here," she commanded. "Lay him here! Beth, go fetch the rubbing alcohol. Cape, bring my sewing kit. Where's Nan?"

"She's putting that spotted horse of his away."

"Well, then . . . after you fetch the sewing kit, bring a little cup of that soup off the stove for the dog."

"It ain't done yet."

"It isn't done," she corrected. "But this dog won't mind, I assure you."

"A bobcat did this?" she asked as she cleaned out the wound with a clean cloth and alcohol.

"Yes, ma'am."

"Please call me Sal," she requested.

"I'm Nathan."

"I know . . . the girls told me everything. You might not want to watch this," she suggested.

Nathan, starting to feel sick to his stomach, turned away from watching. "I think you're right."

"Your dog's lost a lot of blood."

"Yeah . . . I know, Miss . . . Miss Sal."

"If he has any chance of living, he'll need constant rest. I'm going to sew him up now. I don't suppose you have any preference on what color thread I use. Here's a charcoal gray . . . this should work."

While he was waiting, the girl named Cape brought him a plate of fried eggs and homemade bread, thick with butter. She handed it to him without speaking and returned to the house.

He went over to the recently filled wash basin on the porch, cleaned his face and hands, and then sat down to eat the meal. About the time he finished, all the girls gathered on the front porch as Sal tied off the last of the stitches. She tried to force some warm stew juice down Tona's throat.

"Do you think he'll pull through?" Nathan asked.

"That depends on how much blood he's lost, whether that wound's clean, how much fight he has left in him, and what the Lord wants to do with him."

Sal stood up, brushed out her apron, and then came over to the steps to sit down next to Nathan.

"Now . . . ," she said with a sigh, "who are you, and what in the world are you doing out here?"

"I'm Nathan T. Riggins. I live in Galena with my parents. My father's the marshal there. I'm working for a freighter this summer, greasing axles and tending his livestock. We're hauling goods up to 10. Did you know about the town of 10?"

"Yes," she said nodding.

"Well, we were back there at Bobcat Springs when my dog, Tona—"

"Is that Shoshone?"

"Yes, ma'am . . . eh, Miss Sal. Anyway, he got tore up by that cat in a fight, and I was desperate to find some help for him. So I hope I didn't impose too much. Now I'll load him up and be on my way."

"You'll do nothing of the kind," she replied.

"What?"

"You'll have to stay for dinner. To do less would be to insult the Rialto name."

"But you just fed me!"

"That was merely a snack."

"I've got to get back to the wagons."

"We'll show you a shortcut to 10."

"You've been there?"

"A couple of times a year. We go up and sell our sewn goods and produce."

"You haven't told me your story," Nathan prodded.

"Well," Sal began. "I'll let Beth tell you. I need to cook. Besides, she's our schoolteacher anyway."

The tall, brown-haired Beth stepped out into the yard so she could turn to face Nathan. The five other girls scampered down and sat on the steps next to Nathan. The one called Cape sat closest.

"All of us were born right here in this house. But Mama died when Babe was born. Then three winters back Father got stuck out in a blizzard and froze to death. Well, we talked it over for a long, long time and decided this is right where we wanted to stay. So we just divided up the chores and settled in. We don't get much company, but we don't get bothered either."

"Yeah," Babe reported, "if anyone tries something on us—boom! Nan blasts them!"

"I haven't shot anyone yet!" Nan protested. "But we sure enough scared a few!"

"So," Nathan asked, "who does what chores?"

"Well," Beth reported, "Sal's eighteen, so she's the boss. She does most of the cooking, looks after the house, does the doctoring when we're sick, and makes sure we take baths."

"And she reads the Bible to us and prays," Babe chimed in.

"I'm next, at sixteen, and my job is to teach the others. We have school everyday. We can all read, write, and do mathematics."

"Plus Beth is teaching us Latin," Cape reported.

"Latin? Where did you learn that?" he asked Beth.

"From my mother. She went to school in New England. Also, I'm helping them all learn how to sew. Then there's Nan—she's fourteen, and she's in charge of the barnyard animals."

"I help her," Nina blurted out.

"Nan milks the cows, pulls calves, smokes the hams—"

"And I do most of the butchering," Nan boasted.

"Then there's Cape—she's twelve, and she's our cowgirl. We've got twenty-two head of cattle and sixteen sheep. She drives them out to pasture and rounds them up to bring them back at night."

"I help her, too!" Nina offered.

"Jerri here is ten, and she's taken over the gardening chores. She had to plant, weed, carry water, and pick the garden."

"I'm next!" Nina called out.

"And Nina, the bashful eight-year-old—she's everybody's helper. She likes being outdoors, so she helps most often with the animals."

"Don't forget me!" Babe insisted.

"And Babe . . . well, she's a very mature six. Her job is to gather eggs and bring in firewood for the stove."

"Now you know all about us," Nina added. "But Cape still don't like you."

"Nina!" Cape fumed. She stomped to her feet and ran back into the house.

"There's one thing I don't know," Nathan ventured. "How did you get your names? Did I hear Babe say her name was Babylon?"

Beth broke into a wide smile. "Yes . . . mother and father gave us all Biblical names. Sal is really named Jerusalem. I'm not Beth, but Bethlehem. Nan is for Nazareth. Cape is for Capernaum, Jerri for Jericho, Nina for Ninevah, and you already know about Babe."

"Yeah," Nina bubbled, "coming here is like visiting the whole Bible!"

The immense dining room was spotless, and the linen-covered table piled with food when they all sat down to dinner and waited for Sal to say prayers. Nathan figured the only woman on earth who could cook better than Sal was his mother, and even that was very close.

After dinner and lots of talk and giggles, Nan brought up Onepenny, and Nathan prepared to leave.

"You can't take Tona," Sal reported. "If he has any chance of living, he's got to stay here a while."

"I sure do appreciate it." Nathan tipped his hat after

he sat down in the saddle. "I'll check on him next time through."

"We shall look forward to your visit, Nathan T. Riggins," Sal added.

He had turned Onepenny to the east when Nina yelled out, "Nathan, do you have a girlfriend back in town?"

"Eh . . . sort of . . . I think," he stammered.

"See, I told you I didn't like him!" Cape huffed as she turned her back on him.

The other six Rialto sisters waved until he could no longer see them.

Nathan knew he was late, but Onepenny was well watered and rested, so he rode hard along the shortcut that Miss Sal had described. Right before sunset he caught sight of the wagons camped in Wild Horse Meadow. Actually he heard gunfire before he spotted the wagons.

Holding his Winchester in his lap, he approached with caution, getting close enough to hear shouting.

"If there was a tree within ten miles, I'd hang you right now!" A man was tied spread-eagle to the large rear wheel of one of the freight wagons.

Is this Quickly? Push-Bill's caught up with Quickly!

S I X

It's about time you showed up, Nate!" Push-Bill hollered. "Hop down and grease them wheels. Then tend to the mules."

Nathan pointed at the man strapped to the wheel. "Is that Mr. Quickly?"

"That there?" Push-Bill nodded. "That there is not a mister. That's a dead duck."

"Son!" the man shouted at Nathan. "Listen, talk to Push-Bill, will ya? He seems to be a tad riled."

"Riled? Riled, am I? Oh, no! I get riled if a mule runs off at night. I get riled if an axle breaks. I get riled if someone tries to make me lower my prices on the goods . . . but this! The entire Apache Nation has never been this mad! You'd be better off being Custer in the hands of the Sioux. Quickly, you'll hang on the first tree you see between here and 10!"

"Son . . . talk to him!" Quickly pleaded. "I offered to pay him back the money—and more!"

Nathan pulled the saddle off Onepenny and walked closer to Quickly. "What do you mean you offered to repay?"

"I came ridin' right up to camp on my own and offered him $500."

"I thought you only stole $300."

"I think of it as a loan," the man corrected him. "And Push-Bill is entitled to interest."

"He didn't offer me nothin'!" Push-Bill bellowed from near the smoking campfire.

"I offered you $500 and you know it!" Quickly howled.

Nathan pulled the bandanna off his hand, examined his wound, and then glanced at Push-Bill.

"He rode in here and said he'd pay me $500 for that phony mining stock he gave me! Then when I jumped him and demanded my money, he said he wanted to buy back the stock on credit!"

"What?" Nathan exclaimed.

"He don't have a penny to his name!" Push-Bill bellowed. "I done searched him."

"Look, I had a man offer me $500 for my stock. So I hurried down to find Push-Bill. I'll take the stock and ride back to 10. Then I can cash it in and have the money waiting when you two roll into town!"

"You mean there's some value in that stock?" Nathan asked.

"At least this old boy thinks so," Quickly called out.

"Well . . . it don't matter, because I don't have the certificate. I chucked it on the floor of the Bucket of Blood . . . and besides you ain't never goin' to live to see 10 again!"

"Wait a minute," Nathan cried. "You came riding into the camp of a man you bushwhacked and wanted to buy back gold stock on credit? You've got to be the craziest man I ever met!"

"I didn't want to bushwhack him. It was those two that cheated me. They was goin' to kill me . . . and Push-Bill too!"

Push-Bill pulled out his revolver and waved it under the bound man's nose. "You should have let 'em kill ya! It would be a might more pleasant than what I aim fer ya!"

"Wait!" Nathan called. "I've got the stock certificate! It's in my saddlebag. I just remembered. I snatched it up when Push-Bill throw'd it down!"

Push-Bill spun back toward Nathan. "You did?"

"Go and see, boy. It's powerful important!" Quickly pressured.

Nathan dug through the papers which included the scraps of mining claims he had purchased from the man near Bobcat Springs.

"Here it is! One hundred feet of the All-Is-Lost Mine!" Nathan shouted.

"That's it!" Quickly yelled. "Now just untie me and let me ride up to 10 and get your money!"

"You ain't goin' nowhere!" Push-Bill commanded. "You done robbed me once. You ain't goin' to rob me again!"

Nathan handed the paper to the freighter. "Maybe we ought to just tow Mr. Quickly along with us. Then you could go with him and get your money when he sells the certificate."

Push-Bill threw a handful of coffee into the pot on the fire and nodded at Nathan. "I was just startin' to think the same thing, son. That way if it's all a big stretcher, I can hang him from the cross beam at the Colorado House."

"No, no! You can't do that!" Quickly protested. "If I don't get back there by tomorrow night, I'll lose the sale! We don't have time to wait for these mules! You've got to let me go, Push-Bill. I won't let you down this time!"

"You worthless snake-eyed skunk! I'm not untyin' ya until I get my money, or you're hangin' from a tree!"

"Look! There won't be any money for that certificate if you don't let me go back now! You got my word on it! I swear . . . I swear . . . on Kit Carson's grave. I'll do it!"

Push-Bill rubbed his whiskers, stirred the fire, and stared at the flames.

The long silence was broken by Quickly.

"Son . . . you've got to believe me. If I'm not back, I lose the sale. Talk to him."

"It isn't my hand to play." Nathan shrugged.

Lord . . . there's got to be a solution that doesn't involve anyone dying! Help Push-Bill deal with his temper.

Nathan tied the horses and mules to the picket line and unloaded the food boxes while Push-Bill continued to gaze at the fire. He couldn't tell if it was the calm before the storm or the calm after it.

It was getting dark when Nathan finally spoke up. "Push-Bill, do you want me to cook some supper?"

"Huh? Oh . . . no, I'm the cook. I'll do it."

The old freighter pulled out his Green River knife and cut two slabs of salt pork for the frying pan.

"There's three of us, Push-Bill." Nathan nodded at Quickly, still tied to the wagon wheel.

"Oh . . . yeah." He nodded and cut a third slice without protest.

"You been staring at that fire an awful long time," Nathan prodded.

"Son . . . did you ever read about Kit?"

"Yes, sir, I did. He got sick and died down in New Mexico after he took that big trip to Washington, didn't he?" Nathan asked.

"He died in southern Colorado actually." Push-Bill nodded. "Well, one time . . . years ago when we was young and raw, me, Dirty Ed McGinnis, Reynolds, and Quickly there . . . left Ft. Hall to go up into Blackfeet country and look for gold on a creek where Quickly claimed he knew an old boy who picked up nuggets as big as your thumb.

"Anyway . . . everyone at the fort told us not to go, that the Blackfeet would murder us the first night out. Well, we was too mountain-dumb to know better so we go ridin' off.

"Three days out we come over a draw, and about fifty Blackfeet meet us lookin' for war. We made a run for the rocks, but they shot my horse out from under me. I hollered, but the others was too far ahead and too scared to hear.

"I started runnin' across the prairie and wonderin' if I ought to blow my own brains out so I don't have to face no torture when a rider in buckskins comes thunderin' down from the bluff. He fired at the Blackfeet, and they reined up like they was facing the whole army.

"The man in buckskins reached down and pulled me up behind him. We cut a nine in our tails and rode for the rocks with the others. Well, son, we held out for three days, and then them Indians just up and disappeared. So we lit shuck for Ft. Hall."

"Was the man who rescued you Kit Carson?" Nathan asked.

"Yep. He came into Ft. Hall after we had left and heard that four crazy greenhorns had rode off into Blackfeet country, so he headed out to turn us back. There just weren't many men like ol' Kit, no sir! So when Quickly there swore on Kit's grave . . . well, it just caused me to do some thinkin'."

"You think that claim really is good then?" Nathan asked.

"Yep . . . I reckon it is!"

"So are you goin' to let me go on back up to 10 and sell it?" Quickly clamored.

Push-Bill turned to the man tied to the wheel.

"No!" he shouted.

"But . . . I thought . . . ," Nathan stammered.

"I'll tell you what I am goin' to do, Nate. I'm goin' to send you and the spotted horse on up to 10 with the certificate. You sell it to the man and then wait at the Colorado House until I get to town."

"You can't do that!" Quickly protested. "He don't know who the buyer is."

"Don't matter." Push-Bill insisted. "If one man will pay $500 for it, so will another. He can just peddle it on the street."

"No! You won't get top dollar for it, don't you see. It ain't general knowledge how rich that strike is. They might not want to buy it at all! I've got to go!"

"You ain't goin'," Push-Bill insisted. "So either you tell Nathan where to find your buyer, or he'll sell it on the street."

"You're not serious?" Quickly started to protest, but his voice trailed off. Determination ruled Push-Bill's eyes. "How do you know you can trust the kid? Maybe he'll sell it and then ride on off himself."

Push-Bill's piercing brown eyes blazed into Nathan's. "You goin' to steal my money, Nate?"

"No, sir, I'm not going to steal it."

"There, Quickly. There's still some of us that is good to our word!"

"He'll have to ride all night!" Quickly complained. "He don't know the trail."

"He's got a good horse," Push-Bill responded.

By the time supper was finished, the details of the plan were settled. Nathan was to ride straight through to 10, stopping only to rest Onepenny. Once he got to town he would go to the Colorado House Cafe and ask for Chance Aragon, make the sale, hang around town until Onepenny rested, and then ride back out and meet them on the trail.

Mounted on Onepenny, Nathan turned back to Push-Bill.

"You promise you won't kill Mr. Quickly while I'm gone?" Nathan asked.

"I won't kill him," Push-Bill assured him, "unless the polecat tries to escape."

"Mr. Quickly, you aren't going to try to escape, are you?"

"You got my word on it, son," Quickly replied.

"His word ain't worth a wet buffalo chip!" Push-Bill scoffed.

"Don't take a penny less than $500 for that claim, keep an eye out for the Shoshone and Bannocks, and don't take no chances with pilgrims on the road. If they think you have anything valuable, they'd just as soon relieve you of it."

"Yes, sir . . . I can do it," Nathan insisted.

He hadn't ridden thirty minutes in the dark shadows of early nightfall before he began to question his wisdom.

Lord, I'm . . . well, I'm not doing this for me. I just want to do what's square for both Push-Bill and Quickly. Lord, nobody ought to lose their life over this . . . especially me!

Nathan pulled his Winchester out of the scabbard and laid it across his lap as he rode along.

"It could be worse, boy." He leaned over the saddle horn and patted Onepenny's neck. "The moon's almost full . . . there are no clouds . . . the breeze is fairly warm so far . . . I can see the road. There's no dark forest or trees to ride through. We could see someone if they were riding along, couldn't we, boy?"

And they could see us! What if there are Indians? Or outlaws! Or wild animals like . . . like . . . no, I guess not. What about Onepenny tripping and falling? I could get smashed in the rocks . . . or I could fall asleep and tumble down a canyon and break my leg, and no one would find me . . . and I'd be lying there in pain for days, and the ants would crawl all over me and . . .

A sudden chill shot up Nathan's back.

"Maybe I'll grab my coat when I stop to let you rest," he said to the horse. "What's that up there?" he whispered and pulled up on the reins. Leaning with his face against Onepenny's neck, he studied the dark silhouette on the ridge of mountains to the west.

"It's probably just a boulder or sage or something." He spurred Onepenny, and again they loped down the trail.

Nathan rode for what he guessed was about two hours. Then he climbed down, loosened the cinch to allow some air to flow under the saddle, and walked along leading Onepenny by the reins.

He carried the Winchester over his shoulder. Even in the darkness he saw Onepenny's ears suddenly twitch and point forward. He thought he heard hoofbeats in the distance.

"What is it?" he whispered. "Is a horse coming, boy? Come on, let's get off the road."

Nathan led Onepenny off to the side and down into the dark shadows of a ravine where he could still view the road in the moonlight. As he waited, he pulled on his jacket.

Now Nathan heard nothing at all. So he waited a little longer.

And a little longer.

Finally, when Onepenny began to doze off, Nathan jerked the cinch tight and remounted. Back out on the road, he noticed the wind had picked up and now whistled through the barren hills.

It was on this third cycle of walking Onepenny that he spotted movement on the high western slope. It was just a slight motion. Then a soft noise. Then another movement in the shadows.

Lord, I don't know what's up there, but I can't hide this time. There's no cover. Whatever it is must know I'm here! Lord, help me!

Nathan couldn't tell if the object was man or animal, and he couldn't tell if it was getting closer—or staying the same distance. Even though his forehead was cold, sweat rolled down his face. He pulled off his hat and brushed his eyebrows, forehead, and hair on the sleeve of his jacket.

Lord, I've got to do something!

Nathan slowly cocked the lever on his Winchester. Then without much thought and still with his finger on the trigger, he raised the gun high in the air over his head.

If that's a person, at least he ought to know I have a gun and am ready to use it!

Suddenly, on a ridge about 200 feet to the west, the silhouette of a braided rider appeared against the night sky.

Indian!

The rider held a rifle above his head and waved it back and forth. Then he turned and rode over the crest of the mountain away from Nathan.

He's leaving! He had a cocked rifle, too! Maybe he was worried about what I would do. Lord, do Indians ever get scared at night? I sure would like to see some daylight. Do you suppose you could hurry this along?

Nathan figured it was at least another long, numbing hour before the sky turned a lighter shade of dark . . . then charcoal gray . . . then a light gray . . . a pale washed-out blue . . . and finally the sun rested on the eastern mountains, and the sky turned blue.

Thanks, Lord. I'm glad You don't go to sleep!

The sun was straight up when Nathan first spotted 10 clinging to the side of White Eagle Mountain.

"That-a-boy. We made good time . . . look at that!"

All morning they'd been passing a string of people and

wagons still flooding into the mining town and a trickle of folks leaving it. He nodded, but spoke to no one. He walked Onepenny most of the way up the steep road, but remounted to enter town so that he might look across the crowds of people and find his way to the Colorado House.

"Now how in the world am I going to find someone named Chance Aragon?" he mumbled in the confusion of the crowd that had lined up to attack the midday dinner at the hotel cafe.

Mr. McSwain! I'll go up to McSwain when he comes out to collect dinner tokens, and I'll ask him.

Nathan hung back of the crowd and allowed them to stampede through the doorway as the cafe opened for the next shift. Then, as the hired help tried to cut off the surging throng, Nathan scooted up to the gray-bearded man who was holding a flour sack full of tokens in his hand.

"Mr. McSwain," he shouted, "I work for Push-Bill, and I'm looking for a man named Chance Aragon."

"You ain't goin' to find him here! You got a token?"

"No, I don't want dinner. I want to find Mr. Aragon!"

"Check up on the top of City Street! If you don't have a token, you don't eat, son."

By the time he finished the sentence, Nathan was back out in the street and climbing up on Onepenny. "Man, there's no way I'm going to eat there again!" He spurred his way through the crowd.

Nathan remembered that the place where they had unloaded the wagons was on City Street, but he couldn't remember what was above the corrals. As he turned up the mountain, the crowd thinned, and he saw several men unloading a freight wagon. One of the men glanced up at Nathan.

"Hey, do you work with Push-Bill?"

"Yeah," Nathan hollered back.

"Did he make it back already?"

Nathan rode closer to the man. "Nope, he sent me ahead. He'll be here tomorrow."

"Well, tell him I'll pay double what I paid last time."

"Double?"

"Yep."

"Why?"

"Prices went up, that's why! They struck pay dirt in one of the mines."

"Which one?" Nathan asked.

"There was an explosion at the Antelope Flats Mine. One man died, but it uncovered a huge vein."

"Antelope Flats? Where's that?"

"Over near the All-Is-Lost."

"Listen, speaking of the All-Is-Lost, I'm looking for Chance Aragon. I heard he was up at the top of City Street."

The man's mouth dropped open. "Eh . . . yeah, I guess you could say that."

"What's up there anyway?" Nathan quizzed.

"The cemetery." The man shrugged.

"Cemetery? He's dead?"

"Yep. He's the one that got killed in the mine. Some say it wasn't an accident . . . anyway there's no time to investigate."

"But . . . I need to see him. I'm supposed to sell him . . . "

"Sorry, son, he's dead, but I'll buy all of Push-Bill's goods."

"No, this was, eh . . . a mining claim."

"Which mine?"

"Eh . . . the All-Is-Lost."

"That's too bad. Antelope Flats is going for $500 a foot."

"A foot? What about the All-Is-Lost?"

"I hear it's creeping up a ways on account of being in the same neighborhood. I think it hit $10 a foot, but that can change at any moment."

"Where can I sell the claim?" Nathan asked.

"Just go down in front of one of the assay offices and start shouting. Someone's bound to make you a deal."

Nathan turned Onepenny around.

"Son! Be sure and tell Push-Bill I'll buy his goods. And listen . . . if you rake in some cash on that deal, you better get out of town or hide that money. It ain't too safe around here at night."

Nathan nodded and rode back down toward the crowded street. He found a noisy shouting match in front of the Northern Nevada Assay Company. He dug out the stock certificate and waved it around shouting, "One hundred feet of the All-Is-Lost!"

After several unsuccessful attempts to attract attention, he rode Onepenny through the crowd and up onto the wooden sidewalk. Then he climbed up and stood on the saddle and shouted at the top of his voice, "One hundred feet in the All-Is-Lost!"

There was a moment of silence as everyone stared up at Nathan. Then instantly everyone began to yell and scream.

"Get that horse off the sidewalk!"

"Move it, kid!"

"I'll give you $5 a foot!"

"What?" Nathan dropped back down into the saddle and leaned over to a man wearing a tall silk hat. "How much?"

"$5 a foot."

"It's worth $10!" Nathan shouted.

"Says who?" the man pressed.

"Me!"

"$5 is my last offer," the man called out.

Suddenly, Nathan felt someone tugging at his other leg. He leaned over to the opposite side of the saddle.

"Son, you still got the All-Is-Lost?"

"Yep."

"I'll give you $6 a foot!"

Nathan sat back up and yelled down to the first man, "He'll give me $6!"

"$7!" the man shouted back.

Then the one on the left yelled, "$8!"

"He's a fool," the first man shouted.

Nathan was about ready to concede to the $8 price when the first man suddenly roared, "$10. I'll give you $10 a foot!"

"It's a deal!" Nathan shouted.

The man began to scribble something on a paper.

"I want cash, Mister," Nathan called.

"Cash? Well, I don't—"

"Cash, and now!"

"But that's not the way—"

Nathan pushed back his hat. "Cash!"

Mumbling in the roar of the crowd, the man dug out a poke of gold coins and counted out fifty coins.

Nathan handed the man the paper. He held it up for inspection. Then he handed the coins to Nathan, who shoved them into his saddlebag and buckled it down.

Determined to make it out of town as soon as possible, Nathan spurred Onepenny down off the sidewalk and through the crowd. As he left, he heard the man who had bought the stock yell, "One hundred feet in the All-Is-Lost! Only $15 a foot!"

He didn't look back. He hurried out of town and started

back down the road. Most of the rigs and horses were still pulling into the hillside town, but a few, like Nathan, were leaving. He didn't think much about the people around him until he noticed two unshaven men riding about thirty feet behind him.

They're following me!

SEVEN

Nathan didn't look back again, but when he crested a hill and calculated that he was out of their sight for a moment, he pulled his carbine out of the scabbard and laid it across the pommel of the saddle.

Lord, money fever is crazy! Everybody wants more and more until they begin to act without judgment. The only reason in the world for the existence of 10 is so that someone might get rich. It's like gambling . . . only instead of chips, you put your life on the line.

Lord, I can't face these men down like my father can . . . so you've just got to help me!

Several miles out of town the road dropped down into a dry creekbed where one lightning-struck cottonwood tried to survive. The limbs were dwarfed close to the broken trunk, and the leaves were turning prematurely yellow. Next to the tree was a parked stagecoach. Two men were making repairs to a rear wheel, and the passengers, all women, were sitting in what shade the tree offered.

He rode right up to the women and blurted out under his breath, "Ladies, I'm Nathan T. Riggins of Galena, and I think a couple of bushwhackers are following me. Could you pretend like you know me, and maybe they'll ride on by." His eyes searched their faces for sympathetic eyes. In the background he could hear hoofbeats coming closer.

This is dumb! They have no idea what I'm talking about!

Suddenly, the dark-haired woman in the bright yellow dress stood up and called out, "Why, Nathan, honey! How good it is to see you! Come on down and give Kay Lynn a hug!"

He had hardly hit the ground when the woman threw her arms around him and squeezed him blue. "How am I doin', kid?" she whispered.

All Nathan could do was nod.

"How's your mama and daddy doin' down in Galena? Or did they move to 10? If they're in 10, we'll have to have a party tonight. Girls, this is my good friend, Mr. Nathan T. Riggins!"

Nathan peeked down at a girl who looked about eighteen or nineteen.

"They're gone, Kay Lynn. You can cut the play actin'." She shrugged.

Nathan glanced around and saw the men far on down the road to the south.

"Thanks, Miss . . . eh, Kay Lynn."

"Who were they?" she asked.

"I don't know, but they've been following me awful close for several miles."

She stared Nathan right in the eyes. "Why?"

"'Cause folks in 10 are gold crazy . . . and, well, they thought I might be carrying some color."

"Are you?" one of the other girls asked.

"Of course he is!" Kay Lynn scolded. "Why else would a young man like this come riding straight up to us." She glanced over at the men working with the broken stagecoach. "Foshee, how long until we're on the road?"

A red-faced man glanced over at the women and grumbled, "I'm workin' as fast as I can. I told ya, I'll get you up to 10 before dark . . . now I'll do that if I have to carry you on my back!"

"Well, Nathan," she continued, "I think we'll probably be here a while. Why don't you just stay with us a spell and give the men a chance to get on down the trail?"

She's got to have one of the best smiles I've ever seen . . . next to Leah's! "Yeah, I could use a little rest. I rode all last night," he managed to reply.

"Well, pull up some shade and take a nap!" she invited him, smiling broadly.

Nathan hitched Onepenny to the back of the parked stagecoach, jerked off the saddle and blanket, and carried the heavy saddlebags over to the shade. He noticed the women glancing at the saddlebags.

"Eh . . . just thought I'd use these for a pillow," he explained.

"Your poke's safe with us, Nathan T. Riggins. At least," Kay Lynn grinned, "with most of us."

He could smell a strong perfume that reminded him of a rose garden. "Why are you going to 10? It's a lousy place for ladies . . . I mean, it's a lousy place for anyone!"

"A man named McSwain hired us out of Denver to come and wait tables and serve food in his fine hotel," Kay Lynn replied.

"McSwain? You mean the Colorado House?"

"Yes."

"Oh, no!"

"What's the matter? We hear it's the foremost hotel in 10."

"Eh . . . yeah, I guess you could say that." Nathan shrugged. "It's a busy place—that's certain . . . lots of hard work."

"He promised us room and board and $65 a month. That sure beats teaching school." She nodded.

Nathan laid back on his saddlebags and closed his eyes. Several of the women asked him other questions about 10.

His answers came slowly as he drifted off to sleep, trying to imagine the excitement a coach load of pretty women would stir up in the town of 10.

When he finally opened his eyes, the sun had disappeared in the western mountains, but plenty of daylight reflected off the blue summer sky. Miss Kay Lynn was shaking his shoulder. She held a lemon-colored parasol over her shoulder, and he noticed for the first time that she didn't have any lines drawn tight around her gray-green eyes, like his mother did.

"Nathan T. Riggins! We're pulling out. Did you want to ride back to 10 with us?"

Nathan propped himself up. "What? Oh . . . no. I need to go on down the trail. I've got to get this money . . . I mean, I've got to find Push-Bill." He flung the saddlebags over his shoulder, making sure he heard the coins rattle.

"Oh, they're still there." Kay Lynn smiled. "All fifty $20 gold pieces!"

"How did you . . . ?"

She lifted her light brown eyebrows. "Not all of us used to be schoolteachers!"

By the time Nathan had saddled Onepenny, all he could see of the stagecoach was a trail of dust to the north. With no one within sight, Nathan crammed papers from his saddlebags into his pockets and dropped twenty-five coins in each boot, pulling his trouser legs back over them. He could hardly walk with the added weight rattling around on each foot, but he scooted over to the dry creekbed and filled his saddlebags a third of the way full of pebbles. Then he awkwardly climbed aboard Onepenny and trotted back onto the road.

"If Push-Bill's made it to his usual camp, we should be coming across him about dark," he mumbled.

Nathan proceeded slowly, carrying his carbine in his lap. Every hill became a possible hiding place. Every big sage, a reminder of ambush. Every ravine, a threat. It was a good hour and a half later that he pulled up at the top of a steep downward grade.

If I was going to trap someone on this road, this would be the place. A couple of men could hide against that mountain on the left, then charge whoever's on the trail. Folks would naturally pull off to the right and make a run for those rocks, but that's the edge of a canyon. They could trap somebody over there and . . .

"Wait!" he blurted out to the horse. "If they're over there watching, I can't go to the left, and I can't slip by on the road unnoticed. Maybe we could ride right out along the edge of the canyon on purpose! No one would look over there!"

The evening shadows were starting to fade when Nathan turned Onepenny off the trail and toward the edge of the canyon.

Nobody in his right mind would come out here on purpose . . . that's why it's a safe route!

Nathan rounded the boulders and slowly picked his way along the rocks, hoping to put a few of them between himself and the road. Constantly glancing over at the road and the hills beyond, he let Onepenny find his own way.

While he was still gazing over his shoulder, without

warning a man jumped out in front of him, waving a revolver and screaming, "Don't lift that carbine, boy!"

Nathan reacted by spurring Onepenny to the right and suddenly found himself trapped at the canyon's edge. Northern Nevada's great basin stretched out in front of him. He whipped the horse around to look for an escape and found himself facing two men on foot, with guns drawn.

"Don't raise it, boy, or you're dead!" one shouted.

"Sure was nice of you to ride right up to us. We had given up on you and camped over here for the night."

"Yep," the other one agreed. "We thought for sure you rode back to 10 with that load of women. But you waltzing into camp like this makes a man believe in divine Providence, now don't it?"

"Now just toss us that saddlebag of coins, and we'll let you ride away!" the other demanded.

Nathan didn't attempt to raise his gun. "It doesn't belong to me. I can't give it away!"

"Well, now . . . if it don't belong to you, it sure ain't worth dyin' fer, is it?"

"I promised to deliver it to a friend!" Nathan pleaded.

"Well, you didn't promise to git yerself killed over it."

"If I give you the saddlebags, you'll let me go?"

"Sure 'nough, won't we, Janton? We ain't got no use for you."

"But I can't ride away. You got me blocked in."

Peering through the evening shadows, Nathan continued to search for a way out.

Lord, You promised never to leave me or forsake me. Well, where are You now?

One of the men waved his arm at the other, and both men scooted over to the north.

"Drop the saddlebags right where you sit and ride on out to the south."

Nathan slowly transferred the rifle to his left hand so he could more easily cock it if he needed to. "You won't shoot me in the back, will ya?"

The man impatiently shifted his weight and pointed his revolver at Nathan's head.

"I'm going to shoot right where you sit! Now throw down that gold!"

Nathan reached back and lifted the rock-heavy saddlebags. At the same time that he held them out to the left of Onepenny, he shook his right boot to make it sound like the coins were in the saddlebags.

"Throw it down, boy! It's your choice!"

"No!" Nathan spoke slowly and softly. "It's your choice."

"What?"

"You can follow the saddlebags, or you can follow me!" he shouted.

With that, he flung the heavy saddlebags over the edge of the canyon and spurred Onepenny. As he did, he swung around the horse's neck, which shielded him from the outlaws.

Two shots fired into the air, but Nathan was flying through the shadows within seconds. He turned onto the road at a full gallop and ran Onepenny for about fifteen minutes before giving him a rest.

Neither of them will want to leave the other with those saddlebags. They won't chase me until they find the pebbles.

It was a long, dark, cautious, menacing hour before Nathan recognized some wagons in the moonlight and noticed two familiar white mules on the picket line.

"Let's take it easy, boy. I don't want to startle Push-Bill and his scattergun."

As they sauntered a little closer, Nathan noticed the freighter had his shirt off and his hands up in the air, and Quickly had an armlock on him.

He's got Push-Bill!

Slipping off Onepenny, he scooted his coin-filled boots along behind the freight wagons, holding his Winchester in hand.

He heard bones crack.

"Wagh," Push-Bill screamed, "you like to killed me that time!"

Nathan dove under the wagon and rolled up on his feet, shoving the barrel of the carbine into Quickly's back.

"Turn him loose, or so help me, I'll pull this trigger!" Nathan shouted.

"Whoa, boy, whoa!" Quickly hollered releasing Push-Bill.

"Nate?" Push-Bill called. "Back off there, son. I was jist havin' Quickly straighten out a crick in my neck."

"What?"

"He was helpin' me . . . at least he was a tryin'," Push-Bill insisted.

"Oh," Nathan sighed, "I thought he was—"

"We know what you thought," Push-Bill interrupted. "We got worried about you bein' so late and all."

"I was bushwhacked."

"No! Did they hurt ya?"

"Nope."

"Did they get your goods?" Quickly pressed.

"Only a saddlebag full of rocks."

"Who was it?"

"One tall, one short. I think I heard the name Janton."

"Janton and Claymore! The two ol' boys that cheated me and lifted your poke!"

Quickly stepped toward the fire. "Did you find Chance Aragon?"

"Yeah."

"Did he buy the certificate like I said?"

"Nope."

"No!" Quickly gasped. "But he promised he would—"

"Aragon's not making any more deals. He's lying six feet under. But I sold the claim on the street."

"You did?" Push-Bill pulled on his shirt and walked over to Nathan. "How much did you get?"

Nathan pulled off his right boot and poured the contents into Push-Bill's hands.

"$500? You got $500?"

"Nope." Nathan hobbled over to Quickly. Then he pulled off his other boot and poured the contents in front of the man. "I got a thousand. This part is for Mr. Quickly."

Quickly jumped to his feet. "A thousand! Didn't I tell you it was a winner!"

Push-Bill and Quickly danced around the campfire. Finally, when they calmed down, Nathan told the whole story.

At daylight Quickly saddled up while Nathan and Push-Bill hitched up the team. "Got to go down to that new silver strike in Arizona before the rush!" he called to them. "You was really goin' to hang me, weren't ya?"

"Yep," Push-Bill replied.

"Well, boy . . . keep that old man alive. His temper will bring him down one of these days." Quickly tipped his hat to Nathan and rode off to the south.

"Do you think those two will be waiting for us up on the trail?" Nathan asked.

"Nope. They sound like a couple of sneak thieves that don't do nothin' unless it's at night and they got good odds. Out on the trail in daylight will be all sorts of folks headin' up to 10. Besides, from what you described, they're probably still trying to find a way to get down the canyon to retrieve those saddlebags!"

The trip back into 10 with the freight wagons was uneventful. Nathan and Push-Bill left town the moment they unloaded. They camped that night not far from where they had the previous morning.

"We won't be staying in Galena for three days this time," Push-Bill announced. "We've got to get back up here while the prices are high."

"I need to go out to the Rialtos' and get my dog," Nathan mentioned.

"You take that shortcut the girls showed you tomorrow, and then meet me at Bobcat Springs," Push-Bill suggested. "Measure them narrow parts and see if a wagon might pull through. I ain't very thrilled about blazing trails with a freight wagon, but if I could save half a day, it might be worth the risk."

"Yes, sir."

"And don't be dallying around with them girls. It's time to make big money. I'll pay you double wages as long as this boom holds up."

Nathan pulled the mining claims out of his pockets, started to turn and pack them back in his saddlebags, and then remembered he didn't have any. Looking at each claim closely, he stuffed them one at a time back into his pockets.

"What you lookin' fer?" Push-Bill inquired.

"I was wondering if one of these was for the Antelope Flats Mine. It was selling for $500 a foot! Hey, look at this!"

"You got one?"

"Eh . . . no, but I found twenty feet of the All-Is-Lost. I didn't know I had that! I could have sold it for $200! But maybe the price will go even higher! If this one goes to $500 a foot, that would be . . . $10,000! I could buy a ranch with that!"

"Well, don't go buyin' nothing on speculation. When we return to 10, you can sell all the scraps of paper you want."

It was a little before noon when they came to the cut-off, and Nathan rode down toward the western mountains. The trail seemed longer than before. He found himself wanting to hurry to the ranch.

Turning down the row of trees, he glanced behind every one trying to spot the girls. Finally, he saw some slightly dusty toes peeking out from one of the tree trunks.

"Is that you, Babe?" he called.

The six-year-old poked her head around the trunk. "I wanted you to see my toes." She grinned.

"Where are your sisters?" Nathan asked. "I expected to see them out here with a shotgun."

"They're busy with chores. So they sent me out. Sal said it was only that Nathan boy, so there was no reason for them to stop work."

"You want to ride with me?" Nathan asked.

"Yep," she giggled. "Can I ride on top those spots?"

Nathan pulled her up behind him and let her sit on Onepenny's rump, holding onto the cantle.

"How's Tona?" he asked.

"Nan says he's mostly dead, but Sal thinks he might pull through. He can't eat or walk, but Cape gets up in the night and makes sure he gets some broth."

Nathan rode silently for a while.

Lord, maybe I should have . . . I just couldn't, Lord. I mean, he's been . . . he's just too . . .

"Hey, are you crying?" Babe blurted out.

Nathan wiped his eyes. "No . . . it's the dust. Just something in my eye," he mumbled.

Riding into the yard, he saw several of the girls ambling over to the front porch.

"Boy, your dog isn't going to make it," Nan announced. "Here, let me take your pony."

"He is too going to make it!" Babe cried out as she slid down off the back of the spotted horse.

"I think he'll be o.k." Cape nodded as she brushed back her blonde hair. "But he's still feeling poorly."

Nathan crouched over Tona who was lying on some blankets in a large crate on the porch. The dog didn't even try to raise up. He didn't turn his head or move his eyes. But his tailed thumped several times against the wooden box.

"That-a-boy . . . you just rest!" Nathan patted the back of the dog's neck and scratched his head. "You've got to pull through, Tona. I need you!"

Lord, he's dying, isn't he?

When Nathan looked up, Sal stood beside him. "He's doing a little better, but we can't get him to eat on his own."

"I've fed him every night since you left," Cape informed him.

"I sure do appreciate it. You ladies looking after my dog. It's . . . *I am not going to cry.* . . . it's one of the . . ."

"Can you stay for supper?" Sal invited. "We would

enjoy the company. Perhaps you could spend the night. There's plenty of room in the barn."

"I really need to take Tona and get back to Bobcat Springs. We're in a hurry to get another load up to 10. Prices are going crazy, and it's a good time to sell freight."

"Well," Sal said thoughtfully, "maybe this would be a good time for us to ride up and sell the produce from the garden. But you can't move that dog. He's just living a day at a time, and there's no way he could make it back to Galena."

"But I can't ask you to . . . I mean, I just don't feel right having you take care of him."

"We don't mind, really," Beth insisted. "Tona has become kind of a project for us."

"Well . . . let me pay you something. It's really worth a lot to me and—"

"Nathan, that would be insulting to our hospitality," Sal insisted.

"But . . . listen!" he protested. "Look, if you're going up to 10 . . . " He jammed his hand into his pocket and pulled out a wad of crumpled papers. "Look, I got all these little mining claims for a sack of beef jerky. I know one of them's worth $250, but you take them all. Sell them in 10 and keep the money!"

"How many do you have?" Cape asked.

"I think there's eight of them, but like I said, I don't know if any of them are worth anything except for that one."

"Which one is that?" Sal asked.

"The All-Is-Lost Mine," Nathan replied.

"Well, we couldn't—," Sal began.

"Please," Nathan persisted. "It would insult my sense of fairness if you didn't take something. I mean, I don't know how long Tona will have to stay here."

"I'd like to own a gold mine," Babe said giggling. "Then I can buy a doll and a red hat and a book with pictures!"

Sal glanced around at the girls who waited with expectant faces. "Well . . . Nathan, if you will take back this All-Is-Lost claim, we'll divide up the others. Each one can have one."

"But . . . I don't think they're worth—"

"That's the reason we're taking them. It will be fun for us to speculate, and you can have a clear conscience about leaving Tona here."

"Well, I . . . ," Nathan mumbled, "that's fine with me, but I don't think you know how much that dog means to me."

"The tear streaks across your cheeks have told us that." Sal smiled.

"Those aren't tears! He just got dust in his eyes," Babe explained.

Nathan drank some fresh milk and ate six warm oatmeal cookies before he climbed on Onepenny and left the Rialto ranch. He rode past the lane, crossed the plain, and entered the hills, climbing up toward Bobcat Springs. But his mind was still on the Rialto sisters.

Lord, Mr. and Mrs. Rialto did an awful good job with the little time you gave them. I suppose you got a pretty nice setup in Heaven for folks like that. Keep the girls safe, Lord . . . and help them not be too bothered looking after Tona.

"Tona!" Nathan muttered aloud. Suddenly Onepenny pulled his head around as if looking for the gray and white dog.

"He's not here, boy." Nathan patted the horse and rode on up the hill. He remembered how lifeless Tona had looked.

Tona's fought lots of bigger animals! He's whipped dogs five times the size of that bobcat. It's just not fair for him to get so ripped up. Lord, why did You have to create bobcats so mean?

Nathan rode into the springs ahead of Push-Bill. He built a small fire, waiting for the wagons to arrive. It was near dark before he heard the shriek of the wheels and Push-Bill's shout.

After camp-making chores were finished, they settled in for supper.

"Well," Push-Bill mumbled through his plate of beans, "every day that dog lives gives him more time to heal up."

"You should have seen him. He looks awful," Nathan admitted.

"Well, you and him learned a big lesson. Don't never dance with a bobcat! Now you just got to trust the good Lord's timing. You don't get to keep any animal forever . . . not that dog . . . not even that spotted horse."

"Yes, but . . . " Nathan's voice trailed off. "I was kind of hoping Tona would stick around until he died of old age." Nathan put down his supper plate and picked up his carbine.

"I'm going down by the springs," he announced.

"With your gun?"

"Maybe I'll shoot a rabbit."

"You ain't goin' rabbit huntin'," Push-Bill said knowingly.

The sky was black, and the moon was out. Nathan crouched by the brush at the side of the springs—five cartridges in the chamber, the lever cocked, and his finger tensed on the trigger. Just as he was about doze off, something moved near the springs.

Out of the brush stalked the bobcat. Nathan pulled back the hammer with his thumb, and at that tiny click the bobcat broke for cover.

Blam!

Blam!

Blam!

Blam!

Blam!

Nathan lowered his gun and shoved in more cartridges. He threw his carbine to his shoulder to fire again.

"Nate!"

He spun around to see Push-Bill standing behind him.

"Give it up, son. You cain't shoot what you cain't see."

"I'm going to kill that Bobcat, Push-Bill! I'm going to kill it for Tona!" Nathan felt his voice tighten, and tears welled up once again.

E I G H T

Leah Walker was sitting on a bench in front of her father's barbershop when Nathan, aboard Onepenny, led the freight wagons back into Galena. He rode straight up to her, slid down off the spotted horse, and brushed the road dust off his shirt and trousers. She wore the new green dress and a matching ribbon in her hair.

"Hi, Nathan!" she called.

"Are you waiting for someone?" he asked, glancing inside the barbershop window and waving to Mr. Walker.

"Maybe I am, and maybe I ain't."

"Is that Kylie guy around?"

"No, he went home last week. You know'd that," she answered, shading her eyes from the afternoon sun.

Nathan cleared his throat. "Leah, I want to talk to you right now."

"What about?"

"Well . . . I been figuring . . . it's time you made up your mind."

She looked down at the wooden sidewalk. "About what?"

"About me or Kylie. Listen." Nathan cleared his throat and swallowed hard. He didn't want his voice to sound high and squeaky. "It's either me or him. You're my girlfriend or you're not. But if you are, you can't go around sayin' that you're going to marry Kylie. Now that's all there is to it. You make up your mind."

Leah didn't answer.

"Well," Nathan urged, "who are you going to choose?"

She wrinkled the freckles on her nose and sighed deeply. "You come ridin' in here like some Saturday night cowboy and want me to have an answer just like that?"

"I don't have much time. We're leavin' at daylight. Leah, it's been grindin' on me every night."

"Ever' night? You been thinkin' about me ever' night?"

"Yeah, it nags at me like a chore that needs doing," he replied.

"So . . . it's a chore to think about me?" she teased.

Nathan could feel his face flush. "No . . . that's not it! But it has been on my mind most all week."

"Well, then, I ought to have a week to think about it, too, Nathan T. Riggins!"

"But it will be nine days before I come home again!"

"I'll let you know when I'm good and ready." She stood up and spun around toward the stairs that led to her house. "I thank you kindly for your offer, and I shall consider it presently," she announced and then ran up the stairs.

Nathan plunged into a hot bath, changed his clothes, and ate a supper of fried chicken and mashed potatoes with his parents as he tried to explain everything from Tona's run-in with the bobcat, to the Rialto sisters, to selling the mining claim in 10. However, he didn't mention the bushwhackers.

"And I've got to go help Push-Bill load tonight. We're pulling out at daylight. He says we've got to get back while the prices are high. Did I tell you he's payin' me double on this trip?"

When he finished his second piece of yellow cake, he

cleared his plate, brought his mother an arm load of wood for the breakfast fire, and ran out the door. Rounding the corner of the Mercantile, he was surprised to find Push-Bill organizing two complete teams of mules and two wagons behind each team.

"Is somebody going with us?" Nathan asked.

"Son," Push-Bill called, "I got a big favor to ask. I got a deal on a second wagon and team. And you, yourself, know how crazy prices is in 10. Well, I want you to drive one team, and I'll take the other."

"Me? I don't know—"

"I've seen you with the mules, and I know you can do it. I'll lead the way on this new team, and you can bring mine up. Old Rosie can lead them by herself—you know that. Besides, they'll be tired and not apt to act up. Now what do you say?"

"But . . . but . . . what about greasing the axles and the extra mules and—"

"I've already hired a couple of kids to help out," Push-Bill announced.

"Kids? Who?"

"Friends of yours, they said. The banker's son agreed to ride along, and—"

"Colin? You hired Colin?"

"Yep. Is he a good worker?"

"Eh . . . well, he's a—"

"No mind. He'll be a good worker after nine days with us."

"Who else did you hire? Most of the older guys are working in the Shiloh."

"Well, now, you're right about that. The second helper was a stickler, but I worked it out while I was getting a haircut."

"A haircut? At Walker's? You don't mean . . ."

"Yep. I hired a girl named Leah. She was rarin' to come along, and her daddy said it was all right as long as you were on the trip."

"But you can't—"

"I did."

"But she can't . . . "

"Cain't what? Don't tell me she ain't a good worker either."

"No . . . no, Leah will work hard. It's just—"

"Good, that's settled," Push-Bill announced. "Besides, I'll only need them for this one trip. I hired Fergusen to round up a couple of clerks to work late and load all four wagons. You and me need a little rest, and then we'll start hitchin' up about 5:00 A.M. Are you up to it?"

"Eh . . . yes sir, I'll be here."

And he was.

Sleepy-eyed, tired bones, raspy voice, and all—Nathan was hitching up the wheel horses and mules at 5:00 A.M.

At 5:30 A.M. Leah showed up wearing a faded long gray dress and heavy leather work gloves.

"Mornin', Nathan."

"Mornin'."

"Ain't it exciting that Colin and me get to go? Say, since you'll be on the team, can I ride Onepenny? I mean, I can take my dad's old mare, but I was thinkin' . . . "

Nathan gaped at Leah. She didn't look anything like the barefoot Leah he had first met the previous summer.

"Did you decide an answer to that question I asked ya last night?" he probed.

"Not yet. Can I take your horse?"

"Sure."

"Really?"

"Yep. You go get him out of the livery, saddle him up, and meet us right here. We're leaving at 6:00 A.M. you know."

"I'll be back."

"Leah," Nathan called, "roust out Colin. He's supposed to be here by now."

At 5:45 A.M. Push-Bill had his team ready to roll. It was 5:50 when Nathan drove his rig up behind the other. Leah came riding up on Onepenny at 5:55 and announced that Colin was on his way.

At 5:59 Colin Maddison, Jr., (with two *d*'s) arrived at the wagons wearing woolly chaps and riding a black gelding. He carried a biscuit in each hand.

Push-Bill dropped his pocket watch back into his vest and signaled them to roll out at exactly 6:00 A.M.

The heat off the high Nevada basin drifted straight up, leaving a trail of dust hundreds of feet in the sky behind the wagons.

There were no bubbling streams.

No cool breeze.

No shade.

Just yellow-brown dust that caked Nathan's clothes, face, eyes, nose, and tongue.

By 9:00 A.M. Colin had pulled off the woolly chaps, Leah had tossed on an old broad-brimmed hat she borrowed from Push-Bill, and Nathan was getting comfortable with his own team.

Most of the time Leah rode alongside Nathan, and Colin plodded along next to Push-Bill. Only the creaking of the wagon wheels broke the silence of the empty landscape.

By noon Nathan had caught Leah up on most of the events of the previous trip. He talked to her while keeping focused on the team, but out of the corner of his eye he noticed her gazing at him. He wanted to whip around and catch her staring.

But he didn't.

"Is it like this for the whole nine days?" she asked.

"Oh, it gets steep further up. And more crowded. Folks coming off the train take the stage route that joins up above the springs."

"Is it pretty at Bobcat Springs?"

"The water's clear and cold . . . and there's still a little green grass. That's about it."

"And there's a bobcat."

Nathan instantly reached down for his carbine and then realized he didn't need it. "Yeah, well, it won't be there much longer. I told you, I'm goin' to blow its head off!"

"Nathan, why do you keep goin' on and on about that old cat. That must be the sixth time today you talked about killing it."

"When you see Tona, you'll understand."

"Are we going out to that Rialito rancho?"

"Rialto ranch," Nathan corrected. "I think Push-Bill might want to try the shortcut. Anyway, I'm going to kill that cat before we get to the ranch."

"You sound just like Colin with that coyote last fall."

"This is different, Leah. Tona's not your dog. You wouldn't understand."

"I'm tryin' to understand, Nathan T. Riggins! But you ain't helpin' much."

The rest of the day was routine as long as Nathan didn't mention Kylie Collins and Leah didn't speak about the bobcat. All four were worn out that evening, and they crawled into their bedrolls right after supper. Push-Bill didn't even light a pipe or tell a single stretcher.

The second day started out identical to the first. About midmorning Colin rode back to Nathan.

"Is this it? Is this all we do? Mile after mile after mile of boring sagebrush and desert?"

"This is it."

"For nine straight days? You got to be kidding!" Colin groaned. "Maybe something exciting will happen up over that pass."

It didn't.

Their wagons squeaked into Bobcat Springs about sunset, and everyone enjoyed washing up in the cold water.

After supper Push-Bill began a series of "ol' Jim Bridger" stories about a country that had petrified trees, petrified birds, a petrified sun, and petrified songs. Colin's eyes grew wide, his mouth dropped open, and he didn't move as he got caught up in the story.

"I'm going down by the springs," Nathan announced, grabbing his Winchester.

"I'm going with you," Leah called. "I ain't never seen a bobcat."

"I'll bring it back to you, and you can make mittens out of the pelt," Nathan offered.

"I'm comin' anyway," she asserted.

It was humid by the springs, and the moisture felt better than the daily dirt. Nathan scooted onto a rock amid the brush where he could look out across the springs. Leah scrunched up beside him.

"We can't talk," he whispered. "They're real skittish. No movement and no sound."

After about a half-hour, Leah leaned her head on Nathan's shoulder. A few minutes later she was asleep.

Lord, I really like being around Leah. She's fun, and she listens when I talk, and she makes me want to do things right. I think she's a good friend for me.

Lord, you know . . . if I'm honest, well . . . I like the way it feels when she holds my hand or grabs me around the waist when she's riding behind me, or now with her head on my shoulder. It feels real good, Lord . . . there's nothing wrong with that, is there?

In the shadows Nathan spotted an almost familiar movement.

Here he comes! I can't see him, but I know he's there.

Silently Nathan lifted the carbine to his shoulder. The trigger felt cold to his finger, the stock extra hard against his cheek. He closed his left eye and took sight with his right. Then slowly he lifted his thumb and pulled the hammer back through the first muffled click to the second click.

He spotted movement—silent, eerie, like a floating shadow. A nose, an ear, then a head appeared. Finally, Nathan could see the bobcat's complete silhouette. He squinted and lined the sights behind its ear.

Then he heard a soft, warm whisper against the same ear where he could feel Leah's warm breath.

"Nathan! No! 'Vengeance is Mine, saith the Lord.'"

He lowered the Winchester an inch and peered out over the sights. Slinking up next to the adult bobcat was another about one-third its size.

A baby? This is the mother? I thought this was the father! Is this the same one? Did Tona stumble onto a mother and her kitten?

Just the thought of Tona brought back visions of the emaciated dog struggling for breath at the Rialto ranch. He raised the gun back up as the two bobcats cautiously drank from the spring.

Once again the soft breath in his ear.

"Please, Nathan . . . You don't need this!"

He paused, with dead aim on the bobcat who alternated between licking her paws and licking her kitten. Finally, he laid the gun silently across his lap. Leah's head still snuggled on his shoulder.

For a long time they sat there. The bobcat cared for her kitten. Just as the cat turned away from the spring, a shout pierced the quietness. Nathan and Leah jumped to their feet.

"Hey, you two! Push-Bill says it's time to come back!"

The bobcat and kitten disappeared. Nathan and Leah hiked back to the camp.

"Did you see a bobcat?" Colin asked.

"Yeah." Nathan motioned. "A mother and a baby."

"I didn't hear any shootin'? Couldn't you get off a shot?" Push-Bill asked.

"Oh, I could have . . . I guess I just sort of got tired of hating bobcats. You know what I mean?"

"Yep." Push-Bill nodded. "I guess hate of any type just eats away at a man's soul. You let it go long enough, and you ain't got nothin' in there worth savin'."

"Well, I guess Leah talked some sense into me," Nathan admitted.

"Me? I didn't see no bobcat. I slept through the whole thing."

"Slept?" Nathan hooted. "What about all those words you whispered in my ear?"

"I told you I haven't made up my mind yet between you and Kylie, so don't go puttin' no words in my mouth," she insisted.

"But . . . you told me . . . the bobcat and her kitten . . . you said—"

"A kitten? She brought a baby? Why didn't you wake me up!"

"Wake you up? Wake you up! You were awake and talking to me."

"Nathan, don't you go 'round makin' up stretchers about me. I was asleep and you know it! I'm going to bed."

"Come on, Leah . . . you leaned over and put your lips right to my ear and whispered—"

"I did what?" Leah exclaimed.

"You said not to do it because I didn't need it, and you quoted from the Bible about vengeance."

"Nathan T. Riggins, I ain't never whispered in no boy's ear, and if I ever do, it won't be no Bible verses!"

"Maybe you were talking in your sleep. Maybe . . . maybe—"

"Maybe you was the one dreamin'," she huffed and stormed toward the last wagon.

Nathan couldn't think of what to say next, so he pulled out his bedroll, yanked off his boots, and crawled under his blanket.

Nathan stared at the stars and listened to the crackle of the fire. In the background he could hear Push-Bill telling another "ol' Jim and me" story to Colin. Somewhere, way off to the west, he heard a coyote howl at the moon.

Lord, this is sort of . . . peculiar. I distinctively heard Leah speak. I felt her warm breath. I remember the sound of her voice. It was deep and confident, crystal clear, yet soft and light . . . it was . . . . Lord, somebody spoke to me. You know I'm not making it up. You know that's why I didn't pull the trigger . . . Lord? Was that You? Did You . . . I mean, did You sort of . . . maybe speak . . . or maybe use Leah even though she was asleep?

Nathan was still awake when Colin tossed his bedroll

down beside him. He was still staring at the stars when Push-Bill poured coffee on the fire and trudged off to sleep near the animals. He was still awake when the moon was high enough to reflect off the canvas wagon tops, making them glow like white ashes in a pine fire.

He didn't toss and turn like usual, trying to find a comfortable spot on the ground. He felt rested without sleep. A quietness stilled his mind. He had a deep sense of everything being right.

Lord, I can't remember feeling this relaxed in a long, long time. I'm glad I didn't shoot that bobcat. It was just being what you created it to be. Tona . . . I really want Tona to live. He helps me, Lord. You know, he reminds me about loyalty and being a good friend and bravery. But I'll just let You decide about that. I just wanted You to know I think I can take it now . . . no matter what You decide about him.

Nathan had started the fire and boiled the coffee before Push-Bill finished tending the horses and mules.

"You rolled out early," Push-Bill rumbled.

"Yeah. I was all rested and ready to get going. Are we going to take the shortcut through the Rialto ranch?"

"Well, according to your measurement we might have eight to twelve inches to spare, so I guess we'll give her a try. The main road will be so crowded with wagons I won't be able to pass nobody from now on. Roust 'em out and hook up your team while I fry some breakfast. The quicker we get on the road the better."

No one said much as they broke camp, scraped down some breakfast, and hitched up the teams. In fact, Nathan hadn't said more than a dozen words by the time they stopped the wagons to rest the animals at the trailhead leading back to the Rialto ranch.

Leah greased the axles on Nathan's wagons and walked up to where he was checking the rigging on the lead mules.

"Nathan, did you really think I was talking to you last night at the springs?"

"It's o.k., Leah. Maybe I just thought I heard you speak."

"You ain't mad at me, are ya?"

"Nope."

Nathan noticed that she had her hair in two long braids, and her hat was pushed back on her head. "Is that the Rialto ranch, over against them hills?"

"Yeah . . . it's further away than it looks, but we'll be there by noon."

"Who lives there?" she asked.

"Didn't I tell you about all the . . . " He paused mid-sentence.

"All about the what?" she pressed.

"All the, eh . . . trees they planted along the driveway and the big garden and the animals and the horse barn and the—"

"No, you didn't tell me nothin' about it. You told me that some lady that reminded you of Miss D'Imperio was lookin' after Tona."

"Yeah, well there is one other thing . . ."

"What's that?"

"You'll see." Nathan nodded. "Let's roll 'em out."

"Nathan, you ain't goin' to embarrass me, are you?"

"No, it's more like a surprise." He grinned.

It was a long, hot, dusty ride to the Rialto ranch. All four pulled bandannas over their faces to block the dust. No one felt like talking.

Push-Bill stopped at the entrance of the long, tree-lined drive. He signaled Nathan to take the lead into the ranch. Leah rode up beside him.

"I see what you mean. These trees sure do look out of place. It's like one of them oasis."

Nathan pointed to the trees. "You're about to meet some of the children who live at the ranch."

"Where? I don't see nobody."

Nathan pulled his bandanna down around his neck, whistled, and then called, "Come on out!"

Instantly, a small brown head peeked around one of the tree trunks.

"Hi, Babe!" Nathan called. "Who's with you?"

Blonde-haired Nina, carrying a shotgun, stepped out behind her. "Just me, Nathan. Are you taking the back road up to 10?"

"Yeah, do you mind if we noon it at the ranch?"

"No! I'll go tell Sal." Nina turned and began to run down the long driveway well ahead of the team. Babe skipped up to Nathan's wagons which continued to roll along.

"Nathan lets me ride on them spots!" she announced.

"Well," Leah said smiling, "that sounds like a good idea." She reached over and pulled the six-year-old up behind her on Onepenny. "Is your name really Babe? Or does Nathan just call all pretty girls by that name?"

"My real name is Babylon Rialto, but everybody just calls me Babe. I'm the youngest, you know."

"How many are in your family?"

"There's seven of us," Babe replied.

"Well, that sure gives you lots of friends to play with."

"Yes, I know," Babe said.

By the time the wagons rolled into the yard, Babe had slipped down and run to her sisters on the front porch.

"All seven children are girls?" Leah asked in astonishment.

"I told you there was a surprise!" Nathan laughed.

"Their mother and father must have their hands full."

Nathan stopped smiling. "Their mother and father are dead."

"Both of them? You mean, they live here all by themselves?"

"Yep. Come on." He signaled. "Let me introduce you."

Nathan and Leah scooted off their mounts and walked toward the waiting sisters.

"Leah, this is Sal, Beth, Nan, Cape, and Jerri, and you met Nina and Babe." They all smiled and nodded at Leah.

"And this is—"

"I'm Leah Walker," she announced abruptly. Then slipping her arm into Nathan's, she disclosed, "I'm Nathan's girlfriend."

"Wh-what?" Nathan stammered.

"I'm ready to decide," she said under her breath. "And I choose you."

NINE

For the next hour the only stationary living thing at the Rialto ranch was Tona. After Nathan checked on his dog, Nan and Cape helped him and Push-Bill run the teams out to the corrals. Sal and Nina dashed to the kitchen to prepare dinner. Leah scampered off to help them, and Nathan saw her point at him, giggle something to Sal, and disappear into the house. Jerri and Cape latched onto Colin, who offered no protest as they enlisted his help to set up a big table in the front yard.

Beth saddled a horse and galloped toward a hilltop behind the ranch. And Babe bounced around the whole yard in delight as if it were Christmas.

Nathan and Leah finally met on the front porch at Tona's crate.

"He don't appear good," Leah admitted.

"Well, he did lift up his head once," Nathan informed her. "He lost a lot of blood. He just can't seem to get his strength back."

"He's got a good place to rest. I allows they all like caring for him."

Nathan glanced around at the Rialto sisters. "They're an incredible family, aren't they?"

"Sometimes I wished I had some sisters," Leah said softly. "And if I did, these would be good ones to have. How come their mama and daddy had to die, Nathan? It don't

seem fair. I thought it was bad not having my mom around
. . . but at least I got my daddy."

"I don't know, Leah . . . I guess we all have different
trails to follow through life."

"Well, I ain't going to complain anymore."

A fierce ringing of a dinner bell interrupted them. Babe
beat the iron triangle with great enthusiasm.

Beth had just returned from her ride, and she organized everyone around the table. When the ladies were seated,
Nathan, Colin, and Push-Bill also sat down.

"Well," Sal announced, "we usually take turns saying
grace. But I think we should yield to our guests. Perhaps Mr.
Horn will do us the honor."

"What? Oh . . . ," Push-Bill stammered. "Miss, thank ya
fer offering, but I get to trippin' over my words when I pray.
Nathan there, he's the one to do it. Go ahead, son." There
was a pleading sound in the freighter's usually commanding
voice.

The girls reached out, and everyone held hands. Nathan
grabbed onto Leah and Babe.

"Eh . . . well, Lord, bless this food and help us all to gain
strength from it. And we thank You for our friends, the
Rialtos. Keep them safe and healthy. In Jesus' name, amen."

The second he raised up his head, Babe blurted out, "If
you don't want your bread pudding, I'll eat it!"

It took a good while before anyone was ready for
dessert. By the time the bread pudding was served, most
everyone could only manage a small portion, even Babe. Only
Colin loaded his plate.

"Miss Sal," Push-Bill began, "if they ever make this
shortcut the main route, you ladies should open up a business
and serve meals. Half the men in 10 would pay $2 apiece
for food like this."

"And the other half would pay it if they had $2," Nathan amended.

Push-Bill banged the table. "Now ain't that the truth!"

Suddenly, one single, long, loud bark burst out of Tona. Nathan jumped to his feet.

"Tona's feeling better!" Leah said.

"Someone's coming!" Nathan said. "I know that bark."

Without saying anything, most of the girls scampered away from the table toward the barn and the trees in the driveway.

"Is something wrong?" Colin asked, taking another helping of bread pudding. "You know, this stuff is really good, especially if you put the cherry preserves on top of it!"

"We don't like taking chances," Sal explained. "I don't see anyone on the drive. They must be on the shortcut."

Nathan and Push-Bill rushed over to their wagons for their guns.

"I don't see nothin'," Leah confessed as they returned to the table.

"That's what worries me," Sal warned. "Friends ride up in plain sight."

"Tona could be wrong," Nathan declared, "him being so bad off and all."

She looked right at him. "Has he been wrong before?"

"Eh . . . no, not really."

"Then they must be watching us from somewhere out there," Sal instructed. "Leah, pick up some dishes like you're cleaning the table and take them into the kitchen and stay there. Colin, keep eating. Maybe they'll think we don't know they're watching."

"Yes, ma'am . . . I mean, miss."

"Nathan, you and Push-Bill keep those guns under the table. Let's wait for them."

"Do you think it's Indians?" Colin gasped.

"I don't know," Push-Bill answered, "but I'd better mosey out back and stand guard at the barn. I cain't afford to let 'em steal the stock."

Just as Push-Bill left, Nathan noticed a column of dust on the cut-off road. "One rider coming in from the north. Don't look back," he advised. "He's coming right over the ridge. It's . . . it's Janton!"

"Who?" Colin gulped.

"One of the guys that tried to rob my poke! He'll recognize me for sure!"

Sal stood and walked straight at the oncoming rider, causing him to stop before he came near the almost deserted dinner table. Nathan sat frozen, turning his face away from the rider. His hands clutched the Winchester under the table. He could hear every word.

"Hello, I'm Sal Rialto. Can we invite you in for dinner?"

No! Don't do that! Tell him to leave!

The man's right hand rested on the handle of his holstered revolver. His eyes scanned the grounds.

"I need to talk to your pa," Janton growled.

"I'm afraid you'll have to speak to me," she said.

"Look, woman, I saw an old man go over toward those mules. Tell him to come out here."

One glance at Colin's eyes, and Nathan knew the man was staring at them.

"Oh, yes, he's a guest; he's not my father."

"Well, go get him and your father! I'm in a hurry, lady!"

"Would you like something to eat while you wait?"

"Just go get 'em!"

A shout and a gunshot rang out from the barn. Then the

mules bolted across the corral. Nathan didn't have time to lift his gun.

"Janton! Looky here what I found. If it isn't the old freighter himself!"

Nathan looked up to see the one named Claymore holding a gun on Push-Bill as they walked slowly back into the yard.

"Well, now . . . it's not every month that you get to rob the same man twice!" Janton crowed. He dismounted and drew his gun. Walking toward Push-Bill, he seemed to be overlooking those at the table. As he got closer, he suddenly twirled and pointed his revolver at Nathan's head.

"Drop the carbine on the ground, boy. And stand up real slow!" he commanded. "We know who you are, and you ain't pullin' no tricks on us this time."

"Shoot him, Janton," the other man called.

Ignoring his partner, Janton nodded at the other place settings. "Now jist call the rest of them back out here. We saw all them girls scatter out like chicks."

"Well, if this is the way you're going to react to our hospitality," Sal replied, "we'll have to ask you to leave."

"Leave? Do you hear that, Claymore? She asked us to leave."

The man holding a gun on Push-Bill spat tobacco juice on the ground and sneered. "When and if we leave, it will be with a pack train of them mules loaded with wares, our pokes stuffed with gold coins, and a couple of them girls tied to the back of our saddles!"

Suddenly, Push-Bill rammed his elbow into the man's rib cage and grabbed for the gun. It discharged into the air. Claymore pulled back and slammed the barrel of the gun into the freighter's head. Push-Bill dropped to the dirt.

At the same time, Colin dove under the table, and

Nathan grabbed his carbine. But before he could lift it, Janton punched his revolver into Nathan's back. "You want to be a hero? I planned on only having to kill the old man, but if you want to die, too, that's all right with me."

For some reason Nathan could never explain later, at that very moment he felt as relaxed and peaceful as he had the night before, looking up into the stars. It was almost like a different voice that came out of his mouth.

"There's worse things than dying with a friend," he said calmly.

Sal swept her arm back toward the buildings and spoke clearly in an unhurried voice, "You understand, Mr. Janton, that you will have to kill all of us. We will all survive, or none of us will. And being gunmen, I assume you are aware of the capability of shotguns? You girls stick those barrels out a little more, please," she called in a loud voice.

From all around the yard the purposeful rattle of guns could be heard. Nathan glanced around and counted seven guns pointed at the men.

Seven? That means that even Leah and Babe are armed!

"You're bluffin'," Claymore called out. "They're bluffin', Janton! They can't use them guns."

"We were all ranch-born and raised. I assure you, we can and will use these weapons," Sal replied.

"Miss Sal," Nathan called out, "you give the signal, and we'll drop to the ground. There's no use us getting caught in the cross-fire."

"I was thinking the same thing, Nathan. Oh, and, Mr. Janton, if you don't mind, please stand back away from the table a little more. I wouldn't want to get blood on the linen cloth."

"What?" Janton stormed.

"Girls," Sal called, "do be careful not to hit Nathan or Colin!"

Hearty replies echoed from all over the yard.

"I got a bead on the one pointing his gun at Nathan!"

"Should I aim for his belt buckle or his head?"

"You aim at his feet, and I'll shoot the head, Nan!"

"Leave some for me! I want something to shoot at!"

"Let's just get out of here," Claymore suggested, straining his neck to see where the voices were coming from.

"I ain't letting a pack of girls bluff me out of nothin'!"

"We will see that you get proper burial and that your families are notified," Sal continued.

"Wait!" Claymore called. "I'm leavin'. Janton can do what he wants, but I'll jist ride right on out."

"I'm afraid that's impossible, Mr. Claymore," Sal continued. "You see, you assaulted Push-Bill, and now you will have to stand trial in 10."

"Stand trial? They don't have no sheriff, no judge, no nothin'!"

"I'm sure they have a miners' court—right, Nathan?"

"Yep," he replied. "'Course Push-Bill being a good friend of most everybody, they might be mighty tough on 'em."

"I ain't standin' trial nowhere," Janton insisted. "Claymore, you shoot the woman. I'll shoot this kid, and we'll break for the horses."

"I ain't shootin' no woman. Every man in Nevada would come gunnin' fer me if I did that. Besides, if we shoot them, we give the others a clear shot."

"Well," Sal added, "there is one other possibility."

"What's that?" Claymore called.

"Reparation."

"What?"

"Yeah," Nathan responded, "you could pay Push-Bill for damages, and then there would be nothing against you."

"Pay him?" Janton cried. "You're crazy . . . we're the ones holding the guns!"

"What do you think is fair, Nathan?" Sal ignored the gunmen.

"Well, I'd say two revolvers, two rifles, and plenty of ammunition would be a good start."

"Yes, but I thought maybe two pairs of boots should be added to that," Sal replied.

"Yep, you're right." Nathan nodded. "Now if you will just throw down your guns, we'll get you on your way."

"Look, you ain't gettin' nothin' from me," Janton growled.

Sal nodded at Nathan, and the two of them dropped to the ground.

"Oh, blast it!" Claymore called, throwing his gun down. "Don't shoot, girls. I'm unarmed!"

Janton broke for the horses, but Nathan slammed the barrel of his carbine around, cracking into the fleeing man's shins. Janton rolled to the ground, screaming in pain.

"Nan," Sal called, "come put a gun on Claymore. The rest of you stay put."

Within moments they had retrieved the rifles and extra ammunition from the bushwhackers' saddles, picked up the revolvers, and pulled off the men's boots.

"You cain't take them. It's stealin'," Claymore complained bitterly as he mounted his horse barefoot.

"We'll pack them up to 10 and leave them with the miners' court," Nathan informed him. "If you have a complaint, just go up and tell them about it."

Janton glared over at Claymore. "You ain't tellin' nobody about this . . . ever!" he growled.

Sal handed Claymore a half-filled flour sack.

"What's this?"

"You men will need some supper."

Nathan spied a trail of dust moving quickly toward them from the west. "It looks like we have some more company."

"Maybe it's some cowhands from the XL Ranch," Sal guessed. "We invited them over for dinner. Now you two better ride hard in the other direction. I'm afraid the XL boys won't be quite as generous as we were."

Janton and Claymore kicked their ponies and galloped south. As soon as they left, the girls poured out of their hiding places, and Sal tended to Push-Bill.

"Who is coming in?" Nathan asked Beth.

"It's Beth's beau, Emery!" Babe blurted out. "He works at the XL, and Beth rode up on the hill this morning to signal him over."

"Signal him?" Nathan asked.

"With mirrors," Beth explained. "We have a little code, and when he sees it, he comes over. I expected him by dinner time, but he probably got caught with chores."

Leah came out to Nathan carrying a fireplace poker.

"What are you doing with that?" he asked.

"It's my gun." She smiled. "Babe was holding a pipe, but the rest had real guns. We bluffed 'em, didn't we?"

In less than two hours the yard was cleared, the teams were hitched, and Push-Bill had recovered. Emery received introductions all around, and Tona wagged his tail every time he heard Nathan's voice.

Push-Bill Horn made one last check of the wagons and

mounted his wheel horse. Most of the girls gathered on the front porch. Sal, Beth, and Emery walked out to the wagons.

"Mr. Horn," Sal began, "Emery agreed to watch the place for a few days just in case those men decide to return. The girls and I were wondering if you could give us all a lift to 10. We've got vegetables, preserves, and sewn goods to sell and some mining stock to check on."

The old freighter, sporting a linen bandage instead of a hat, flashed a broad smile. "It would be our privilege, ladies. How much time do you need to get ready?"

"About thirty minutes. Can you wait?" Beth asked.

"Wait? You bet we'll wait!" Push-Bill roared. "That'll give me time to eat that bread puddin' that I missed earlier. Tie 'em up, Nate! We're goin' to sit a spell."

TEN

All afternoon the freight wagons creaked along the cut-off route with Rialto girls hanging all over them. Sometimes they rode on the wagons, sometimes on the mules. Sometimes they walked along beside.

Babe spent most of the afternoon riding the other wheel horse next to Nathan. Sal and Beth chose Push-Bill's first wagon. But the rest changed places so often Nathan couldn't keep track of them.

The heat and the dust were just as bad as always, but in the happy confusion everything seemed more bearable. Hardly a moment passed that he couldn't hear laughter and giggles. Leah traded off, letting each of them ride Onepenny. That night, quartered at Wild Horse Canyon, the girls took over encampment. They stretched a tarp between the four wagons and made that their "cabin," banishing Push-Bill, Nathan, and Colin to the fire ring and the livestock. They prepared a meal from supplies left over from the noon dinner at the ranch. After supper they started singing, and it was a good two hours before any of them decided to stop.

It was Sal and Beth, as always, who got the girls rounded up and headed for bed. For most of the evening, Leah had so blended in with the others it was as if she were an eighth Rialto girl.

Finally, with Push-Bill and Colin down with the mules, it was just Nathan, Leah, and Sal sitting at the fire.

"You two sure acted calm out there with those outlaws today," Leah remarked.

"Well, don't let it fool you," Sal replied. "I was pretty scared . . . only . . . "

"Only what?" Leah pressed.

"Well, sometimes you just know what you have to do. Part of being scared is not knowing what you should do next," Sal offered. Then she turned to Nathan and looked him in the eyes. "Were you scared?"

"I prayed awful hard," he admitted. "But I've been more scared than I was today. I don't know why. It was just kind of peaceful."

"Peaceful? Peaceful!" Leah gasped. "You could have been shot to death right in that yard!"

"Yeah, well . . . ," Nathan stammered. "I don't really know how to explain it. But I just knew that I would have to stop them from hurting any of the girls. The way I figure, it was kind of like my assignment."

"Assignment from whom?" Leah pressed.

"From the Lord, I guess." Nathan shrugged. "I don't know. Do you know what I mean, Sal?"

"Yes, I believe that's how I felt, too. We made a pretty good team, didn't we?"

"We sure did, Miss Sal."

"Nathan's my boyfriend," Leah reminded her.

"Well, I'm glad because if you hadn't come into the picture, I think Cape and Nan were going to come to blows over him. We don't get too many visitors back at the ranch."

"Cape and Nan?" Nathan exclaimed. "They don't like me at all!"

"You'll have to excuse him, Miss Sal," Leah commented. "He don't know much about girls."

Sal smiled and poked at the fire with a long stick. "Well, now they are arguing over Colin."

"Colin?" Nathan choked.

"Yes. There seems to be some fascination with a bank owner's son."

Nathan stirred the fire for a long time after Sal and Leah wandered off to bed.

Lord, I've sure had lots of adventures since I moved to Nevada. Some of them have been pretty scary . . . and some pretty happy. And sometimes I've had both on the same day. I'm grateful You were there every time.

He stood above the fire watching the coals pop and sizzle as he poured the coffee over them. The smoke and steam boiled up around his head. Suddenly he felt sleepy.

Stretching out on top of his bedroll, he used his blanket for a pillow and started to count the stars.

He fell sound asleep somewhere between six and seven.

The next morning they found the road up to 10 packed with prospectors and pilgrims, freighters and foreigners, grocers and gamblers. True to form, Push-Bill passed half the rigs on the road, and Nathan had to struggle to keep up. The girls were all riding on the mule teams as they pulled up the last grade with the town in view.

"Why's he in such a hurry?" Leah asked Nathan.

"Well, for Push-Bill, minutes mean money. If all the wagons arrive at the same time, prices will drop. And if the mines go bust, there will be no market at all."

Colin came riding back to Nathan and Leah to report. "Push-Bill said he wants to roll right through town up City Street to Jacob's. He wants to sell and unload first thing. He said the girls can hop down at the assay offices and see if anyone wants to buy their claims. Then we'll all meet up at the Colorado House for supper."

"The Colorado House?" Nathan moaned. "These girls can't eat there!"

"That's what he said," Colin reported.

"I'll tell the girls," Leah offered.

In a few minutes she came riding back to Nathan.

"Sal said they would take their goods to sell also. There's a market next to one of the assay offices."

"Did you tell her about Push-Bill wanting to eat at the Colorado House?"

"Yeah. She said it was the best place in town to eat," Leah related.

The final climb into 10 was steep, and the teams were barely trudging as they entered the town.

"They're building sidewalks!" Nathan called out to Leah. "Last week there wasn't a sidewalk in town."

"Looks like a school or something's being constructed, too," she reported.

"A school?" Nathan called.

"No, it's going to be a church," Leah shouted. "Look, there's the steeple!"

"In 10? A church? That's unbelievable," Nathan gasped.

"You know, the streets are pretty smooth, too."

"It's all so different. What did they get, a mayor or something?" Nathan wondered.

The crowds at the assay offices were just as boisterous as ever, but Nathan noticed a marked improvement in the way the men dressed. Many now sported silk hats and ties, and several looked as if they had shaved and taken a bath recently.

The wagons ground to a halt as Push-Bill tried to part the crowd. Sal, Leah, and the others slid down and unloaded their produce and preserves. Leah handed Onepenny's reins to Nathan.

"Can you take him to the corral?" she asked.

Nathan nodded and dug into his pocket. "Listen, you take this claim and sell it for me. Last week it was worth $10 a share. Maybe it will be more now."

"You mean, I'll be holding $200?"

"Or more!"

"I ain't never had that much money before."

Nathan teased. "Well, if you're going to hang around me, you'll have to get used to big money."

The girls stepped toward the new sidewalk, and the whole crowd of men drew back and gave them plenty of room.

Push-Bill, Colin, and Nathan rolled into Jacob's, and within a matter of minutes they were unloading the wagons. About an hour later the task was done. Nathan and Colin led all the animals into the corrals.

"What's the thing on this Colorado House?" Colin asked. "The old man says the food's great, and Leah said you didn't like the place."

Nathan closed the corral gate and walked back toward Jacob's. "Well, the food is good, but you have to fight a dozen hungry miners for every bite. It's kind of like a war."

"What do you mean, a war?"

"You'll see," Nathan assured him.

Suddenly both he and Colin were engulfed by the massive arms of Push-Bill Horn.

"Well, boys, let's go get some supper. I'm buying for ever'body. I sold my wares for double the price and the extra wagon and team for triple what I paid. I ain't takin' no chances. I sent my profit down to Galena by Wells-Fargo. Now let's go get us a fine supper at the Colorado House."

"Push-Bill, do you think that's the kind of place to take girls?"

"They don't get no better in 10," he bragged.

As they came closer to the Colorado House, Nathan was astounded. The crowd outside stood in an orderly fashion, waiting in what looked very much like a line. A wide wooden sidewalk now graced the front of the restaurant, and several men in white shirts and ties sold dinner tokens.

"Looks like McSwain upgraded things a tad." Push-Bill elbowed Nathan.

"I don't believe this! Why would he change?" Nathan peeked through the window at the tables all set and waiting. "Tablecloths? They have tablecloths?"

"It's them women that's ruined the place!" a big voice boomed behind him.

Nathan turned to see one of the hefty miners he had squeezed in next to on a previous trip.

"Women?" Nathan asked.

"Yep. Ever since McSwain brought in them serving girls from Denver, the place has started to be respectable. If this keeps up, 10 won't be a fit place to live." Then the big man paused, and his brushy beard parted into a wide smile. "But them gals sure is purdy . . . mighty purdy."

Nathan walked up to Leah and the others.

"This place looks all right," she announced.

"Yeah . . . well, it's changed. Trust me. Could you ladies sell any of those claims?"

"Yes!" Babe shouted. "And we sold our produce, and we bought some things! I got my very own feather duster. Sal says I'm old enough to dust! And I got some candy and a book with pictures!"

"You know," Leah added, "they offered Sal triple the usual price for the produce, but she wouldn't take it all. She said it wasn't right for anyone to have to pay that much for food."

"Did you sell my . . . it's our turn already? Now remember, grab all the food you can because . . . what's this?"

"I guess they seat you at a table now," Push-Bill mumbled. "Ain't this somethin'?"

The whole party of eleven stepped into the restaurant, and a uniformed serving girl showed them where to sit.

"Say, aren't you that Nathan boy?" she asked.

"Yes, ma'am."

"Well, we met down at that draw when the stage needed repairs."

"You ladies really changed this place!" Nathan added.

"Oh, my yes, you wouldn't believe how horrid it used to be!"

Nathan turned to Leah. "See? I told you it used to be awful."

When everyone was seated, the waitress began to bring them their food. As they settled down with meat and potatoes, Nathan suddenly sat straight up.

"The claims! I forgot about the claims. Could you sell any of them? Leah, what did you get for my claim?"

Leah glanced over at Sal, then back at Nathan, and then back at Sal.

"Eh . . . we'll give our report first," Sal offered. "I had seventeen feet of the Lucky Seven, and I got $9.10. I spent it all on yardage."

Beth was next to speak. "Well, thanks to Nathan, I had twenty-two feet in the Alligator, and I received $22, which I already spent on primers and new slates for the children."

Then it was Nan's turn. "Mine was the twelve feet of the Pretty Nugget, and it brought $8.

Blonde-haired Cape spoke next. "This guy offered me $3 a foot for my Root-Hog-Or-Die footage, but I told him that none other than Nathan T. Riggins of Galena, Nevada, had told me it was worth $10 a foot and so—"

"No, that wasn't the one worth $10 a foot!" Nathan corrected her.

"Well, anyway, I made the man give me $10 a foot."

"How many feet did you have?" Nathan asked.

"Six. Now I've got three gold coins that are all mine, and I'm never ever going to spend them . . . until I get married, of course."

Jerri stood as if to give a formal speech. Her black braids bounced as she spoke. "I had twenty-one feet of a worthless hole in the ground, but a man got to feeling sorry for me and offered me $5, so I took it and bought some new shoes. Now I'm as tall as Cape!"

"You are not!"

"Am too!"

"It's my turn!" Nina called out. "I had twelve feet in the Broken Nose, and they gave me $6. I gave half of it to the church building fund, and with the rest I bought stick candy!"

"What kind of candy? What store sells candy?" Colin chimed in.

"Well," Babe announced, "I had six feet of some old mine, and this man with a tall hat said I reminded him of his daughter, and he gave me $6!"

"And," Sal offered, "we all want to thank Nathan for his generosity!"

"That's great!" he replied. "I didn't know those were

worth anything at all! How about you, Leah? What was my claim worth?"

"Eh . . . well, you said it should bring $10 a foot, right?"

"Yeah, what did you get?"

"That was the price last week, right?" she asked.

"Yeah, right. Now what did you—"

"Well, something happened over the weekend at the mine."

"What?" Nathan spoke rapidly. "Did the price go up like the Antelope Flats?"

"Eh, no," Leah replied. "They broke into an underground stream, and the mine filled with water. They've abandoned it. Now the certificate is worthless!"

"Worthless? You mean, nothing?"

"Zero."

"They can't do that! I sold some last week for $10 a foot!"

"I'm sorry, Nathan," Sal replied, "but Leah's right. Look, if you need these other claims back, we can—"

"No, no, no." Nathan sighed. "They're yours. It's just . . . just . . ."

"It's a crazy business, ain't it, boy! Welcome to the mines!" Push-Bill joined in. "Mr. Maddison with two *d*'s, would you pass that cherry pie?"

All of a sudden a smile broke across Nathan's face, and he started to laugh.

"You ain't mad at me then?" Leah frowned.

"No." He grinned. "I was just thinking about that mine. It proved to be true to its name. I should have known better than to hang onto something called the All-Is-Lost."

"Nathan!" a feminine voice shouted from across the room.

Suddenly he found one of the serving girls throwing

her arms around him and hugging him. He recognized the strong perfume.

"Honey, why didn't you come look me up when you came to town?" she teased.

"Eh, Kay Lynn!" he stammered, caught up in her flashy eyes. *She just might be the most beautiful woman in the whole world!*

"Me and Nathan were almost family," she said with a laugh.

"Listen," he hurried to explain, "this is the lady that helped me out when the bushwhackers were following me! Kay Lynn, this is Push-Bill Horn, Colin Maddison, Jr. (with two *d*'s), the Rialto sisters—Sal, Beth, Nan, Cape, Jerri, Nina, and Babe . . . and this is Leah Walker."

Leah stood up, placed one hand on her hip, tilted her head, and spoke with authority. "I'm Nathan's girlfriend, and I can tell you right now, he ain't never goin' to marry nobody but me!"

BOOK SIX

Hawks Don't
Say Good-bye

ONE

Colin, quick! Head him off! He's coming over by the dry goods!" Nathan shouted, scrambling out from behind a pickle barrel. The unpainted wooden floor was slick from years of heavy use. "No . . . no, there he goes! Leah, he's coming your way. Grab him!"

"With my hands?" Leah gasped. She backed away from the coffee bin and bumped against a string of garlic hanging from the rafter.

Scooting around a stack of ready-made shirts on his hands and knees, Nathan hollered, "Leah, throw your hat on him!"

"Not this hat! I ain't throwin' this hat on no rat." She backed across the room to the glass candy case.

"Mouse," Nathan corrected. "It's only a mouse. Ah, hah! I've got it cornered! Colin, hand me something to clobber it with."

"You mean a broom or perhaps a—"

"Anything! Hurry!" Nathan shouted.

Colin tossed him a pair of rubber galoshes.

Nathan grabbed the overshoes and slammed them down on the fleeing rodent.

"We did it! Another successful hunt."

"Well," Leah pouted, "you seem to have more fun chasing rats than you do spendin' time with me."

"Mouse. It's only a mouse, and besides I only do it every other day."

"Young man!" a stern voice scolded from the front counter of the Galena Mercantile. "I believe, Master Riggins, that you are employed here. Are you not?"

"Eh, yes, ma'am," Nathan stammered, standing to his feet with the overshoes in one hand and the mouse in the other.

"Well, then, I hope you see fit to attend to my order, or I'll have to tell Mr. Anderson that you were shooting marbles in the corner when you should have been working."

"Marbles?" Colin choked. "Actually, he was—"

"I'll be right with you, Mrs. Kearny," Nathan interrupted, quickly dropping the dead mouse into the rubber boots and replacing them on the shelf.

It took him about fifteen minutes to gather Mrs. Kearny's supplies and pack them out to her rig. He pulled a tarp over the goods and then lashed them down. Helping Mrs. Kearny into the wagon, Nathan untied the team and brought her the lead line.

"Thank you, Nathan. Tell Mr. Anderson I'm sorry he wasn't here so that I might say goodbye," she added, pushing her floppy green hat back out of her eyes.

"Goodbye? Are you pulling out?" Nathan asked shading his eyes from the noontime sun.

"Yes. I'm afraid Henry has the wanderin' fever. His brother's raising cherries in California, and Henry's decided what with the Shiloh cutting back, we're going to become cherry farmers."

"Well, ma'am, I'm, eh . . . sorry to see you go." He waved to her as she slapped the reins and rolled the rig down the street, each wheel leaving a cloud of dry yellow dust.

Leah and Colin were lounging on a bench in front of the store by the time he stepped back up on the raised wooden sidewalk. He unbuttoned the sleeves of his shirt and rolled them halfway up his forearms.

The hot Nevada sun blistered his face, and he squinted his eyes until he reached the cover of shade. Plopping down on the bench next to Leah, he grinned.

"Sure is a pretty hat, Miss Leah."

"Oh . . . sure, I'll bet you say that to all the other girls, too."

"What other girls?" Nathan kidded.

"Riggins, look down Main Street." Colin pointed. "What do you see?"

Nathan wiped the sweat off his forehead and stared down the street. A couple of horses stood tied at the Drover's Cafe. There was a broken buckboard parked in front of the Paradise Dance Hall, which had been closed since November. And he spotted old Ezree Mullins asleep on a bench beside the Welsh Miners' Hall.

"Eh . . . I don't see anything. I mean, it just looks like Galena, Nevada," he answered.

"Precisely!" Colin proclaimed. "That proves what I've been saying all along."

"Do you know what he's talking about?" Nathan asked Leah.

"Me? I never know what Colin's talkin' about. He came with you."

"With me?" Nathan teased, "I thought he came with you."

"If you two are quite finished, what I'm talking about," Colin Maddison (with two *d*'s), Jr., explained, "is that this town is absolutely dying!"

"Oh, it's just been a slow summer. I hear they might have found some color up on Crazy Woman Mountain. If they did, then—"

"Riggins, you sound like Henderson down at the post office and the miners sitting unemployed in front of the Miners' Hall! Take a good look. Does this look like the town you arrived at two years ago?"

Nathan glanced at the businesses along Main Street again. At least half of them were boarded up.

"Well, it's just a slump. These things happen, but we'll pull out of it. My dad says—"

"Your dad's a great marshal," Colin acknowledged, "but he isn't a businessman. The town's dying, and now's the time to exit. There's no use waiting until everyone goes broke."

"Come on, Colin, it's not that bad," Nathan insisted. He pulled off his left boot, straightened his sock, and then yanked it back on. "Sure, it's a slow summer, but that doesn't mean we'll dry up and disappear like Willow Springs or something. The cattle froze out last winter, and some of the big ranches shut down, but they'll be back. I've heard some folks say they enjoyed not having the town shot up every Saturday night."

"I don't know, Riggins." Colin pulled out a small folding knife and began to clean his fingernails. "Miss D'Imperio said if five more kids don't come to town this summer to make up for those that have moved, we won't have school in September."

"They'll move in. You'll see," Nathan encouraged him. "I've been praying that the Lord would move some large families into Galena."

"Oh, like them Rialto sisters, I'll bet. You been prayin' that all seven of them will move to town, have you?" Leah accused.

"No, but that's not a bad idea. Why, I'll bet they look even—"

Leah slugged him in the arm. Nathan tried to avoid the punch and ended up crashing into Colin, knocking him off the bench to the sidewalk.

"Hey, watch it!"

"Sorry, Colin."

Leah scrunched her nose and wrinkled the freckles across her face. "But what if the Lord don't want Galena to go on?" she asked.

"I don't know about your prayers," Colin added, "but I personally happen to know that my father has considered closing the bank."

A shock of alarm shot down Nathan's back. "He can't do that! It's the last bank in town."

"He most certainly can do it. He owns the entire bank, you know."

"Yeah, we know it," Nathan moaned.

"What would your daddy do for a livin'?" Leah asked. "I mean, if he didn't have the bank? Jobs in town is kind of hard to find."

"Why, we'd move to another town and open another bank," Colin explained. "You don't think we'd want to stay here, do you? Father mentioned opening a bank over in White Pine County perhaps."

"I like it here," Leah said softly. "This is the best place I ever lived in my whole life. You ain't goin' to move, are you, Nathan?"

"Nope, not us. 'Course it has been a little tougher since they only pay Daddy part salary. He was saving up to buy a ranch, but now it looks like we've been using some of that savings just to get by on."

"Oh, come on, you two, it ain't the end of the world! It's just a lazy July day, that's all," Leah insisted. "By September folks will be linin' the streets, and we'll wish they would all move on. It's happened before."

Nathan stood to his feet and stepped to the edge of the sidewalk. "Well, Colin's right about one thing. Two years ago there were freight wagons parked three deep and lined back out to old man Blanchard's place. You were lucky if you could cram into a cafe for a meal. Now you're lucky to find a cafe open. Look at the Mercantile. Remember when they had eight clerks working here? Now it's me, Tony, and Mr. Anderson."

Leah jumped to her feet and twirled on the sidewalk. "Well, I don't have to listen to all of this bad talkin'. I'll see you after work . . . I mean, if that's all right with you."

"I'll come by your house," Nathan promised.

She smoothed her long cotton dress with the rich brown velvet bows on the shoulders and hiked off toward her father's barber shop.

Nathan stood in the doorway and watched her walk away.

"Towns do die out here, don't they, Nathan?"

"Yeah . . ." He nodded at Colin. "They can dry up and completely disappear."

"You know, my grandparents live in Boston," Colin remarked. "They've lived in that two-story white house for over fifty-three years. And I suppose someday my uncle and then my cousins will live there too. But out here nothing stays the same very long, does it?"

"I reckon not." Nathan retreated to the doorway of the store. "I sure can't imagine Galena being around fifty years from now."

"Precisely."

"Are you comin' inside?" Nathan asked, running his hand along the rough, unpainted door jamb.

"I think I'll go home and pour a bucket of well water over my head," Colin reported.

"Really?"

"Of course not. It's just a saying when it gets so hot. Nobody actually pours water over their head," Colin explained. He turned to cross the street.

"I do," Nathan muttered under his breath, entering the Mercantile. The comfortable, familiar mixed smells of freshly ground coffee, peppermint stick candy, and new leather greeted him.

Lord, this is not the way I had things planned, remember? I asked You about that ranch and cattle, and when we're older, You know . . . me and Leah. And Colin would be the banker. But now everything's up in the air. Everyone's moving or worried. Nobody in town laughs anymore.

His thoughts were interrupted by Miss Phillips and another woman entering the store.

"Can I fill an order for you ladies?" Nathan asked.

"Why, young Mr. Riggins. I see Mr. Anderson has left you in charge today."

"Only until after he has his dinner," Nathan reported.

"Well, this is my sister, Mrs. Krause, from Charlotte County, Virginia."

"Howdy, ma'am." Nathan nodded. "Pleased to meet you. Are you plannin' on movin' to Galena?"

"Oh, my word, no!" she exclaimed.

"I'm afraid my sister could never leave Virginia," Miss Phillips reported. "Nathan here is the marshal's son. Did I mention Marshal Riggins, Delia? He's a very fine Christian man, you know. Anyway, we're going down to the river tomorrow to escape this dreadful heat, so we thought we'd do a little shopping today. Don't mind us, Nathan. We'll signal if we need some help. We'll just poke around. Maybe over there in the barrel of parasols."

"Yes, ma'am . . . eh, nice to meet you, Mrs. Krause." He smiled and went back to the counter where he began to uncrate some enamel-coated tin dishes.

"My, such a polite young man," he heard Mrs. Krause murmur.

You see, Lord, I like it out here. It's kind of scary not knowin' where you're going to be living. Everyone has to be somewhere and, well . . . this is where I want to be. It's . . . it's comfortable—like an old pair of boots. And it's so quiet and peaceful. It's the kind of place—

A piercing scream shredded his thoughts. He dropped a stack of tin plates.

"A rat! There's a rat in the boots!" Miss Phillips shouted, and she struggled to hold up her trembling sister.

Running to the women, Nathan grabbed up the rubber galoshes and jammed his hand into the boot. He clutched the dead mouse, jerked it out, and scurried to the back door. "I'm really sorry, Miss Phillips. I'll get rid of it right now."

"My word," Mrs. Krause gasped, "did that young man grab that rodent with his bare hands?"

"The children grow up rather leathery out here, don't they?" Miss Phillips brushed down her sleeves and then called out to Nathan, "Mr. Anderson should get a mouser!"

"Yes, ma'am, I'll mention it to him." He dumped the mouse on the dirt beside the back door and then turned a small empty nail barrel over the top of the animal.

By the time he finished waiting on Miss Phillips and her sister, they had both regained their composure and were so busy chattering that they almost walked out the door forgetting their purchases.

"Miss Phillips, your bundle," he called.

"Oh, my heavens . . . yes." She smiled. "Please tell your mother I said hello."

"Yes, ma'am. Thank you."

Nathan finished unpacking and stacking all the tin dishes without another customer entering the store. For several minutes he stood in front of a floor-length mirror and tried on several new hats that he had unboxed earlier in the day.

You're too skinny, Riggins. You grew too fast this year. It's all right to be five feet, ten inches, but you need some girth. Mom's right. I need my hair cut. If Mr. Walker's not too busy, I could get it cut when I stop by and see Leah. Look at this one! Nathan T. Riggins, riverboat gambler. No . . . this is it. This black one. Riggins, you dog, you could be mistaken for . . . for Stuart Brannon himself!

Pretending to be the famous gunman, he sauntered up to the mirror wearing the black hat. "Excuse me, Miss, I'll just mosey on out to the street and face down them fourteen desperados. Then I'll be back and finish my pie."

Glancing at the clock on the wall, he put the hat back on the shelf and walked over to the cash drawer.

Harris Anderson returned to the Mercantile at exactly 1:00 P.M. He looked at his pocket watch, listened to the wall clock chime once, and examined the cash drawer.

"Looks like you had some cash sales. That's a good sign. Go grab yourself some dinner, Nate. You can finish putting up stock later."

Nathan pulled off his heavy ducking apron, hung it on a peg by the back door, shoved on his floppy gray hat, then stepped outside, moved the barrel, and picked up the dead mouse. He ambled down the alley behind the buildings and turned up the hill to the boarded-up Heartford Hotel.

Shading his eyes with his hat, he strained to focus on the roof line of the hotel.

"All right, Domingo . . . I see you up there!"

Nathan reached to his back pocket and pulled out a heavy, worn leather glove and slipped it on his left hand. The gauntlet extended almost to his elbow. Then he held his arm straight out in front of him and let go with a shrill whistle.

"Come on, Domingo! Come on, boy . . . it's dinner time."

Nathan watched for a few moments until the large, brown-winged bird swooped down off the shingles of the hotel and glided to a rest on Nathan's gloved hand.

"I don't know how you do it. How do you have such a soft landing? You're a big boy, but you always feel so light. Have you had a lot to eat today? I hope you aren't too full for a mouse meal. Are you ready?"

The brown hawk swiveled its neck and stared at Nathan, then swiveled back and looked down the street. Nathan could tell he was about ready to fly away.

"Wait . . . wait. Here it comes!"

With his right hand, he tossed the dead mouse high into the air. He felt the hawk kick free from the perch and flap his wide wings. Nathan could hear the beating sound and feel the breeze they made as the powerful bird winged towards the tumbling rodent. The bird's talons snatched the mouse in midair, and with several long flaps of the wings the bird returned to its perch on top of the building.

"Yeah . . . well, you used to come back and say thanks," Nathan called. "That's a big dinner, so I won't be back tomorrow."

He's going away, too, isn't he, Lord? When it gets cold, he'll be gone. Off to someplace sunny. Off to someplace where there's a lonesome lady hawk.

Nathan strolled home thinking about the day he had found the baby hawk in the hayloft above Onepenny's stall. First, the bird nested in a coffee can half full of straw, then in an empty nail barrel, then in the abandoned chicken coop, and finally Nathan had turned him loose and found that Domingo preferred the roof of the Heartford Hotel.

Walking across the dirt yard in front of his house, Nathan was greeted by a tail-wagging, limping gray and white dog.

"Tona, you don't have to come out in the sun. Stay back there and rest up. You're all stove-up today, aren't you, old boy?" He rubbed the dog's ears and scratched its head. The dog sniffed him up one arm and down the other.

"It's a mouse. You smell it, don't you? It's okay, don't worry. I fed him to Domingo."

The dog struggled back into the shade of the porch and flopped down on a small, worn braided rug that had become his permanent dwelling place ever since Nathan brought him back from the Rialto ranch early in the spring.

He washed his hands in a basin on the porch.

"Nate," his mother called, "bring in a couple more sticks of wood for the cookstove."

On entering the kitchen, he heard the sound of meat frying and crackling in the skillet, and he smelled the aroma of ham.

"How was work this morning, dear?" she asked, pouring herself a cup of coffee.

"Really slow," he reported. "It's like everyone's out of town today. Oh, Miss Phillips came in and said to tell you hello. Did you know her sister came to visit her?"

"Came to help her move, I hear," Nathan's mother responded.

"Move? Miss Phillips is moving from Galena?"

"So I hear."

"Did you know the Kearnys are leaving too?"

"No. Where did you hear that?"

"Mrs. Kearny told me herself. You know, Mom, town will perk up next fall, and all these people are going to regret cashing in so quickly," Nathan reported.

"Well, I certainly hope so." His mother set a bowl of boiled potatoes on the table and then forked the sizzling meat onto their plates.

"Where's Dad?"

"He went to Austin."

Nathan sat up straight. "Austin? He didn't tell me he was going! What's he doing in Austin?"

"Looking for a job."

"A job? He has a job!"

"Well, not any more." His mother sighed.

With a chunk of ham only inches from his mouth, Nathan's head swung up with surprise. "What?"

"The mayor stopped by and said they can't afford to pay him anymore, what with everyone leavin'. So they are going to have to call a posse whenever the need arises."

"But . . . but he's just got to be marshal!" Nathan protested. "This whole town's going crazy. I don't get it. Why's everyone leavin'?"

"I suppose, Nathan T. Riggins, that they all like to eat, too."

Nathan's afternoon blurred as he stocked shelves and waited on customers at the Galena Mercantile. His mind kept racing over the idea that his family might soon be one of those to leave Galena. It hung like a drooping hat over his head even as he entered Walker's Barber Shop several hours later.

"Hi, Mr. Walker. You got any time for a haircut?"

Leah's father looked up from a newspaper and glanced at his otherwise empty shop.

"Time? Nathan, I have time to cut hair for the entire U. S. army. Hop in the chair, and I'll give you a trim."

"Thanks. Is Leah at home?"

"Well, son, if she's not with you, chances are mighty good she's upstairs, but I ain't seen her since dinner."

"Sure is a quiet summer, isn't it?" Nathan mentioned as Mr. Walker strapped his scissors.

"Quiet? Nearly dead, I figure. If things don't perk up this fall, I don't suppose there will be many left that winter out."

"How about you, Mr. Walker?"

"Well, Nate . . . a man's got to go where there's customers. And lately I haven't been cuttin' much hair or pullin' many teeth, that's for sure. I've thought about takin' a look at Silver City."

"In Idaho?"

"Yep."

"Isn't that where that Kylie Collins guy is?" Nathan asked.

"Well, I reckon you're right."

"I ain't goin' to no Silver City!" a voice boomed from the back door.

"Leah!" Nathan blurted out.

"Daddy, I told you I made up my mind. I ain't ever goin' to marry that Kylie Collins. I think we should stay in Galena as long as . . . well . . . you know."

Nathan watched in the big mirror as Mr. Walker ran a comb though his dark brown hair and clipped it shorter. "As long as that good-lookin' Riggins boy lives here. Was that what you were goin' to say?"

"Daddy!"

"Now, Nate, let me tell you about this Leah-girl. She's sort of like those Gila monsters down in Arizona. Have you ever seen them?"

"Eh . . . no, sir."

"Well, they're nothing but a huge fat lizard. Some grow to two or three feet. Anyway, when they get mad and lock their teeth into you, they never let go. You got to literally hack them to pieces with your huntin' knife to get them to turn loose. Now ol' Leah-girl . . . she's clamped her iron will down on Mr. Nathan T. Riggins. I'm afraid you don't have much chance of ever gettin' loose."

"Daddy! I ain't goin' to stand here and be humiliated. Supper's ready if you're hungry, and Nathan can stay if he wants to." Leah turned to leave.

"Eh . . . I, eh, you know . . . need to check with my mother. With Dad gone, she might not want to be alone."

"She ain't alone," Leah offered.

"What do you mean?"

"She's upstairs at the supper table waitin' for us."

"What? She didn't tell me that we were havin' supper over here."

"Well, that just goes to show you don't know everything, Mr. Nathan T. Riggins!" Leah turned and scampered out the back door of the barber shop.

"There you have it, Nate—one very opinionated young lady."

Nathan swallowed a lump in his throat. "Mr. Walker, Leah sure is a good friend for me. I really do like her."

"Son, I appreciate you sayin' that. 'Cause that little lady thinks the sun rises and sets with Nathan T. Riggins."

Nathan was afraid to glance in the mirror. He knew his face would be burning.

"Your daddy out chasing outlaws?" Mr. Walker asked.

"Eh . . . no, he's . . . he's down in Austin."

"Had to go to the courthouse, huh?"

"Well . . . maybe. I mean . . . actually, Mr. Walker, they laid him off as marshal. Said they couldn't afford a lawman anymore. So Dad's down in Austin lookin' for a job or something."

"You don't say! I didn't know." Mr. Walker brushed Nathan off and sprinkled some talc on the back of his neck. "Well, this is . . . it surely does cause a man to consider driftin' on out."

Nathan handed Mr. Walker a quarter.

"Oh, no, it's my treat, what with your daddy being out of work and—"

"No, sir, Mr. Walker!" Nathan insisted. "I'm still workin'. Besides, my mama would skin me alive if I didn't pay my own way."

The barber glanced at Nathan, then smiled, and took the quarter. "You got good folks, Nathan. I hope you remember to thank the Lord for 'em."

"Every night." Nathan nodded.

"Well, I'm closing up and sweeping the shop. Tell the ladies I'll be right up."

"Yes, sir, I will."

The following day Nathan didn't have to go to work until 1:00 P.M., so he saddled up Onepenny at the first sign of daylight. Then he slid his carbine into its scabbard, put some biscuits into his saddlebags, and strapped his canteen over the saddle horn.

Tona limped out into the middle of the dirt yard to watch him.

"You want to go, boy? You can't keep up anymore. You know that." He stared at the sad face that seemed to be Tona's permanent expression.

"Okay." Nathan shrugged. "Come on . . . Onepenny can carry us both. He'll like some company." Lifting the crippled animal, Nathan struggled to climb into his saddle and situate the dog in his lap.

"All right, gang. Let's go huntin'."

They rode down Main Street without seeing any sign of life. The July air was dry, still, and already losing any coolness the night might have brought. An aroma of dust and sage hung heavy about them.

In a little over an hour, they had swooped down through the valley, crossed Lewis Creek, and begun to climb up into the Shoshone Mountains. He finally left the barren hills and hit the chaparral at Rabbit Springs where he climbed off Onepenny. He loosened the cinch and hobbled the spotted horse to graze on what little grass was near the pool of water.

Tona slumped over to the shade of a scrub cedar, circled three times, and then lay down where he could watch the horse and the springs.

Nathan stared at his dog.

Lord, Tona hurts all the time. I kept prayin' all last summer that he'd live after that bobcat tore him up. And You answered my prayers, but . . . maybe it wasn't so good an idea. He can't hunt. He can't run. He can hardly watch over me. Lord, either let him regain his strength, or . . . or, You know . . . well, I just can't watch him hurt so bad every day.

His canteen strapped around his neck, his Winchester carbine in his left hand and two biscuits in his right, Nathan hiked up the mountain past the piñon pines on the north side of the slope. Reaching a jagged row of rocks above the tree line, he sat where he could look to the east, west, and north.

Munching on the biscuits, he watched the horizon for any sign of the pronghorn antelopes that he'd seen several weeks earlier.

Lord, well, I'd like to shoot an antelope and show Mom and Dad I can contribute to the food supply. But really I guess I rode out here to think a little bit. All I ever wanted was to be with Mom and Dad. I remember how I wandered around this country two years ago lookin' for them. I said then if I found them, that's all I would ever ask for.

But this time it seems different. I've got friends . . . good friends like Colin and Leah. I don't want us to all move away. When I get old, I want to be able to say to someone, "Remember when we were kids?"

It's crazy out here, Lord. Everyone's in a hurry to get rich . . . they run to Virginia City . . . they run to Bodie . . . they run to Eureka . . . they run to Belmont. You can live your whole life and never get to know anybody at all. It's like you're always visitin' . . . never stayin'.

Someday, Lord, someday I'm goin' to buy me a ranch and never ever move. My kids will spend their whole life in that same house, no matter what.

I mean, if Leah doesn't mind.

Sudden movement caused Nathan to jerk his head to the right and lift his carbine to his shoulder. Trailing the metal sights of the gun across the horizon, he followed the dust of what looked like several animals running at the lower edge of the chaparral. He lowered the weapon and continued to watch until they dropped over the western horizon of the mountain.

A rifle with a Vernier sight maybe, but not with a carbine—not at this distance. Last week they ran up on top . . . now they're down there. It's like they always know where I'm going to be.

It was over an hour later when Nathan gave up the hunt without firing a shot and hiked back to Rabbit Springs. Tona greeted him with one lone bark. He thumped his tail but didn't bother getting to his feet.

Nathan remounted with Tona and rode back to Galena. It was almost noon when they reached the north/south road and turned up the mountain. The windswept town looked deserted from a distance. There were no rigs on the road, no prospectors' tents scattered about the hillside, no noise from Shiloh's stamp mill. No dogs barked. No children shouted.

As he drew closer, he noticed a number of men talking in front of the bank and several women walking down toward the church.

"Well, Tona, at least it's dying peacefully. Just slowly, a

little at a time—nothing painful. Someday we'll just wake up, and no one will be left."

He pulled the tack off Onepenny and turned the spotted horse out in the corral. Then, with Tona tucked under his left arm and his carbine over his right shoulder, he hiked down the back alley to his house. He cradled the dog on its rug and stuck his head through the doorway.

"Mom, I'm home. I didn't have any luck with a pronghorn, but it was a nice ride."

"Do you want some dinner?" she asked.

"Nah. Thanks. I'm stuffed with all your biscuits. I'm going down to the store. Maybe I'll stop and see Colin on the way. Will Dad be in for supper?"

"That all depends on when and where he finds work. He did say he would be home by Saturday, no matter what."

"Good. I want to talk to him."

"About what?"

"About stayin' in Galena rather than moving."

"Nathan, you know we'll have to do what your father thinks best."

"Yes ma'am, but I aim to use my best logic to persuade him to stay."

As was his custom, Nathan stayed off Main Street as he tramped over to the Mercantile. Swinging up the hillside, he purposely detoured by the Heartford Hotel.

"Domingo? Did you go off huntin'? You won't be able to eat it, and you know it. You'll come back and hold a mouse for two hours and then drop it down for the cats to find . . . just like last week." He searched the sky, but he couldn't find the hawk anywhere. "Well, I just hope you don't go down to Swifty's chicken coop again. He'll plug you with that shotgun."

He picked up a couple of small rocks and tossed them across the dusty street. Then he trotted down to the back door of the Mercantile.

The door's locked? Am I late? Did Mr. Anderson close for dinner? Where's Tony? He always works the noon hour on Wednesdays.

Scooting around to the front of the store, he noticed a fairly large crowd of people now gathered in front of the bank.

"Hey, what's going on here? What happened?"

"Nathan!" Leah yelled from across the street. "Where have you been?"

They met out in the center of the street.

"Eh . . . I went huntin' in the Shoshones. What's all the fuss?"

"They robbed the bank, that's what!"

"Maddison's bank? Who did it?"

"Nobody knows."

"Did anyone get hurt?"

"Colin's daddy was hit on the head, and Mr. Melton was tied up, but they didn't get shot."

"How about Colin? Was he there?"

"He got locked in the safe."

"In the safe!"

Leah walked with Nathan closer to the crowd. "I heard he was yelling at the outlaws that Marshal David Riggins would chase them down and shoot them dead, and they shoved him into the safe."

"But he's okay now? Right?" Nathan pressed.

A big man who smelled like black powder turned and

looked at Nathan. "I hear they can't get the kid out. The dial got jammed when they busted it open."

Nathan pushed through the crowd. "But . . . he'll suffocate in there!"

"That's for sure." The big man nodded.

The crowd ended at the door. Brady Wheeler blocked it with the strength gained from a life of hammering and drilling hard rock.

"Mr. Wheeler, have they got Colin out of the safe?"

"Not yet, Nate. Mr. Maddison's workin' his fingers off tryin'."

"Can we help or anything?"

"Nah, there's nothin' you can—"

"Nathan! Leah! Let them in, Brady!" Mr. Maddison shouted.

They pushed their way into the bank where the smell of gunpowder hung in the air.

"Mr. Maddison, how's Colin? Is he . . . I mean—"

"Nate, the door on the safe is jammed just enough to let a little bit of air inside. Colin will be all right for a while. But the dial is so smashed that we had to send up to the CP and get some equipment for busting it open."

"What can I do?" Nathan asked.

"Talk to him. Just stay with him. He's pretty scared."

"Yes, sir, I'll do it. Who's goin' after the robbers?"

"The mayor said he'd wire the sheriff."

"In Austin?"

"Now that we don't have a marshal, it's about all we can do. Forget the money, Nate. Just help Colin relax and stay calm."

"Yes, sir, I'll stay here as long as I need to." Nathan swung toward the safe and then turned back.

"Leah, can you run over to the Mercantile and tell Mr.

Anderson why I'm not coming in? The back door was still locked, so he might be at dinner."

"Until straight up 1:00, right? I'll tell him."

Nathan scooted over to the five-foot door on the safe and found it barely open—not enough to let in much direct light, but enough to allow a little fresh air to filter in.

Holding his ear to the opening of the door, he could hear Colin crying.

"Colin, can you hear me? It's Nate!"

The crying continued.

"Colin, hold on . . . your dad's gone to try and get a fresh air pump from the Shiloh mine. It'll help you breathe easier. You've got to relax. Colin, do you hear me?"

"I am relaxing!" Colin wailed. "I've never . . . been so . . . so relaxed . . . in my life. Get me out of here, Riggins!"

"Listen, Colin, it won't be too long, and I'll stay right here."

"I want my mother! Get my mother!" Colin screamed.

"Your mother's in Carson City, remember?"

"I want out of here! Right now!"

"Colin . . . eh . . . listen, did you get a good look at the bank robbers?" Nathan quizzed.

He heard the sobbing stop.

"Is your father chasing them?" Colin hollered.

"No," Nathan shouted back, "he's down in Austin. But they'll get caught."

"And hung," Colin added.

"Listen, try not to be upset. Just, well, why don't you close your eyes and pretend you're asleep," Nathan suggested. "This will all be just a bad dream."

"And why don't you jump down a mine shaft, Riggins! This is a living nightmare. Get me out of here!"

"Do you want me to sing?" Nathan suggested.

"Get an iron bar and rip open this door!"

"It's too big. Only the Central Pacific has tools that strong."

"Then get the Central Pacific down here immediately. I want my father . . . where's my father?"

"Colin, is there any money left in there?"

"What did you say?"

Nathan leaned over close to the safe's door. "Is there any money in there?"

"How would I know what's in . . . hey . . . hey, Nate!"

"Yeah?"

"I think there's a couple of gold bars back here. Yes, I'm sure of it. Those jerks didn't even find the gold!"

"What else is in there?"

There was a long pause.

"I want out, Riggins. Quit changing the subject."

"You'll be all right, Colin . . . just don't panic."

"Don't panic? Don't panic! Riggins, if I can't panic now, when on earth am I allowed to panic? Why do these things always happen to me?"

He began to bawl again.

"Colin . . . hey . . . what would Stuart Brannon do if he were in there?"

"What?"

"Brannon . . . what would he do?"

Again he stopped crying.

"Brannon would shoot his way out . . . no, he'd pick the lock with his penknife."

"Brannon doesn't carry a penknife," Nathan yelled.

Leah rushed up to him. "Nathan! Hey, no one's over at the Mercantile."

"What time is it?"

"It's 1:15, and Mr. Anderson ain't been home for dinner neither. I asked Mrs. Anderson."

"Is the front door locked?"

"Yep."

"I've got to go check it out. Come here and talk to Colin until Mr. Maddison gets back."

"Talk to him? What do I say?"

"Tell him to relax. Tell him that help is on the way. Tell him not to try something dumb and injure himself."

"Colin, this is Leah . . . are you really in there?"

"Where's Nathan?"

"He'll be back."

"What are you doing here?"

"The whole town's here." Nathan heard Leah shout as he crashed out the front door and into the brightness of the early afternoon sun.

Pushing through the crowd, he ran to the Mercantile and rattled the front door. He placed his face to the glass and screamed, "Mr. Anderson? Are you in there?"

He heard nothing and started to turn to go back to the bank when he noticed something strange on the floor of the store. With a sudden reckless lunge, he rammed the tall double doors with his shoulder, and they swung open.

"Mr. Anderson!" he hollered, running to the side of a man lying in the aisle between the dry goods and the hardware.

THREE

Nathan pulled the gag out of Harris Anderson's mouth and fumbled at the ropes that tied the store owner. The hemp burned into his fingers as he tugged at the knot.

"What happened?"

"Three of them . . . they got the jump on me . . . took mainly cash and guns. Tony's tied up in the back room," he panted.

"Must be the ones that robbed the bank," Nathan surmised.

"The bank? They got the bank? Did anyone get hurt?"

"Eh . . . well . . ." Nathan hesitated. "No one's in too bad a shape. I mean, no one got shot. You all right? Should I go find the doc?"

"Nate, I'll take care of Tony. Is your daddy still down at the county seat?"

"Yes, sir. He's in Austin."

"Lettin' him go was the dumbest thing this town ever did!"

"The mayor said he wired Austin about the bank, so I guess the sheriff will be coming up. I'll go tell them about the Mercantile."

"Nate, go up and down Main Street and see that no one else has been robbed also."

"Yes, sir . . . eh, Mr. Anderson, is it all right if I don't work today? Colin's stuck in the safe at the bank, and I promised to stay with him until they get him out."

"Stuck in the safe? How in the world did he—"

"Eh . . . it's just the kind of thing that only Colin can do," Nathan reported.

"Listen, stop by in the morning. I'm goin' to close up and take inventory to see what else might be missing. Then I'll stir up a crew of men and see if we can find some tracks before the wind blows them all to Utah."

Nathan passed word of the holdups to all the other businesses. None had been aware of the robberies.

Then he returned to the bank. Mr. Maddison and Brady Wheeler were unbolting the back of the safe from the stone wall. Leah stared in fascination, twirling her brown hair on her finger.

"Mr. Maddison, what are you doing?" Nathan inquired.

"The Central Pacific telegraphed and said the only tools that could do the job were fastened to a mail car in Battle Mountain Station. If we get the safe to them, we can use the tools."

"You're goin' to take the whole safe to Battle Mountain?"

"Yes, it seems to be our only choice."

"Can you lift this thing? I mean, what freight wagon can hold it?"

"How about Abel Mercee's Buffalo Tight #1?" Leah shouted.

Nathan's eyes lit up. "Thunder's wagon? Sure!"

"Is it still around?" Mr. Maddison asked.

"Yeah, but it will be rusted. Mr. Mercee left it here when he moved to Bisbee," Nathan reported.

"Brady, I'll finish this up. Go see if you can get that wagon in rolling shape," Mr. Maddison commanded.

"Should I go help him?" Nathan asked.

"No . . . no. You talk to Colin. Keep talking to him."

Trying to stay out of the others' way, Nathan crawled up by the safe door and shouted into the crack.

"Colin! It's me, Nathan. They robbed the Mercantile, too!"

"Did anyone catch them yet? Don't let them hang them until I get out. I want to see them hang."

"No," Nathan hollered, "they haven't been caught. What did they look like?"

"Mean!"

"What?"

"They were mean-looking—bandannas, guns, dirty hats, tobacco stains on their vest . . . you know the type."

"Colin, did you know we're taking the safe to Battle Mountain Station?"

"Yeah, but . . ."

Nathan could hear Colin begin to cry.

"What is it? Colin?"

"I'll die in this steel box out in that heat!" he sobbed.

"Tell him we're not going until after dark," Mr. Maddison reported as he pulled the last bolt from the wall.

"Colin . . . we aren't going until after dark."

"What if the wagon breaks down? What if we're stranded? I'll bake like a turkey!" he moaned.

"It won't happen . . . we'll get you there," Nathan assured him.

"Are you going with us?" Colin hollered.

"I'll be there. Now sit still! They're going to try and pull the safe off the wall."

"Don't let the door close all the way," he shouted.

"It's all fixed. Don't worry about that."

"Nathan!"

"Yeah?"

"I'm hungry!"

"That's good . . . that's good, Colin."

"Why?"

"'Cause you're thinking about something other than this lousy safe."

Nathan spent the rest of the afternoon at the bank next to the safe. About 4:00 P.M., Leah brought him a loaf of fresh-baked bread, some slices of roast beef, and a bowl of boiled turnips and cabbage, which he ate quickly.

Nathan was reading a book to Colin entitled *Stuart Brannon and the Argentine Outlaws* by Hawthorne H. Miller when Brady Wheeler came in and announced it was time to load up.

"Did you tell my mother what's going on?" Nathan asked Leah.

"Yeah, she sent your coat, your canteen, and your carbine. She said to be careful and tell ya she was prayin' for you and for Colin."

Praying? Lord, how come I haven't been praying? Please keep Colin alive . . . You've got to help him!

"Listen, we should be back tomorrow afternoon. Could you tell Mr. Anderson what I'm doing, and, well, could you take some . . . meat scraps and—"

"And feed that chicken-killing vulture?"

"Domingo's a hawk. Just toss the meat up into the air. He'll come get it. Please? He needs to eat every other day."

"Oh, all right." Leah sighed. "Nathan?"

"Yeah?"

"I'll be prayin' for you and Colin, too."

"Thanks."

"Nathan!" a muffled voice shouted.

"It's all right, Colin . . . they're going to load you up now."

The evening sun had dropped behind the western hills when the safe was loaded by eight strong men into Abel Mercee's Buffalo Tight #1 wagon. A six-up team of mules led the way with Brady Wheeler driving. Mr. Maddison sat next to Nathan in the back of the wagon, which no longer sported a tailgate. Two other men rode horses behind.

"It's getting darker in here, Nathan!" Colin shouted.

"It's gettin' darker out here, too. Maybe you can get some sleep."

"No!" Colin shouted. "I won't sleep . . . I can't sleep."

"How come?"

"'Cause I'm afraid I won't wake up," he sobbed.

Nathan reached over and spun the broken dial on the safe. It twirled free like nothing was happening on the inside.

"What are you doing?" Colin yelled.

"Just twisting the dial. You want me to stop?"

"No . . . no! Keep it up. Then I know you're really out there."

For the next two hours Nathan and Mr. Maddison took turns talking to Colin and spinning the dial on the safe. Sometime after the sixth time Mr. Maddison sang through "Amazing Grace," Nathan nodded off.

He dreamed about sitting on top of the Heartford Hotel and watching three men rob the bank. But instead of riding horses to get away, they rode pigs. Huge, ugly, long-tusked, wild pigs.

"Nate." Mr. Maddison poked him. "Can you take a spell? I keep dozing off."

"Oh . . . yes, sir . . . is Colin asleep?"

"I'm not asleep, Riggins. I happen to be starving to death! Are you out there? How come you're not twisting that dial? Are you eating? I can smell ham. Maybe you could slip a slice of . . . a really thin slice of ham in here! Nathan? Are you there?"

Nathan's voice was hoarse, and every bone in his body ached for sleep as the wagon creaked its way up the Battle Mountain Station road. One of the outriders had switched with Brady Wheeler to drive the rig, and Nathan could whiff the smell of tobacco in the man's pipe. The summer night sky, painted with stars, seemed much brighter with the absence of a moon.

Suddenly he stopped twisting the dial as the heavy metal object fell like a brick into his hand.

"Hey!" he yelped. "It broke!"

"Nathan?" Colin called. "I don't hear you twisting the dial. Nathan!"

"I'm here, Colin. The thing broke. I'm sorry, but the dial broke off—or something."

"What do you mean it broke? It can't break."

"I didn't mean to do it. It just fell off in my hand, that's all. Listen, I'll tap on the safe."

"Nathan, is there a hole in the safe where the dial was?" Colin asked.

Nathan probed in the darkness with his hand. "Yeah . . . but, I mean, there's another metal plate. It doesn't go clear through," he reported to Colin.

"I know that. Now reach in there and see if you can feel a steel rod."

"A rod? What do you mean, a rod?"

"You know . . . about the size of your thumb. It should be sticking out where the dial used to be, but pointing to the right."

"Yeah," Nathan hollered. "I found it. Now what?"

"Pull it."

"Pull it? What do you mean, pull it?"

"Pull it in the direction it's pointing. Pull it, Nathan!"

"I can't pull it! It doesn't budge, Colin."

"Wait, Nathan! Wait until I wiggle the door. When I'm wiggling the door, you pull the rod."

"Hey! It's moving, Colin! Keep shoving the door . . . yeah, it's moving."

"Nate?" Mr. Maddison shook himself awake and stood up at the back of the rambling iron wagon. "What's happening?"

With a tandem effort, Nathan shoved the rod another inch just as Colin thrust at the door. Suddenly the heavy safe door swung open, catching Mr. Maddison in the chest as he started to stand up.

"It's open!" Colin shouted, gasping for fresh air.

Stumbling, trying to catch his balance, Mr. Maddison shoved the door away from him. The heavy door crashed closed. And Mr. Maddison tumbled off the back of the wagon.

The driver, who had been half asleep, reined up the team, and the outriders trotted up.

"What's goin' on?"

"Maddison's on the ground."

"We had it open. The door was open!" Nathan cried. He heard kicking from inside the safe, and immediately he grabbed the pin and shoved it to the right. Once again the door flew open. This time Colin dove out into the night, rolled off the back of the wagon, and crashed into his father who was being helped to his feet. Both plunged full-spraddle onto the packed dirt roadway.

For fifteen minutes shouts, hugs, tears, and an occasional joyous gunshot filled the night air like a Fourth of July celebration in a gold camp.

An hour later, the wagon was well on its way back to Galena. Nathan and Colin sat side by side next to Mr. Maddison who was driving. Colin's hands still trembled as he clutched Nathan's canteen in his lap.

"I can't believe you didn't bring any food! You could have starved to death out here. What if you took a wrong turn and got lost?"

"There aren't any turns on this road," Nathan replied.

"Well . . . there could have been a storm. If a blizzard blew in and all of you were stranded, what would you eat? My word, you've got to think about these things!"

"Colin, it's July! We won't get a blizzard. Besides, we'll get back to Galena before daylight."

"I haven't eaten since breakfast, and I can't get my mind off food."

"Well," Nathan said searching for an idea, "tell me about . . . eh, safes. How did you know what was inside that dial?"

"I collect them."

"You collect safes?"

"No. I collect books about safes. Companies are always sending catalogs to father, and I collect them. Did you know they once made a safe so heavy that when they placed it aboard ship, the ship sank?"

"Eh . . . no, I didn't know that." Nathan shrugged.

"Well, there's a lot of interesting things about safes you don't know, so I'll tell you."

And he did.

Somewhere between the story of a man who kept fake snakes in his safe and daylight, Nathan fell asleep.

Galena bustled with confusion when they arrived back in town. The streets streamed with loud, noisy people. Everyone talked of the holdups, but no one seemed to know what to do next.

Except Colin.

He went to the Drover's Cafe, ate two orders of ham, eggs, biscuits, and gravy and then trotted home and went to bed.

Mr. Maddison tried to put some order back into the bank and began to determine how much the thieves had stolen. Down at the Mercantile, Mr. Anderson, although extremely pessimistic, was open for business again. And everyone was demanding that the mayor and the whole city council resign for dismissing Marshal Riggins.

Several men had combed the countryside looking for the outlaws, but they returned without any clues whatsoever. As far as Nathan could determine, no one saw the men enter town, and no one saw them leave. Most figured that the Mercantile was robbed first, but even that was debated. A number of merchants, including Mr. Anderson, threatened to pull out of town if they didn't get better protection.

Nathan filled in Leah and Mr. Walker on the nighttime ride in the former buffalo wagon. He was just leaving to go home when Leah called out, "Your old hawk ain't there, so I threw the scraps to the dogs."

"Domingo isn't there?"

"That's what I said."

"But he knows that I feed him every other day. He wouldn't—"

"Well, he ain't there. Maybe he lost his calendar. He probably flew off to the mountains like all decent hawks ought to."

"He'll be back later. I'll check on him after I get something to eat."

"You goin' to go get some sleep?" she asked.

"Nah. I'm not that tired. I'll probably go see if I can help Mr. Anderson at the Mercantile."

Nathan left the barber shop, cut down the alley beside the closed Oriental Cleaners, and traveled up the back street to his house. Tona performed his ritual of limping halfway across the yard to greet him and then returned to his rug.

Nathan fell asleep between the second helping of potatoes and a double serving of apple cobbler. He sort of noticed his mother leading him off to bed.

His father's voice startled him awake. His dad and mother were having a discussion in the kitchen.

"Dad!" Nathan shouted running into the room where his parents sat at the table drinking coffee. "Did you hear about the holdups? And Colin got locked in the—"

The shining badge caught Nathan's attention.

"They made you marshal again?" he asked.

"Nope. I hired on with the county sheriff. I'll be the deputy in charge of this end of the county."

"Can we still live in Galena?"

"For a while. If the town plays out, we might need to move."

"Are you going to catch those outlaws?"

"I'm going to take a look at it, but they've got over a day's head start, and from what I hear, no one has any idea which way they went. Anyway, eat some supper and I'll be back shortly. I've got to catch Mr. Maddison before he and Colin pull out."

Nathan's father yanked on his hat and hurried out the door.

"Supper? Is it that late? Hey, what did Dad mean about Colin pulling out?"

"Mr. Maddison has decided to pay off the depositors the best he can and shut down the bank. He's leaving Mr. Melton to settle up here. He and Colin are riding up to the Central Pacific and will meet Mrs. Maddison in Carson City."

"They're taking a vacation?"

"I'm not sure they're coming back," his mother replied.

"What do you mean? Just because they were robbed? What if father recovers the money? They aren't leavin' for good, are they?"

His mother came over to the table and rested her hand on Nathan's shoulder. "Well . . . if I were you, I'd skip supper and go talk to Colin."

"Eh . . . yes, ma'am, I mean, is it all right with you?"

"Go on." She nodded.

Nathan ran right down the middle of Main Street and whipped around the corner to Colin's big two-story house. There was a buggy parked out front and several large trunks loaded in the back. The front door of the house stood open.

"Colin!"

"Up here!" came a shout. "Come on up."

Nathan ran up the stairs two at a time and burst into

Colin's room. His dark-haired friend stood staring out the window.

"What's all this about leaving? You guys aren't leaving for good . . . are you?" Nathan pleaded.

When he reached the far side of the room, he could see that Colin was crying.

Lord . . . I don't . . . I don't know what to say. Help me not say something dumb.

Suddenly, Nathan began to cry. He tried to stop. He brushed his eyes on the long sleeves of his shirt and blurted out, "Colin, I don't want you to move!"

"I've got to . . . I've got to, Nathan . . . I can't stay."

"But, I mean . . . your dad can . . . he can start a new bank, or open an assay office, or sell mining stock, or work for the Central Pacific."

Colin brushed back his tears and turned to face Nathan. "We lost most of our money in the robbery. Father's been loanin' out a lot, and people have moved off without repaying. We've got just about enough to settle accounts."

"But my dad can catch those robbers. You'll get the money back!" Nathan insisted.

"Maybe, but this town's dying, and Father says now it's time to move."

"Let me talk to him. Maybe I can change his mind," Nathan pleaded.

"It's not just him, Nathan. I want to move, too."

"What? Why?"

"I got real scared in that safe, Nate. No, really, I'm afraid to live here. I want to go somewhere that has policemen and incandescent lights and indoor plumbing . . . I'm scared out here. I've always been scared. Nathan, I've never been brave like you are. You know that. You and Leah tease me about it all the time."

"But we didn't mean anything. Colin, you're my very best friend in the whole world! You can't go!"

"One of your two best friends," he corrected.

"Are you leavin' tonight?"

"We're leaving just as soon as your father gets through talking to mine."

"Couldn't you wait for morning? How about Leah? Does she know you're going?"

"I don't think so."

"Listen, I'm going to go get her. She'll be mad at me if I don't tell her. And you know what she's like if she gets mad."

Colin broke into a smile. "Yeah, go get Leah."

"You won't leave until we get back?"

"I promise."

"Are you sure you can keep your father from pulling out?"

"You've seen me throw a tantrum, haven't you?" Colin grinned.

"You're the best," Nathan teased.

"Thank you." Colin bowed. "Now go get Leah. This is my last valise to pack."

FOUR

Nathan could feel the dust fog up to his face from the pounding of his feet as he ran up Main Street shouting at the top of his voice, "Leah! Leah!"

She bounded down the stairs with one black boot laced up and another in her hands.

"Nathan T. Riggins, you better have a good reason for screamin' at me!" she hollered, flopping down on the bottom worn wooden stair and pulling on her other boot. "What are you hollerin' about anyway?"

"Colin . . . it's Colin!" Nathan panted, bending at the waist to catch his breath.

"He ain't caught in the safe again, is he?"

"No . . . no . . . he's leavin'. Colin's leavin'!"

"Where's he goin'?"

"He's movin', Leah! The Maddisons are moving out of Galena!"

"You mean . . . he won't be here for school or nothin'?"

"School?" Nathan shouted. "He won't be here for breakfast! He's leavin' town right now! Hurry!"

Nathan grabbed Leah by her hand and pulled her out into the street. They began running toward Colin's house.

"I can run jist fine without you holdin' my hand," she puffed, trying to keep up. Nathan started to drop his grip, but Leah squeezed his hand even tighter. They arrived out of breath and still hand in hand. Colin and his father stood by the loaded carriage talking to Mr. Riggins.

"Are you really leavin' us?" Leah blurted out.

Nathan noticed that Colin had washed his face and now seemed to have regained his composure.

"Well, it was bound to happen. Gold mining camps are so unstable, you know," Colin pronounced.

"I don't want you to move," Leah protested.

"My word, now, you aren't going to get emotional, are you? You see, Riggins? Women just can't handle a goodbye."

Just then Leah threw her arms around Colin's neck, hugged him tight, and kissed him on the cheek. "Well, I'm goin' to really miss you, no matter how snobby you act!"

When she pulled back, Nathan could see Colin's face blush red and tears flood down his cheeks.

"Good heavens," Colin choked, "the dust sure is bad this evening!" He wiped his eyes on his sleeves.

"It's time, Colin," Mr. Maddison called, climbing into the carriage and lifting the reins.

For a moment Nathan and Colin just stared at each other.

"Well," Colin swallowed hard, "you surely aren't going to kiss me, too, are you?"

Nathan threw his arms around Colin's shoulders and hugged him tight. Both boys had tears streaming down their cheeks.

"You got to write to me and tell me where you're living," Nathan demanded.

"I will, I promise."

"And . . . and you'll let me borrow your latest Brannon book," Nathan added.

Colin climbed up into the carriage.

"I will. You know I will."

"You can come back and visit," Leah called out as the carriage pulled away from the house.

Both Nathan and Leah ran alongside of it as it rolled down Main Street.

"Maybe we'll see each other again." Colin was crying unashamedly now. "Thank you, guys, for treatin' me square. You two were the best friends I ever had."

Unable to keep up with the wagon, Nathan and Leah stopped in the middle of the street. Colin turned around and stared at them. Then he shouted, "And don't forget when you write to me that it's Maddison with two *d*'s!" The words faded as the carriage disappeared in a cloud of dust and with the high-pitched squeak of wheels.

Nathan looked away from Leah and wiped his face and eyes on his bandanna.

Leah slipped her arm into Nathan's as they walked back toward Walker's Barber Shop. They didn't say anything until they sat down on the edge of the raised wooden sidewalk. Leah released her arm from Nathan's and rested her elbows on her knees, her chin in her hands.

"Well, the Lord sure does have surprises every day, don't He?" She sighed.

"It just doesn't seem real," Nathan added. "It all spins around in my head and makes everything confusing."

"Yeah, that's it." She nodded. "You jist keep hopin' that things is goin' to settle down quick, but they don't."

"I keep thinking about when it will be our turn."

"Yours and mine?"

"Yeah. Dad said we weren't movin' for a while since he got hired on as a deputy sheriff, but if this town keeps goin' down, the day will come when we move."

"I suppose more folks will move with the bank gone."

"Yeah, they'll get awful tired ridin' into Battle Mountain Station to do their banking. What do you think, Leah—will your dad stay through the winter?"

"I don't know. Every day he reads them out-of-town papers more and more. And every day there seem to be fewer customers. Are you workin' tomorrow?"

"Yeah, I think so. I'll go check with Mr. Anderson in the morning . . . after I find Domingo and feed him."

"I told you he ain't there."

"Oh, he's probably back on his perch at the Heartford right now."

They looked at each other. Then Nathan bolted down the street toward the abandoned hotel.

"Nathan . . . wait! I cain't run fast in this dress . . . wait up!"

Suddenly Nathan slid to a stop and turned back toward her. "Well, hurry up!" he called.

They continued to the Heartford walking side by side.

"That's the first time you ever done that." She smiled.

"Did what?"

"Stopped and waited for me."

"Oh . . . well, it just seemed to be the right thing to do."

They rounded the corner by the closed Central Nevada Assay Office and hiked up to the hotel.

"See, I told you that old hawk was gone," Leah said triumphantly.

"Well, he might be over on the other . . ." Nathan trotted to the far side of the building with Leah right behind him.

"He's gone, Nathan. That's all there is to it."

"This is a good time to hunt. He'll be back later."

"I thought you said hawks like to hunt in the mornin's."

"Sure . . . normally . . . but I've not been around, and he's probably worried about—"

"Now don't you go tellin' me that hawk is worried about you!"

Nathan strained to gaze at the twilight sky. "No, he's probably worried about his next meal. I'll come feed him in the morning."

"And I say he should be off in the wilderness some-place."

"Sure . . . when he's a little more mature, he'll—"

"He'll what? You think he's going to fly down and shake your hand and promise to write. Come on, Nathan. Hawks don't say goodbye." Leah turned and started walk-ing back toward Main Street. Nathan tagged along behind.

Lord, not two of them in one day. Domingo was just a bird, but he was part of my routine, part of daily life. I just don't want it all to fall apart at once. Please, Lord. I got to at least say goodbye to that hawk.

The next morning the topic of conversation on the side-walks of Galena centered on just how long each person was planning on staying before they moved elsewhere.

Many held on to the hope that the Shiloh Mine would reopen by August. At the height of the gold mining activ-ity, sale of mining stock had flowed without control. Although Nathan didn't really understand the details, right after Christmas the Shiloh's production fell off, the mining certificates drastically lost their value, and the principal owners were forced to sell out to a company in

San Francisco. Company officials came to town and closed the mine, saying they would reopen soon under a new ownership.

But that was February. It was now July, and the only rumor they had from San Francisco was that the company who purchased major interest in the mine had sold it to some foreign investors. The only thing operating at the Shiloh were the huge steam-driven pumps that kept the lower tunnels from filling with water.

Meanwhile, many in Galena were waiting, hanging on to see what would happen to the mine. With the departure of its last bank, a good number in Galena, even those who still held some stock in the Shiloh, had decided it was time to move.

Even Mr. Anderson talked about closing the Mercantile.

"It's like kicking a man when he's down," he told Nathan the next morning. "You know, two years ago, if I got held up, I could recoup the losses in a couple of weeks. But now it will take all year if the money and firearms aren't recovered. That is, a whole year at the present rate of sales. If things slide more . . . well, I've moved and started a store before. I suppose I can do it again."

Nathan tossed his hat on a worn wooden peg by the back door of the store and pulled down his clerk's apron.

"Eh . . . Nate," Mr. Anderson continued, "what I'm leadin' to is this—I just can't afford to have you work here anymore, at least not for a while. Tony has a family to support, and now that your daddy's the deputy sheriff, you'll have groceries on the table . . . well, I hope you understand. You're a good worker, and I'll hire you any time I can afford it but . . ."

Nathan put the apron back on the hook.

"Yeah . . . sure. I, eh . . . I understand," he stammered, yanking his hat back on his head. "Just . . . eh, well, let me know if you'd like me to fill in for you or anything."

"Sorry, Nate," Mr. Anderson apologized. "I hope to have your pay by Saturday night. I don't have much cash right now, if you can wait 'til then."

"Huh? Oh, yeah. Sure. That's fine," Nathan mumbled as he slipped out the back door.

Scooting up the alley to Main Street, Nathan plodded along, head down, watching the cracks in the weathered wooden sidewalk.

Lord, it's gettin' worse. Every day things just keep falling apart. I don't understand. Why is this happening?

"Well, Mr. Nathan T. Riggins, you plannin' on marchin' right by me without speakin'?"

"Leah! Oh . . . hey, I'm sorry. I was just . . . thinkin'."

"Why ain't you at work?"

"I was laid off. Mr. Anderson can't afford to pay me anymore."

"No! Well . . . well," Leah stammered. "Did you feed that chicken hawk yet?"

"Eh . . . he wasn't there this morning. Maybe he is gone for good."

"Let's go for a picnic!" Leah beamed.

"What?"

"Saddle up Onepenny, and let's ride over to the Shoshones. I'll pack a dinner."

"I just lost my job and all you can think about is a picnic?"

"I cain't do nothin' about gettin' your job back, but I been wantin' a picnic all month. So why not today?"

"Well, I, eh . . . need to look for another job, and—"

"Do you want to go with me on a picnic or not?" Leah demanded.

A big smile broke across Nathan's face. "How come you can get me thinking about something else so quick?"

"'Cause of my absolutely irresistible beauty," she teased.

"Nope, that's not it," Nathan replied and dodged as Leah swung wildly to clobber him in the arm.

Within thirty minutes Leah, riding a gray mare that belonged to her father, and Nathan on Onepenny rode across the valley floor toward the Shoshone Mountains. When they crossed the river, Nathan turned back and glanced at the distant town of Galena in the western hills.

"They just come and go," he sighed.

"People or towns?" Leah questioned.

"Both . . . I guess. Maybe the luckiest people in the world are the ones that live in the same place all their lives. All their friends are always right there with them."

"And all their enemies," Leah added.

Nathan tuned back toward the Shoshones and spurred Onepenny to a trot. Leah bounced her way along trying to catch up.

"Well, I don't think it's so great to stay in one place your whole life," she hollered as she gained ground.

"Why not?"

"'Cause if you would have stayed in your home town, you'd still be in Indiana, and we would never have met."

"Did I ever mention this girl I knew back home? She would always say that one day we—"

"Don't you go tellin' me about some old Eastern girl, Nathan Riggins!"

"You brought it up," he insisted.

"I did not," she corrected. "I mentioned Indiana, but I

didn't say nothin' about no girl! I'll race you to Rabbit Springs!"

"There's absolutely no way you can beat me," Nathan bragged.

In a haze of dust the two galloped up the gradual slope of the Shoshone Mountains.

Twenty minutes later, with Onepenny worked at full lather, Nathan pulled up near the springs and waited for Leah. She crashed into the clearing and ran the mare straight into the water of Rabbit Springs.

"I won!" she shouted.

"What do you mean, you won? I've been waiting for several minutes."

"Yes, but you were waiting ten feet from the springs. I got to the water first."

"That doesn't count!"

Leah stuck out her tongue and wrinkled her nose, causing the freckles across her face to wiggle. "It does too count, Nathan T. Riggins. You're just a poor loser."

Nathan slid off Onepenny and began to pull off his saddle.

"Is this where we're havin' the picnic?" Leah asked.

"No, let's leave the horses here. I know a place up at the top of the chaparral that will be great for a picnic."

"You been here before?"

"Yeah, I was just here two days ago—right before the robbery."

"How come you ain't never asked me to come out here before?"

Nathan ignored her question and hiked on up to the lookout rocks where he had spotted the pronghorns.

By the time Leah caught up with him, he was poking at a fire circle that smelled of a fairly recent campfire.

"I think someone was camping here last night," Nathan reported.

"Well, I don't blame them. Look how far you can see!" Leah pointed to the west. "Is that dark spot over on those distant mountains Galena?"

"Eh . . . yeah," Nathan muttered, "but what were they doin' camping here?"

"Well, it's a free country. They got just as much right as we do, don't they?"

"Yes, but this has always been my own private—"

"Nathan, you don't own this place."

"But . . . I wanted it to be my own private spot to come and think and plan and pray, you know?"

"You brought me up here," Leah pointed out.

"Sure, it can be for both of us. But now some strangers—it looks like they had several horses—have made it their camp too."

"They're just passin' through. I can't imagine why you're makin' such a big concern out of it. Shall I spread dinner right here?"

"Eh . . . yeah . . . sure. That's fine. But it doesn't make sense to me to camp up here. Down by the springs is the best place to put up for the night. You got a better view here, but it's not nearly as comfortable."

Nathan sat cross-legged and watched as Leah unrolled a small canvas tarp and began to pull fried chicken and biscuits out of a tin box.

After several minutes of talking about nothing but food, Nathan leaned back against a large boulder and stared out across the high mountain desert below them.

"Leah, do you think the Maddisons might return if we got their funds back?"

"We? You mean, you and me?"

"No, I mean if anyone was able to recover what was stolen from the bank, would they come back?"

"I don't know . . . once you say good-bye and all, it's kind of hard to return, don't you think? Besides, I don't think Colin's mama ever liked livin' here. Did you notice how she was always takin' trips and wantin' to go somewhere else?"

"Yeah . . . I suppose you're right. Anyway, I'm going to try to help Dad find the bank robbers. It's for certain they won't come back without the money."

"I thought your daddy didn't have a clue as to who they were."

"Well, perhaps I can dig around town and find out a little more. I don't know . . . I've got to do somethin', and since I'm not workin', it's a cinch I can't come up here for a picnic every day."

"I don't see why not," she teased. "Unless you don't like the company."

Nathan stared out across the desert and poked at the dead ashes in the rock fire ring with a short stick that had been burned on one end.

"I like the company. You're the only friend I've got left."

"That's why you tolerate me," she puffed. "I'm the only one left in town."

"Hey! Look at that!" Nathan pulled a short, light blue bottle out of the ashes. "They tossed something away."

"Nathan, that's one of them special Heartford Hotel liquor bottles. You know, the type they give when you stay in one of them big, old upstairs rooms."

"How do you know that?"

"'Cause Miss D'Imperio stayed there a little while, remember? 'Course she didn't drink none, but she did think the bottle was cute and had it sittin' right there on her dresser."

"But the Heartford has been closed for months. Where did they get this bottle?"

"They could have stayed there last fall and just emptied it yesterday."

"But it's only a little sample. Men who are camping out horseback wouldn't carry a sample of liquor around for months."

"What are you sayin', Nathan?"

"Well . . . maybe they took this from the Heartford recently."

"But it's closed."

"They could break in and steal stuff."

"Who would want to do that?"

"The same ones who robbed the bank and the Mercantile!" Nathan shouted.

Leah quickly looked around at the boulders. "You mean, we're sitting where them bank robbers spent the night?"

"Maybe. Let's go back and check out the Heartford. If we find out they stole things there, then maybe this is the trail."

"But," Leah questioned, "that was two days ago. They would have left a lot sooner than that."

"Uh . . . yeah, well . . . maybe they got lost or circled around. Yeah, that's it! Perhaps they went north to throw everyone off and then circled east! Let's go back to Galena."

"Right now?" she protested. "We ain't even finished the cake."

"We can eat it on the way home. Pack up the goods. I

want to mark their trail with rocks, you know, just in case Dad wants to ride out here and look at this camp."

"Well, Nathan T. Riggins, you surely know how to show a girl a grand time."

"Huh?"

"Oh, nothin'!" Leah sighed in disgust.

F I V E

Nathan wanted to ride right up to the Heartford Hotel and look around immediately.

But there were chores to do.

He rubbed down Onepenny and then Leah's mare. He grained them, checked their hooves, and put all the tack carefully in its place. Leah had hiked down the street from the livery to her house to put up the picnic supplies.

Then Nathan checked in with his mother.

"You're back early," she observed.

"Yeah . . . I, eh, we thought we might—," Nathan mumbled.

"You were nice to Leah, weren't you?"

"Huh? Oh . . . sure. I'm always nice to Leah. Say, where's Dad?"

"He said he heard that Big-Fist Tom might have seen some strangers pass his way a couple of days ago, so he rode out to visit with him."

"South of town? No, they didn't go south. They went . . ."

"You know something about this?" his mother asked.

"Well, actually, not yet . . . but maybe. We did find a new camp over in the Shoshones. It could have been the bank robbers."

"Or any of 1,000 other people in this county. Now don't you go meddlin' around and get into trouble."

"No, ma'am. I think I'll go down to the Heartford now."

"I don't want you too disappointed if that hawk's flown off. It was bound to happen."

"That's what Leah keeps telling me."

"Before you go, split some wood for the cookstove for supper."

"Yes, ma'am."

Ten minutes later Nathan came in carrying an arm load of split white pine. "Mother, did you notice that Tona's not even getting up anymore? He just lays there. He'll get all stove-up if he doesn't move around more."

"I'm afraid Tona's doing the best he can, Nathan. He's just . . . well, Nate . . ." His mother looked away. "Your father thinks Tona's dying."

"No! He's just having a bad spell. It's probably the heat. Come fall he'll be running around again," Nathan argued.

"I sure hope so. Are you leaving now?"

"Yeah, Leah and I thought we would—"

"Leah's going with you?" she asked.

"Eh . . . yeah. That's proper, isn't it?"

"You're spending a lot of time with that young lady this summer."

Nathan pulled on his hat and turned to the door. "But everyone else is moving away."

"Do you know what I hear from the ladies around town?" she asked.

"What?"

"They say, 'My, your Nathan and that Miss Walker certainly make a handsome pair.'"

Nathan could feel his face flush. "That's okay, isn't it?"

"Oh, it's quite acceptable when you're sixteen. But you're barely fourteen," she reminded him.

"So . . . you think I shouldn't . . . spend so much time with Leah?"

His mother took a deep breath and sighed. "Well, no, that's not it. I just . . . I want you to treat her proper. She's not merely some neighbor kid down the street. She's special, and if I ever hear of you being mean, well, your father and I will both take you out behind the woodpile."

"Yes, ma'am. I'll be home for supper." He left the house making sure to close the front door as quietly as possible.

Lord, I think Mom's kind of worried about everything lately. Help her to relax and trust You more about leading our family. And, Lord, I surely do want to treat Leah proper.

Nathan stepped into Walker's Barber Shop and noticed that Leah's father was busy with a customer.

"Excuse me, Mr. Walker, is Leah upstairs?"

"Yeah, but I, eh . . . don't think—"

"I'll go see her."

"Well, you might want to . . ." Mr. Walker hesitated.

"Thank you, sir." Nathan spun at the front door and ran back outside. He heard Mr. Walker say, "That's the lad I was tellin' you about."

Telling him what about me?

Nathan's boots tromped up the rough-cut wooden stairs on the outside of the barber shop to the house above. He knocked on the door. Leah's stepmother met him at the door.

"Oh, hi, Mrs. Walker. I was lookin' for Leah."

"Yes?"

"Well, is she here?"

"Yes, she is, Nathan."

"Oh . . . I mean, could I visit with her a minute? I wanted to . . . we were—"

"Nathan, Leah's not feelin' too well right now. Perhaps you could stop back later?"

"But we were going to—"

"I'm sorry, she's resting," Mrs. Walker added with finality.

"Yes, ma'am. Well, could you please tell her I stopped to see her? Tell her I'm headin' down to . . . feed Domingo."

"I'll tell her."

Nathan sauntered down the steps, pausing several times. *This doesn't make any sense. We just spent the morning together. She was feelin' fine. We laughed and raced. She promised to go with me to the Heartford. Did I miss something, Lord? What did I say?*

Hiking down the alley to the Heartford, Nathan reviewed the morning and remembered the little blue bottle in the ashes near Rabbit Springs.

"Well, I'm goin' to look around the hotel," he mumbled.

Not finding any trace of Domingo on the roof of the Heartford, Nathan circled the old building. The front door was boarded shut, as were all of the windows facing the front porch. Hiking up the hill and around to the back of the building, he noticed nothing unusual until he found a mint plant that had been struggling to grow on the shady side of the building just outside a kitchen window. The plant was withered and looked as if it had been stepped on recently.

Poking at the window, Nathan couldn't get it to swing out. He pulled out his folding knife and slipped a blade between the frame and the sill. The window swung out freely.

"That's how someone could get in." He pulled himself up to the window and climbed through. "Now, Lord, I don't normally crawl into someone else's building. But they say that the McBrineys just walked away and abandoned this hotel. I don't have any idea who to ask for permission."

The kitchen was dark and the air stale. He could see boot tracks in the dust across the wooden floor. "Man, he must be wearin' big spurs 'cause look how those rowels are draggin'."

He walked out into the dining area of the hotel and then to the parlor.

I didn't think they left all the furniture. Everything's still sitting right where it used to be. There's Mr. McBriney's desk. It seems funny not to see him there chewing on that cigar and sorting through those statements.

Well, I've never been upstairs, but Leah said that's where they gave away those little blue bottles.

At the top of the wide, dust-caked mahogany staircase, Nathan discovered a long hall and sixteen doors, each door looking as if it led to a hotel room.

One at a time he entered the rooms. Most were the same. A bed with linen folded and stacked at the foot, a dresser with an empty wash basin, a small wardrobe closet, and padded seat chair. Some of the rooms had several pictures and mirrors. Others had none at all. All the rooms had a liquor sample in a blue bottle sitting by the wash basin.

Nathan was working his way east down the hall when he thought he heard a noise in the next room. Scurrying into the room at the southeast corner of the two-story hotel, Nathan was shocked at the sight.

"Domingo! But what . . ."

The hawk was walking across the floor toward Nathan. Then it turned and scooted behind the bed. Glancing around, Nathan noticed that there were feathers and bird droppings scattered around the room.

"You've been in here for two days! How'd you get in here? You sure didn't open the kitchen window with your pocket knife, did you?"

Nathan reached to the back of his trousers and pulled

out the heavy leather glove with the long, fringed gauntlet. Then he whistled at the bird.

"Come on, boy. I'll get you out of here. Come on, Domingo, come on!"

The bird hopped out from behind the bed, walked toward Nathan, lifted his wings about halfway, and then put them down without flapping them.

"You about worn out? You must be starved . . . and thirsty. There's no water in here!"

Nathan got down on his hands and knees and laid the gloved arm in front of the bird. Domingo took a couple of steps and hopped onto the glove.

"Okay. Now you just hang on, and I'll get you outside."

Nathan scooted out of the room with Domingo teetering on his arm. Gliding down the stairs as smoothly as possible, he pushed his way into the kitchen, hustled past the chopping block, and threw open the window.

"All right, boy, you fly out there to someplace safe, and I'll find you something to . . ."

The big hawk spread his wings and glided to the ground, but did not try to fly.

"Are you hurt? Hungry? You're starving to death, aren't you?"

Nathan crawled back out of the hotel and bent low to the ground, allowing Domingo to hop back on his arm.

"Well, I can't leave you on the ground 'cause the dogs would get you, and you can't fly, so . . ." Scouting around, Nathan ran up the hill behind the hotel to the privies. Lifting the bird high, he jiggled his arm, signaling the bird to jump off.

"You stay up there on the outhouse roof. I'll get you some water and food. You wait for me, you understand?"

Nathan ran all the way home. Finding his mother gone,

he filled a tin cup with water from the pump and grabbed a cooked pork chop lying under a towel next to the sink.

Arriving back at the Heartford, Nathan was relieved to find Domingo standing exactly where he had left him. He propped the water cup on top of the roof, and the brown and white hawk hopped over for a drink. Taking out his knife, Nathan sliced small bites off the pork chop and sprinkled them across the shake roof of the outhouse.

Domingo quickly swallowed several of the portions, took another drink, and then hopped up to the top ridge of the outhouse.

"You going to be all right now? What were you doing in there anyway? Somebody had a window open. That's it. There had to be someone in the hotel to open a window! I sure wish you could talk. On second thought, you'd just bawl me out for leavin' you in there for two days."

Nathan shoved his penknife back into his pocket and tramped down to the hotel, once again climbing in through the kitchen window. Leaping the stairs two at a time, he returned to the room on the southeast corner. Other than Domingo's droppings, Nathan couldn't find anything unusual about the room.

Even that little blue bottle is still by the basin. Maybe Domingo found a hole in the ceiling and—

"Look at that!" he blurted out. "You can see the front of the bank from here. A guy could sit here and see just who was coming in and going out. And the back door of the Mercantile!

"You could signal others when to go in and even which way to ride out of town. 'Course, you'd have to open the window to signal. Someone could sit up here and direct both holdups."

Leaving the corner room, Nathan swung open the door

of the room directly across the hall. It was the one room he had not checked out earlier.

"Hey . . . this is it! Someone's been staying in this room!"

He smelled cigarette smoke. In the corner were assorted empty air-tight fruit tins. Stale bread littered the floor, and there was an empty whiskey bottle lying on top of the mattress. Nathan pulled out the drawers of the dresser and found a heavy cotton sack with "Dr. Barker's Horse Liniment" printed on the front, under which was hand-written ".44-40."

"That's the Mercantile's loose bullet bag! The ones that robbed the store were up here!"

Nathan hustled down the stairs carrying the empty sack. Climbing out the kitchen window, he carefully closed it and ran up the alley toward his house.

"Domingo, when you feel strong, you better get back on the roof of the Heartford," he yelled as he glanced back at the privy.

His mother was sitting on the front porch doing needlework when he huffed his way into the yard. Tona lifted his head and beat his tail on the porch.

"What's the matter?" his mother asked.

"Is Daddy home yet?"

"Not yet. Why?"

"I found some evidence from the outlaws."

"What kind of evidence?"

"The cotton sack Mr. Anderson used for the loose .44-40 bullets at the Mercantile. It was stolen along with some revolvers."

"Where did you find it?"

"Upstairs in one of the rooms of the Heartford Hotel."

"Nathan Riggins, what were you doing up there? That

hotel is private property. I mean, someone somewhere owns it. I think."

"I was letting Domingo out. He got caught in one of the rooms, and I brought him out. But I found this up there."

"I'm sure your father will be very interested in it. But he won't be home for a couple more hours."

"A couple hours! Maybe I'll ride out to Big-Fist Tom's."

"You'd better go see Leah first."

"Leah? I went over there, and she was sick or something. Her stepmother said she couldn't visit."

"Well, she was over here a short while ago and quite upset, I might add. What did you do or say?"

"Me? I didn't do anything! We had a great time, and then she turns up sick."

"Well, stop by and see her on the way out to Big-Fist Tom's."

"Yes, ma'am, I will."

Tona looked up at Nathan and let out a faint, high-pitched bark.

"Nathan, I think he wants to go with you."

"Mom . . . I'll have to carry him the whole way."

"Well, whatever. But it seems like Tona's earned a free ride over the years that he's watched over you."

Nathan looked down at the dog whose only hint of happiness was the slapping of his tail on the porch.

"Yeah, you're right. He can have a ride any time. Wait here, boy, and I'll go saddle up Onepenny."

"Why don't you take your carbine," his mother urged. "You might see a varmit along the way, and Tona would enjoy the hunt."

"Eh . . . yeah, I'll take it."

As he saddled Onepenny, he wondered why his mother was suddenly so concerned about Tona's happiness. At her insistence, he tied his jacket on behind the cantle, lashed the scabbard and carbine to the left side of the saddle, and hoisted Tona into place.

"Did you get your canteen?"

"Yes, ma'am, it's in my saddlebags. But I'm just going to Big-Fist Tom's."

"Well, Tona might get thirsty. He hasn't felt too good today. I stuck some biscuits in the pocket of your jacket."

"Tona doesn't eat biscuits."

"Those are for you and your father. He probably skipped dinner. And don't forget to stop by and see Leah."

"Yes, ma'am."

Nathan rode up to Walker's Barber Shop. Carefully setting Tona on Onepenny's rump, he climbed down out of the saddle.

"Now you two wait for me . . . understand?"

Nathan left the reins dropped to the dirt road. Onepenny stood motionless, and Tona laid his head on Nathan's jacket and closed his eyes.

He had just started up the outside stairs when Mr. Walker called to him from inside the barber shop.

"Nathan?"

"Yes, sir?" He spun on the step and ducked into the barber shop. Nathan noticed that the man who had earlier been getting a haircut now sat on a bench inside the shop. There were business papers spread across a little table.

"Nathan, are you still lookin' for Leah?"

"Yes, sir. Mama said she stopped by after I was here. Is she feelin' any better?"

"I don't think so. That's what I want to talk to you about."

"Mr. Walker, I can't think of one thing I did or said

that would upset Leah. I promise you, I've always treated her square."

"No, no." Mr. Walker smiled. "She's not upset because of you. You've been the best influence she's ever had in her life. From the time you bought her those black shoes to the way you helped her know about God. In fact, I guess you two have got along too well."

"What do you mean," Nathan asked. "What's troubling her?"

"Well, I promised to let Leah tell you, but I'm worried sick about her. So don't let on that you know anything. You see, this is Mr. Hiram Silverman from Salt Lake City, and he just bought my barber shop."

"What? You sold out?"

"Yep. I figured it was time."

"But . . . what are you goin' to do? You aren't going to move, are you?"

"Yes, we'll be moving by the end of the month."

"But where?" Nathan moaned.

"We'll take a look at Austin and White Pine County. Maybe we'll try Arizona. Just not sure, Nate."

"But . . . but Leah can't move! I'll . . . sorely miss her!" Nathan gulped. "This just about breaks my heart."

"Well, there's a young lady who feels the exact same way, I assure you."

"Can I go up and see her?"

"Now it's not that easy. She's not home."

"Where is she? I've got to see her!"

"That's the problem. When she couldn't find you at home, she said she was goin' to saddle the mare and ride to where she could think and plan and pray. When I asked her where that was, she said it was a secret place, but you would know."

"Over by Rabbit Springs! We were just out there this morning."

"I'm surely glad you know where it is. Would you have time to ride out there and make sure she's all right?" Mr. Walker asked.

"Yes, sir, I've got Onepenny, and I'll . . . . Dad! Listen, Mr. Walker, I was on my way out to see if I could find my dad. He is out toward Big-Fist Tom's place. I think I found some evidence that will help catch the bank robbers."

"Oh . . . well, maybe you should go ahead and—"

"No, sir. Leah's more important than all the bank robbers on earth. If you see my dad come through town, tell him I found out that the outlaws holed up in the old Heartford Hotel before and after the crime. I think they camped near Rabbit Springs, which means they're probably in Utah by now." Nathan turned toward the door. "And . . . eh, would you tell him where I went?"

"I'll tell him, Nate. And thanks for going after Leah."

"Mr. Walker, I've never met anyone I like bein' with more than Leah—you know, other than my mama and daddy."

Nathan wanted to race off toward the Shoshone Mountains, but instead he set a pace that he knew Onepenny could keep up. Tona rode in his lap. The hot breeze dried his face even as the sun started its gradual summer descent. When he crossed the river, he pushed his hat back and let it hang by the stampede string on his back.

Lord, this is like a horrible, horrible nightmare. It's like everything and everyone important to me is being taken away. It's not fair! I don't want to . . . I can't imagine . . . Lord, do You know what it's like when all your friends just take off at once?

After a long pause, Nathan glanced up at the blue sky.

Yeah, You know, don't You? They all ran away and left You there on the cross. And You went ahead and did what needed to be done. Well, You're goin' to have to get me through 'cause in my heart I feel like I'm dyin'.

As he expected, Leah had hobbled the gray mare near Rabbit Springs. Nathan loosened the cinch on Onepenny but left him saddled. He took Tona to the spring to give him a drink and then placed him in the shade.

Pulling his Winchester .44-40 carbine from the scabbard, he hiked up the hill to the rock-pile lookout.

At a distance he spotted Leah waiting for him.

When he got closer, he could tell she had been crying.

"He told you, didn't he?" she called as he approached. "Your daddy?"

"Yeah, I asked him to let me tell you."

"He told me. Leah, he was worried sick about you and didn't know where you had ridden off to."

"Well, it's okay 'cause I couldn't figure out what to say to you. It's all I can do to even mention it now."

"I know. When he told me, I felt like . . . like—"

"Like you been robbed?" she asked.

"Yeah . . . that's it." Nathan sat down on the rocks next to Leah. "It's crazy. It's like someone picked up the whole world and is shakin' it out. Everything that used to be here is fallin' over there. Nothing's the same. Everything's different."

"I ain't movin', Nathan."

"What?"

"I done made up my mind I ain't movin'!" she insisted.

"But your daddy said that—"

"If he makes me move, I'll jist run away from home and come back to Galena."

"But what would you do? Where would you live?" Nathan asked.

"I'll get me a job at the Drover's Cafe and rent a room of my own. Maybe your mama would rent me that back room at your house. Do you think she'd rent it to me?"

The tears streamed down her face.

"Leah, I don't think either one of us believes that story."

"Well, it ain't fair. Nathan, I been prayin' and prayin' and prayin' that you and me wouldn't have to move. I didn't ask for money or jewelry or to be famous or to be beautiful. All I ever wanted was for you and me to have a chance to grow up in the same town. Nathan, that wouldn't cost God nothin'. Why won't God answer my prayer?"

Nathan stared for a long time across the high desert floor beneath them.

"I don't know, Leah. One time, two years ago, when I was lost out in these mountains and couldn't find my parents, I thought God had forgotten me completely. But when it was all over, I looked back and realized that God was with me all the time. Maybe it's the same now."

"Yeah, well, if God's doin' it," she asked sniffing, "how come it hurts so bad?"

SIX

Leah stood up on top of the boulder and stared out at the valley floor. "Nathan, how many times have you ever moved?"

"Eh, just once. You know, from our farm in Indiana."

"That's it? You only lived in two places?"

"Yeah. How about you, Leah? How many houses have you lived in?"

"Twenty-three. But I wouldn't call all of 'em houses. We lived in a tent here in Galena before the barber shop was built."

"How come your daddy moves so often?"

Leah jumped off the boulder and stumbled toward Nathan. He reached out and caught her. Then she pulled back and brushed off her blue dress. "He says it's his Indian blood."

"Indian blood?"

"My grandma was half-Indian, you know."

"I didn't know that. How come you never told me that?" Nathan asked.

"'Cause most kids make fun of me when I tell 'em. Besides, there are other things you don't know about me, Nathan T. Riggins." Then she broke into a wide smile. "'Course, there ain't many things you don't know."

"Your father said maybe you'd move to Austin," Nathan added. "With my daddy being a sheriff's deputy now, we might have to move to Austin someday."

"Yeah, he also said we might move to Tombstone. Talk about a dumb name for a town! You know, when I was little, I liked movin'," Leah continued. "Every new place was a new adventure. There was new streets to explore, new kids to play with, and always the hope that things would be better than the last place. Well, Galena is the place where they all got better." Leah's eyes teared up again. "What are we goin' to do, Nathan?"

"I, eh, I think," Nathan stammered, "well, I think we ought to just pretend that nothing's different. Maybe you will move in two weeks . . . maybe you won't. Maybe *I'll* be the one to move first. Who knows? In the meantime, we ought to go ahead and do what we would be doin' if you weren't moving. Maybe it's our last two weeks of living in the same town, but they ought to be fun weeks and not sad ones. Right?"

"Yeah, I like that." Leah reached down and snapped off a tiny red flower growing on a leafless plant that hugged tight to the mountainside. "What would we be doin'?"

"I think we ought to search for the trail of those outlaws who camped up here."

"How do you know it was outlaws?"

"Because of the dragging Spanish rowel. The same track was in the dust at the Heartford where I found the bullet bag."

"The what? The Heartford? Were you in the Heartford?"

"Yeah, listen, I'll tell you all about it while we look for some tracks," Nathan suggested.

Nathan explained his discoveries in the Heartford Hotel as they hiked over the crest of the hill.

"Are we goin' to track 'em down then?" Leah asked.

"I don't want to . . . you know, catch up with them,"

Nathan admitted. "But it wouldn't hurt to mark their trail for a while before the wind blows it away. Let's get the horses."

Within minutes they were following the hoofprints of five men who had ridden east from the campfire. Nathan leaned over his saddle horn, searching for prints on the rocky desert hillside. Tona curled up in Leah's lap as she rode the gray mare.

"Tona don't look so good, does he?" Leah asked.

Nathan sat up straight in the saddle. "Maybe I should have left him out there with the Rialtos. Then I wouldn't have to watch him go down."

"I like Tona," Leah commented.

"Well, the feeling's mutual. You know how he doesn't want anyone to touch him but me and you."

"And them Rialto girls."

"Yeah, them too."

"Maybe when I run away, I could go live with them," Leah said pondering.

"You can't run away."

"How come?"

"'Cause the Lord would hound you to go back home, and you know it," Nathan insisted. "Hey . . . look at this!"

"I don't see nothin'."

"The tracks split. Can't you see it?"

"What do you mean, they split?"

"Well, two horses turned straight east."

"Over them mountains?"

"I guess."

"How about the other three?"

"They're pointing south."

"There ain't nothin' south of here, is there?" Leah asked.

"Not that I know of . . . until you get to Pony Canyon and Austin."

"Well, what are we goin' to do now?"

"I think we ought to mark both trails and go home. It's late, and I ought to tell my dad what's happening."

"Can I eat supper at your house?"

"Eh . . . sure, I mean, I'll have to ask my mother, but she's never turned anyone down for a meal. How come you want to eat at our house?"

"'Cause all they'll be talkin' about at my house is movin', and I don't aim to sit around all evenin' with that on my mind."

Neither said anything for several minutes as Nathan slipped off Onepenny and piled rock markers in the directions of both sets of riders.

They turned the horses west and began the descent back to the valley floor.

"Colin was lucky," Leah blurted out.

"Lucky?"

"Yeah, they just up and moved. He didn't have to think about it very long. Maybe that's the way to do it. Maybe I should tell Daddy that we should just up and move tomorrow."

"Tomorrow? No!" Nathan exploded.

"How come? You're the one that gets to stay in Galena," she reminded him.

"Yeah, but Galena won't be the same without you. You were just about the first one I talked to and . . ."

"And what, Nathan T. Riggins?"

"Well, you know . . . we had some good times . . . and I'll really miss you," he blurted out.

Again they rode in silence.

Stopping at the little creek, they let the horses drink.

Nathan poured a handful of water from his canteen and let Tona lap it up. Then he took a deep breath and filled his lungs with the pungent smell of sage.

"What you been thinkin' about?" she asked him.

"About that time you slipped off the back of Onepenny and fell in the mud." Nathan laughed.

"Oh, that's real nice. I'm all sad about movin', and you're pokin' fun at me."

"You know what I like about you?" he probed.

"What?"

"Nothing's ever boring when we're together." Nathan pulled off his bandanna and wiped the dirt out of the corners of his eyes.

"You know what I been thinkin' about?" she asked.

"No, what?"

"Writin' letters. I ain't too good at it. You won't shame me if I spell them words all wrong, will you? I am gettin' better, you know."

"I promise I won't be critical. But I don't want to talk about you movin'."

"Well, whether we talk about it or not, it's goin' to happen."

"I'm prayin' you'll stay."

"That would take a miracle." She shrugged.

"The Lord's pretty good at miracles," Nathan reminded her as he spurred Onepenny across the creekbed.

Some of the lanterns were already lit when they made their way back into Galena. After returning Tona to the braided rug on the porch, Nathan put the horses away and

walked Leah back to her house. He waited at the bottom of
the outside stairs next to the barber shop.

Bounding down the stairs, Leah was all smiles. "I kin
have supper with you! Guess what?"

"You're not moving?"

She wrinkled her freckle-covered nose. "No, but it is
sort of good news. Daddy and Mr. Silverman are goin' to
Austin to file some papers. My stepmother is goin' with
them."

"Are you going, too?"

"Nope." She grinned. "They said I didn't have to go."

"They're goin' to let you stay here by yourself?"

Leah dropped her smile and frowned.

"No, they ain't goin' to let me stay by myself. I'm goin'
to stay at your house."

"My house? Really? Did you ask my mother already?"

"Nope, but she'll agree to let me stay, won't she? It's just
for a few days."

"Well . . . I, eh . . . sure, I reckon she will."

She did.

That evening Nathan told his father the whole story
about finding the bullet bag in the Heartford and the tracks
near Rabbit Springs. Nathan and Leah made plans to ride out
the next morning with Mr. Riggins and see if they could find
the trail.

Leah helped Mrs. Riggins with the dishes. Then all four
of them retired to the coolness of the front porch. His mother
started to sing "Shenandoah," and soon the others joined
in. For the next two hours they talked, sang, laughed, and

teased. Mr. Riggins finally signaled that it was time to turn in for the night.

Leah and Nathan stayed on the porch for a few minutes after his parents re-entered the house.

"You know why I like comin' over to your house?" she asked him.

"How come?"

"'Cause everybody likes everybody, and there ain't no drinkin', and there ain't ever no yellin' or nothin'."

"Well, we don't . . . have that much fun all the time. I mean, sometimes it's pretty boring," Nathan admitted. "Too bad you weren't my sister. Think of all—"

"That's dumb," Leah interrupted. "I don't want to be your sister!"

"No, no, what I meant was that—"

"Nathan T. Riggins, I cain't understand how come you are so smart in school and so dumb about other things!"

Later that night Nathan lay in his own bed and stared out the window at the star-filled night.

Lord, how come I always say things that make Leah mad? And . . . You know . . . if You wanted to change her daddy's mind about movin', well, I would really like that.

Nathan fell asleep and dreamed that he was walking down Main Street in Galena, but it was totally empty. Everyone, including his parents, had moved away, and he couldn't even find his house. The next morning he woke up with his nightshirt wet with sweat.

Nathan dressed and scooted outside to gather an arm load of wood for the cookstove. He noticed that Tona was breathing heavily, but the dog didn't wake up as he walked by. The morning air felt dry and stale. The mountains to the east could barely be seen through the dusty haze.

"Mother, I think that trip yesterday wore Tona out. Maybe I better not take him anymore."

"Perhaps you're right. Nathan, your father went to Austin this morning," she announced.

"He what?"

"A telegram came in early stating that the sheriff had been shot in a gunfight with some bank robbers. They need him in Austin."

"But we were . . . I mean . . . the sheriff's shot? Is he dead?"

"The telegram only said he was shot. Your father thinks it might be the same men who robbed the bank up here. But he did have a job for you."

"What's that?"

"Well, you said the trail looked like three men went south from Rabbit Springs?"

"Yeah, and the other two went east."

"Yes, he wants you to ride out and follow the two east just to Coyote Creek. He wants to know if they kept going east after the creek or if they turned some other direction."

"He wants me to do that?"

"Yes, he said you're the best tracker he has, but he doesn't want you following them any further than the creek."

"Yes, ma'am. Eh . . . Leah can go with me, can't she?"

"That's why I'm packing you two a lunch," his mother answered.

"I've got to go check on the horses and feed Domingo."

"I thought you fed that hawk yesterday."

"I did, but after not eating in a while, I figured he might need a little extra."

In the livery Nathan pulled down some hay for the horses in the corral and pumped up a little more water for the trough.

Lord, keep Dad safe. I think Mother gets more worried every time he goes out. Help her to relax, too.

Main Street was almost deserted as he hiked up the hill toward the Heartford Hotel. Someone across town was banging a hammer, and the sound drifted up the street. A lone horse tied in front of the Drover's Cafe swished its tail, providing the only movement in sight.

He scanned the roof line of the hotel.

"Okay, Domingo, where did you go? Did you stay on the privy all night?"

Running to the back of the hotel, he searched everywhere for the hawk.

Well, I don't see any feathers, so I guess nothing ate him. Maybe he just flew off for a hunt. I thought he'd probably be hungry. One more pass around the hotel revealed no clues as to the hawk's location. Nathan trudged up the alley to his house.

He didn't say much on the ride back out to Rabbit Springs. Mainly he listened to Leah, who seemed to be in a hurry to shove three years of conversation into one morning.

"See, I reckon to have a house with fruit trees out back

and a shade tree in the front large enough to have a push
swing. You know the kind I mean? Like some folks have on
their porch, but I want one out in the yard. Those on-the-
porch ones don't swing very high, and I figure why have a
swing if it don't swing high? You like to swing, don't you?

"I knew a girl once—her name was Priscilla P. Preston
. . . no, really, that was her name. Well, she got sick every time
we got in a swing. I mean, she'd lose her lunch right there
on the porch. I ain't never knowed anyone else who got sick
in a swing, did you? Well, I don't guess anything like that
makes me sick. I got sick one time on top of a barn. Did I
ever tell you about when I was stuck on top of a barn all night
long?"

Nathan started to speak.

"I didn't think so," she barged on. "See, I was going to
run away from home when I was about six, but there weren't
no place to go. So I decided to hide in the barn and pretend
like I run away. But then I got scared that Daddy would find
me in the hayloft, so I crawled up on the roof of the barn. You
know, it had one of them cupolas up on top, so I hid up
there.

"Well, I heard them a callin' and callin', but I wasn't
about to let on where I was. But when it started to get dark,
I realized that I couldn't get down. When I started easing
down the roof, I turned and looked at the ground. I got so
scared I threw up all over the roof."

"You were up there all night?" Nathan asked.

"Not exactly all night. My daddy came out after dark
and started yellin' for me again. That's when I hollered at him
that I was on the roof."

"What did he do?"

"He got me off the roof, washed me up, whipped my

behind, gave me a hug and a kiss, and then tucked me in bed."

"Did he swat you hard?"

"I don't remember." Leah shrugged. "But he kissed me tender. I remember that. I think he was more scared than mad."

Leah continued the nonstop conversation all the way to Rabbit Springs and beyond. When they came to the marker where the outlaws' trail divided, Nathan slid down off Onepenny and examined the tracks.

"How come you ain't been talkin' much?" Leah asked. "What you been thinkin' about?"

"Oh, I've been listening to you . . . and thinking about . . . well, if those three that robbed the bank in Austin are part of this gang, maybe they'll ride back up here to follow these two."

"You mean there might be bank robbers on the trail?" she asked.

"Yeah. Maybe the kind that shoot sheriffs."

"They wouldn't ride back up here, would they?" Leah asked.

"*¿Quién sabe?*" Nathan shrugged.

He climbed back on Onepenny, and they followed the tracks of the two riders east until they came to Coyote Creek, which was no more than three feet wide.

"Which way did they go?"

"It looks like they went north." Nathan motioned. "They weren't worried about being followed. Look at all the tracks they left."

"Where would they go to the north?"

"Maybe Elko . . . maybe to catch the train—"

"Or rob it!" Leah suggested. "Are we going back now?"

"It's about noon. Let's rest the horses and eat. Then we can head back," Nathan recommended.

"What if them robbers are still out here?" she asked.

"If you were an outlaw, would you camp right out here in the open?"

"Eh . . . no, I don't guess I would. I'll spread out dinner. Your mama sure is a good cook, Nathan. Do you think she'd teach me how to cook? I got two weeks before we move. I think I could learn a lot in two weeks. Did your mama ever teach anyone to cook? I heard of a boy once whose mama taught him. I don't think a boy ought to cook. 'Course, I don't mean around a chuck wagon. That's different and . . ."

Nathan was still listening to Leah when he finished eating and began packing the supplies back on Onepenny.

"Hey," he shouted, "did you see that?" He waved wildly to the north.

"What?" Leah jumped to her feet and stared.

"Pronghorns! I think I saw some over toward those hills!"

"You saw antelope? I don't see nothin'."

"They're up there, I tell you. Can't you see them? A dark brown spot two-thirds of the way up the mountain. Come on, let's go hunting."

"Hunting? I don't want to go—"

"Come on, Leah. I've been wanting to get one for months."

"I ain't goin' to shoot none, but I'll watch you. Me and that old mare cain't keep up with you two. So go on, and we'll catch up. But don't you go leavin' us stranded."

"See those trees up on that distant hill?" Nathan pointed.

"I don't see no trees."

"That dark green color on the side of that range? See it? That's some kind of trees. I'll meet you there. Can you finish cleaning up?"

"Oh, sure, eat and run. That's the way you boys are, never takin' time to listen to what a girl has to say," she teased.

"I've been listening all morning long," Nathan reminded her.

"But I ain't got to the important part yet," she protested. "Go on. Go hunt your antelope."

"I'll see you at the trees," Nathan shouted as he swung up into the saddle and pulled his carbine from the scabbard.

"Oh, I'll meet you in them trees, providin' I don't get a better offer," she pouted.

Nathan whipped around and looked back at Leah.

She stuck out her tongue.

For some reason he couldn't explain, he stuck out his tongue in return.

Within seconds he was galloping north.

Pulling up at the bottom of a draw, Nathan checked on the wind, felt it blowing in from the northwest, and then rode east.

No reason for them to catch my scent before I get a little closer.

On an incline to the east he looked back and could see the animals grazing on a small dry meadow near the juniper grove.

"Okay, boy, you wait here." Nathan slipped down from the saddle and let Onepenny's reins drop.

He cocked the lever on his Winchester carbine and slowly stalked around the hillside, approaching the short juniper trees.

If I can make it to the trees, I'll sneak right up to the edge and pick out a good-sized one!

Crouching behind the first few trees, he kept his eyes focused straight ahead. He stepped slowly, lightly, and then lifted the carbine to his shoulder. He could feel the plate on the stock press tight against his right shoulder; the trigger felt cool to his finger; the gun felt light . . . one more tree and Nathan would come within view of the prey. They would see him, too, but he knew he would be close enough to get off a good shot. Nathan held his breath and . . .

"Drop the gun, kid, or you'll never live to see your mama!"

The man with the rough voice jammed a Colt .44 into Nathan's ribs.

S E V E N

The hairs on the back of Nathan's neck bristled; a heaviness hit the pit of his stomach, and a lump welled up in his throat. He let the hammer down slowly on the carbine and then bent over and laid the gun in the dirt. Turning, he found himself staring at a thin man, almost six feet tall, holding a cocked revolver against Nathan's side. The man's wide-brimmed hat was pulled low, covering dark eyes. His face was unshaven, and his cheek bulged with tobacco.

"Who . . . who are you?" Nathan choked out.

"Don't matter none who I am. What matters is who you are and why you are sneaking up on our camp with a cocked gun."

"You . . . you . . . your camp?" Nathan stammered. "I, eh, I didn't see any camp. I was just hunting those antelope over there."

"Do those look like antelope?" the man growled. "There ain't nothin' over there but our horses."

"I can see that now . . . but from a distance . . . I thought I was . . . I mean, I'm sure I saw some pronghorns."

"Kid, you're wasting my time. I want to know what you was after!"

"I was huntin'. Honest!"

"Well, you found more than you bargained for, I can tell you that."

The man reached down and scooped up Nathan's carbine and shoved him back up the hill toward a thick clump of junipers.

"Where are you takin' me?" he protested.

"As if you didn't know." The man shoved the barrel of the revolver hard into Nathan's back. A sharp pain racked his ribs, and he stumbled forward.

"J. T., I'm bringin' in a snoopin' kid!" his captor hollered out as they came close to a fire circle and crude camp in a small clearing back in the junipers.

A hatless man in a dirty brown vest stepped out from behind a short tree. A shotgun rested across his left arm, and Nathan could see that the thumb and index finger of his right hand were missing.

"What's he doin' out here?" the man asked.

"Says he was huntin' antelope."

"Antelope? Now ain't that a coincidence. Here we are huntin' antelope, too. But we ain't had much luck, boy. Ain't nothin' around here close. Sit down . . . you want some coffee?"

"Eh . . . no." Nathan sat next to a fire circle that had long before been extinguished. "I thought there were some antelope just outside your camp, but I didn't know you were here."

"I say he's been spying on us, trying to steal our horses. Maybe we should just plug him," the first man suggested.

Ignoring that comment, the one with fingers missing asked, "Where you from, boy?"

"Eh . . . Galena. I live in Galena."

"Galena? Don't reckon I've ever heard of that one." The man looked Nathan straight in the eyes. "Is that near here?"

"Oh, it's over there to the west about . . . well, it's not all that far," he finished. "I'm really sorry for bustin' into your camp. I'll just be on my way now, and I promise I won't come over here again."

"You ain't goin' nowhere, boy. You see, we're the kind of fellas that like our privacy. Now you go traipsing back into Galena and telling everyone about the . . . eh, antelope hunters you seen out here, and, well, every Sunday hunter in the county will come ridin' this way poppin' off their repeatin' rifles. So we'll jist sit you here a spell."

"You got to let me go home!"

"I don't got to do nothin'! You understand that?" the man barked back.

Nathan heard the horses whinny on the other side of the junipers and turned to look. He counted at least a half-dozen unsaddled mounts.

"Go check on them horses. They ain't settled into that rope corral yet," the one called J. T. commanded.

"What you goin' to do with him?"

"Tie him to a tree and wait for Clayton and the others, I suppose."

Others? How many others?

After the first man went up the hill, the other turned to Nathan. "Where'd you tie your horse, boy? Now don't go tellin' me you walked all the way over here from Galena."

"Town's not all that far," Nathan tried to explain.

"I know how . . . anyway . . . where's your horse tied?"

"I, eh . . . didn't tie him. I was . . . I thought I was chasing antelope, and I left him over by the south edge of the trees. I don't know if he's still there."

"Well, now, that surely ain't very smart."

"I was huntin' antelope."

"And I say you was tryin' to steal our horses. Say, you ain't part Indian, are ya?"

The other man came back into the clearing.

"Brushy, you hike over and see if this boy's pony is on the south edge of the junipers like he said."

"He doesn't warm up quick to strangers," Nathan warned.

"If the cayuse gives ya any trouble, jist shoot it," J. T. called out.

"No! You can't do that!"

"You don't seem to understand, boy. You come sneakin' around camp, flashin' a cocked weapon, and tryin' to steal horses—I kin do anything I want. That's the rules."

"What rules?" Nathan protested.

"The rules of who holds the gun."

"J. T.," Brushy called out as he returned to the clearing, "I cain't find no horse out there."

"I told you, I didn't tie him up."

"Well, that's no matter. We got plenty of horses anyway."

"It looks like some riders coming up from the south . . . or maybe a dust devil blowin' out there," Brushy reported.

From the south? It's Leah . . . Lord, don't let her come up here! Keep her safe.

"Tie him up, and I'll go check on who's comin' in," the man with the missing fingers commanded.

Brushy shoved Nathan back against a short juniper. The boy sat down and felt his arms jerked around behind his back and tied to the trunk of the tree.

Lord, if these are the bank robbers, then they don't mind shooting sheriffs . . . I want to get out of here. I want to get out real bad!

"Hey, Brushy! I think it's Clayton and the others. They're settin' a pretty good pace."

"Anybody followin' them?"

"Nope."

"That's a good sign." Brushy walked over to the edge of the clearing and stared south. "You suppose they pulled it off?"

"Yep. Ain't nothin' will stop Clayton but a bullet."

"How much you suppose they got?"

J. T. looked back at Nathan and then whispered a few words to Brushy. Then both men laughed and glanced back at him.

The others are coming in from Austin! They're killers! Don't let them find Leah!

Nathan tugged at the rope that secured him to the tree, straining to see who was approaching. He watched the column of dust come closer until all three men rode into the clump of junipers. He tried to hear the conversation, but he could only make out shouts, boasts, and laughter. He thought he heard one of them mention the word *sheriff*, which was followed by a curse and then some more laughter.

Finally all five men walked into the clearing.

"So this is the hombre who was tryin' to steal our horses?"

"I wasn't tryin' to steal your—"

"Boy, didn't your mama teach you not to lie?" he gruffed.

"But I—"

"Shut up, kid! Now, boys, pull your saddles and slap 'em on some fresh mounts. I don't figure to stay in this country any longer. Grab yourself some grub 'cause we got a long ride."

Nathan searched around for some way to escape. Every time he yanked on the ropes, they seemed to pinch tighter on his wrists.

If I could get free, I could dive for my carbine over next to the fire circle. Then I could ... then I could get myself shot!

Maybe this is a bad dream, Lord. Like the other night when I thought everyone had left Galena. This would be a real good time to wake up in my bed and—

"You did a good job of gettin' horses, J. T.," he heard Clayton call out. "They look fast enough to run all the way to Utah!"

Suddenly, all five came back into the clearing with fresh horses.

"Well," J. T. laughed, "the old man felt mighty bad about givin' up such fine animals."

"Yeah," Brushy added, "but he ain't feelin' sorry now. He ain't feelin' nothin'!"

The one called Clayton glanced over at Nathan, and all the men lowered their voices. "You got camp packed up?"

"Yeah, I figured we'll take the roan for a pack horse," one of the men called. "You want me to turn these others out?"

"Nah . . . we'll drive them ahead of us."

"We could shoot them two lame ones," J. T. suggested.

"That might attract buzzards and who knows what else."

"How about the boy?"

"Same thing."

"He'll die all tied up like that," Brushy observed.

"Yeah, but not for a day or two," Clayton replied. "Besides, I'm sure a kid like that can figure out how to get loose sooner or later. Tough luck, boy. You jist came ridin' in to the wrong grove of junipers. But don't fret. When they write the history books, maybe they'll list you as one of the victims of the Blue Mountain Boys."

"Blue Mountain Boys? Is that the gang that goes around killin' children?" Nathan hollered.

Riggins, you jerk, why did you say that?

"I don't need no lip." Clayton pulled his revolver and pointed it at Nathan.

Expecting the sound of gunshot and piercing pain, Nathan grimaced. He heard a completely different sound.

"Well! There you are, Nathan T. Riggins! Try to ride out on me, will you? I'm certainly glad you men hogtied him! I would have done the same thing myself, but it didn't seem ladylike!"

Nathan's mouth dropped open as he saw Leah ride into the clearing. He noticed several guns yanked from holsters and pointed at her.

"I ought to jist leave you out here. It would serve you right! But I don't know how to find my way home. Besides, when my brothers get ahold of you, you'll wish you was tied to a rope and dragged all the way to Wyoming!"

Brothers?

"Who are you?" Clayton huffed.

"Well, until an hour ago I thought I was his girlfriend. Do you know what he did? Did he tell you? I don't suppose so! Well, he invites me out here for a ride in the country and a picnic. Don't that sound nice? I thought it sounded mighty swell. He says he's got to talk to me about something important. Do you know what it was he wanted to talk about?

"I'll tell you what it was. He up and tells me he don't want to be my boyfriend. Says he likes that Tashawna girl. Do you know her? She's got that stringy, curly hair that looks like a matted cow's tail. She's as skinny as a fence post to boot! Now I ask you, isn't that a fine thing for a boy to do? There are lots of boys in Galena who think I'm quite the looker, Mr. Nathan T. Riggins! Mister, I ain't all that bad-lookin', am I?"

"What's goin' on here?" Clayton mumbled.

"Then he leaves me there cryin' and says he's goin' to

hunt some antelope. I ain't seen no antelope out here. Have you men seen any antelope? Of course not! He was just tryin' to dump me. Can you imagine anyone so vile as that? We get back to Galena, and my daddy's goin' to whip you, boy. He'll whip you until you got to stand in the stirrups 'til Christmas."

She's bluffin' them! You can do it, Leah!

"But that ain't nothin' compared to what my brothers will do." Then she turned to Clayton. "They is kinda hot-tempered, you know what I mean? They ain't all that smart, but they kin shoot a lizard from a hundred yards. I've seen 'em do it." Then she turned back to Nathan. "And if you don't git me back home soon, they'll be ridin' out here after me. You know that, don't ya? Mister, kin ya jist unfasten him from the tree and leave him tied up? I'm goin' make him walk all the way back to Galena. I don't care if it takes all day. There ain't no boy alive who can jist dump me like that for no Tashawna."

"You want me to tie her up, too?" J. T. offered.

"Of course he don't want you to tie me up," she protested. "Could you men tell me the direction of Galena? This here boy got me all turned around. I think he's kind of lost, too. He told me that Galena was out there somewhere." Leah waved toward the west. "But I think it's this way, right?" She pointed south.

A wide smile broke across Clayton's face. "That's right, darlin', that's the way home, and don't let this rascal tell you otherwise."

"See there. I told you I could find my way home." She turned and stuck out her tongue at Nathan. Then she looked back at the man. "Thanks, mister, I'm much obliged."

"Cut him loose, but leave his hands tied," Clayton commanded.

Leah bowed her head. "Thank you kindly. I tell you, I learned my lesson good. I ain't ever goin' to ride out in the country with some boy who wants to talk to me. If he cain't tell me right there in the middle of Main Street, I don't want to hear. No, sir, you ain't goin' treat me that way no more."

Nathan pretended to protest. "You aren't going to turn me over to her!"

While cutting the rope around the tree, J. T. laughed. "Yeah, Clayton, we ought to show this boy some mercy. Let's just shoot him and take him out of his misery."

The men laughed as the last of them mounted their horses.

"I don't envy you, boy," Brushy called out as they rode up the mountain toward the east.

Nathan and Leah watched the men until they were out of earshot.

"You did it!" Nathan called out. "Those are the bank robbers! They shot the sheriff down in Austin, and you talked 'em out of shooting me."

Leah took a big, deep breath and sighed. "Yeah . . . I did, didn't I? I guess I'm good at somethin', Mr. Nathan T. Riggins."

"I thought he was goin' to shoot me."

"Yeah, so did I."

"They could have shot you, too," he reminded her.

"I know."

"Why did you take a chance?" Nathan asked.

"I got lost in the trees and followed them three to this clearin'. When I saw what was happenin', I prayed real hard for the Lord to show me what to do."

"And what did He tell you?"

"He told me that there was worse things than dyin' alongside a good friend."

"I'm sure glad you listened to Him. Where did you come up with that story about brothers and all?"

"Well, I tried to think of something without lyin', but I couldn't think fast enough. I jist couldn't think of nothin' else. The Lord will forgive me for lyin', won't He?"

"If you ask Him, He'll forgive you for anything. You know that. Now, how about climbing off that mare and untying me. I've got to go find Onepenny."

"I tied him up behind that rock pile down yonder. I was afraid they might try to steal him."

"Great! You thought of everything! I can't believe this. You saved Onepenny, too. Now, come on, untie me," Nathan insisted.

"I kind of like havin' a captive audience," she giggled.

"Leah!"

"No, really. If those men turn back, they could see you was loose. We don't want them comin' back now, do we?"

"Leah, you aren't serious. They can't see us from there."

"Maybe they got a spyglass."

"Leah, get down right now and untie me!" Nathan shouted.

"Don't you raise your voice at me. I just might go back to Galena and leave you out here," she threatened.

"Leah, come on, a joke's a joke. Untie me!"

"Not until we get to the rock pile." She slid down off her horse, picked up his carbine, and then remounted the white mare.

"Okay, Riggins, start hikin'," she ordered.

Nathan began to trudge out toward the rock pile.

"When are you movin' anyway?" he teased.

"Keep walkin', Riggins! I ain't ever had a boy all tied up before."

"You aren't goin' to tell people in town about this, are you?"

"Maybe I am, and maybe I ain't." She smiled.

"Look." He motioned with his head. "They're clear over that mountain now. They can't possibly see us. Untie me!"

"I ain't untyin' you until we get to them rocks!"

And she didn't.

Finally, mounted on Onepenny, Nathan spurred the spotted horse toward the west.

"How come you keep lookin' back?" Leah asked.

"'Cause I keep having this feeling that they're going to change their minds and come riding after us. I can't believe you talked them into letting us go."

"Well, it's a cinch you weren't doin' too good, them pointin' the pistol at you and all. What do we do now?"

"I've got to get word to Dad. They're heading out through Eureka and Elko Counties. Maybe he can wire ahead and have someone cut them off before they get to the White Desert. Once they get out there, no one will find them."

"Are you sure they're goin' to go east?"

"Wouldn't you?" Nathan asked.

"Yeah . . . I guess so. Is it goin' to be dark before we get home?"

Nathan scanned the sky. "I reckon."

The sun had dropped behind the western mountains when they stopped to water their horses at Rabbit Springs.

It was dark enough to see the lights of Galena on the distant mountain slope as they trudged across the valley floor. Nathan could feel the hot summer air begin to cool at their 4,000-foot elevation. He pushed his hat back and let it dangle by the stampede string. Then he picked up Onepenny's gait to a lope.

Lord, there for a while I sure didn't think I'd be coming home tonight. You sure did send Leah at the right time. Thanks!

"Nathan?"

"Yeah?"

"You goin' to go back out and help your daddy chase down them bank robbers?"

"Eh . . . no," Nathan admitted. "I've had all I want of that bunch. I don't aim to be that scared again for a long, long time."

"Do you think they had the money from Colin's daddy's bank right there in camp with them?" she asked.

Nathan slowed down the pace of the horses as they started the climb up to Galena.

"I never thought about it much. But I imagine they did. Sometimes I read about outlaws burying their take, but that never seemed too smart to me."

"I miss Colin, but I was kind of glad he wasn't out there with us. That ain't very nice to say, is it?"

Nathan grinned at Leah. "Oh, I know what you mean. Colin doesn't always know the right thing to say." He took a deep breath and sighed. "I miss him, too."

"You know what, Mr. Nathan T. Riggins? We carried on all afternoon and hardly talked about me movin' at all."

"That was nice, wasn't it?" Nathan sighed.

"Yep. And who's going to take care of you when I'm

gone? You're liable to get yourself shot without me around," she bragged.

"Oh, I suppose some pretty girl with curly hair will move to town and feel real sorry for me," he teased.

Nathan didn't see Leah swing the canteen until it hit him in the stomach. He bounced back over the cantle and would have tumbled off the horse if Onepenny, sensing trouble, hadn't shut it down and come to a sliding halt.

"Don't you ever go teasin' about other girls, Nathan T. Riggins!" she hollered. Then she kicked the mare and galloped on into Galena.

By the time he reached the livery, Leah's gray horse was waiting to be groomed, but she was nowhere in sight. Nathan hurried through the chores and put up the horses. Then he sprinted home.

Nathan spent a full hour telling his startled and anxious mother everything that had happened with the Blue Mountain Boys. After he ate some navy bean soup and a handful of gingersnaps, he went to the Express Office to send his father a telegram.

He found the front door locked and the "closed" sign posted. Scooting around to the back door, Nathan yelled in through a screened window, "Mr. Fernandez? It's me, Nathan Riggins. I need to send a telegram."

"We're closed up, son."

"This is an emergency!" Nathan called.

"Everyone has an emergency. I'm just sittin' down to eat my supper. Come back in a half-hour if it's still an emergency," the agent hollered.

"But I've got to let Dad know that the bank robbers aren't down in Austin anymore. They're out on the other side of Rabbit Springs."

Suddenly Mr. Fernandez popped his head out the door. "Are they headed this way?" he asked.

"No, they're going east into Utah Territory. That's why I've got to reach my father. Maybe he can get someone to stop them."

"You sure it's them bank robbers?" Mr. Fernandez quizzed.

"Yep. It's the Blue Mountain Boys. You ever heard of them?"

"My word, there's a sizable reward posted for them! . . . Come in, come in, come in. Let's see if Richards is still in the office down in Austin.

About an hour after the telegram was sent, Mr. Fernandez came puffing up the dimly-lit dirt street where Nathan and his mother sat out on the porch.

"Evenin', ma'am," he began. "I just got word from the marshal . . . I mean, from Mr. Riggins. Thought you should see this." He handed the telegram to Adele Riggins and then turned to Nathan. "Your daddy and a posse are riding all night to get here. They aim to track those bank robbers themselves!"

E I G H T

Deputy Riggins and six well-armed men rode into Galena about ten o'clock the next morning. Nathan and Leah described all the events of the previous afternoon, including details about the men and horses.

"You going to chase them all the way to U. T.?" Nathan asked.

Mr. Riggins put his arm around Nathan's shoulder. "Well, I hope not. The sheriff up in Elko County is sweeping down this way with a posse. We hope to trap them in the middle somewhere, but they've got a good head start."

Nathan walked his father to the front door of the house. "But they're pushing that remuda. Won't that make it easy to track?"

"Sure, we can follow a band of horses. But they can drop off one at a time, and it would be hard to spot. Then if we get close, they can scatter the whole bunch, and we'd have to be mighty smart to know which tracks to follow."

Mr. Riggins glanced back at Leah, then at Nathan. "Now I don't want you two riding off to Rabbit Springs until this matter is settled."

"Eh . . . no, sir, we won't," Nathan assured him. "I don't feel much like leavin' town for a while."

Mr. Riggins grinned. "If you do have to ride off, be sure and take pretty Miss Leah with you so she can get you out of trouble."

Leah broke into a wide smile.

"Well . . . actually . . . I could have . . . it was just . . . I, eh," Nathan stammered. His father jammed on his hat, stooped to kiss his wife, and then pushed his way through the front door.

"Now don't you go anywhere without 'pretty Miss Leah,'" Leah teased. "You ever notice how your daddy calls me pretty? Maybe there's still hope you'll turn out to be like him."

"I'm going to go feed my hawk and tend the horses. Does 'pretty Miss Leah' want to come with me?"

"It ain't sayin' it that counts," she scolded. "It's how you say it. Your daddy knows how to say it and make a girl feel good. But I'll go. Someone's got to look after you."

"Oh, brother, am I goin' hear that the rest of my life?"

"Nope. Jist for two more weeks," Leah reminded him.

It was almost noon when they hiked up to the Heartford to look for the hawk.

"Domingo! *Venga aquí.*" Nathan searched the sky. "I don't see him. Do you?"

"There ain't no bird on the hotel, I can tell you that much," Leah replied.

"He's not on top the privy either. He's got to be here. It's time to feed him. He wouldn't miss a meal. Maybe someone else came to feed him."

"And maybe he moved to Carson City," Leah teased.

Nathan continued to search the sky. "He's not goin' to leave a good deal."

"I don't know what's such a good deal about gettin' locked into a hotel room."

"Oh, he'll be back by afternoon. You wait and see."

"Well, I ain't goin' to wait right here. Let's go see if the mail's got put up yet," Leah suggested.

Nathan snatched up a pebble and chucked it up the

hill. "Does, eh . . . 'pretty Miss Leah' want to race to the post office?"

She lifted her nose. "Ladies don't go runnin' down city streets." Then she spun on her heels and slammed the palms of both hands against Nathan's shoulders, causing him to stagger back and fall to one knee. "But girls do!" she shouted. She hiked her dress above her ankles and raced up the street.

"That's cheating! That's cheating, and you know it," Nathan hollered. By the time he started to sprint, Leah had turned the corner on Main Street, her long brown hair flowing behind her. Nathan didn't try to catch up, but slowed to a walk instead. As he passed the Mercantile, he noticed a full freight wagon parked out front.

"Tony, did Mr. Anderson get some new goods?"

"They ain't comin' in, Nate. It's all goin' out. A fella's openin' a store up in Idaho."

"That's a big sale."

"Mr. Anderson's sellin' out, Nate," Tony explained.

"You mean he's quittin' business?"

"Yep. Says he's goin' to retire in San Diego."

"The Merc's closing? Really?"

"That's the way it goes." Tony shrugged.

Leah was sitting on a bench in front of the post office holding some mail.

"Did you know the Mercantile is closing?" he asked.

"That ain't all that's closin'," she sighed. "Read this."

Nathan unfolded the letter and turned it so that reflected sunlight struck the page.

"Miss D'Imperio? She's not coming back! She's goin' to teach in St. Louis this year? But . . . but we . . . ."

"She don't think they'll even have a school in Galena,"

Leah reported. "It's all over, ain't it, Nathan? I guess maybe it's time for us all to move on."

"Well, you aren't moving for two weeks, so I'm not going to get sad 'til then."

Leah glanced up at Nathan. "Will you be sad then?"

"Yeah," Nathan said softly, "I don't think I will want to live here anymore either." He stared down Main Street. "Hey, what's going on over at the bank?"

"Mr. Melton is goin' to pay folks off, I think. Ain't that what Colin's daddy said?" Leah glanced down at her lap. "Colin! I almost forgot . . . You got a letter."

"Already? But he's only been gone—"

"Read it to me!" She handed him the slick brown envelope.

Dear Nathan,

We are here in Carson City. Father is settling up financial matters. He says Mr. Melton should soon have enough money to reconcile all accounts in Galena. I think perhaps we might buy a house here. Father has been offered a nice position with the U. S. Mint, and mother has some family in Virginia City.

Guess who I saw today? Tashawna! She wanted to know how you were doing. (Maybe you'd better not let Leah read this.) She promised to show me all over town. You should see her. She really, you know, grew up.

Please try to come to Carson City this summer. I'd really like to see you. (And so would Tashawna.)

Say hello to Tona and Leah for me.

Your friend,
Colin Maddison, Jr.

"You ain't goin' to Carson, Mr. Nathan T. Riggins. If Colin wants to see you, he can just come to Galena . . . or wherever. 'Say hello to Tona and Leah'?" she mimicked. "I get mentioned down there with the dog!"

"Let's go see Mr. Melton. Maybe he knows if the Maddisons plan on coming back any time soon." Nathan sprinted across the dusty dirt street and then spun around and ran back to Leah.

"I'm not in that big a hurry," he sheepishly admitted. "If you promise not to push me down, I'll walk with you."

"I ain't promisin' nothin'." Leah grinned. She stepped out into the street with her head tilted slightly upward. "Hey, is that your old hawk up there?"

"Where?"

"Way up there." She pointed high in the blue sky above the Mercantile.

"Yeah . . . it's a hawk all right! That must be him. That's Domingo!"

"How can you tell from here?" she questioned.

"I'll show you. I'll whistle him in." Nathan pulled the heavy leather glove out of his back pocket and slipped it over his left hand. Even though Nathan's whistle was loud and shrill, the hawk continued to circle.

"That ain't him," Leah decided.

"It is too. He'll come. Just wait."

"Well, if it is, he jist flew off toward them mountains."

"But . . . but . . . maybe he didn't know it was me."

"And maybe, Mr. Nathan T. Riggins, that ain't your old hawk in the first place."

Nathan searched the sky for another glimpse of the bird. "Maybe you're right," he mumbled. "Maybe that wasn't Domingo. He wouldn't just fly off."

Mr. Watson was helping two men wearing double Colts

unload a couple of locked metal boxes when Nathan and Leah walked up.

"Is that a shipment from Mr. Maddison?" Nathan asked.

"Oh, Nathan . . . yes, it is. Say, did I hear that your daddy got back in town this morning?"

"Yeah, but he already rode off with a posse after the bank robbers," Nathan reported.

"Are they around here?"

"They're out in the Shoshones headed toward Utah Territory."

"That is some comfort." Mr. Melton wiped the sweat off his forehead. "Although I'd feel better if your dad were in town."

"What's the matter? You ain't expectin' no trouble, are you?" Leah quizzed.

"No . . . no, not really. It's just . . . well, the safe is all busted up, and I'll have to baby-sit these funds until everyone comes in to collect. By noon tomorrow everything should be reconciled."

"You goin' to stay here until then?" Leah asked.

"Yes, I see no other option."

"Kin we bring you some dinner and supper? I'm stayin' with Nathan's mama, and she's one of the best cooks in town."

"That's mighty kind of you, Miss Leah. I'd be obliged. And say . . . if you two happen to see any suspicious types hanging around town, let me know. The Maddisons had to go into debt to raise these funds, you know. But that's the way they are. They pay their debts."

"Are you open for business now?" Nathan asked.

"Not 'til mornin'," Mr. Watson replied. "I've got to get the paperwork done."

"Mr. Watson, do you know if the Maddisons will be coming back to see that everything is taken care of?"

"I don't think so, son."

"We'll bring you some dinner after a while," Leah promised.

"Thank you, Miss Leah."

Leah and Nathan hiked home.

"It don't seem fair. Them robbers take all the money, and Mr. Maddison has to pay it off. Some bankers would just ride off and forget Galena," Leah noted.

"Nobody but a thief would do that. A man pays his debts. That's the code," Nathan replied.

"What code?"

"Well . . . you know. It's just the way good folks operate out here. You know . . . the code."

"I don't think I'm goin' to marry a banker. That Tashawna can marry the banker. Now wouldn't that be a pair? Mr. and Mrs. Colin Maddison (with two *d*'s), Jr. He could make the money, and she could spend it."

Nathan turned to Leah with a wide grin. "Hey, that does sound fine, doesn't it? Then every time we went to visit Colin, we could—"

"Forget it, Riggins! I ain't ever goin' to visit her, even if I'm an old lady."

"Now, now, pretty Miss Leah. I think you'd better learn to be more trusting."

"And I think you better figure out which subjects not to tease about," she huffed.

All the rest of the day, Leah and Nathan got along fine, providing they didn't talk about moving or a girl whose name started with T. That evening after a supper of fried steak, boiled red potatoes, and applesauce, Mrs. Riggins, Leah, and Nathan sat out on the porch.

"It isn't coolin' off much tonight, is it?" Mrs. Riggins commented.

"Nope, it's almost hot enough to soak the sheets," Leah offered.

"Do what?" Nathan asked.

"One summer we lived down in west Texas, and it was so hot at night we pulled our beds right out on the porch. But we still couldn't sleep, so my daddy soaked a sheet in cold water and then wrung it out real good. We pulled it over us, and we went right to sleep . . . until the sheet dried out, of course."

"Did you have to do that all summer long?" Mrs. Riggins asked.

"Nah. We didn't stay there that long. We moved to Lincoln, New Mexico . . . but it weren't no better there in the summer." Leah reached out and scratched Tona's head as he sat in front of her.

"Look at that!" Nathan motioned to his mother. "Tona sure does pick up with Leah around. I think he's feelin' better . . . don't you?"

"Well, he's certainly more active. Maybe you two could take him for a little hunt tomorrow. Just up behind town. If he got tired, it would be a downhill walk all the way home," Mrs. Riggins suggested.

"I ain't goin' very far away from town. I got all the scare I wanted yesterday," Leah declared.

"Let's get up real early and hike up toward the old Copper Basin mine. There's always some rabbits up there," Nathan suggested.

"How early is early?" Leah demanded.

"Oh . . . daylight."

"How much daylight?"

"Breakin' daylight."

"Oh, all right. I ain't never went for a walk with a boy at daybreak."

"Well, it's not exactly a walk," Nathan protested.

"It ain't? You mean we got to run?"

"No . . . what I mean, it's a huntin' trip where we walk, but it's not a . . . you know, a walk."

Nathan was on the front porch the next morning scrubbing his face at a wash basin when Leah came out.

"Ain't you ready yet?"

"I thought you'd need . . . a little more time," Nathan stammered, drying his face.

"Well, you thought wrong," she asserted. "Tona! That-a-boy! Come on. Let's walk down and feed the horses while we're waiting for slowpoke."

"Slowpoke? I'm ready! I just need to pull on my boots, grab my hat, my carbine, a handful of shells, and maybe some biscuits."

"I have the biscuits!" she announced. "Me and Tona will be down at the livery."

Nathan ran back into the house, put on his boots, grabbed his carbine, and then took five minutes looking for a dozen .44-40 cartridges to shove into his pocket.

By the time he reached the livery, Leah had pulled down the hay and was holding an oat bucket for Onepenny.

"He sure is a purdy horse. I'm goin' to miss him, too."

"You aren't going to start the day sad, are you?" Nathan asked.

"Nope. Let's go shoot a snake or rabbit or somethin' ferocious."

Nathan was surprised that Tona traipsed up the hill well ahead of them. He never got out of sight, but he only slightly limped, and his eyes seemed to perk up.

"He's definitely feeling better," Nathan remarked.

They roamed up the hill about two hundred yards above the town and then headed west along the slope of the mountain. They walked slowly, visiting as they hiked. Tona stayed about twenty feet ahead of them. Nathan carried the carbine, loaded with three shells, over his shoulders, with each arm resting on the gun.

The sunlight just creased the top of the mountains, and Nathan watched it gradually slide down the hill until they walked in daylight. He figured daybreak in the summer was the best time of the day in northern Nevada. Looking south, he could see mountains one hundred and fifty miles away.

"I ain't seen nothin' to shoot," Leah complained.

"It doesn't matter." Nathan shrugged. "It's mainly just a walk for Tona. Hey, let's sit on these rocks and have a biscuit. Tona! Come here, boy," he called.

They sat on the rocks and ate biscuits and salt pork. Tona sniffed around the sagebrush and disappeared.

Leah nodded toward Galena. "If we had a spyglass, we could sit here and watch what was going on in town."

"Yeah . . ." Nathan gazed off at the western mountains and then back at Galena. "Most of the time it's a windy, barren spot up here. I mean, if it weren't for gold, no one would ever want to live in this country."

"What do you think will happen to town?" Leah asked.

"Oh, a few will hang on for a while . . . they might even open the Shiloh again. But sooner or later it will look like Willow Springs. Empty buildings without window casings or doors. Snow and rain blowing through rooms. Then one day it'll catch fire and burn to the ground. The ashes will drift away; the sage will grow back . . . and by 1910 nobody will even remember there was a town here."

"Boy, that ain't very cheerful."

Nathan climbed up on the rocks and looked around for Tona.

"Well, I guess I'm kind of in a sad mood. It might not be that depressing."

"Sort of reminds me of some folks' lives."

"What does?"

"You know, their lives just sort of flash by. Then they die, and nobody remembers that they were even around. You ever notice how many markers in the cemetery don't have a name on them?"

"Yeah . . . well, it doesn't have to be that way. I think the Lord has more in mind for us than that."

"Nathan, do you ever think about Heaven?"

"Sometimes . . . how about you?"

"Yep. I think about it all the time. Sometimes I wish we could hurry up and get there," Leah said pondering. "Is it true that there ain't no marriage in Heaven?"

"That's what I read in the Bible." Nathan nodded.

She grinned. "Well . . . well, I think maybe I'll wait a few years before goin' there."

"Hey!" Nathan shouted. "Tona's found a rabbit!" He quickly cocked his carbine and, looking down the metal sights, followed the darting jackrabbit as it scampered several feet in front of a puffing Tona.

Squeezing the trigger, Nathan heard the report, felt the kick, and saw the rabbit turn a somersault and fall lifeless on the mountainside.

"You got it!" Leah shouted.

"Yeah, it's kind of a big bullet for the target." Nathan shrugged. "Look at Tona pounce on it! You'd think he was a pup."

The dog carried the rabbit in his teeth and began to trot back to town.

"I think Tona's through huntin'," Leah remarked.

"How about you?" Nathan asked. "You want to go back to town now?"

"Sure. Your mama promised to show me how to bake some french pastries. And we ought to take Mr. Melton some breakfast."

As they hiked down the hill, Nathan noticed that Tona often stopped and dropped the rabbit, caught his breath, then picked up the animal, and continued the descent.

They were within a hundred feet of town when Leah called out, "Hey . . . ain't that an open window at the Heartford Hotel?"

"What window?" Nathan asked.

"The one in the corner. It's a little bit open at the top . . . see? Maybe a couple, three inches or so. Didn't you close it the other day?"

"No, I didn't close it. I didn't even know it was open. I guess I was so excited to find Domingo that I—" Nathan stopped suddenly. "Domingo! He could have crawled back in that room and now can't get out! That's it. I bet he's stuck back in the hotel. Let's go check it out."

"I ain't crawlin' into no boarded-up hotel. Me and Tona and what's left of the rabbit will wait out here."

"I'll be right back. Hold my carbine. I know he's in there."

Nathan ran to the back of the hotel and lifted the window. He pulled himself into the musty kitchen and scooted through the darkened lobby of the hotel.

"Domingo?" he shouted as he ran up the stairs. "Hey, Domingo, are you stuck again?"

He shoved open the door of the corner room and scampered toward the slightly open window.

Suddenly someone grabbed the collar of his shirt, and he felt a revolver pressed to his back.

"Well, well, boys, look at this," a gruff but familiar voice snarled. "If it ain't the horse-stealin' antelope hunter himself!"

NINE

Nathan swallowed hard and gasped, "The Blue Mountain Boys!"

"Ain't that nice? The boy remembers who we are." Clayton snarled, "I should of plugged him out at Rabbit Springs."

"Don't shoot him in here," J. T. warned. "A shot might bring the whole town out."

"This town ain't that quiet, is it?"

J. T. walked over and glanced out the window. "Well, it surely ain't boisterous like the old days. You can hear dogs bark clean across town."

"I still figure most every man with nerve enough to pull a trigger is in that posse out chasin' our remuda."

Regaining his breath, Nathan glanced around the darkened room and could spot only four of the five men. "What are you doin' here? I thought you were headed to Utah."

"Yeah, that's exactly what we wanted you to think. Then you'd come runnin' back to Galena and send the authorities out after us," Clayton reported.

"Then," Brushy continued, "while all the law is out chasin' Wesley and that band of horses, we slip into town and scoop up anything that's left over from the other day."

"Tie him up, J. T.!" Clayton ordered. "You see, kid, that banker will bring in new funds to pay off his accounts. I know the type—they're fanatic about payin' everyone back. So as soon as they open that door this morning, we'll make a withdrawal."

Don't they know the safe is broken? Or that the Maddisons have left? If they'd known that, they could have broken in last night.

"Yeah, I bet that banker wished he had what's in these saddlebags!" J. T. laughed as he pushed Nathan to the dusty, dirty floor and tied his hands to the bedpost.

They've got the bank money here? Dad and the posse could be a hundred miles away by now!

Clayton tramped over to the corner window and glanced down toward the bank.

"I cain't figure why that banker hasn't showed up."

"Them banks don't open until late," Brushy mumbled.

"But he's got to come down and set things up for the day," Clayton reasoned.

"The bank's closed," Nathan shouted out. "The Maddisons moved to Carson City."

Why did I say that?

"Closed?" J. T. snapped. "That ain't the way I heard it at the Drover's Cafe. They said the bank's goin' to open this mornin' to pay folks off."

"But if it ain't the banker, who are we lookin' fer?" Brushy questioned.

"Well, I can tell you one thing," Clayton announced, "the first person that walks through that door who knows the combination to the safe is goin' to get some visitors real quick like." Then turning again to Nathan, he demanded, "What were you doin' in the Heartford anyway?"

"I was, ah . . . hunting for my hawk."

"Hawk? Nobody owns a hawk." Brushy laughed.

"That hawk that flew in here last week? It was yours?" Clayton asked.

"Uh . . . that's the one. Is it in here again?"

"Nah, we ain't seen him this time," J. T. began. "Clayton! Come here! Folks are headin' into the bank."

"Folks?"

"Yeah . . . ordinary town people."

Clayton stormed to the window and glanced down at Galena's Main Street. "How'd we miss the banker? Well, boys, let's get down there before they give away all our money. Brushy, gather up those saddlebags and, Milt, you bring the horses around."

"We ain't comin' back here?"

"Nope, not with this kid snoopin' around. J. T., stick a gag in his mouth. Boys, we've got to move smooth, and we've got to move fast. If someone gets in your way, shoot 'em."

"Ain't nobody goin' to shoot nobody!"

Nathan and the men looked up to see Leah, with Tona by her side, standing in the doorway holding Nathan's .44-40 carbine.

"Leah!"

"Oh, no, not that mouthy girl! Don't you ever git tired of buttin' in?"

"You untie Nathan, or one of ya is gettin' blasted!"

"That's it. I've had it. Kids ain't got no respect anymore." Clayton reached up and pulled his black hat down tighter.

"I ain't bluffin', mister. I'll pull this trigger! Tell 'em, Nathan. Tell 'em I ain't bluffin'!"

"Leah, run! Warn Mr. Melton that they intend to rob the bank again!" Nathan shouted.

"Ain't nobody goin' nowhere!" Clayton marched straight at Leah.

Lord, save Leah! Don't let her get hurt!

When Clayton came within five steps of Leah, he

reached to his side to pull out his revolver. Suddenly, Tona let out a deep growl and leaped at Clayton's right arm. His teeth had just broke skin when Clayton let out a yell, dropped his gun, and slung the dog to the floor.

Immediately, Brushy whipped out his Colt and shot Tona. The gray and white dog fell dead after the first shot. There was no response when the second shot punctured his body.

"No!" Nathan yelled.

"Tona!" Leah screamed.

Clayton lunged at Leah and grabbed the carbine. The gun discharged wildly and shattered the hotel window. The other men dived for cover. Then Clayton shoved Leah into the middle of the room. She tripped over Tona's body and fell to the floor beside Nathan.

"Why did you do that? Why did you kill my dog?" Nathan cried. He could feel the tears streaming down his face. He was trying to catch his breath, but the sobs grew uncontrollable. He tried to pull free from the bindings but only managed to hurt himself more.

"I'm sorry, Nathan. I'm sorry," Leah wailed. "I shouldn't have brought Tona up here. It's all my fault! I'm sorry . . . oh, Lord, I feel so bad I want to die!"

"Clayton! There's some folks headin' this way. They must have heard them shots!"

"Tie her up with the boy. Milt, run get the horses and bring them around back. Let's get out of here."

"How about the bank?"

"Forget it. The odds just switched, and it ain't worth gettin' killed over. There'll be other banks."

The tall man called Milt ran out the door, and Nathan could hear his boots tramp down the hallway.

Then they heard several shots. Clayton stuck his head out the doorway.

"Milt, what's wrong?"

"They were takin' down the boards over the front door. But that should cause them to think again."

"How about in the back?" Nathan heard Clayton shout.

Two more shots blasted from somewhere downstairs.

"They've got us surrounded, boys. We'll have to shoot our way out. Come on downstairs, and we'll try to break through."

"How about these kids?" J. T. called as he scooped up the saddlebags with the bank money.

"Leave 'em tied. We might need them alive later on."

"Well, I ain't leavin' this carbine again!" J. T. scooped up the gun and ran out of the room, slamming the door. Someone locked it.

A few more shouts and two more gunshots . . . then silence from downstairs.

The gunfire had diverted Nathan's attention. He finally had control of his sobbing. He glanced at Tona's lifeless body and then over at Leah who hung her head down. He could see tears dripping onto her dress.

"Leah? Leah . . . it's okay . . . Leah . . . please stop crying," Nathan tried to comfort her.

He heard her sobs lessen. Finally she lifted her head and took a deep breath. Still not looking at Nathan, she spoke in a slow, soft voice.

"He wanted to come in . . . honest, Nathan."

"What?"

"Tona," she explained. "You know how he don't like to ever go into buildings? Well, you was gone so long that

Tona barked and barked at that kitchen window. I ain't heard him bark that much in a year. Did you hear him?"

"Eh . . . no, I guess not . . . well, maybe."

Nathan heard shouting from somewhere down in the street. Then the men downstairs yelled something in return.

"What's happening?" Leah asked.

"Sounds like the people in town have the hotel surrounded. They must have heard the shots."

"What people? Your daddy's out there chasin' . . . chasin' that band of horses, I guess."

"Harris Anderson, Brady Wheeler, Tony, and Briggs at the freight office, Mr. Fernandez—men like that."

They both sat silent for a few minutes listening.

Finally, it was Leah who spoke up. "Nathan?"

"Yeah."

"It breaks my heart to see Tona layin' there. You know that, don't ya?"

"Yeah. I hurt real bad, too."

"You know what I think?" she continued. "I think shootin' Tona might have saved the bank from being robbed again."

"It might be that they won't even get away with the money they stole in the first place," Nathan added.

Tear streaks had dried on her face. "That sort of makes him the town hero, don't it?"

"Yeah . . . you're right!" Nathan took a deep breath of the dusty, stale air in the hotel room.

"See, Tona started barking, and when I climbed into the kitchen to come look you up, he pitched such a fit I had to bring him along . . . really! Do you think he knew you was in trouble?"

"I don't know, but . . . wait . . . did you hear what they shouted? I think they mentioned us."

"They goin' to shoot us?" Leah asked.

A gunshot punctuated her sentence. The two waited a long time before speaking. Finally, Leah whispered, "What are you thinkin' about?"

"I guess I was kind of prayin' about Tona, you know, asking God why this had to happen."

"What did He say?"

Nathan waited a minute. Two of the bank robbers argued with each other down in the lobby.

"Well, I don't know if it was the Lord. But I got to thinking about how much Tona's been hurting lately—ever since the bobcat tore him up. Well, I don't think he's had a good day since last summer . . . until today."

"You call gettin' shot a good day?" Leah tugged at the curtain sash that tied her hands.

"Tona got to go huntin'. He got to tote a rabbit home, and he died." Nathan could feel the tears rolling down his face again. The knot in his throat made it hard to talk. "Leah, he died doing exactly what he liked doing best, protecting me and you. The first time I met Tona, he saved me from that crazy bear up at Willow Springs. Huntin' and protectin'—I think it was better than slowly dyin' in pain on the front step."

They both stared at the lifeless Tona and listened again to the argument below.

"We've got to get out of here!" Nathan tried fumbling with the knot. "They'll get around to using us as shields to make a break for the horses. Leah, it looks like they just tied your hands behind the bedpost. Can you slide down the post and scoot out from under it?"

"I can't lift the bed."

"Maybe I can lift the whole bed. Then you see if you can slip out."

Nathan twisted himself around to an awkward position and placed his shoulders under the frame of the hotel bed. By shoving straight up, he was able to raise the bed a couple of inches.

"Quick . . . there . . . hurry . . . I can't hold it much longer!"

"I'm hurryin', Nathan. I'm hurryin' . . . I can't get loose . . . I can't!"

"Try!" Nathan insisted.

Suddenly, Leah's ropes popped off the bedpost. "There! I did it!"

"Someone's coming!" Nathan whispered. "Sit back down. Quick! Pretend you're still tied to the bedpost."

Clayton unlocked the door and burst into the room with his Colt .44 held tight in his right hand. "What's all the noise up here?" he shouted.

"It was me," Nathan announced. "She's drivin' me crazy with all her talk. Can't you put me in another room so I don't have to listen to this?"

"We could toss you out this second-story window," Clayton sneered. "If you two make another fuss, I'll gag you both!" He walked over to the corner window. "Ain't that somethin'? I didn't reckon there were that many folks left in this town. There must be a hundred folks down there. Most of 'em pointin' guns. I don't know how they got down here so blamed fast!"

"What are you goin' to do with us?" Leah asked.

"Well, don't worry none for a while. As long as you sit tight, we ain't goin' to do nothin'. Once we told them folks we had you two in here, we got them scared of shootin' just in case they hit you. So we'll just hole up 'til dark. Then we'll let you help us escape."

"We ain't goin' to help you," Leah protested.

"Darlin', you'll help. All I have to do is stuff a rag in your mouth and tote you right in front of me to stop bullets."

"Don't you ever call me darlin'!" she fired back.

"Girly, I'll call you—"

A shout from down below ended his sentence. Clayton hustled out the door and tramped down the stairs.

"Leah, can you scoot over here and untie me?" Nathan asked.

"My hands is tied tight. I cain't get down under that bed and untie nothin'."

She awkwardly struggled to her feet and walked softly over toward the window. After glancing out, she scooted back to Nathan.

"They got wagons and rigs and people all over down there!"

"Well, don't get too close to the window. If folks see you and cause a ruckus, the robbers will see it and come running up the stairs before we figure out how to get out of here. We've got to get untied."

"There's some scissors on this dresser," Leah announced. "But I don't rightly see how I can use them behind my back."

"You've got to try," Nathan encouraged her.

Backing up to the mirrored dresser, Leah bent forward and raised her bound arms. Nathan watched as she stood up and attempted to cut the rope.

"Come on, Leah! We've got to hurry. They could be coming back up here any time!"

"I'm hurryin'! Oh!" she cried.

"Are you all right?"

"Yeah . . . I'm hurryin' . . . honest, Nathan, I'm hurryin'. There!"

Nathan watched as she pulled her hands around in front of her and pulled off the rest of the curtain sash. Blood oozed down the back of her hand and dripped to the floor.

"You cut yourself."

"Yeah . . . but I hurried."

"Leah, I didn't mean you had to—"

"I been hurt worse." She scooted next to Nathan with the scissors still in her right hand.

"Don't worry, I won't cut you. I can see what I'm doin' now."

"I wasn't worried. I'm . . . I'm sorry for makin' you hurry and cut yourself," he apologized.

"Well, we're both free! Now what?"

Nathan stood and rubbed his wrists. Then he knelt down beside Tona and petted the fur gently.

"We aren't going anywhere without Tona."

"We cain't carry a dead dog."

Nathan glanced up at Leah.

"Oh . . . well, yeah . . . we'll take him. How are we going to carry him?"

"Look in the wardrobe for a box or something." Nathan motioned toward the free-standing closet. "Well, old boy, you've been a good dog . . . and you taught me some things about loyalty and life and . . . Well, you should've picked out some other kid to follow around. Someone smart enough to not let you go chasin' bobcats and bank robbers. But I loved you, Tona." Nathan began to cry. "You know I loved you."

"Nathan," Leah said softly, "there ain't no box, but I did find this valise."

She handed Nathan a medium-sized worn leather suitcase. He gently scooped up Tona and carefully laid him inside the valise. He closed it up and lifted it with his right hand.

"It isn't very heavy. Tona's been awful skinny since last summer," Nathan commented.

"Tona was always skinny." Leah shrugged. "Now where do we go from here? There ain't no outside stairway, is there?"

"I think one of the rooms has a ladder sort of built right on the outside wall. You think you can make it down a tall ladder?"

"I'll make it." She nodded. "Which room is it?"

"One of 'em on that back side."

"How we goin' to get there without being noticed?"

"I don't think they locked the door the last time out, so I think we'd better crawl on our bellies down the hall. Maybe they won't be looking our way."

"If they come chasin' us, what do we do then?"

"Start praying, I guess," Nathan advised.

"Start prayin'? I been prayin' like crazy the whole time."

"Okay, come on! We'll head down the hall into the middle room. No matter what, don't say anything until we get there."

Nathan dropped to his hands and knees and scooted the suitcase with Tona alongside him. Motioning with his hand for Leah to follow, he swung open the door, dropped down to his stomach, and crawled across the hall. He smelled dust and stale liquor. Nathan had almost reached one of the middle rooms on the back side of the landing when he heard voices. Someone was coming up the stairs.

"We got to make a break, J. T. More and more people are comin'. This is suicide sittin' in here."

"Brushy, we bust out now, and we'd be shot down in a minute. Clayton's right."

"I'd rather die in the fresh air with a gun in my hand than be hung by a rope with a bunch of old ladies lookin' on. I'm grabbin' those kids and leavin'. You can stay if you want."

Lord, he's going to see us! No! Help us, Lord, help us!

"Brushy! Come back down here!" J. T. yelled. "We've got to stick together on this thing. Come on, Brushy, you don't want to face them guns by yourself."

Nathan saw the top of the man's hat spin and disappear down the stairs.

"You and me had nothin' to do with shootin' that sheriff. They can't blame us for that one, can they, J. T.?"

"Come on, Brushy. By mornin' we'll be ridin' north to Wyoming. By Friday we'll be playin' Faro in Cheyenne. Just stay by your window and don't let no one go sneakin' up on us."

The distant voices sounded muffled as Nathan shoved open the door of the hotel room and scooted inside. Once Leah made it into the room, he locked the door with a skeleton key that had been left in the lock.

"We made it!" Leah whispered.

"So far," Nathan cautioned.

He stood up and went to the window, peering out on the right side of the dusty lace curtains.

"It's here! There's the ladder!"

Leah glanced out at the people who filled the mountainside behind the hotel. "How do we get out there?"

"Just open the window and . . . Leah, it's stuck! I can't get the window open!"

"Just beat on it with something. It will open."

"I can't beat on it. Someone downstairs will hear."

Leah stepped over to the corner of the room next to a broken rocking chair.

"Here's a curtain rod." She motioned. "Pry it open with this."

Nathan jammed the rod under the window at the right corner and pushed down on the rod. It began to bend. Then suddenly the window broke free. The wooden-cased window flew wide open and crashed into the side of the hotel with such impact that the glass shattered and tumbled to the ground below.

They heard someone running up the stairs.

T E N

Leah, you go first. There might not be time for us both to get down."

"You go. I'm scared of them steps. They don't look too safe!"

"You got to do it. Stay close up against the building when you get down there. Then we'll figure out how to get to the wagons! Go on!"

Nathan helped Leah crawl out the window to the ladder steps. They stretched all the way from the ground to the roof of the building.

She clutched each rung with white knuckles and inched her way down the outside of the hotel.

"I'm scared, Nathan!"

"You can do it! Keep going!"

Nathan grabbed up the valise with Tona and placed one foot out on the steps. The one-by-four wooden slats had white paint flaking off, revealing dark gray weathered wood beneath. The suitcase, now swinging on his right arm, seemed unbearably heavy. He heard a loud crash from inside the hotel room. The door swung open.

"Get back in here, kid!" J. T. screamed.

Nathan had descended only a couple of steps. The bank robber, being careful not to expose himself as a target in front of the window, pointed his Colt right at the boy.

"Crawl back in here or you're dead!" he commanded.

Nathan glanced down. Leah had made it safely to the

ground and was scrunched up tight against the side of the hotel, out of sight of the gunmen in the hotel, but in full view of the townspeople.

Without thinking about it, Nathan moaned, "Lord, help me!"

"That's right, boy, say your prayers because if you don't get yourself back in this room, you'll be goin' to meet your Master."

Nathan looked up at the outlaw holding the gun. The man squinted his eyes, making tight creases around them.

"Mister, you men tied me up, threatened me and Leah, robbed a bank or two, stole some horses, shot a sheriff, and killed my dog. You've proved there isn't much about you that's decent. Well, I'm going to find out if you're low enough to kill an unarmed kid while the whole town's looking on 'cause I'm not crawling back in there."

Nathan eased on down the ladder.

Lord, if I got to die, well, I sure hope I can be as brave as Tona.

He heard several shouts and curses, but no shots were fired out the window. By the time he reached the ground, his right arm ached. Sweat dripped off his forehead.

"Were you talkin' to one of them?" Leah asked.

"Yep."

"What did he say?"

"He told me to crawl back in there or he'd shoot."

Leah scooted next to the building and sat in the dirt. Nathan plopped down beside her.

"What did you tell him?"

"I told him I didn't think he was the type to shoot unarmed kids in front of the whole town."

Leah took a deep breath. "Well . . . I guess he wasn't. What are we goin' to do now?"

A roar of noise rose from the townspeople. Several

shouted at them to stay put. This was followed by several bursts of gunfire at the front side of the hotel.

"What are they doin' around there?" Leah asked.

"I suppose they're trying to get the bank robbers' attention so we can escape." Nathan searched the distant crowd to see who was among them. Most remained safely hidden from sight. A man inched his way closer to the building. "Tony's trying to get to us!"

"Maybe they're all around front," Leah guessed.

Several rifle shots forced Tony to dive back behind a wagon.

"Then again, maybe they ain't," she added. "Which one was up in that room?"

"The one they call J. T."

"That Clayton fella wasn't in there, was he?"

"Nope."

"Well." Leah took a deep breath. "If J. T. didn't shoot you while you was on the ladder, maybe he won't shoot us if we run for it."

"No, we can't . . ." Nathan heard more gunfire from the front. "Well, maybe . . . just maybe we can. You really want to try it?"

"Do you?" she asked.

"Yeah . . . sort of. Yeah, let's do it!" Nathan maneuvered to his feet but stayed tight against the building. Leah stood alongside and brushed off her dress. Nathan straightened his hat and picked up the valise.

"Which way are we going to run?"

"Straight ahead—toward that freight wagon."

"Together?"

"Yep," Nathan asserted. "But we aren't running. We're going to walk right out there and not look back. If they're going to shoot us, they can do it if we run or walk. I say we walk with our heads up."

Leah looked up at Nathan and scrunched her nose just enough to make the freckles wiggle.

"Will you hold my hand?"

"What?"

"I'll walk by your side if you hold my hand."

"All right." Nathan took another deep breath and then prayed aloud, "Lord, this is Nathan and Leah . . . and we're scared. Walk with us, Jesus. Please walk with us."

Nathan ignored the shouts of the townspeople and began walking toward the freight wagon. Leah laced her fingers into his left hand, and with his right he carried the leather suitcase containing Tona.

Without looking over at Leah, he called out, "Keep your head up."

"My head is up."

"Don't look back."

"I ain't lookin' back."

"Don't get in a hurry."

"I'm not in a hurry!"

Nathan could feel the sweat drip from his forehead. "Just a few more steps . . . oh, Lord . . . just a few more." When they came close to the wagon, Nathan dragged Leah by the arm and dove to safety.

Suddenly, a throng of townspeople swarmed around them, and a great cheer went up. Leah and Nathan got pulled in two different directions. Mr. Walker was there hugging Leah, and tears streamed down her face.

Nathan felt familiar arms surround him, and he looked up to see his mother's relieved face. Taller than she, he stooped over and laid his head on her shoulder. Finally, regaining her composure, his mother spoke, "Nathan, I was very proud of you. The way you walked out of there, taking care of Leah, and all. It's the kind of thing your father would have done."

"Mama . . . they killed Tona." Nathan started to cry again. Then he stood up and wiped his eyes and looked at all the townspeople staring at them. "He was trying to protect me and Leah, and they shot him twice even though the first bullet killed him. I've got him in the valise."

"In there?" His mother pointed.

"Yep. I wasn't goin' to leave him in the hotel with them."

"I'm really sorry, Nathan." His mother tried to console him.

"It's all right, Mother. Leah and me talked it out . . . and . . . well, I can take it now."

Nathan knew the words sounded right, but tears still streamed down his cheeks.

"Well, come on. We're going to get you home. Your father can take care of this matter now." She tugged him back up the street away from the hotel.

"Daddy's here? But I thought he was—"

"He picked up their trail last night and rode two horses into the ground getting back. He and the others rode up about the time you started crawling out the window. He's the one who got the diversion going around front. Mr. Walker got back to town this morning, too."

"Yeah, I saw him."

"Are you hungry?" his mother asked.

"Well . . . actually . . . yeah, I am," Nathan admitted.

"I thought so." Mrs. Riggins slipped her arm into Nathan's, and they walked side by side through the crowd of people.

Nathan and his mother ate dinner on the front porch while a steady stream of people stopped by to congratulate

Nathan for his bravery and bring the latest report from the standoff down at the hotel.

At about three o'clock they heard several rounds of gunfire. Then word came that one of the bank robbers was wounded, and at least two of them wanted to surrender. A few minutes later there was a loud cheer, and Tony ran up to Nathan, who now stood in the street.

"They surrendered to your daddy!" Tony yelled. "It's all over, and the bank got its money back! They got it all back!"

The following hour was a confusion of visits and reports. His mother insisted that Nathan stay near the house. She wouldn't let him out of her sight. His father came home for only a few minutes to announce that he and the posse were immediately hauling the prisoners to Austin.

Nathan hardly had time to hug his father and tell him about Tona.

"You bury him up on the hill, Nate. Don't be leavin' him around here overnight."

"Yes, sir. When will you be back?"

"Can't say. If it's going to be long, I'll send a telegram. Take care of your mother."

"Yes, sir . . . I will."

That evening Nathan hiked up the hill behind Galena to a small grove of junipers. In one hand was the suitcase, still containing Tona. In the other was a shovel. For several moments he dug in the rocky ground. The soil was dry and had a yellow tint that made the dust-laden air taste bitter.

He had just finished the hole and was about to lower Tona into it when he heard footsteps and spun around. Leah was standing there wearing a new blue dress.

"Leah! You look . . . I mean, that's a pretty dress."

"Is it respectable if I come to the buryin'?" she asked.

"Sure. I would have gone to get you, but I figured you needed to be with your father."

He lowered the whole suitcase into the hole and began to fill the dirt in over it.

"You buryin' him in that?"

"Yeah, it's like . . . you know, a coffin."

"Ain't you goin' to say no words over him?"

"I'm sort of . . . all cried out." Nathan stopped shoveling. He hiked up his brown duckings, pulled off his hat, and cleared his throat.

"Lord, Tona was a good dog for me. I thank You for the years we had together, but I surely wish he could have stayed around longer. And I do thank You that he isn't hurting any more. In Jesus' name, amen."

"Amen," Leah echoed. "You were right about me needin' to talk to my daddy. We are movin' to Austin, Nathan."

"When?"

"In the mornin'."

Nathan felt a wave of shock sweep through his whole body. "But I thought you had . . . two more weeks."

"Daddy bought a barber shop, and he wants to open up the day after tomorrow. So we're startin' to load up things in a wagon. Daddy said you can come help load if you have a mind to."

For the next two hours Nathan helped Leah, her father, and her stepmother load a large farm wagon parked in front of the barber shop. When most of the household goods were packed, Nathan and Leah sat down on the wooden bench on the raised sidewalk. Light from the setting sun struck only the tops of the buildings on the east side of the street. There were no clouds in the sky. The daily breeze began to dwindle. The excitement of the day had died down, and only a few people could be seen on Main Street.

"I don't suppose Colin's daddy would want to come back and open the bank now that all the money's been recovered?" Leah questioned.

"Come back to what? Look at this, Leah. It's the summer that a town died."

"I guess it ain't much of a town, is it?"

"It's freezing cold in the winter, blistering hot in the summer. There's no trees, no grass, not much water that's fit to drink, and the wind blows every day of the year. It's a lousy place for a town."

"But we had some good times, didn't we, Nathan?"

"Yeah," he sighed. "That's what makes a place home. It's not the buildings or the location or the wind. It's the people. When the people you really like move away and all you've got left is a wood-frame house that leaks during a heavy storm, where marbles roll toward the fireplace . . ."

"I remember the first time I saw you." She smiled. "You crawled off that stage lookin' like an orphan calf."

"Me? How about you? Barefoot and wearing a dirty dress."

"It wasn't dirty," she protested. "I just . . . used it a lot."

"You were about the only one in town who would talk to me," Nathan replied.

"We were still livin' in the tent then," Leah added. "Daddy says he got us a nice house up on a hill in Austin."

"Everything in Pony Canyon is on a hill!" Nathan laughed.

"They got a good school, too. Daddy says I can either go to school or get me a job. I think maybe I'll try some more school. What are you going to do, Nathan?"

"I don't know. Mama said she might fill in teaching those kids that are left up here. There's always a chance we'll move to Austin, too. If Daddy ever became sheriff, then we could still be . . . uh . . . friends."

"Well, I'm goin' to pray every night that you move to Austin!" Leah stood up and stared across the street. "This is a crazy conversation," she announced. "It's like I'm up in the air staring down at us talkin'. It's just not real. It can't really be happenin'. This ain't the way I planned my life at all."

Nathan stood up and walked over by Leah. "Well, maybe it's the way the Lord planned it."

"If so, I don't think I like the plan," she said softly.

"Maybe not, but it's a better plan than if we'd never gotten to meet each other in the first place." Nathan turned his head toward the stairs. "I think your mother's calling you."

"My stepmother," Leah corrected him.

"I'd better go get my supper, too. What time you pulling out in the morning?"

"About sun-up, I guess." Leah turned to go up the stairs.

"I'll be over here on this bench at daybreak. You won't leave town without saying goodbye, will you?"

"Nathan T. Riggins, if you ain't over here to say good-bye in the mornin', I'll march up there and drag you out of bed in your nightshirt!"

"I'll be here." He laughed.

"Well, it's a good thing!" She grinned and ran up the stairs just like he had seen her do hundreds of times before.

Nathan climbed out of bed before daylight. It had been so warm during the night that he slept on top of the covers. After dressing and carrying in an arm load of wood, he scooted out the front door. Even though it was mostly dark, he stepped over to check on Tona. Then he remembered. Tears welled up in his eyes.

"Well, ol' boy . . . it's going to take me a while to get into a new routine. Now I don't have anyone left to really talk to—except maybe Onepenny."

He walked along the darkened street. The wind twirled dust in his face. There was no boom and vibration of the stamp mill, no shouts and shots from McGuire Street, no dogs barking, no roosters crowing, no kids playing tag on the sidewalks, no freight wagons circling the Mercantile.

Thanks, too, for Galena, Lord. I had a good time here. The history books won't ever remember it. But I will. I was here. And most of all, so were You.

Leah sat on the bench in front of the barber shop wearing her new dress.

"Mornin', Nathan."

"Mornin', pretty Miss Leah."

"Don't you go teasin' me!"

"I'm not," he replied, looking down at his boots.

"Maybe next time your daddy comes down to Austin, you can come with him," she suggested.

"Yeah, and . . . and you could come up and visit us. Mama said you could stay with us anytime."

"Sure, that would be fine, wouldn't it?"

"I'll write to you, Leah. You got to promise to write back."

"I will, but I told ya, you cain't make fun of my spellin'."

"I won't."

For several moments neither said anything.

"Nathan, what are you going to do today?" she finally asked.

"I don't know. Maybe I'll go for a ride on Onepenny."

"Out to Rabbit Springs?"

"No, I think I'll find a new place. Some place that I've never seen before. Some place where there aren't any memories. Memories can sure hurt sometimes."

"Boy, you can say that again," Leah agreed. "Well, here they come." She pointed to her father and stepmother toting a couple of large green valises.

Nathan walked Leah over to the wagon. She spun around and threw her arms around Nathan's neck and hugged him tight. "I don't want to let go!" she cried. Surprising himself, Nathan kissed her on the cheek next to the field of freckles. She pulled back with a wide smile on her face. Then he helped her climb into the wagon.

"Thank you, sir." She smiled.

He tipped his hat. "You're welcome, ma'am."

"It's like the last page in a book, ain't it, Nathan?"

"Yeah. One of those that you don't want to end, and you've been trying to read real slow so's to make it last."

The wagon started to roll south.

Leah looked frantic. Tears rolled down her cheeks.

"Cowboy!" she called. "You know I ain't never goin' to marry nobody but Nathan T. Riggins, don't ya?"

Nathan pushed his gray hat to the back of his head and waved to her.

"I know," he called back. He stared at the wagon until it pulled around the corner. Then he turned toward home and wiped his eyes on his dusty shirt sleeve.

Epilogue

TASHAWNA CHOLACH
At the age of eighteen, Tashawna joined BUFFALO BILL'S WILD WEST SHOW AND CONGRESS OF ROUGH RIDERS OF THE WORLD and made two tours of Europe as a trick rider. Returning to Carson City, Nevada, she became active in local theater productions. She married Colin Maddison, Jr., on July 4, 1895. They lived in a large home on the mountain just west of the city.

COLIN MADDISON, JR.
Majoring in business, Colin graduated from the University of California at Berkeley and then returned to Carson City, Nevada. At the age of twenty-five, he purchased the Ormsby State Bank. The bank was moderately successful. In 1903 he invested heavily in mining stock at Goldfield, Nevada. Selling out in 1905, Colin's profits were of legendary proportions, earning him the nickname "Lucky" Maddison. He and his wife (the former Tashawna Cholach) had one child, Colin Maddison III (with two *d*'s).

ONEPENNY
The talented spotted horse served Nathan (and his children) for thirty-two years. At one time it was the best-known horse in Lander County, Nevada. When Onepenny died, he was buried in the family grave site near the Salmon River in Idaho.

LEAH WALKER

Leah graduated from Nevada Normal and taught in a mission school in the Hawaiian Islands for two years. She then returned to the mainland and taught in rural schools in Nevada and Idaho for twenty-six years. Leah and her husband had six sons of their own and adopted three daughters. She contributed to the Federal Writers' Project on the History of Nevada and also to the project on the history of Idaho. She and Tashawna Maddison became the best of friends.

NATHAN TIMOTHY RIGGINS

Three days after Thanksgiving, Nathan and his parents moved to Austin, Nevada, where Mr. Riggins served as acting sheriff. Nathan received a one-year diploma at Mr. Dwight L. Moody's Bible School in Chicago, Illinois. He then took classes at Nevada College of Agriculture and Mining. In 1893 he married Leah Walker in Austin. It was estimated that 640 people attended the wedding. Soon after, Mr. and Mrs. Nathan Riggins moved to central Idaho where they formed Tona Land & Cattle Company and began a ranching career. The sprawling two-story white clapboard ranch house they built in 1902 is visible from U. S. Highway 95.

For a list of other books by
Stephen Bly

write:

Stephen Bly
Winchester, Idaho 83555

More Great Fiction for Boys & Girls!

THE LEWIS AND CLARK SQUAD ADVENTURE SERIES

They're not just a summer basketball squad—they're a lean, clean, adventure-finding team!

Cody Clark, Feather Trailer-Hobbs, Jeremiah Yellowboy and Larry Lewis are used to lots of excitement on the court. But it's the teammates' many adventures off the court that keep this fun-loving foursome on the move and learning more about themselves, friendship and the Lord. Ages 8-12.

Book 1: Intrigue at the Rafter B Ranch
Book 2: The Secret of the Old Rifle
Book 3: Treachery at the River Canyon
Book 4: Revenge on Eagle Island
Book 5: Danger at Deception Pass
Book 6: Hazards of the Half-Court Press